Marginally Human

Outliers in a post-apocalyptic dystopia

By

Vidyut Gore

To creativity and kindness.

To my son, who taught me cheerful resilience, and Neerabai Shinde, who cares for his needs, so that I may chase my dreams. My mother, Nisha Gore, my first companion for reading and writing. My father, Vishwas Gore, who scavenged vast quantities of pre-loved books for me to devour on a factory worker's budget. My grandmother, Nalini Godbole, who taught me kindness and collecting interesting wordplays, and Balwant Godbole, my grandfather, who put artistic tenacity and music into my blood.

To schoolmates who never snitched, when I hid story books inside textbooks to read in class. And teachers who knew it.

To the varied interesting people, both real and imaginary, who caught my imagination and enriched it.

To the folks at Critique Circle, for their generosity with their time and attention. They elevated my writing from inspired incoherence sans punctuation to merely fashionably erratic.

Thank you.

Books in the Sarovar Series:

Marginally Human
Terminally Immortal

Table of Contents

The great economic crisis of 2053 is widely recognised as the first event of the Enduring War, though a few think it was the failure of antibiotics. The global population of the old world is believed to be an astonishing eight billion. The Enduring War wasn't a single event, but a peculiar era that changed the course of human history forever.

Collapse of law and order magnified the chaos in the wake of depleting resources like water and food resulting in entrenched local conflicts called civilisational incompatibilities (CI). The much feared Third World War, a mere blip in the late twenty-first century, ended inconclusively, with the collapse of participating countries, setting off a domino effect.

By the time the Enduring War ended in 2167 with Abrahamha's Ultimatum, the meaning of the word 'war' itself had evolved to include any fight for human survival. A mere ninety million humans remained worldwide, most of them clustered in twenty-two cities and three domes.

Humanity was saved from extinction through the fortuitous discovery of symbiontic microorganisms in the bodies of humans who enjoyed extreme longevity and, in rare cases, extraordinary abilities. They were cultured in order to save the surviving population. Humans became functionally immortal.

But *Homo symbions,* as we are now known, are very far from reaching population numbers that guarantee long-term survival.

Every city and dome now guarantees food, clothing, shelter, access to communication, education, healthcare, and more to every human, without exception, as a part of a Global Agreement.

PROLOGUE

Disgruntled wrestler attacks three, injuring a teenage girl badly. Ekta Dorm management promises a crackdown on illegal fights. Dome & Dorms, Thursday, July 4, 2430

~~*~*~*~*

AAXYL: EKTA DORMS CLINIC

"Blink if you understand me." A paramedic with moustache-grade eyebrows waved his hand close enough to take her nose off.

Aaxyl blinked her still working left eye.

She lay in a medical bed with her leg elevated. A soft, familiar child stuck to her left side like an extra splint.

Aameh.

The grey walls and scent of lemon disinfectant teased her memory. She was in the Ekta Dorms clinic. The rest of the room would be meticulously utilitarian, like everything in the Dorms of Dome 91-110: the bare minimum provided efficiently.

HealSYMB suffused warmth through her body. If symbiont microorganisms could save humanity from extinction, they could fix one beat up teenager.

Aaxyl tried to stroke Aameh's back.

Pain blinded her. Her arm was fine, but her shoulder wanted a vote.

"Ow." Her voice caught.

"You've been admitted for severe injuries and are under a pain block. You should be comfortable as long as you avoid movements that still feel painful." Eyebrows waved his hand again. How long was he planning to do this? "You were at an illegal fight."

A match hadn't landed her in this predicament. A deranged brute with AthSYMB-enhanced strength had slammed into her while her sponsor briefed her on upcoming bouts. A blur of vicious blows blindsided her before nature administered the oldest anaesthetic of all: unconsciousness.

Eyebrows lectured her on the perils of the fights. *Symbionts can't cure death* and other pearls dripped like acid on her ears. Another paramedic, not Eyebrows, urged her to consider the little girl, as the men prepared to move her. She had. Aameh *was* why Aaxyl participated in fights.

Something clacked out of her line of sight, and a wheel squeaked. Eyebrows talked over his shoulder as he loomed to detach her from the treatment bed. "We don't need the gurney to get to the ambulance. Use your hoverboard." He examined her records. "The patient has no family. The little girl can't go to the hospital."

But they were a family. Aaxyl and Aameh: AxAm. Just not on Dorms records.

"No!" Aameh shrieked and Eyebrows jumped. "Let go of me!"

Not-Eyebrows had tried to remove Aameh from the bed but she'd worked her arms around Aaxyl, wrapped her legs around Aaxyl's elevated left leg, and clung.

Aaxyl wanted to calm her, but Aameh escalated to ear-splitting screams. Not even Aaxyl heard her own feeble moans.

"Get your hands off me right now!"

This wasn't why Aaxyl had taught her to shout that.

The paramedics sympathised, but there was only one way this would end.

Not-Eyebrows released Aameh.

Screams tapered into hiccoughs.

He crouched before her. "We can't take you with us, sweetheart. We'll get arrested if we take a child out of the Dorms without an authorised guardian."

Aameh whimpered.

Eyebrows devolved to unconcealed bribery. "Tell me your name, and we'll fly my hoverboard all the way to your dorm. Your friends will be jealous."

As bribes went, this one ranked high.

Aameh wouldn't budge. "Take me with her."

If they left her behind, she'd try to find the hospital on her own.

"No hospital!" Aaxyl croaked.

Three faces leaned close—paramedics Eyebrows and not-Eyebrows in their brown uniforms, and a white-haired rotund symbiontist with a slight stubble over a double chin.

"Let's give them some time together," the symbiontist said. "We still have a few hours."

"You're joking!" Eyebrows burst out, kicking off an argument. "Are we babysitters?"

The crux of their issue was that the clinic was open in the day, but Aaxyl needed supervision overnight.

Aaxyl's issue was that she had an eight-year-old appendage who refused to detach.

"This is your clinic and your decision," not-Eyebrows concluded. "Send her to the hospital, or stay back to monitor her. If there's no patient to transport, our work is done."

"Call us if you change your mind." Eyebrows headed for the door.

"But..." Symbiontist Softie would lose. First to the paramedics, and then Aameh would wrap him around her little finger.

AxAm now became Softie's problem.

Aaxyl struggled to remain awake. Aameh needed to sleep for everyone's sanity, but she wouldn't, if Aaxyl slept. According to Aameh's documentaries, one member of a herd always remained alert for predators. Aaxyl had been stuck with her 'herd' seven years ago, when her mother had left a toddler with her. They'd go to some place called SYMBTech when she came back, she'd said.

Her mother never returned.

Aameh never left.

~~*~*

"Let me stay!" Aameh's insistent tone verged on hysteria, awakening Aaxyl. Small arms still held on. The child had a bladder a wasteland camel would envy.

A low voice reasoned with her. She tried to see the speaker, but forgot rule number one: *do not move*. Her swollen shoulder had cemented her neck into place and shards of pain broke through the block.

"I'll eat dinner if you promise." Everyone made honest promises in Aameh's world.

~~*~*

A soft voice roused her later. "How is she?"

Crap.

Leela, soon-to-be Director of Ekta Dorms, was the closest they had to a parent. She wouldn't appreciate Aaxyl's arguments on the legality of her fighting.

Aaxyl imagined them standing and staring. *Exhibit A: How not to exit a fight.*

Softie broke the silence, "If she can't return to her room tomorrow, we'll send her to the hospital."

Aaxyl hated disembodied voices of doom. Everyone stood on her right, because hers was the farthest bed from the door. She opened her right eye and spied the grey ceiling enhanced with watery depth of field. There, that was good, wasn't it? Her neck still wouldn't turn enough.

"I can send a medic assistant for the night," said Leela.

Aaxyl didn't need anyone. The pain block discouraged movement very convincingly. But a dormer volunteering for a better SociCred score beat a professional symbiontist paid in universal money. She'd never hear the end of it if Softie billed unimon because of her.

"Her condition needs a hospital or a trained medic," said Softie.

"Very well. I'll check on her in the morning." Leela's heels clacked to the door.

"Wait," Softie said. "This little girl here. She won't leave."

Leela sighed, and Aaxyl's memory supplied the exasperated expression to go with it. "She may stay."

Aaxyl stroked the tangled mop of hair by her side. To the overwhelming gratitude of Aaxyl's left leg, the clingy menace had exhausted herself to sleep.

Leela's voice rose. "Aaxyl, if I ever find you around those fights again, I'll send Aameh to a dorm on the other side of the dome." Heels faded to silence.

The bed moved as Softie picked Aameh up and put her somewhere. Hopefully, in a bed, though Aaxyl wouldn't blame him if he put her in a box and locked it.

"You heard Leela." Softie dragged a chair over to Aaxyl's left.

He had the caring expression of one who knew nothing about her, but was confident that she was wrong.

"I'm Hersh. Must I tell you that the fights are forbidden?"

"You will, anyway." A lecture loomed.

"You're sixteen with an entire life ahead of you," he said, as though nobody could possibly have told her this before. "You scared the little girl."

"Aah-may," said Aaxyl.

"What?"

"Her name is Aameh. She's eight. She feared losing me. She won't." Half-dead was a hundred percent alive.

"Why are you doing this?"

"SociCred for Aameh's upgraded meals."

"Doesn't look like she wants meals more than you."

"She needs them. She doesn't heal."

Hersh snorted. "You aren't recovering on your own. HealSYMB—"

"—doesn't work on her."

"HealSYMB works on all *Homo symbions*." Hersh sounded more confident about that than he'd be in ten minutes.

"That's what the last symbiontist said. Check her history."

She told him Aameh's identifier. She didn't need to see the first event the Synthetic Intelligence System would list. Aaxyl had slept in a top bunk to evade the persistent toddler.

Hersh gaped at the SIS screen. "Eight vials of HealSYMB for a fall from a bunk!"

"Still took a week. I'll bounce back faster from this. Nutrition helps."

Hersh pondered this as he slouched more comfortably. "Why not do a job for SociCred then?"

"The job pays for our room."

"A room?" Hersh's voice rose like she'd purchased prime property.

"She searches for me at night—half asleep, climbing into bunks. We get separated in age-appropriate Dorms."

"Why won't she adjust to children of her age? Adults complain about coffin-dorms, but kids love them."

The basic accommodation stacked ten bunks on each face of four-sided racks. With twenty such racks to a hall, the 'coffin-dorms' delivered compact claustrophobia that children inexplicably enjoyed. Not Aameh though.

"She's too weak to defend from an impulsive hug, let alone worse. She's terrified of the other kids." And had the agreeability of a know-it-all.

"And what job pays a minor enough for a room?" asked Hersh.

"Sanitation worker." Aaxyl grinned. "Enough for a shared bed in an eight-bed room. That's why no dorm-supervisors called for her. She lives in a room."

"Minors in sewers can't be legal!" He got off the chair and went out of sight.

"Laws are for paid work, not volunteers." Aaxyl said, before he could alert anyone. SociCred dodged minimum age and wage, by rewarding *volunteer* work for the community. It was just a score, not unimon, even if it was the currency of the Dorms.

A drawer scraped as Hersh continued. "New tissue takes time to strengthen. I can't clear you to work in sewers, let alone fight."

No other work for her age and skills earned enough to upgrade accommodation for two people. She fought panic.

More drawers rattled. Aaxyl tried to see what he was doing, but the pain block disagreed.

"Why can't you use a proper pain block?" Aaxyl lashed out.

Hersh strolled back into view. "It isn't an anaesthetic. You're pain free if you don't aggravate the injuries. If you can't sense an increase in pain, you'll re-injure yourself. Pain is nature's warn—"

"I get the idea." Aaxyl's eyes watered.

"So." Hersh returned to his chair. "You didn't reply. You can't work in sewers or fight. What will you do?"

Aaxyl's voice wobbled. "I promised Am we'd never return to separate coffin-dorms."

Hersh held up a booklet—*Clinic Protocols*. "Work here." He tossed it on her bed. "You're young and under-qualified. Keep the place clean, learn on the job, prove yourself."

"Why?" Aaxyl rasped over the doubt tangled with hope in her throat.

"I'm new, and need an assistant. You need a break. It's an opportunity, not a guarantee." He settled low into the chair, heavy feet propped on the rails of her bed, and closed his eyes. "Promise me no more illegal fights, and I'll cover your current accommodation and Aameh's food."

Orphans of the State

Dome 91-110 reports more births than deaths for the tenth year in a row. Feather in President Damodar's cap. Dome Times, Wednesday, October 1, 2442

~~*~*~*

AAXYL: AxAm's room

Aaxyl ran all the way from the Ekta Dorms to the SecPro station: Aameh had been arrested.

Stay out of trouble was AxAm rule number one. Aaxyl had never seen the residential area at night, let alone getting into trouble with SecPros.

The SecPro station was surrounded by residential towers and brightly lit streets unlike the dim Dorms. A commotion was underway in the parking area. Half a dozen SecPros barrelled out toward a scuffle.

She shrank out of their way, then hurried inside to a waiting area before four desks manned by SecPros. Barely a dozen men waited in the chairs at this time of the night. She walked through and approached the desk she'd been told to report to. "My name is Aaxyl, and I'm here for Aameh."

The potbellied SecPro verified Aaxyl's identification. "You're *twenty-eight*?"

"Is that relevant?" Aaxyl asked.

"Only to *logic*. She's twenty. You can't possibly be her *parent*."

"I adopted her." Aaxyl had done so on turning twenty-five to end the *no relatives on record* problem once and for all. "Is she okay?"

"She's fine. *We* are furious. *You* are responsible for her."

Aaxyl nodded in relief. "What did she do?"

"She's been *harassing* us with nuisance theories about some super-villain called The Whisperer." Potbelly was hitting his stride, when his comm blinked. He raised a finger to prevent her reply, and turned away, murmuring into it.

The Whisperer was Aaxyl's childhood name for a scary voice only she heard. She'd been too busy for imaginary voices since Aameh toddled into her life. Why was Aameh complaining about it two decades later? She might as well complain about shadows under the bed.

Potbelly finished his conversation and turned back to Aaxyl. "She has filed thirty-eight complaints. *Thirty-eight.* She tried to break into the commander's office here to submit another one in person."

"Well, you are SecPros. It's your job to investigate..." Aaxyl had no idea what Aameh had done to deserve arrest. Surely they didn't mean breaking in... Best stick to generics.

The man pushed his chair back and ducked below the desk, grunting as he came up with Aameh's backpack and set it on the table with a thunk. "This is her complaint. She's not the aggrieved party. She doesn't know any victim or their friends or family personally, she doesn't have a single witness who can describe a single crime or claim to know any of the victims. She doesn't know the identity of this supposed super-villain or what he looks like. Her complaint is two thousand pages long." He checked the display before him. "*Two thousand, three hundred and six* pages."

Aaxyl was impressed Aameh managed to lug it into the station.

Speaking of the crazy one, Aameh's indignant voice floated out from a door into the bowels of the station. "I am not mentally impaired! I'm smarter than all of you combined. I have a symbiont disorder not a mental one."

Aaxyl let out a sigh.

"She just won't stop arguing." Potbelly grumbled.

An irritated voice said something Aaxyl couldn't hear.

"Everybody's needs should be special. I pity you if you don't think yours are,"

Heads turned to the corridor. Was Aameh closer?

"Well then, you're sane enough to stand trial for your crime, and clever enough to convince the Judicial SIS," a voice boomed back. A hefty SecPro with a chest like a continent hauled the lanky Aameh in by her arm and Aaxyl fought to not launch herself at him to protect her. That grip would leave welts, but both of them getting arrested wouldn't improve their lives.

"Yes, I am," Aameh said.

"No, you're not," Aaxyl snapped. She turned to Potbelly, slipping flawlessly into the persona of a long-suffering caretaker of a nutcase. It wasn't hard. "Let her go, please. She's harmless, just... insistent."

"*Harmless*?" Potbelly slapped Aameh's bag indignantly. "She tried to break into the commander's office. That's a crime. Actual humans will have to go through her numerous complaints to file a closure report." He thumped Aameh's bag again. "Filing nuisance complaints is *punishable by law*."

"No, Ax!" Aameh rolled up her sleeve. "Don't listen to him. They have hurt me. Mistreated me, to cover up crimes. Look at the evidence."

Aaxyl rushed to her. There were just the welts from the SecPro holding her as he towed her in. The weirdo had probably resisted just to acquire them. Aameh's intelligence might be off-the-charts, but her grasp of reality was more like a touch. With the back of one finger.

Potbelly looked at Continent in shock.

"I didn't do that!" Continent said in alarm.

It would be a matter of time before the they realised how easily Aameh bruised. Her symbiont issues left her mildly anemic. Before they did, it gave her a bargaining chip.

"Look, I know you didn't mean to hurt her," Aaxyl said. "She has a symbiont disorder. What wouldn't matter to us can endanger her. Be reasonable. She can't handle prison."

"I'm sorry," Potbelly said. His face was now kind. "But I don't have a *choice*. If her complaints aren't a nuisance, then I'll have to assign several SecPros for *weeks* to get through this. She's refusing to withdraw them or even stop." He waved a *case-in-point* at Aameh's bag, sitting between them.

"You don't know Am," Aaxyl sighed. "You're going to have to do that anyway, because she'll ask you in court how you knew her complaints were a nuisance without reading it. And she'll know the details in and out and fight you every inch of the way. You know I'm not lying. She doesn't give up. Then she'll claim you injured her, which you did, even if unknowingly."

"If you think that will *motivate* me to—"

"This will." Aaxyl leaned forward. "I'm her legal guardian. I have the authority to withdraw any complaints she has filed as long as they aren't against me. I'll withdraw them. You never have to see her again."

Scientists estimate it will take five thousand years to reach pre-Enduring War populations. Research Watch, Thursday, October 2, 2442

~~*~*~*

AAXYL: AxAm's room

Aaxyl hurried out of the bathroom in a towel and fast dissipating cloud of steam. The secret to a satisfying shower in twenty-five litres of hot water eluded her. She shivered her storage locker open, reaching for... no clothes. Aameh's locker had no clothes either. Nor did their shared one. The fourth probably had clothes, but it contained the belongings of their friend Scharada and was locked. "Am, tell me you did the laundry."

Aameh sat cross-legged on the spare bed surrounded by a blizzard of paper. She held up a few sheets and leaned over to put them on the table. She could lug a two thousand page complaint all the way to the residential area, she could paint naked men on the ceiling of their room, because some old world fellow did it, but apparently she could not carry laundry down the corridor to machines eagerly awaiting it.

"Aameh! You said you'd wash the clothes."

Aaxyl tightened the towel as she scanned their room: two beds and a spare, a table and a chair, and barely any space to walk.

Aameh gestured absently at the table. An unfamiliar pile of welfare clothes sat on it. The T-shirt was fine, and she wore it. The flimsy, elastic-waisted trousers wouldn't do. Like the bland food paste, and cramped coffin-bunks, the welfare clothes met needs, but not aspirations.

She checked the dorm tag. "You got these from Scharada's coffin-dorm. Where are *my* clothes?"

Aameh turned to her. "They will look very flattering on you."

"I don't want to be flattered, I want pockets I can put stuff into without the weight undressing me if I jump." Aaxyl could pack a universe in the pockets of cargo pants, which these were not. "Where are *my* pants?"

Aameh freed a leg to the floor and reached under the bed to pull out a bundle of unwashed clothes tied by a shirt. "I'll do them in a bit. I know how to find the *The Whisperer*."

She'd known better than to argue the SecPro complaint issue, but clearly she hadn't given up.

"Why would you want to?"

Aaxyl pulled her unwashed cargo pants free, sniffing at them. Hersh was very particular about punctuality. Aaxyl dressed. Her comm snapped onto its strap on her wrist: 9:33. She reached for her FastSprints.

"Listen to this." Hazel eyes gleamed conspiratorially. "Family and friends said 'he talked to himself', 'someone needed help and was calling him', 'he went to meet someone only he could hear'."

"Whose family and friends?"

"The Whisperer's victims! Your nemesis is kidnapping people!" Aameh pushed a printed paper at her. It was one of those lengthy analytical articles in the *Dome Times* about unsolved missing persons cases. Dead boring.

"I'm not missing," Aaxyl said drily.

"What if you'd answered him? You only stopped hearing him because your mother injected you with my blood."

Whoa. Where had that come from? Aaxyl thudded the shoes to the floor, turned the chair to face the spare bed, and sat. "I'm not certain of that!" Aaxyl pushed her feet into the FastSprints, bending to tighten the straps. "I used to say it, because you followed me like you wanted your blood back. It was a joke, Am."

Aameh caught her hand as she straightened. "Ax, if she knew symbionts don't work in me, she could have done it to protect you from him."

"Well, we'll never know."

"Some of his victims showed up in the Null Dorms or morgue, Ax." Aameh handed her another paper. "The list matches dome notifications of unidentified bodies and nulls."

"I don't have time for this." Aaxyl dropped it on the table unseen.

While immortality brought respite from the fear of extinction, symbionts could keep bodies alive without a functioning mind. Comatose immortals were stored in life support boxes in the Null Dorms. All she knew about them was dormer sarcasm: the only difference between nulls and the dead was that the dead could be disposed of. And oh, care for them ate up the Dorm budget that could be spent on the living. Aameh was elbow-deep in obscure records, otherwise read only by governance provider employees paid to maintain them.

"Notice anything?" Aameh jiggled the paper. Notes decorated the margins of a list in Aameh's distinctive calligraphy.

Aaxyl loved Aameh, but.

Aameh thumped the paper triumphantly. "They're the *same* people, kidnapped once, found several times." She pulled out *more* sheets of paper. "Descriptions of missing residents, dormers, descriptions of unidentified..."

"Is this some project?" Aameh freelanced for artistic or analytical projects to retain *creative space t*hough this sounded personal. Aaxyl, on the other hand, had an actual job, and no intention of letting Hersh down. "What does all this have to do with us?"

"I'm taking a job in the Null Dorms to find out."

"What?" Aaxyl hated it when she sounded shrill. Composure was power. Too late.

Aameh stacked the ignored sheets of paper. "The job is safe. I checked."

"Not the job, Am. Criminals. *If* the Whisperer is real, he's dangerous. If anyone is kidnapping anyone, they are dangerous. Give this to the journalist who published the article."

"I couldn't trace the journalist who wrote the story." Aameh squirmed sheepishly. "He quit his job. Used up both our comm quotas trying to find him."

Aaxyl rarely used comms beyond messaging Aameh. It was the inquisitive one who'd miss her wasteland documentaries and information about anything and everything until Monday.

Aaxyl asked as calmly as she could. "And that doesn't sound suspicious to you?"

"It is!" Excitement laced Aameh's voice as she folded the article into the back pocket of Aaxyl's cargo pants. "At least read this when you have time."

"We'll discuss this in the evening, but you definitely aren't investigating anything on your own." Aaxyl drummed *bye* on the door with a quick roll of her fingers, and dashed off to work.

Despite inner residents equating the Dorms with squalor, they ensured the welfare of sixty percent of the dome population through a meticulous system of incentives and management. The precise layout located manufacturing and offices adjacent to the dome wall on each floor, and accommodated dormers as close to their place of work as possible. Staggered shifts ensured negligible risk of stampedes. At this time of the morning though, a crowd of dormers still ambled to work at a comfortable pace, because they were well-adjusted people without Aameh delaying them with her weirdities.

She shouldered through the crush of dormers at the elevators, and barrelled down the five levels of stairs. Or tried her best. With each floor adding to the horde heading down, Aaxyl jumped the railing with one level left, earning profanity from the dormers below.

She jogged through the labyrinth of shops and offices on the ground floor to Hersh's clinic, slowing to a pace befitting a medic assistant as she entered. Twelve years here and she still felt like an impostor, a dorm-rat with wiry muscles and rough palms better suited to a labourer.

A few dormers sat in the waiting area she breezed past to the clinic. Equipment and a treatment recliner gleamed on one side and treatment beds lined the other. She headed straight through to the shelves behind Hersh for her medic assistant's uniform.

He took one look at her, and asked, "What did Aameh do now?"

"Long story."

The waiting patients entered at 10:00, filling four of the six beds.

Three needed HealSYMB. This was almost the entirety of their practice. The symbionts competed with pathogens, even as they repaired damage to the host bodies. This single culture combined with an adequate nutrient intake had relegated most diseases to medical history and made humans functionally immortal. The surplus symbionts would help patients recover faster, and die out over time, returning to sustainable levels.

The fourth dormer needed AthSYMB to work on dome repairs. Aaxyl assessed him for risk of violence. Such precautions resulted in a misbelief that AthSYMB caused aggression. It didn't, but strength boosts allowed violent people to inflict more damage.

Hersh and Aaxyl settled into a well-rehearsed routine as more dormers drifted in. They checked medical records, transfused symbionts, attached nutrient drips, and sent people off once they recovered from the energy drain from the initial healing.

Empty of patients, the clinic looked like what it was: a partitioned section of a dorm hall. The other three housed paediatrics, gynaecology, and assorted medics. Each section inherited a massive door, turning them into convincing independent facilities.

By the time Aaxyl sank into the treatment recliner for a breather, it was almost time for lunch. Aameh's paper crumpled in her back pocket.

Aaxyl scanned the article and was relieved it had no similarities to The Whisperer until... damn it. The reports of victim behaviour did sound familiar.

Aaxyl folded the article into an arrowhead and slung it at Hersh to get his attention. "How acquainted are you with telepathy?"

"Telepathy is a rare symbiont effect. Why?" Hersh unfolded her origami.

"Fifty-six unexplained missing persons over two decades. Most turned up as nulls or in the morgue. Investigators are stumped. Aameh thinks the kidnapper is telepathic."

"Not likely," Hersh said. "Telepathy isn't common and requires both recipient and sender to be telepaths. Such powers emerged when the symbionts were still adapting to us in the early twenty-second century. There are very few survivors of those symbionts. Modern folks just have enhanced healing or occasionally, superior strength."

Most dormers were more than two hundred years old, but they'd received HealSYMB to become immortal. They had no powers as described in the stories of the original ancients.

But, on the other hand, "Telepathy still exists, even if not common?"

"Less than seven hundred thousand dormers live here in Ekta Dorms. Multiply it by seven Dorms. Add a generous hundred thousand for the Null Dorms." He grabbed a pen and scribbled exasperated math. "A maximum of five lakh in the Dorms, plus three lakh inner city residents. With this generous overestimation, there are eight lakh people in the Dome. Maybe one or two in a lakh are telepathic. Let's exaggerate that too to three. How do you kidnap fifty-six telepaths out of a population with only twenty-four telepaths?"

Hersh tossed the math enriched article back. Aaxyl dived nimbly to save it.

"If not telepathy, then what?"

"No clue. Something is off, but hard to say what. She should give this to SecPros," Hersh said.

"She pestered them and they ignored her," Aaxyl said. "Now she's got this in her head and applied for a job in the Null Dorms."

Hersh considered this for a while, then asked, "Do you want me to get her application refused?"

"I could do it myself." For another five years, till Aameh turned twenty-five, Aaxyl owned that bunch of crazy, and could prevent Aameh from doing jobs she didn't approve of.

But it wouldn't stop Aameh's curiosity. The more she was disbelieved, the more the stubborn one would strive to prove herself right.

Aaxyl hated risk when it came to Aameh. It had been all she could do to keep Aameh safe and happy over the years. She didn't want anything upsetting their fine balance. Aameh leaped before she looked.

A small orchestra of beeps and pings chimed. Aaxyl peeked to see what the fire was. Gynaecology wanted a consult for a woman with an ectopic pregnancy and gestational diabetes.

Diabetes had once afflicted almost the entire species until the energy consumption of symbionts all but eradicated it. A bigger concern with blood glucose was low levels, particularly after the administration of HealSYMB, except in low symbiont conditions, like a pregnancy.

Symbionts were the leading cause of miscarriages, long pregnancies due to delayed fetal development, and very low birth rates. It was the ultimate irony that symbionts made humans almost immortal, but seriously hindered reproduction. So much so, it was near impossible to increase the population to a more optimal level for species security and progress.

Another factor hindering birthrates was the greatly diminished population of eligible women in the wake of the violence, disease and desperate poverty after the collapse of the old world. By the time the truth finally became apparent, women were less than ten percent of the population. Centuries later, the world still struggled to meet a replacement rate.

Was it any surprise many women had little interest in reproduction? Even the most determined of breeders tired of the heartbreak of miscarriages.

There was no good answer for this poor woman. If they administered HealSYMB, she was likely to miscarry. If they didn't, the transplanted ectopic pregnancy was unlikely to heal or thrive with the high blood glucose. It would endanger her life. The pregnancy had progressed too far to adapt to in vitro conditions. At least, she had a partner to share her grief.

"You aren't going to be able to protect Aameh forever," Hersh murmured, scrolling through the reports.

From the moment she'd taken Aameh under her wing, Aaxyl had been out of her depth. She didn't understand art, argue about complicated scientific theories or chase mysteries. Given a choice between adventure and safety, Aaxyl wouldn't even consider adventure. She was just a worker responsible for nurturing a genius.

Aameh's horizon extending beyond Aaxyl's capacity to protect her was inevitable. It terrified Aaxyl.

And yet, Aaxyl knew Aameh could just as easily trip down the stairs. "I don't want to limit her. Just..."

Hersh gestured for the article. "I'll talk to Dhrit. He can permit her to examine the Null Dorms records and order an investigation if she finds anything concrete."

Admin Dhrit's father, Saisrisel, was the sole provider of nuclear cores enabling small-scale nuclear gen globally. They were the founding members of the dome. These were important people. As the Administrator of all eight Dorms, if Dhrit Saisrisel ordered an investigation, SecPros couldn't ignore him.

Aameh wouldn't investigate criminals if SecPros did it.

She hoped this would be the end of the matter.

AVANT's Immersia series brings pathbreaking synesthetics to enhance sensory detail in 3D immersive movies and interactives. Tech Edge, Thursday, October 9, 2442

~~*~*~*

AAMEH: D4F2, NULL DORMS

Aameh ran a finger across the SIS screen in bewilderment where she sat hunched at the dorm-supervisor's desk peering at the numbers spewing forth. The Null Dorms records were never designed to be read by humans. Almost all the access beyond admissions was by the machine network that cared for the nulls. Aameh's fourth day at work barely revealed any data classifications to for her to investigate. She'd spent her first two days figuring out how to retrieve name entries from the avalanche of values for each Life Support Unit.

She'd chosen D4F2, dorm four on the second floor, only because it contained the sole living victim of The Whisperer. Reported missing once, but found thrice, he'd stayed put for a year now, but she wanted to keep an eye on him.

There was an extra chair today, for Aameh's backpack. So much better than putting it on the floor.

Aameh liked the Null Dorms and the sense of solitude wrapped around sleeping potential—a hundred thousand non-persons in life support units, their stories locked tight inside them. If a null awakened in her time here, what an experience that would be, to witness someone sleeping for decades, maybe even a century, awakening to a changed world.

The twenty LSRs—Life Support Racks—twinkling with occasional lights beyond the dorm-supervisor's desk, were her companions, minding their business as she conducted hers. The humming mechanical silence suited her just fine.

A throat cleared at the door, and a quiet, thin man with an owlish look entered. Sambit Amdani, the Director of the Null Dorms, sported a brief, thin moustache in a stingy claim to masculinity to go with an impeccably tailored black *prezine* style suit. She'd met him on the day after she joined when he'd escorted the President of the Dome on an inspection. She hadn't expected to see him again. Directors didn't exactly mingle with dormers, but Aameh was staff here. Perhaps Directors met staff more often.

"Good morning!" The chair creaked as Aameh stood and extended her hand.

Sambit walked over with a handsome young assistant in tow. He barely looked older than her, and even more fair-skinned, but with a healthy pink glow rather than Aameh's pale tones.

She hated to disappoint Sambit, when he had given her the opportunity to examine the Dorms records. "I haven't made any findings yet, Director. I'm still familiarising myself with the records."

Sambit waved her words away and turned to his assistant. "This is Aameh, the dormer investigating the missing persons." He turned to her. "NeoJai is Admin Dhrit's son. He'll be verifying your findings."

Introductions made, Sambit left. NeoJai hesitated as he approached her, eyes scanning her section of the desk and returning to her.

Aameh extended her hand. She liked people who hesitated. They wouldn't trample you.

She gave herself a mental once over to check for anything she might have done to give him pause. She was wearing a dress she'd stitched herself. Tiny white, pink and red flowers textured soft black fabric. A ruffled hemline with just the right weight flared if she turned. She turned slightly, hoping he'd notice it.

NeoJai wore a peach coloured formal shirt with a good fit. They'd get along just fine. She waved him to the seat next to hers, facing the LSRs. The dorm supervisor's desks were long enough to seat half a dozen comfortably. There was plenty of room. She took her backpack out of his chair.

"I'd hoped to arrive on time on my first day." NeoJai set a briefcase into a large lower drawer as he ran his eyes over her papers sprawled across the desk.

She hadn't realised she could use the drawers for her belongings. She put her backpack in one as well, in a belated attempt at tidiness.

"I come in early," she assured him. "Usually, it's just me and the LSUs in the LSRs."

"LSUs in LSRs?"

"That's what the staff here calls these." Aameh waved at the nulls. "Life Support Units and Racks."

He ran an indifferent eye across the hall. "Why do you come early?"

"Ax works in the clinic at Ekta Dorms, so she drops me in early to be there on time."

"Ax?"

"My sister, Aaxyl. She's raised me since she was nine and I was one," Aameh said. "She drops me here on the Dorms bus and then runs back to get to work."

"You need to be escorted to work?" NeoJai scrutinised her. "How do you get back?"

"She picks me up," Aameh said. Aaxyl did so much for her, she sometimes felt guilty. Aaxyl had already sacrificed her childhood. Aameh didn't want to take up the rest of her life too. "I can't heal normally. Injuries can be life threatening. She's overprotective, and won't accept I'm twenty now and have to learn to manage."

"She runs between Dorms twice a day so that you can work here?" NeoJai looked impressed.

"She won't spend the SociCred on the bus for herself," Aameh grimaced. "Says she can run back in the time it takes to wait for the bus. Hopefully in a few days she'll see that it's safe, and let me travel on the Dorms bus on my own."

Despite all her objections, Aaxyl hadn't once complained about the added work for her.

NeoJai finally took a seat and activated his SIS screen. "What do you normally do?"

Aameh brightened. "I'm an artist with a special interest in science and analysis. I freelance for the Ekta Dorms Art Department and anyone else who'll give me work and work from my room. I can't afford the compute for final quality outputs, but I'm great at high def graphics. Virtual sets and model detail for immersives, research visualisations, interactivity design and such. Of course, my comm can't handle that kind of load, but I use the C&Cs and if I file bug reports, they reward me with compute time. Even more if I can catch security risks—"

"C&C?"

"Communications and Compute?" Aameh eyed him skeptically. He didn't know the basics. "Dormers get an hour per week of C&C on the Dorm SIS that they can use from their comms or if they don't have comms, from the public C&C booths. They have big screens and are great for art design. And a Dorm SIS of course has plenty of compute power, but that still isn't enough time for me to craft high quality scenes. So I take up partials. I wish I had sculpting gloves—"

"I get it. I have a car. I can drop you back."

SPACERS expects to establish a human colony on Mars in five decades. Modern Science Review, Monday, October 20, 2442

~~*~*~*

AAXYL: DIRECTOR LEELA'S OFFICE

"I need you available to handle emergencies till we can find a replacement symbiontist. We can divert regular cases." Leela spoke without taking her eyes off her SIS screen as soon as Aaxyl entered her office. Her stone-faced bodyguard, Kant, was still closing the door.

Aaxyl had been summoned to Leela's office early in the morning and there she stood, trying to make sense of it. "Where's Hersh?"

Time tiptoed. Replacement, Leela had said.

Leela looked up. "I thought you knew. Hersh resigned from his job last night. Some emergency with his family in 91-600. He doesn't expect to return."

"He didn't say anything?" Aaxyl clutched the back of the chair before her, ears ringing in the silence. What was she supposed to do now? She didn't have a concept of a clinic without Hersh.

Leela shook her head. "Just that he'd update contacts once he'd settled in."

"He was our... he can count... you can count on..." Aaxyl surprised herself with a choked sob and jumped as Kant's huge hand patted her shoulder.

Leela waved Aaxyl to a chair. "Sit. Take a moment."

Aaxyl shook her head. "I'll need to prepare to... for... if I have to open the clinic on time." What was wrong with her? She was beginning sentences without thinking them through.

Aaxyl needed to get away from Leela's sharp eyes. Nobody needed the makeshift symbiontist turning into a soggy mess.

Leela nodded, and Kant opened the door.

Aaxyl swiped at her eyes as she left.

~~*~*~*

NEOJAI: D4F2, NULL DORMS

The biggest tomb in human history housed the living. The world's only facility dedicated to the care of non-persons on a massive scale, the Null Dorms presented an unending quagmire of political controversies, funding black holes, and ethical dilemmas about the rights to life support or termination. And yet, a few nulls woke up every decade, ensuring that the rest couldn't be written off.

The stench of synthetic perfume from the disinfectant wafted from the dim depths of the most desolate place in the Dome. NeoJai had found the scent invigorating on his first day here. Two weeks in, it held all the forced brightness of a desperate sex worker's seduction.

D4F2 housed four hundred non-persons on automated life-support in a standard coffin-dorm layout. The bunk racks managed only half the number of occupants here to accommodate life support. The same eighteen foot desks on thirty-foot-long dorm supervisor platforms sat vacant. Bot bays replaced busy supplies areas. Without the bustle of humans, these dormitories lacked meaningful life.

Most of the non-persons in this one were victims of the Null Dorms Earthquake of 2324. A collapse of the erstwhile Bhumi Dorms killed a thousand. Twenty thousand more never regained consciousness. Brain dead or with minds too damaged to retain enough memory for a personality, their tragedy named the rebuilt Null Dorms as well as retroactively renamed the earthquake.

His grim mood brightened as AxAm's voices broke through the all pervading pseudo-silence of machines at work. He folded up his sleeves and left the top button of his shirt undone to emphasise his neck and jaw, hoping Aaxyl would drop in for a bit. He swivelled his chair toward the door, leaning slightly against the armrest in a nonchalant pose.

Aameh limped in alone. She'd caught her thigh on a medibot a week ago, and bled till her shoes were soaked. She slapped on a dressing before fainting.

He'd rushed her to the Ekta Dorms clinic in a panic, only for both Aaxyl and Hersh to respond calmly, reassuring him. This was why Aaxyl escorted Aameh. He resolved to look out for her better.

"How's the leg?" NeoJai said by way of a greeting, as he had, every day since.

"Hey, NeoJai." Aameh shrugged as usual. "Were you quirking?"

"What's quirking?"

"It's when people do things to grab the attention of those they are attracted to." Aameh pulled her comm off her wristband and attached it to the SIS connector.

NeoJai covered his face with his palm. "Please tell me Aaxyl doesn't know."

"You should talk to her." Aameh slid into the seat next to him, calling up data on the residents in the Dorms. "It's mating behaviour."

Basic social norms suggested that if you noticed someone embarrassing themselves, you didn't immediately give it a label and discuss it. But he didn't mind Aameh's tactlessness. She noticed it. That was all.

"NeoJai," Aaxyl called.

He jolted to his feet hoping she hadn't overheard Aameh, his mind now wiped clean of anything clever to say. Unlike Aameh's easy camaraderie, her sister was quicksilver. Lush hair barely softened features sharp enough to cut a hand that dared caress them. Practical clothes hung on a wiry frame. Everything about her was sparse and efficient, but her grey eyes had worlds living within. He craved to suffer that slight frown for her, freeing her laugh.

"Hi, Aaxyl." NeoJai tugged imaginary wrinkles from his shirt and walked slowly enough to not appear over-eager. He scrambled to think of something witty. "Can I help you?" he asked, like a receptionist.

"We may have a new symbiontist coming in today and I was wondering if..."

Aameh's stories of Aaxyl had inspired him so much, he'd do anything to make her life easier. He'd pick Aameh up too, but Aaxyl had said mornings weren't a problem, and he hadn't dared argue. "Of course, I'll drop Aameh home as usual."

"Thanks!" Aaxyl drummed the door with a quick roll of her fingers. "Just wanted to make sure." She dashed off before he reached the door.

NeoJai slunk back to his chair.

Aameh stood and pushed the button for amplification. Her voice was bright as she waved at their unconscious non-audience. "Good morning!"

She did that every day. She stood like an insignificant speck in front of hundreds of nulls and *greeted* them.

Every day, the racks responded with a resounding silence. He wondered what she'd do if one responded. Who was he kidding? She'd be delighted.

"They can't see you, you know?"

"Us dorm-rats stick together," Aameh informed him. "It's a friendly gesture." Aameh reattached her comm to her wrist, picked up an ear piece and headed for a row of racks. "Meet you for lunch." She stepped off the stage and stood on the lift to access life-support units higher up in the racks. She always began with the same null. Some Boris something.

The metallic whine of the lift faded as Aameh took it into the maze of racks, motion-triggered lights marking her way. She'd go to other dormitories when she was done here. With no problems found with the data, who knew what she did? Probably visited different non-persons to reassure them that they'd be okay. She'd return for lunch. It was their ritual since his first day here, when he'd shared the food his mother had packed for him.

His mother, charmed when he described Aameh's enthusiasm, sent enough for both of them ever since. Every day, Aameh sketched something interesting to send back to her, adding "Thank you" before signing her name.

His mother collected them ever since the first sketch showed NeoJai sitting at his desk. The next one portrayed NeoJai spotlit before the twinkling depths of the dormitory. Two weeks in, his mother had a vivid record of NeoJai's days in the Null Dorms.

As far as work went, the data checked out. Supervisors had no work here. Most dorms didn't even have supervisors. Aameh alone remained busy all day, visiting random dormitories. At first, NeoJai had thought she'd been investigating, but he'd monitored the records for two weeks now. He didn't know why they continued. Probably because he wanted to drop Aameh home daily so that he could be too tongue-tied to talk to a busy Aaxyl one more time.

He went to find Aameh. He needed to do *something*, even if it was... whatever it was that Aameh did. He trudged over to where she was lowering the lift after examining the non-person on the fourth rack of the D side of rack 4-3, which was identical to every rack in every dorm on every floor.

Ironically, this wasn't called a coffin-dorm. It took awake and sarcastic dormers to name things like that.

"How's Boris?" NeoJai leaned against a rack. The life support pod near his shoulder had a bald man in it, oblivious to him leaning a mere foot away from his slack face. Life support indicators illuminated slack face and shoulders with data of *vital* signs in macabre irony.

"Boreil." Aameh flapped her hands at him before putting a finger on her lips and gesturing him to follow.

What now? He trailed her lift to the end of the Dorms Hall, where she parked it next to another as a parade of three service bots whirred past them into the maze. Aameh pointed to where the service bots had come from.

He followed her into the service bots bay housing the stocky green medic-bots that maintained life-support.

"The bots use a machine network unique to the Null Dorms. They report only results into the main system used by humans and don't log speech." Aameh now spoke in a low voice. "We won't be overheard."

"Overheard? I doubt anybody would hear even if we screamed." The entire Null Dorms had a few hundred staff, at best, including everyone from maintenance and security to researchers and management. "Is this necessary?"

"There are inexplicable disappearances of non-persons," Aameh reminded him. "We can never be too careful. Ax will skin me alive if I get into trouble."

"I checked non-persons against records as described in your report. There are no disappearances," NeoJai told her.

"You didn't even bother to read my latest report, did you?" Aameh shook her head. "I've been carrying out the investigation on my own."

"What are you talking about, Aameh? I have one report from you, and I read it, or I wouldn't be here." NeoJai pulled his comm off his wrist and handed it to her. "See for yourself. Accordingly, I've checked the records daily for the past two weeks. No nulls are missing."

Aameh examined his comm, bewildered. "My second and third reports are missing. My requests for meetings are missing." She transferred her reports directly to his comm. "These are my reports. See the submission date."

NeoJai checked. She had indeed submitted them, but they were missing from the SIS. "But there are no anomalies in the records, anyway." NeoJai would have found them.

"That is what my other reports explained." Aameh tapped his comm. "After my first report, the names of the missing nulls were removed from the records, so that all the records matched. I traced them from admission records and alerted Admin Dhrit to hurry, because someone was covering up. After that, the admission records changed too. So I sent my third report."

"So you've been investigating all this time?" He'd fallen for a cover up.

Aameh frowned. "You think I go around checking non-persons because I like riding an ancient platform lift?"

NeoJai hoped she didn't guess the truth—that he had thought she was spending her days *talking* to the nulls.

"But how do you even know which dormers are missing if even the admission records are gone?"

If the admission records were removed, tracking would be impossible. The null wouldn't be on the system to be missing.

Aameh tapped her comm with a smug grin. "As soon as they altered the records the first time, I copied the list. I compare it with the SIS daily and I check any changes in person."

Clever.

"You should have told me. I just sat there all day thinking nothing was wrong. I could have helped you."

Aameh shrugged. "I thought you didn't care enough to take prompt action."

NeoJai stared at her in disbelief. "You eat my lunch every day and this is what you think of me?"

"I didn't mean to offend you. These guys have been comatose for years. Many think they should be terminated anyway." Aameh scanned his face with a sheepish expression. "I'm saying this all wrong. Honestly, I don't know how rich people work."

"Just shut up, Aameh," NeoJai groaned. "Inner or dormer, an investigation is the same."

"We don't investigate in the same way!" Her voice rose to an indignant pitch. "Your father is the Administrator of all eight Dorms. You can force investigators to... to... investigate!"

NeoJai wasn't going to argue. The thought of arguing with Aameh exhausted him. "I'll recommend isolated backups of records. Your list is good for us, but we need authenticated records for evidence."

"See? I can't order that."

UDAY imposes hefty fines on illegal firecrackers, reminds that Dome 91-110 is a no-combustion zone. Annual Diwali art contest at the Octagon on 2nd November. Dome notifications, Friday, October 24, 2442

~~*~*~*

AAXYL: THE CLINIC, EKTA DORMS

Aaxyl hesitated to encourage NeoJai. His eager smile, clean-shaved face, and creamy complexion said life hadn't got around to scribbling on him yet. His admiration intrigued her, but Admin Dhrit's son inhabited a different world from dorm-rats. No point checking out a road to somewhere she had no intention of going.

She raced back to work, letting gravity speed her down the steps, bolted past the security desk and out of the building like a slingshot. The stagnation of the Null Dorms gave way to freedom as she breezed through parking. Across the ring road, the central Octagon—the rarefied stratosphere of privilege—rose beyond the residential area.

NeoJai lived in that direction. Perhaps, if she lived in the residential area, she'd reciprocate, but Aaxyl turned left on the ring road, back to her life in the Ekta Dorms. Less than half of sector populations lived in the spacious residential areas, while the giant welfare dormitories crammed the rest within a fifth of that space, squashed between the ring road and the dome boundary like spectators to the arena of prosperity. A mere one percent of the world population at the time of the great economic crisis of 2053 had remained by the time the Enduring War ended in 2167, but centuries later the Dorms still felt overcrowded.

She sped over the fragrant wedge of the inter-sector park. The Ekta Dorms towered on her left. The glass exterior implied a bright and spacious interior. In truth, these highly coveted windowed rooms were offices and residences of department heads and specialists. Not dormers.

She skidded to a halt around a circle of gawkers in the parking area.

A zeplyn gleamed among the dorm buses and a few cars. While a about the size of a large car or small bus, the agrav-tech made it more practical to park on roofs. Aaxyl had never seen one up close. It was a beauty with paint so glossy, it was hard to discern its colour. There were no wheels. It simply hovered slightly above the ground.

Aaxyl wished she had the time to marvel at the gorgeous thing, but she was late. She ran into the building and through the windowless maze of the main level of the Ekta Dorms, navigating busy corridors with the ease of habit.

The clinic was already open without any staff. Not good.

She slowed barely in time to avoid colliding with a tall man in a bright yellow whatever-that-was waiting just inside the door. Aaxyl blinked. Long hair and beard framed delicate features like a lush mane on a pencil thin lion. The unimon designer clothes suggested Leo had wandered very far from whatever elite bubble he'd escaped from.

"Take a seat," Aaxyl told him as she hurried past. "I'll attend to you in a minute."

The Ekta Dorms SIS logged her arrival, and displayed a notice for medics on the screen on Hersh's desk. Her desk now. It still stung that Hersh hadn't told her that he was leaving.

She scanned the notice as she shrugged on a white coat. She'd never read a notice about an appointment before. They just ran into new people and introduced themselves.

It is my pleasure to announce the appointment of Dr. Sam Ajath of AVANT as the symbiontist at the Ekta Dorms clinic. Dr. Ajath's wealth of experience in symbiont research comes highly recommended by Noir and Mohan, the representatives of Abrahamha himself. His work for AVANT's philanthropic arm, SYMBTech, promises new symbiont based treatment protocols. As a representative of a Superdome organisation, Dr. Ajath enjoys diplomatic status in our dome. We are privileged to be graced with his expertise. Ekta Dorms welcomes Dr. Ajath.

Privileged to be graced with...? Aaxyl did a doubletake as she scratched her head.

Residents of the Superdome on the deserted American continent represented organisations offering free or heavily subsidised products or services toward the continued survival of the human race. They headquartered there independently of all local governments to ensure non-partisan access to all. They had privileges and independence of functioning in all signatories of the Global Agreement.

This diplomat was her new boss? Talk of being overqualified for a job. Dorms symbiontists were medics trained to administer symbiont products safely. It was all they needed.

A symbiontist recommended by both Mohan and Noir... If Aaxyl could impress him with her work, a mentor like that could transform her life.

"Incoming patient," the SIS announced. "Sixty-four-year-old male arriving in two minutes with bleeding gash..." Name, injuries and medical history replaced the notice on Hersh's screen, while it droned on about estimated blood loss and glucose levels.

Aaxyl readied the innermost bed, and assigned Gash's medical data to it, leaving beds closest to the door free for emergencies.

Leo hovered in the door again, like an irritating yellow wasp.

Aaxyl waved him away. "You! This is a clinic. Keep the door clear."

He complied sulkily.

This wasn't a popularity contest. As long as he didn't impede incoming cases, she'd endure his disdain.

The paramedic hovered the patient to the door, smoothly detaching the stretcher onto a waiting trolley. The hoverboard slid out and he turned to leave with choreographed ease.

Aaxyl transferred Gash to his bed. His gash was more like a stab on the left side of his stomach. He was unconscious, but not in danger. He'd perk right back up for more mayhem with some nutrients in him to counter the drain from the HealSYMB. She assigned his medical data to the bed, detached the gurney, and rechecked tubes and wires. This bed placed the sensor cables and monitoring processor under the gurney lock, making them easy to dislodge when the gurney detached. Brilliant beds donated as welfare because they scared the wealthy in private hospitals when alarms wailed about incorrect use and missing vitals.

The paramedics had already cleaned Gash's wound during the transfer and administered HealSYMB. She added a nutrient drip, and contemplated the half-millilitre transfuser of HealSYMB she'd kept ready.

Symbionts died on contact with air, and HealSYMB had been too precious to waste in the early days of immortality. An illiterate teenager had won the design bounty of the twenty-second century with the inexpensive soft vials. The needle broke the seal under pressure to penetrate the skin and deliver the dose. An ingenious single-handed press and pinch design that had endured the test of time and eliminated wastage, quadrupling lives saved overnight.

If an illiterate teenager could be an inventor for SYMBTech, dormers AxAm could work their way out of welfare with the right mentor.

She rolled the gurney back toward the door, when a blow sent her reeling. Gash shoved the gurney out of his way, and bolted for the door with the tell-tale jerky motion of someone unused to AthSYMB.

Leo was in the door again. The crowded main floor lay beyond.

Aaxyl lunged to intercept Gash.

"Call security!" she yelled at the SIS, and rammed Gash with all her strength, tackling him to the ground to restrain him. Someone her size either disabled a crazy on AthSYMB, or got admitted to the clinic herself. She didn't want a repeat of the second option, ever.

At twice her size, Gash stood with her still perched on his back, leaving Aaxyl scrambling for options. She locked her arm around his neck, aiming for a choke hold, and dug her heel into his wound. She hoped the pain distracted him enough that she could choke him before he thought to rip her arm off.

"This is enough chaos for my first hour here." Leo had appeared out of nowhere and she lacked enough free hands to wave him back.

Gash stopped abruptly, and momentum dumped Aaxyl's startled butt to the floor.

Leo caught Gash on his way down with a dancer's grace, smoothly carrying him right back to the bed he'd escaped, adding restraints for good measure.

She forgave Leo for loitering and fell back, heaving great breaths. How had Leo stopped Gash?

His words registered. *His first hour here.*

She should have guessed. Odd zeplyn in the parking lot. Odd announcement of the new symbiontist. Odd creature in the clinic. It added up.

In her defense, she'd never seen a medic who dressed like a colourful bird from one of Aameh's wasteland documentaries. Or, for that matter, grew long facial hair that would be a nightmare to clean after one well aimed blood spurt from a patient.

"You're Sam? Perfect." Aaxyl trudged over to extend a hand. "Sorry for this unorthodox introduction. I hope to learn a lot from you."

Sam glared from her hand to her face. "*Doctor* Sam. What goes on in this place?"

"Well, Dr. Sam," Aaxyl hurried to reassure him, "this is a welfare clinic. There are the occasional incidents, but this is not the norm."

Perfect Sam wiped his hands fastidiously, unbuttoning his bloody shirt. "Not what I meant. Overconfidence. Late for work. Deranged guy high on AthSYMB, being given nutrients before HealSYMB. Medic assistant *fighting* instead of waiting for security."

"I'm sorry."

Unconscious people didn't come pre-labelled as 'deranged' or she'd have restrained him. But she should have let security deal with Gash. He could have injured her badly. And she *had* been late. If the emergency had arrived earlier... Life had taught Aaxyl to pick her battles. Perfect Sam had a point.

Guards wheeled Gash away.

Perfect Sam turned to her.

"I don't work with careless assistants or SYMB-junkies. Leave or I'll file a complaint." Perfect Sam dropped his bloody shirt in the laundry tub and sauntered to the bathroom in a dazzling display of masculine grace.

SYMB-junkie?

Symbionts had no narcotic or addictive effect. Compulsive consumption implied a mental problem, not a reliable medic assistant for over a decade. But if he refused to work with her, she didn't have a job.

How could she tell Aameh that they couldn't afford their room because she'd been fired from the clinic? Aaxyl pinched tears back in, swallowing them with the other useless emotions. What were her options? Crying was out. As was rage, humiliation, confrontation, wishing Hersh was back. Leela would sympathise but not interfere with how a specialist ran his clinic.

Perfect Sam returned, elevating a standard clinic uniform to high fashion. He was *incongruous* in the drab welfare clinic like a compelling puzzle: identify which doesn't belong with the others. Movements like poetry, a voice to listen to forever if it weren't firing her and a skin that belonged on celestial beings. No such thing existed in the Dorms. Aaxyl ogled, reluctantly mesmerised.

"Complaint it is." He accessed applications. She hoped he didn't realise that all he had to do was notify a vacancy and her job would be snapped up in an instant. Forget dormers, the medics would trample each other to work with a prestigious expert.

"Wait. I want to apologise."

"This ought to be interesting." Perfect Sam arched a single eyebrow. How could someone be beautiful and ugly at the same time?

Aaxyl crossed her arms to avoid appearing nervous. She said, "We got off on the wrong foot. I should have been more professional. I appreciate you not filing a formal complaint."

Perfect Sam's eyebrow dropped into a frown. She had his attention.

Recipients of welfare learned to pacify what they couldn't change. "Please don't let one incident influence you. You won't find a better assistant in the Dorms. I've worked here for over a decade. Please verify before you decide."

She waited as Perfect Sam checked her work record. Hersh had told her to prove herself, and she had. Aaxyl had rarely taken days off, willingly and cheerfully going beyond what was asked of her. For the SociCred, sure, but she *was good*. She was a preferred backup by paramedics. Surely that counted.

Perfect Sam glanced up from the screen. "You have today to change my mind."

Aaxyl headed for the bathroom with a medic assistant's uniform, and slumped against the wall. No tears. It wasn't yet over. She had a day to win her job back. She tidied the clinic, hoping it wasn't for the last time, and focused on being the best symbiontist's assistant she could be.

A rush of cases arrived from an accident and Perfect Sam dazzled everyone.

His long hair and beard looked more religion-monger offering profound gems of esoteric wisdom than a science professional. Yet, he knew symbionts and procedures she'd never heard of. He referred one person with a rare profile of symbionts to SYMBTech free of charge.

They remained busy until half an hour before closing, and stopped for a late lunch. She opened her meal packet. One egg with spiced rice. The upgraded meals claimed to be unique, but familiar spices flavoured vegetables, egg, meat or rice, and the same fillings hid in wraps, rolls or breads. Still, it beat food paste.

She cancelled her meals and got SociCred refunded before eating, embarrassed when she forgot to turn off the speech and the SIS asked her if she wanted to cancel her meals.

The day promised hope and actualised disaster.

She checked out available jobs. Dormers could volunteer for any work they were competent at, but like everything else, the best jobs vanished as soon as they were posted. On the other hand, sanitation listed half a dozen jobs. The job didn't matter. She'd done everything sanitation could list and was authorised on all the systems. She chose the best paying one: a snake-bot operator. Snake-bots cleaned small drains and were less icky than working directly. AxAm would retain their room, but additional comforts would depend on Aameh.

"You aren't a SYMB-junkie."

He scrutinised her over a giant tray of food with bowls full of aromas she couldn't name. It wasn't a question. No need to say anything.

"You did good work."

Again, not a question. Aaxyl dug around with a spoon and pretended to eat.

"You cancelled your meals." He sounded bothered.

She grew up on food paste. It was quality nutrition, if not palatable. Meals were the least of her worries, but Perfect Sam wasn't going to let up till they played conversation.

"You're on call as backup for paramedics," Aaxyl said.

"Is that a symbiontist's job?"

"It isn't. I did it," Aaxyl said. "Are you restoring my job?"

Perfect Sam got busy with his food.

Aaxyl put her spoon down and shot to her feet. "What's wrong with you? You admitted I'm not a SYMB-junkie. You admitted I worked well. So why have I lost my job?"

She stalked to the bathroom and slammed the door for effect. She took a moment to compose herself before she dressed to leave. It didn't work. She got the crying out of her system, quietly. Then she collected her dignity, and came out of the bathroom, and... froze.

"Probably no big deal, but it hasn't healed yet and is still painful." A beloved voice and an awkward chuckle.

This couldn't be happening. A star-struck Aameh sat in the treatment recliner and chatted amicably with Perfect Sam. He sat at Hersh's desk, scratching his beard like it had lice, and glaring at the screen. Four empty transfuser vials of HealSYMB lay discarded on the table. Aaxyl wished she could do this day over.

"Hey, Aaxyl," Aameh beamed. "NeoJai reminded me to tell you that he dropped me off at the gate. I was telling Sam about our ambition to train with SYMBTech, like him."

Not even Aameh's innocent match-making could fix her mood. She supposed it was good NeoJai hadn't come in to witness her humiliation.

Aaxyl wished for the opportunity to at least break the news kindly. Aameh had never met someone like Perfect Sam before. Aaxyl never wanted her to.

"You asked me why you've lost your job." Perfect Sam flourished at the empty HealSYMB transfusers. "You weren't the SYMB-junkie. Your sister was."

"I'm not a SYMB-junkie!" Aameh's camaraderie flash-evaporated to indignation.

"Right. You're not a SYMB-junkie." Perfect Sam sauntered to tower over Aameh and Aaxyl fought to not insert herself between them. "You caught your thigh on the corner of a medic-bot last week, and took enough HealSYMB to heal a beheading today."

Aameh gaped like she noticed for the first time that there was something wrong with the man. Aaxyl wouldn't be surprised if that were true. Aameh navigated the world with an assumption of good faith.

"She was hurt." Aaxyl finally understood why toxic creatures in Aameh's wasteland documentaries were so beautiful. "She needs the HealSYMB!"

Perfect Sam scoffed. "Four vials?"

Aaxyl stopped him right there, palm out. "Check her records."

"I've been through the records. Aameh and you have been supplied with extraordinary amounts of HealSYMB for years on end."

"Yes, and check Aameh's records for why," Aaxyl said, pulling them up. "There have been three symbiontists in her nineteen years of medical history. Were they all corrupt? Can a one-year-old be a SYMB-junkie?"

"Hersh knew about her?" Perfect Sam asked.

"Of course!" Aaxyl said. "Both of us have ten vials of HealSYMB for emergencies because he insisted."

"Do you think I did this to myself?" Aameh pulled her dress up to reveal a small, still-healing wound. "I took four vials of HealSYMB and have been in front of you all through. Why is this cut still half-healed? I didn't take any nutrients. How am I still awake after four vials of HealSYMB?"

If Aameh had been normal, she would've lost consciousness from excessive HealSYMB without nutrients for an energy boost, and remained unconscious till she started healing and the HealSYMB didn't have to work as much. The skin around the wound would be flaky and peeling from abnormally fast healing. But Aameh's injury looked normal and she was alert and arguing as usual.

Perfect Sam stared at Aameh's leg like he expected it to explain itself.

"Hersh doesn't have family in 91-600," he said finally. "Hersh is missing."

That had to be the most bizarre response to an injury, but Aaxyl's gut believed him. Hersh hadn't said goodbye.

"He resigned," Aaxyl said shakily. She should have suspected something instead of being hurt that Hersh didn't tell her.

"It's fake." He scrolled through Aameh's medical history again.

"Is Hersh in danger?" Aaxyl should have known Hersh wouldn't abandon them.

"You suspected us," Aameh connected the dots. "You presumed us guilty and concluded we were SYMB-junkies. Motive."

"Look, I'm sorry." Sam ran his fingers through his hair. "You'd been issued insane amounts of HealSYMB. You'd tried to contact SYMBTech for years. You fought in illegal fights! You have to admit, it didn't look good."

Aaxyl needed him to see they weren't criminals to get her job back. "I contacted SYMBTech to bring Aameh to you. My mother had said we'd be going there, but she didn't return. I was a child myself. It wasn't a big deal."

Aaxyl wasn't supposed to tell anyone about her mother or The Whisperer, but she'd be out of a job unless she convinced him.

"What's your mother's name?"

"I don't know." The truth.

"You don't know your mother's name?"

Aaxyl wanted to cry. How did it matter? "I grew up here. She visited secretly a couple of times a year till she brought Aameh. I was nine. I called her Mom."

Perfect frown stayed put. "Maybe your mother hoped we could treat Aameh?"

Every other thought in Aaxyl's head vanished. "Can you treat her?"

"We could identify strains that work on her to create a more potent culture, but it wouldn't contain anything new," Perfect Sam said. "She'd need two vials instead of ten. Space in symbiont labs isn't cheap. If she's tolerating HealSYMB, there's nothing to be gained from the expense. HealSYMB is free. Use ten vials."

Was he starting to believe her?

Aaxyl took a deep breath and hoped as hard as she could. "Please, I need my job back."

Perfect Sam extended his hand with a gorgeous smile. "If we can start with a clean slate. Forgive me?"

SecPros break up Thar Dorms protest demanding mandatory reproduction for women. Five suffer mild injuries. Dome Times, Tuesday, November 11, 2442

~~*~*~*

NeoJai: D4F2, Null Dorms

Aameh had made NeoJai the star of a theoretical physics poster for the new symbiontist in Aaxyl's clinic. She sketched a nerdy T-shirt with *Quaspar Symbiont Hypothesis* on his caricature, and angled squiggly lines into his clever head. He watched her conjure the educational illustration to life.

A security guard brought a sealed envelope for him. NeoJai opened it to find the authorisation for official backups from the President of the Dome. "I'm amazed we got it at all. Damodar hates Admin Dhrit. Dad was the previous President."

"Hmm?" Aameh asked, absently, as she pencilled the word *Symbion* between the wavy intelligence around his head to match *Quantum*, *Ultra*, and *Anti*. "He seemed nice enough."

"You've met the President of the Dome?" NeoJai had never met him.

"He inspected the Dorms on my second day. It was before you started work. He's tall."

NeoJai laughed at her goofy stare upward. "That's because he's an ancient. He was tall to begin with, and they can add an inch or two a century."

"Huh." She got back to her sketch.

NeoJai had a more important question. "Why does Aaxyl avoid me? Have I offended her?"

"Aaxyl likes you," Aameh replied, pencil busy without pause. "She just thinks that you're rich, so there's no point."

"She likes me?"

Aameh grinned. "You drop me home. She likes me to be safe."

He'd hoped for another kind of like. "Why avoid me then?"

NeoJai would deny it to his dying day, but he had no clue what the *Quaspar Hypothesis* said. Squiggles of light now emanated from his head between the words.

"People leave. She cares too much." Aameh found her can of fixing spray and gave the sketch a light layer. "Besides, AxAm rules prohibit romantic attachments with residents."

"AxAm rules?"

"Rules we have for ourselves." Aameh met his eyes. "Women in the Dorms go and live with rich men outside. Then if the man is bad, they have no money and live at his mercy. We don't want to risk it." She took in his shock. "I don't think you're the abusive type."

"Thanks, I guess," said NeoJai.

Aameh examined the sketch from a distance. "Aaxyl is smart. She never chooses bad men. That's my department. I kiss princes and they turn into frogs. Or remain princes I can't kiss."

NeoJai hadn't imagined Aameh had a romantic life. The thought of Aameh blindly trusting dormers alarmed him. The Dorms had even fewer women than the general population. Desperation could cause men to do stupid things, and Aameh trusted too easily. "Bad how?"

He imaged the art to print. His mother would get the original.

"You aren't the only victim of the Dorm divide. I like the new symbiontist. But he's worse than a resident. Global citizen. Out of my league." Aameh pouted.

NeoJai let the *worse than a resident* go. "But you don't date."

"Of course, I do. I'm curious about sex. But Aaxyl says I miss social cues and choose jerks." She extended her hand for the backup chip. "If we talk about my dull sex life, let me make the backups while we do it."

NeoJai plugged in the official chip and gave her the sealed access codes. "Jerks in what way?"

Aameh's fingers flew as she set up the chip and indicated for him to authenticate the access. NeoJai did as told, waiting for Aameh to continue.

"A few months ago, an artist said he loved me. We gave up Ax's chair and got an extra bed. He turned out to be a SecPro. He seduced me thinking I was a dorm artist called the SoulScaper and dumped me thinking I wasn't."

"Men can be jerks." NeoJai noticed her odd phrasing. She so totally was the SoulScaper.

Aameh shrugged. "I didn't love him and the spare bed comes in handy."

NeoJai burst out laughing. "That wasn't so bad."

"Ax can recognise bad people instantly," Aameh said. "She'd have been a much better SecPro than him, if they had the sense to keep her when she applied."

"Ax... a SecPro?" She seemed rather tiny for that. If this was an AxAm tale, NeoJai hadn't heard it yet.

"You don't know?" Aameh handed him the sketch and searched for something on the SIS. "SecPro trainees live at the facility, so don't need unimon. And then they get paid and can rent a place. Ax loves the clinic, but it was a way out of the Dorms without having any unimon."

"So what went wrong?"

"Here. This went wrong." Aameh sent a video to his screen: SecPro selection trials from four years ago. NeoJai didn't like such content. He'd prefer to just hear what happened. The popularity of the combat tests created a bloodsport rather than a fitness test.

"Contestant A ready?" the test asked.

He was about to dismiss the video when he heard her voice. Curiosity stirred.

"Ready." Aaxyl was a tiny speck in front of a building. Her brief on the screen said her rogue SecPro partner had hijacked a security hover. She had to defend the building and minimise loss of life. She was armed with a gun.

"Contestant B ready?" the test asked.

"Ready." He was in an attack hover. His brief was that the facility manufactured illegal weapons and to exterminate everyone and defeat Contestant A. He had a security hoverboard with mounted guns and a shielded base that he hadn't even seen SecPros use inside the dome.

Live commentary criticised the test as blatantly unsporting. B could fly around shooting people like a game, while A's gun couldn't penetrate his hoverboard's reinforced bottom. Contestant B would score a spectacular victory. Contestant A would lose. Skill wouldn't matter.

Aaxyl should have sued them for endangering her life.

The test started with the hover's camera as it flew at the facility and the tiny Aaxyl ran inside.

A shrill alarm sounded to dismay by viewers. "It appears Contestant A mistook the evacuation alarm for lock-down. It will send her charges into the line of fire."

NeoJai bit his nails. That didn't sound good.

"No-no-no, girl, protect the staff, not feed them to the enemy!" a commentator moaned as her opponent started shooting and the first two simulated staff fell in the door on sight.

A gruff voice, labelled a SecPro trainer, remarked, "The participants get younger and stupider with each year! I—"

The cameras switched abruptly to the interior and the commentary hushed. Aaxyl scaled the open door to perch on the top edge. She moved like lightning.

The gruff voice continued. "Great technique on display here. That door didn't move an inch. It's a pity—what is she doing?"

The hoverboard entered the building over the heads of the simulated staff evacuating, bringing the unsuspecting Contestant B right below Aaxyl. She dived straight at him and knocked him off his hover. Just like that, she had won.

The commentary erupted once more with clips of her dive from different angles.

Unexpected... Outstanding strategy, and a brilliant victory to A... The top view highlights a technique so balanced that the door didn't budge... Well done... Exceptional fighter... she makes diving from that unstable perch to a moving vehicle look easy... big beautiful move here... will end up as training material... and this is how it is done.

NeoJai didn't know what the deal was with the door not moving while she climbed it, but he understood that Aaxyl had won a test *stacked* against her in three minutes flat. Commentary clips of replays and analysis poured in for the entire duration of the hour long broadcast. Total media across layers was two hundred hours. NeoJai dismissed the video after a while.

He turned to Aameh. "Thanks for sharing. That's amazing!"

"Yeah?" Aameh asked sourly, without taking her eyes off her work. "Media minted money from her risking her life, and the win was disqualified for being *tampered*."

"Tampered?"

"Her opponent was Rohan, a journalist undercover for *Dome Times*. Someone had tampered with the test to favour him."

Scheduled maintenance of the Ekta Dorms water supply will result in a cutoff of residential water between midnight and 4am. Ekta Dorm Notifications, Tuesday, November 11, 2442

~~*~*~*

AAXYL: THE CLINIC, EKTA DORMS

One client left before lunch, and Aaxyl yawned.

Aameh had invited Perfect Sam to their room for dinner again, and they'd stayed up half the night. This was becoming a ritual. Every few days, Aameh would invite him over, and he'd oblige. He answered endless questions, shared updates on Hersh and enjoyed her transparent affection without judgment. Aaxyl gave up up and slept when the two got into a spirited debate about symbiont theory. Her day job was enough symbionts for Aaxyl.

Perfect Sam looked fresh, while she wilted.

She scanned the application. GymSYMB. Perfect Sam had taught her to administer the culture when he realised she was an athlete. It was SYMBTech's commercial product for agility, balance, and gymnastic skills. Neither essential nor provided as welfare, it earned some unimon for the Dorms and could become a profitable specialisation for Aaxyl when she got out of the Dorms.

Perfect Sam was so conspicuously excellent in the Dorms that the nickname had stuck. The medics section heard her say it once and that was that. She'd even heard Leela call him Perfect Sam.

The client took his time with a 'warm up' of floppy cartwheels and floppier handstands, kicked his legs up in a stumbling-in-the-air motion and plonked down.

Aaxyl planned to discuss applications of symbionts for waste management workers over lunch. Aameh had told her that in the previous year, twenty out of forty-three avoidable deaths at work worldwide were in sanitation. None from the three Domes, but it had remained on Aaxyl's mind since she almost lost this job and chose one in sanitation.

Perfect Sam's eyes met hers, and his merriment aggravated her impatience. SYMB products for vanity were a waste.

But needs were welfare. Wants paid.

Contemplating the challenges of sewers, Aaxyl guided Floppy into the somatic gimbal, transfused the symbionts, handed him the headset, switched on the hypnotics and watched his body relax. She manipulated him into positions to adapt his muscles for gymnastics. Balance or flexibility was tricky to induce, but Aaxyl had tricks. It helped to be able to do those moves and move him not just into key positions, but with the right process. Floppy back-flipped and cartwheeled and hand-stood as she moved him. Muscle memory would help him later.

There, done. Aaxyl switched off the hypnotics and waited for him to be alert, panting from the exertion of Floppy's gymnastics.

"It will take your body time to adapt to—"

"I know. I will have to develop the skill myself." He had it memorised.

Aaxyl wanted to say he didn't need GymSYMB to do a handstand. But this was the service industry. She fixed a courteous smile on her face.

Floppy leaned in. "Explain it to me over lunch?"

Aaxyl could have sexed her way out of the Dorms any time if not for Aameh. She faked regret as she ushered Floppy out. "I'm not allowed to date clients." It was kinder than telling him she wanted to discuss sewage with her boss.

As they opened their meals and dug in, Aaxyl told Sam about her idea for a symbiont culture to prevent the deaths of sanitation workers. She lacked the expertise, but he didn't.

"No." Perfect Sam opened his ginormous food tray with the premium bread-based meal, rice-based meal and some chicken something that looked too much like an actual chicken to tempt her. She liked her food anonymised into pieces.

"Why not?" Even a marginal increase in resilience could reduce mortality.

So far, Perfect Sam had lived up to his name. Saving lives would fit right up there on his halo.

"For the same reason that I don't do GymSYMB."

"What reason?" GymSYMB was vanity. Saving lives was the core of their work.

"Doesn't convince me." He pointed a vegetable wrap at her. "Aaxyl, you should know. They die from inhumane conditions. Many cities still use ancient sewage systems. If the work were dangerous, why aren't any dead in well designed systems of the Domes? How many sanitation worker injuries have you treated?"

"None, but old world designs can be different from us. How would it harm to make workers safer?"

"It puts the onus on the workers and normalises bad conditions. We worry when people die, but we should look at how they live. Humans with ordinary AthSYMB and HealSYMB have survived for ten minutes in space without spacesuits or with faulty spacesuits. Not well, but not dead either. How much tougher do people need to get to survive sewers?"

"Still, you'd take it if you could keep people alive in space for half an hour."

"The first thing you learn when you get into research is to only seek specific solutions," Perfect Sam said. "Needing symbiont transfusions to get through a day of work is too broad. Each time new strains interact, there is some degree of rejection, evolution and adaptation. Rejection can be dangerous, and reckless evolution risks inability to control side effects. AricNova, Abrahamha and Jugaad developed dangerous abilities from extreme exposure, but those closest to them became powerful from adaptation. Their symbionts evolved so readily, new powers manifested from mere intention, but you can't stand next to The Three comfortably. When angry, they could kill those around them inadvertently in spite of hypervigilance, the support of the finest minds and the best tech to assist them. They saved the human species, but can't live among it beyond the occasional interaction when everybody is hyperalert."

He would know. The Three founded AVANT and SYMBTech, the company he worked for. Far be it from Aaxyl to disrespect the sacrifices of The Three, but "what does this have to do with GymSYMB?"

"I'll let you in on a secret if you agree to non-disclosure."

No-brainer. "Agreed."

"GymSYMB shouldn't exist either. All the symbiont strains in GymSYMB are already present in AthSYMB, which is free," Perfect Sam winked.

"I just spent fifteen extra minutes to ensure it worked."

"I know." Sam was so tongue-in-cheek. "Makes this so much fun to tell you."

"I wasted my time?" Aaxyl was dismayed.

"No. Somatics offer real benefits. Training muscle memory intimidates even seasoned symbiontists. Even fewer do it with your insight, but you can do the same with AthSYMB."

Aaxyl punched his shoulder. "Why do it? Why create a bogus product?"

"Can't tell you. Let's call it a combination of a coercive demand and an Abrahamha's Stray who thought that vanity not being welfare, they might as well pay."

So GymSYMB didn't introduce new symbionts into the population. Interesting.

"You know Abrahamha's family as well?"

"I know them all." Sam winked.

Over the centuries, Abrahamha had adopted orphans at risk from their symbionts. In the promos of a documentary about his family, a scrawny boy proclaimed that they were not orphans, they were Abrahamha's Strays. He glared defiance at the camera with his hands on his hips, all adorable hero-pose. AxAm loved the promos because they too were an intentional family of orphans.

Every day Perfect Sam shared such gems. No wonder Aameh adored him. The information junkie craved the fount of interesting information in sexy packaging. Aaxyl looked at the said sexy packaging. Really looked. At some point, the tip of his beard had dragged in his food.

He caught her scrutiny and felt around, smearing gravy further into the hair. "I'll be shampooing it in a bit."

Stormy weather in coming weeks. Minor risk of leakages within Dome.Weather Monitor, Thursday, November 13, 2442

~~*~*~*

NEOJAI: D4F2, NULL DORMS

"I need a favour." Aameh spoke the minute she entered their dorm-hall.

"Anything." NeoJai wondered what it might be. She looked uncharacteristically grim.

"A friend has applied for asylum here," Aameh said. "Can your father approve it?"

He hadn't seen that coming. "Asylum is handled in the Octagon, not the Dorms, but it shouldn't be too complicated. We want to increase our population."

Aameh thunked her backpack to the floor. "It's been a year."

NeoJai didn't know what to say to that. "That might happen if his background checks indicated criminal activity. He probably didn't realise that moving locations wouldn't erase a criminal record."

"She's not a criminal!" Aameh's voice rose with her outrage. "She's an authority on community disorders and authored papers on the Tribist Community Disorder, complacency paralysis and stupidification. She's training psychologists in our Dome."

That made no sense at all. Symbionts healed the brain structurally, but not thought processes. Every place in the world wanted more psychologists. Those dealing with community disorders could state their terms. Plus, she was a woman. They should have approved her application the instant she applied.

"How's she lived here this long?" he asked.

"She's saving her money and living in the coffin-dorms. We store her stuff in our room."

"I meant, how haven't they sent her back?"

"The psychologists here keep sending her invitations to speak at events or train them," Aameh said. "It gives her reason to remain here, and counts as successive work trips."

That was clever, but also puzzling. "She gets invited as a trainer because she's good. She should have been approved." NeoJai reached for his comm. "I'll ask Admin Dhrit to send a recommendation through Sambit."

"Our Director Sambit here?" Aameh synced the list on her comm with the SIS, preparing for her checks.

"He's from Ridnam and used to work in Damodar's office. His contacts come in handy." Also, he owed Admin Dhrit a favour for getting him out from under Damodar's thumb with this appointment. The Null Dorms couldn't vote for their own Director, of course.

"Why do you call your father Admin Dhrit?"

NeoJai wished he could simply tell her, but it wasn't his secret to tell. "I can't keep advertising that he's my father! It would be horribly pretentious."

Aameh collected her comm and an ear piece absently, her eyes still scrutinising his face as though she sensed his lie. NeoJai held her gaze and didn't squirm. Finally, she put on a bright smile for her daily greeting to the non-persons. "Good morning!"

As usual, there was no reply.

Aameh set off on her daily tour, leaving NeoJai to his thoughts. He didn't like lying to Aameh, but she could be indiscreet. His father had been cloned in the wake of an assassination. Calling him Admin Dhrit differentiated him from the others. If Aameh knew this, there would be no end to the questions. He didn't know why the Dhrits didn't want to make the knowledge of the assassination or cloning public, but he had to respect that it was their decision.

Footsteps drummed in the corridor. Seconds later, Damodar walked into the dorm hall, purposeful strides devouring the distance from door to desk. Black eyes swept the life support racks. The man had become the president less than a week after his father's assassination.

Sambit Amdani, Director of Null Dorms, trailed in his wake: a timid mouse scurrying after a lion.

Damodar unnerved NeoJai. It was his first time coming face to face with the President. Aameh had said he was tall, but Damodar was easily seven feet. NeoJai, an inch short of six feet, felt insignificant.

When he spoke, his voice boomed. "Hello, NeoJai."

"President Damodar! I'm surprised you recognised me." Much as NeoJai hated the man, he didn't have the guts to omit his title to his face.

Aameh's platform lift whirred closer in the awkward silence.

"Of course, I know who you are." Damodar spoke warmly, but NeoJai heard the indifference. "Isn't this a lowly job for you?"

NeoJai was trying to think of a reply when Aameh's lift emerged from the racks. "There is dignity in all jobs, President," she said, voice prim with disapproval. "Global icon Abrahamha cared for his bedridden friends in their last days. Surely that teaches us that nobody is above honest labour."

"Aameh, lovely to see you again." Damodar remembered the name of a dorm-rat? Aameh was rather difficult to forget, though. "I've heard good things about you and Aaxyl. My creative team could do with someone like you. Do visit my office if you'd like a job."

NeoJai's heart beat a nervous double-time in his chest. Aaxyl had never met Damodar. No reason for him to know of her or remember Aameh from a previous visit.

"I'm a minor. I'll have to ask Aaxyl," Aameh said abruptly. NeoJai couldn't fault her instinct.

"Do ask," Damodar insisted. "Life in the Dorms can be tough."

"You're the President. You're responsible for all lives in the Dome." NeoJai interjected, his fear washed away in indignation. His father struggled to provide better for the Dorms. "An increase in the budget would improve everyone's lives."

"Your father is the Administrator of the Dorms. Shouldn't you be having this discussion with him?" Damodar asked NeoJai.

"You're the one who designed and built this dome," NeoJai blundered on to his own amazement. "You designed the Dorms to house sixty percent of the population in a fifth of the space of the residential area."

"The people in the residential area paid to build the Dome. Two centuries later, they still bear the cost of providing for the Dorms." Damodar stepped right into his space, towering over him, as NeoJai shrank.

He wished he'd kept his mouth shut.

"I'm sure he didn't intend to offend." Sambit broke in with a warning look at NeoJai. "I'll talk to him later. We should continue your tour."

NeoJai bit his tongue to keep his idiot mouth from digging a deeper hole.

Damodar took a deep breath and noticed bug-eyed Aameh. "No one intentionally overcrowded the Dorms. We built them to offer refuge to those who couldn't afford to buy residences. The Wastelands were much more polluted then. Everyone who could afford it evacuated to less polluted places or moved into protective domes. We had twice as many refugees as residents. This is a gap between intention and ability, not malice."

Damodar turned on his heel and took his inspection elsewhere.

Sambit shook a frown at NeoJai, then hurried to catch up with the royal visit.

"That man gives me the creeps," NeoJai said.

"He does seem over-familiar." Aameh frowned.

"Why does he come here at all? He's followed by media bots everywhere. But not here. Why not cover the President of the Dome visiting the Dorms? It would be great publicity."

"He's the President. He's responsible for everything." Aameh shrugged.

NeoJai gave a cynical snort. There was no requirement for inspections of the Dorms by the President of the Dome. "Don't believe him, Am. He minted money from selling residences to people desperate to shelter in domes. It is true dormers got refuge for free while residents paid, but dormers also provided free labour in exchange for a token score. Why do you think most dormers prefer to live in coffin-dorms? They are done with slogging to meet basic needs and then for it to be called charity."

Aameh's eyes gleamed. "Perhaps it's personal?"

"He has no other family. His cousin is a gangster in Ridnam. These aren't good people. Don't trust him."

Fire in residential apartment in Ravi sector results in a three day drop in air quality.
Dome & Dorms, Thursday, November 13, 2442

~~*~*~*

AAXYL: EKTA DORMS, PARKING AREA

Aaxyl finished up in the clinic and headed out. NeoJai would be dropping Aameh home soon. She jogged out of the building and through the parking lot toward the gate of the Dorm.

A car careened in through the gate and she barely got out of the way in time. "Hey!"

The car had already moved out of earshot. Furious, she glared after it. Beyond the car, closer to the other gate, Perfect Sam headed for his zeplyn.

Most anti-gravitational vehicles parked on roofs, but the clinic was on the ground level. The fancy zeplyn was almost half as big as AxAm's room and shaped like a covered serving dish, with a high-gloss finish conspicuous in the welfare dorm parking, like everything about Perfect Sam. Too excellent for the Dorms.

The car picked up speed as it came closer to the oblivious Perfect Sam.

"Sam!"

The car slammed into Perfect Sam, throwing him into the air, and screeched to a stop. Aaxyl alerted SecPros on her comm as she ran, the world tunnelling. A dozen men got out of the car and surrounded him.

Aaxyl thought they'd help, but they started kicking and hitting him.

Aaxyl screamed, her throat scraping like broken glass. "Stop! SecPros are on their way! Stop!" She pointed her comm at the attack and started recording as she ran. Several of them made stabbing motions at Perfect Sam. A knife glinted against the light of the sun, clutched in the hand of a dark-haired man, and in a terrifying slash it tore down at Sam's broken body. And then there were more. She staggered to a shocked halt. Dormers shouted in alarm. A flurry of flashes, the silver of the knives rising from Sam covered in a deep red.

They outnumbered Sam so badly that she could no longer see him, but his blood made it past them, making an attacker slip. Her mind computed possible attacks. She could do nothing. She'd get herself killed. They returned to their vehicle as dormers closed in. More dormers ran past her to the scene. She followed them in a daze.

The attackers drove away from Perfect Sam and back toward her, accelerating through dormers trying to stop them and forcing them out of the way.

Jolted out of her shock, she ran after the car when it passed her and followed it through the gate and up toward the ring road, but it sped off once it hit the ring road. Angry tears welled as she fixed her eyes on the spot where she'd seen it last, panting, suffocating.

SecPros flew in on hoverboards overhead, followed by wailing and flashing zeplyns. Aaxyl ran back to Sam, but the SecPros were already pushing the crowd behind a perimeter as more SecPro vehicles drove in. The roar of voices around her, some alarmed, some asking questions, washed over her and made no sense.

She pushed through the crowd, but the SecPros wouldn't allow anyone through.

"I'm a paramedic," Aaxyl called out, trying to get their attention. It was only a mild exaggeration. She did help out in the Dorms when they were short-staffed.

"I'm sorry," a SecPro replied. "Nothing you can do. He's dead."

"Let me check! I'm trained." She wasn't trained for anything like this.

"I can't," he said. "If he's a global citizen, this is a diplomatic issue. We can't compromise procedure and risk undermining the investigation."

Aaxyl stood blankly as a forensics team scanned the scene and collected evidence, while another team of SecPro interviewers went around asking witnesses questions. A ringing quiet stifled all the sounds around her.

Aaxyl approached a SecPro again, explaining that she had alerted them. She stammered and choked her way through explanations and showed them her recording.

"We have a dorm-comm video here!" the SecPro spoke into his mic and turned to her. "I'll need your comm for a moment."

"I'll transfer the recording to you." Aaxyl didn't want to let go of the last she had of Perfect Sam.

"I'm sorry, but for it to be used as evidence, I need forensics making a copy with original device markers."

She didn't know how it was different from transferring the recording to them, but she didn't care. She gave them her comm and stood facing the space they left when they took it to forensics. Unmoving.

Sam, Perfect Sam, who helped her with Aameh's investigation mere hours ago, was a mangled lump of flesh. Aaxyl had never seen a dead body. They even sent bad injuries or anyone needing observation overnight to the hospital. And now the symbiontist was dead.

Hersh, missing. Sam, dead.

Aaxyl's brain ground to a halt, then rambled on loop.

AxAm had hoped to become symbiontists and live independently with the help of Perfect Sam. He'd offered to sponsor AxAm with SYMBTech internships once he found Hersh and returned to SYMBTech. Aaxyl hated herself for feeling disappointed that this would no longer happen.

She wasn't sure what she was mourning. A deceased friend or broken dreams?

Aameh had liked what Aaxyl considered a good man for the first time ever.

What would she tell Aameh?

If she had stayed alert, run, reached him in time... she could have helped him escape. Dormers close to him had tried to stop the attackers while she stood paralysed. Everything had happened too fast. By the time they rallied, the attackers were already leaving.

The forensics van left with the body. Smudged, blood-soaked concrete held her transfixed.

A SecPro said something. Aaxyl tried to listen through silence drenching her, blotting out all sound with a tinny ringing.

"Are you alright? Do you need to sit?"

Aaxyl trembled uncontrollably.

Shock, she realised with distant indifference.

That mob had destroyed her self-belief without laying a finger on her. She was athletic, her body forged with physical labour. She was a champion at combat from a young age. She'd trained to be a SecPro. While Aaxyl did not seek violence, she had always imagined that if it came to violence, she would prevail. Instead, she'd stood and watched her friend die.

Aameh emerged from NeoJai's car beyond the SecPros, looking around curiously. She didn't know why they were there. NeoJai followed. What was she to tell them?

Usually, Aaxyl decoded an incomprehensible Aameh, but as Aaxyl stood frozen, Aameh soothed her and tried to talk her into going to their room. Aaxyl didn't want to tell Aameh like this. She pointed to SecPros. "They took my comm."

NeoJai got her comm back from the investigators and escorted them to their room. She showed them her recording. "Sam," was all she whispered.

Aameh broke down crying as she saw Sam curled up against the blows. Aaxyl couldn't cry now. Both of them mustn't lose themselves in grief and be unaware of potential danger. She sat frozen, considering what she should do.

NeoJai stood awkwardly. He accepted their meal packets when the dinner bot arrived and coaxed them to eat. He was shaken too, but he murmured soothing words and hugged them both. Aaxyl broke. Tears overflowed. Heaving sobs followed.

His quiet kindness was what she needed now. She never had a shoulder she could rest her head on when it all got too much. She needed someone to hold her and tell her that it would be okay.

It wasn't okay.

Brutal mob attack in Ekta Dorms, the first this century, kills one. SecPros promise swift action. Dome Times, Friday, November 14, 2442

~~*~*~*

VIDROH: TANK 5, WASTELANDS

The water tank stood in a clearing in the wastelands. Beyond the fence, scrub vegetation and the creatures that lived in it had reclaimed the vast swathes of land vacated by humanity. A bustling city had once stood here.

Today, SecPros secured this water for the Dome. Not because the human population would ever recover to its earlier numbers. It would not. Nor would it ever need this water. They were just doing their jobs.

The high clatter of a distant *tasha* drum swept across the land, blending with rumbling thunder.

tak, tak, tak, tak

ta-tak, ta-tak, ta-tak, ta-tak

taka-taka, taka-taka, taka-taka, taka-taka

Srayoshi had called the distant drumming the most beautiful experience of the wastelands, underpinning the rhythm of life. How appropriate, then, that it played now, as Vidroh mourned her.

The heavier *dhol* kicked in.

dhin tinak dhin, dhadhin tinak dhin

More water flowed in the region than the Dome needed, but those who lived next to it had no right to it. The state recognised nobody as alive in the wastelands to have any right to it.

Srayoshi was a SecPro, but when she had come across a settlement near three interconnected ponds, she had let them be. She had dared to disobey orders.

She had died as she lived, true to her beliefs.

taka-taka, taka-taka, taka-taka, taka-taka

dhin tinak dhin, dhadhin tinak dhin

Vidroh's head nodded in sync to the beat.

The ageless sound had accompanied festivals and weddings till time erased both. The wandering percussionists still entertained wastelanders and SecPros alike, weaving joyous occasions or bored evenings into melodious memory.

taka-taka, taka-taka, taka-taka, taka-taka

dhin tinak dhin, dhadhin tinak dhin

Last week, Srayoshi had perched with him on this rocky outcropping overlooking the valley. As the crops grew, so did the evidence of her betrayal of the state.

"You can't keep doing this, Srayoshi. You must move the settlers out and secure the water. They're irrigating crops."

"*Their* crops. With water from the lakes next to *their* homes."

"The settlement can move out of the patrol areas till we get help. They could even live for free in the dome. Nothing good will come out of this."

"Where will they go? Why should they vacate their own village to live in coffin-dorms and be grateful for it?"

"The settlers can't argue with SecPro weapons, Srayoshi. You don't have an argument that defeats weapons."

"I will die once, not daily."

"In an age of immortality, we may never die."

"We may wish we did."

ta-ta ta, ta-ta ta, ta-ta ta, ta-ta ta

dhadhinna, tak-dhin, tak-dhin, tak-dhin

Against all advice, Vidroh had supported her. He knew better.

Now they said he'd killed by not stopping her. They'd seen it coming.

Vidroh stumbled to the abandoned store room under the tank, where they'd stashed a few items. From it, he dragged out an empty water can. Wedging it awkwardly between rocks, the next time *dh-dhin tinak dhin, dhaginakana dhin* came around, he slapped the can hard for a *THUP*.

He couldn't move his left arm. He only added to the last beat. Turning it into *dh-dhin tinak dhin, dhaginakana THUP*.

He added *THUPs* determinedly. Not that he could have done more with both hands.

She was the drummer.

She was everything.

He only had *THUPs* to give.

The wandering drummers couldn't hear his *THUPs*, of course. If they did, they'd be out of sync, like him.

THUP-dha, dhin-dha, dh-dhin-dha, dhin

The beat syncopated and flowed. Bloody drummers, accepting everything.

But some things couldn't be accepted.

Shouldn't be accepted.

There was no fixing this beat.

taka-tuk, taka-tuk, taka-THUP, taka-tuk-THUP

dhidhinna, THUPdhinna, dhidhinna, THUP

Five days ago, another patrol had found the settlement. Then they'd attacked it to secure the water.

Just doing their jobs.

Five days ago, he'd received the last message from Srayoshi. "They've found us. I'm leading them away. Help the settlers escape. Please, Vidroh."

He did as she asked, and doubled back to help her.

Too late.

She had fought to buy the settlers time to escape. The SecPros had killed her.

They had shot his left arm off.

Just doing their jobs.

And then, obeying protocol with meticulous savagery, they secured his arm in a protective seal. They'd rushed him to the hospital to save his useless arm when a precious woman lay dead.

Still doing their jobs.

taka-tuk, THUP-tuk, taka-tuk, taka-tuk-THUP

dhiTHUP, dhidhinna, dhidhinna, THUP

This wasn't working. He went to find a stick to beat the can properly.

ta-ta ta, ta-ta ta, ta-ta ta, THAK

dh-dhin tinak dhin, dhaginakana, THAK

Mohan had been furious that he hadn't stopped her. Settlers had died because she gave them false hope, he said.

Five days ago, Mohan arranged for his arm to be saved and sent the SYMBTech lawyer to get him out.

Out to what? He had nothing left.

He'd lost his job, because of his unfit arm.

He'd lost his home to pay for fixing his arm.

And now his arm ached as did his heart.

He didn't want their stupid job.

He didn't want a home without her.

He didn't want a world without her.

ta-ta ta, ta-ta ta, ta-ta ta, THWACK

dh-dhin tinak dhin, dhaginakana, THWACK

Vidroh would not rest till the settlement Srayoshi gave her life for had secured water.

He swung harder with his right arm. His left was in agony.

Tears ran down his face. For her. For his arm. It didn't matter which.

Everything was wrong.

ta-ta ta, ta-ta ta, ta-ta tawhooshTHWACK

dh-dhin tinak dhin, dhaginwhooshTHWACK

His left arm was inflamed and excruciating. He was dripping snot and drool and tears. He couldn't fight like this.

He didn't want familiar faces. He couldn't face Mohan's accusation.

Why was he cooperating with this stupid rhythm?

ta-ta whooshTHWACKta, ta-t-whooshTHWACK

dh-dhwhooshTHWACKhin, dhaginwhooshTHWACK

The stick broke.

The can had been in tatters for some time.

The drums had stopped a while ago, but not in his head. Maybe they had always been in his head.

Two days ago he came to the wastelands. Restless. Seeking peace.

Now, he returned to the Dome. Restless. Hoping to find peace there.

Resilience

Exchange offer for residential furnishings. Return furnishings in good condition to get discounts on new selections. Dorm ads, Saturday, November 15, 2442

~~*~*~*

AAMEH: SEXUAL WELFARE SERVICES

Sexual welfare in the Dorms satisfied about as much as paste for food and coffins for beds. It was little more than a coffin-dorm converted into a warehouse of tiny rooms on three sub-levels and offered little more than private space a few times a year. SWS issued registered dormers a couple of tokens a year for fifty-minute allocations of a room to meet their need for privacy. Ten minutes between allocations for staff to tidy the rooms and evict any stragglers.

Coffin-dormers, with no private space to call their own depended on these allocations for intimate time with each other. At least the ones who didn't wander abandoned corridors late at night. The waiting area also served as an informal dating area. AxAm had their own room, of course, but both of them registered for SWS tokens. Aameh out of an interest in sex, Aaxyl, because desperate coffin-dormer couples often traded SociCred for the tokens. *Did Aaxyl earn from sex?* Aameh wondered with an internal smirk.

The common area that was used for meals or a general sitting area in coffin-dorms was a waiting area here. Nothing fancy. The dorm-supervisor desks were converted into desks for booking allocations or sex-ed, counselling, contraception or fertility consultants and resources, and so on. Seating along the walls or clustered around tables hummed with the constant murmur of conversations. There was little else to do other than wait for the previous allocations to be vacated.

She took a seat in a corner and pulled out her sketchbook, carefully avoiding interested eyes. She didn't feel like encouraging anyone who wasn't Perfect Sam. Why was she here?

Sexual welfare, the busy intersection between necessity and dignity was a great vantage point for an artist. Maybe she would sketch what she couldn't have.

A familiar voice intruded her thoughts. "Mind if I sit here?" Scharada asked.

Much as she adored the head-fixer from Ridnam, she didn't want anyone looking too closely inside her head. She hadn't tidied it up yet.

Several men trying to catch Aameh's eye since her solo arrival switched to disinterest with Scharada's arrival. Lesbians weren't too popular in a population of mostly men. You didn't even have to be one. Just having a woman approach you in SWS would do it, apparently.

This was inevitable. "Ax sent you."

"She's worried." Scharada slid into the seat next to Aameh.

"I'll be okay." Aameh understood their concern. She chose men poorly and she missed Perfect Sam. "It isn't every day one transitions from crushing over someone to mourning them. A little time to reorient is reasonable."

Scharada came to her point. "Women stop their friends from doing things they'll regret."

Aameh was glad it was out in the open. Scharada wouldn't leave till it had been discussed.

"I've no clue what I'm doing. Leave and give me a chance to find out." With broad strokes, Aameh sketched a man staring at her. How many lines did it take to capture someone's soul? Aameh looked at him and back at her sketchbook with satisfaction. A dozen or so. "Are you planning to follow me into a room?"

"Do you want me to?" Scharada asked.

"You lack the anatomy I'm missing." Aameh attempted a wry smile and felt her face, swollen from crying, resist. No wonder she was worrying everyone. "I thought I reminded you of the sister you left behind in Ridnam."

A group of dormers caught her eye and she began sketching their animated interactions. One of the men had a birthday and they seemed to be planning to use three tokens to party in a single room. Their boisterous laughter reminded her of evenings when Sam had visited them. A few other couples in the area seemed too impatient to wait for their room.

"I'd go in with her too, if she needed to talk." Scharada gave her a friendly nudge. "Its just an empty room for fifty minutes."

Aameh leaned her head back against the wall. "If you offered therapy for SociCred instead of giving it for free in sexual welfare, you wouldn't need to store your belongings in our room and live in coffin-dorms. You'd have enough room to host sex orgies"

"I can't work for the dorms without the freedom to choose clients or session duration. Talking to you isn't work. You're my friend," Scharada said.

"I have other friends Ax didn't send."

"Okay, so I'm a friend with a specific skillset. I'm still your friend."

"There's nothing you can do." Perfect Sam had infected her with malignant hope and died.

It took some persuading, but finally, Scharada left with a worried frown. Aaxyl would get the full report. That was just what it was.

Aameh scanned the room to see if someone tempted her. None compared with Perfect Sam.

A heterosexual woman never lacked opportunity, but there was an AxAm rule about it. The occasional sex was fine, but there would be no chasing sex at the cost of derailing their goals. They had seen other women spend chunks of their life in a hormonal fog of male attention without any achievement to their name. AxAm wouldn't do that.

But right now, Aameh just didn't want to feel so desperately bereft. Abandoned.

She headed over to the dorm supervisor's desk. A sleek Sexel logo punctuated the purpose of each counter: matchmaking, directory of dormers offering sexual services, room allocation, information and at some distance, a display with contraceptives, toys and other items. Sexel, leaders in global sexual commerce, sponsored a skeleton staff in the Dorms as social service. The man at the information counter leaned forward as she approached.

Aameh asked, "I lost someone I cared about. Do you think sex with someone else will help?"

His eyes filled with compassion. "It varies."

"Should I do it?" Aameh's heart sank as he delayed an answer. If a sex worker expert enough to counsel others struggled to answer, how could Aameh figure it out?

"It won't bring the person back, but if you enjoy sex, it can distract you. Or it can feel wrong." He stood. "Would you like a hug?"

"Yes, please."

He came around the desk and gave her a wonderful hug, embracing her securely without any demand or pushing advice at her. A clean hug.

Aameh stepped back when satisfied. "Thank you."

He smiled back. "Take all the time you need to decide. I'm right here."

Someone else approached his desk and Aameh returned to her seat, looking at the men looking at her.

Aameh's assumptions of good faith scaled poorly across sexes. Men wanted sex, but disliked her weirdities. As one put it, she was *complicated*. As if that were a bad thing. Perfect Sam had enjoyed being with her. He didn't mind her odd thoughts and endless questions. She was sad, because he mattered. It would be wrong to shrink the hole he left. He deserved to be missed.

Life. Kiss a hundred princes, find ninety-nine frogs and one dead prince.

Aaxyl never let her love life ruin her happiness. She would never sit in a waiting area feeling sorry for herself because the man she really wanted died.

Aameh had lost something before she understood it.

Ultimatum Day festivities at the Octagon to begin at 6pm. Dome Times, Sunday, November 16, 2442

~~*~*~*

AAXYL: EKTA DORMS

Aameh blamed herself for bringing danger to Hersh and Sam, and wanted to interrogate dorm lowlifes for information on the attack on Perfect Sam.

Not wanting her to feel alone, or worse, do something on her own, Aaxyl played along, but Aaxyl worried about Aameh's recklessness. She hesitated to refuse a grieving Aameh, but someone needed to do it. She messaged Leela explaining the situation and asking her to talk to Aameh in the morning before following Aameh down the dark corridor in the manufacturing section.

It had been so much simpler when Aaxyl could ground Aameh.

Opportunistic scum lurked in isolated corridors after midnight, away from busy stairs and coffin-dorms, hoping to snatch belongings or extort SociCred. Unease skittered through Aaxyl as she saw Aameh approach a man most sane people would avoid as though he were an information booth. He would likely have a partner skulking in wait.

Aameh was supposed to let Aaxyl handle any interrogation.

Now Aameh shied from Brute-1 towering over her. His friend, Brute-2, closed in on the duo, trapping her. Aaxyl slunk closer in the shadows. They had cornered Aameh.

Aameh's voice rose. "Who attacked the symbiontist? Was it you?"

Aaxyl coiled with tension in the shadows, waiting for the right moment.

"You think we'd murder someone?" The enraged man grabbed Aameh's arm.

That was quite enough. Aameh getting manhandled crossed every line of tolerance Aaxyl had. This ended now. No one knew anything, but Aameh would get into trouble by provoking people.

Aaxyl sprang at the second man and put all her weight into a single punch. Brute-2 out.

Taking advantage of the distraction, Aameh jerked her arm forward and out of the gap between Brute-1's fingers and thumb like Aaxyl had taught her. She gaped when it worked before scampering away and providing Aaxyl with a nicely distracted Brute-1.

Divided between Aaxyl and Aameh, Brute-1 swung unexpectedly at Aaxyl. She blocked it poorly at the last moment, before backing away from his second punch and getting in a flurry of hard kicks, all of which landed. These were bullies, not fighters. They lost before they fought. Soon, Brute-1 joined his friend on the floor.

Aaxyl raised her arms and stretched. If she were honest, there was catharsis in punishing bad guys.

"I can't believe that worked," Aameh commented, rubbing her arm as she returned. The fool didn't have the smarts to run for safety and had simply lurked, watching. She would have a bruise just from that grip.

Aaxyl checked the men for injuries. "If he were on AthSYMB, he'd have broken my arm. You shouldn't even be here. What's wrong with you, Am? How does any of this help Perfect Sam?"

Aameh probably believed there was a cosmic club of thugs who all knew what the others did.

Aaxyl kicked the man she'd just checked for injuries. He was fine. He needed the rest.

The lights came on, making them blink. Heels tocked as Leela came around the corner.

"Beating up people in the corridors at night, healing them in the clinic in the day?" Leela stood with her hands on her hips, Kant behind her.

AxAm looked at each other. Busted. Aaxyl hadn't expected Leela to react this fast.

"What's going on here?"

Uni-silence.

It was like being a nine-year-old again, except Leela was now the Director of the Ekta Dorms instead of a supervisor in Aameh's toddler-dorm. Same, just scarier.

"Follow me. Both of you."

She strode off with Kant, leaving AxAm to follow her to the lift. Leela's office was on the first floor, but they went all the way up to the top floor. They turned into a bright side-corridor with just two doors. It looked like a residential space rather than a Dorm. A beautiful carpet covered the floor, and even the light fittings were decorative.

Kant stepped in their way, blocking their entry as Leela entered a small office and sat at the desk. The other door, presumably leading to her suite of rooms, stayed shut. Kant's face showed no recognition.

A single gesture from Leela moved Kant out of their way. AxAm entered when told and stood looking around while Leela took her time checking the SIS.

The three walls around them each had a portrait of the founders of the modern world: AricNova, Abrahamha, and Jugaad. The fourth was even more intimidating. There was no wall. A huge glass window framed the brightly lit residential area. Only the most important people had rooms with windows.

They sat when told. Aaxyl sneaked a glance at movement in her peripheral vision to find Kant glaring holes into the backs of their heads.

"Start talking." Leela's voice whipped her attention forward.

Uni-silence.

"No? Let me try." Leela leaned her elbows on the desk. "First time I spotted you two trouble-magnets, your age was in the single digits. Aameh would not stay away from you and screamed her head off. I managed to help you stay together. True?"

They nodded.

"You came up with demands you didn't have SociCred for." Leela spoke true. "I helped the best I could, allowed you to share a bed, get a room, keep Aameh safe. Was that so you could pick fights against men twice your size? Why bother to keep her safe if this is where I'll find her?"

"Wait." Aameh caved. The traitor. "It's not a big deal, Ax."

True, but Leela wasn't going to like the truth either. Aaxyl tried to put the Aameh genie back into the bottle with her eyes.

Leela rapped the desk, snapping their attention back to her. "Don't even look at her, Am. Start at the beginning. Why are you two picking fights?"

Aameh blurted in a pathetic close-to-tears voice, "We wanted to know who killed Perfect Sam."

Fantastic.

"The attackers came and left in a car. What makes you think they were from here?" Leela asked them, and nodded to Kant.

Kant skirted them to take a seat by Leela's side. "You work in the clinic. Are you seeing injuries from such attacks coming in?"

Aameh answered for them both. "We were just ruling it out. Both Hersh and Sam were symbiontists here."

"You idiots! Did you stop to consider what would happen if you lost a fight? If Aameh got hurt?" Leela looked torn between relief and fury.

"I don't lose fights!" Aaxyl defended what little dignity remained. "I don't pick fights I can't win." When Aameh started picking the fights, Aaxyl asked for help, but that wouldn't fly after Leela caught them fighting.

"I've seen your recording," Kant said. "Did those people look like opponents you could defeat? Why didn't you save Perfect Sam if you could win against them?"

Aaxyl flinched.

"What if you found the men?" Kant had a point. "Beat them up too? And then what? Check for injuries? What if your victims recognised you and attacked Aameh?"

Leela spoke into the silence that followed. "Aameh, your food upgrade is cancelled for a day, and you can thank me you aren't in the coffin-dorms and stripped of every comfort for this stunt."

Kant added, "Aaxyl, you will stop assaulting people. Leave investigations to SecPros."

"Yes." Aaxyl agreed.

"Why are my meals cancelled, but Aaxyl's are not? She knocked them out! Besides, those men deserved it!" Aameh had a strong sense of injustice at inconvenient times.

Aaxyl hoped Leela wouldn't reveal that Aaxyl had tipped her off.

"The men deserving it is the only reason you two are here instead of arrested. And you're the bigger fool, Aameh. Unlike Aaxyl, you can't defend yourself and would end up in the hospital if the man landed a stray hit on you. But yes. Aaxyl's food coupons are cancelled too."

"Okay." Aameh nodded. Weirdo.

"You aren't Aaxyl." Aaxyl glared at her.

"But if we both are punished, I'm okay with this." Aameh nodded again. Her sense of proportion was satisfied.

Leela rubbed her forehead. "I'm closing the clinic short of emergencies till we have a new symbiontist. You will continue to hold the role and the SociCred. You need trauma leave in any case."

Aaxyl nodded.

"Leave. Now."

AxAm left.

As soon as the door closed behind them, Aaxyl pushed Aameh in irritation. "Why did you get me punished? You wanted this because of what happened with your Perfect Sam."

"I don't want to talk about it. And don't call him my Perfect Sam." Aameh's voice caught.

Sometimes, you had to talk about everything except the truth. "I'd have given you my food, dummy. Leela knew that. She was punishing me."

"Oh."

*Beware the crazy man yelling outside the clinic door. He reeks! Ekta Dorms
Grapevine, Monday, November 17, 2442*

~~*~*~*

AAXYL: THE CLINIC, EKTA DORMS

The dorm grapevine had news: a huge, filthy man had stumbled to the waiting area of the clinic, shouting profanities when the door wouldn't open.

Aaxyl came to investigate. So much for keeping the clinic closed.

His clothes were torn and stained. She spotted caked mud streaked over more grime. Ignoring well-meant suggestions to go to the medics or the hospital, he sat outside the door, oblivious to stares. He reeked of something unidentifiable. Rotting organics, perhaps. Unwashed, definitely.

Aaxyl thought he might be Brute-1 from the previous night. Ever since Leela pointed out that the lowlifes could recognise them and retaliate, Aaxyl couldn't unthink it. He had the size, but he wasn't Brute-1. Dorm life didn't wreck a person like this. Even if you lost everything, you claimed a bed in a coffin-dorm, clean clothes, and food paste.

Dead eyes glanced up blankly at her approach before ignoring her.

She opened the clinic and waved him in, making a virtue out of patience as... Blank took his own time.

She hoped the sight of a bathroom triggered some latent instinct. If not, she'd hose him down the best she could. When Blank failed to respond to a "come this way," she put a gentle arm around his back to steer him to the bathroom.

He recoiled from her touch.

Aaxyl raised her hands and backed away. Had he been assaulted or abused? His size and aggression suggested otherwise, but size could be deceptive, and aggression could be a result.

She kept her voice reassuring. "I don't intend you harm."

It was absurd, because Blank towered over her, and no one intending harm confessed it.

"Have you been assaulted? Should I call SecPros?" she asked directly, choosing not to guess her way out of ignorance at his cost.

A brief scowl animated his face before he lost focus again.

"I'm not going to touch you. There are clean clothes on the shelf and the bathroom is through that door. When you're comfortable, we can see why you need the clinic, okay?"

Blank left a chip, picked up a medic assistant's uniform, and zombied his way to the bathroom.

She could give him a patient's robe instead, but it wasn't worth the bother.

Aaxyl inserted the chip and waited for his data to load. The SIS hadn't recognised him. The chip either meant it was his first time here, or he opted out of the Dorm records. Most people just kept a copy on their comm, but she hadn't seen a comm on him.

A tormented howl erupted from the bathroom. Sobs followed. Despair and denial crescendoed out, filling the clinic, and subsided back into that bathroom.

Perfect Sam's first day at work flashed through her mind, when the deranged patient had caught her unawares. "Sedative... just in case." Aaxyl sniffed. Something had got in her eye. She rubbed at it.

She mustered professionalism as the bathroom door opened, releasing a generic floral scent.

"How are you doing"—she checked his records—"Vidroh Trinis?"

He'd have cried in front of her if he wanted her to know, so she pretended not to have heard it. It was a dormer's working concept of privacy.

Vidroh had composed himself.

Far from a disorganised mess, he filled the clinic uniform with authority, and radiated discipline.

He started taking off the top as he sat on a treatment recliner. Aaxyl intended to object, but the view wasn't objectionable. She hadn't read his file. She transferred it to the recliner and went over.

His left arm was all wrong as he struggled to take off the top. Stiff. Swollen. Discoloured. That explained why he hadn't fastened the top. She wondered why put it on at all, only to torture himself removing it now.

She helped him free his hand, as she scanned his file quickly. His surgeons had inserted a bio-fabricated connector and transplanted his original arm below it. Transplanting limbs was complex, but to do it twice with such seamless precision verged on surgical swagger. She felt guilty about her excitement, but the technique, developed by SanJeevan, the undisputed legend in modern medicine, had human surgeons and surgical nanobot clusters working in tandem. It wouldn't need much rehabilitation. His body would replace the prosthesis over time, giving him his original arm back.

That single surgery probably cost more than the clinic itself.

How could he be such a mess?

He glared back at her.

His eyes looked feverish. Was it expected after a transplant? The recliner readings confirmed the fever.

Vidroh grunted as he lay back in the recliner. "I was expecting to meet... Sam."

Of course. He was no dormer with that transplant. He'd have come to SYMBTech's best. This was probably not a good time to tell him Sam was dead. "Did you know Sam?"

"Yes, but better for my peace of mind if he isn't here."

Aaxyl transfused HealSYMB.

"This is brilliant work. The only thing better is not losing your arm. It must have cost a fortune. So why are you neglecting it?"

Was it weird to protect a brilliant surgery from its recipient?

"I'm fine." Vidroh sat up. "Just give me painkillers."

Aaxyl attached a nutrient drip for the HealSYMB and added an antipyretic. "The HealSYMB is exhausting you and failing to fight the infection. You're malnourished and fatigued. Eat. Sleep. More eat, more sleep."

"I can't sleep. I'm not over-working. I did a few hours of composting for a lower bunk because I don't want to climb twelve feet into a bed slot."

Perhaps that had been part of his enigmatic stench. His situation sucked, but agreeing wouldn't help.

Aaxyl went over to the supplies drawers. Wait... "As a disabled person, even temporarily, you have a right to an accessible bed. Why are they assigning you higher bunks?"

"For entertainment? SecPros are not popular in coffin-dorms."

Ah. "You're a SecPro."

"Not anymore," Vidroh said, slowly.

There should have been slings in this drawer. She slammed it shut with more force than needed as she stood. She examined her mental list. A two-faced scum of SecPro had hurt Aameh. SecPros invalidated her trial. SecPros refusing updates on Sam's attack . Yeah, she had SecPro issues. She rummaged in another drawer and found a sling.

Vidroh recognised her. "You're the participant from the invalidated trials. Brilliant moves! Became a thing in SecPro circles."

She grinned back, but he closed his eyes and stretched his neck. It was probably stiff because of his arm. The sling would help. He'd moved on from her stunning win. Dang.

"Your surgical team has flagged your file for consults for any additional medications to manage the transplant."

She checked for contacts. The lead surgeon was SanJeevan herself, from AVANT. Aaxyl wondered if she was dreaming. Sadly, the file had no contact information for the legend, or that consult would have been a story to narrate to rapt medics for life. It listed one "Katie" for follow-ups.

Vidroh tested his arm. "Just give me the painkiller. I don't want to talk to the surgeons."

Aaxyl took the sling over and helped him put it on. His stubbornness had more heft without the fever cooking his brain.

"You'll get the pain block last because then you'll leave. Add it to your woes. The medic assistant forced you to sit while she solved some of your problems."

"I can't afford the SociCred. I worked to secure only enough for a lower bunk."

"You need the sedative if you can't sleep. I can give you a free consult about the revolutionary 'eat more and rest more' approach to symbiont-supported healing. It was revolutionary three centuries ago."

"The food paste isn't edible." Vidroh's scowl was losing conviction. "What's in it?"

"Cranky dormers." Aaxyl smelled imminent victory.

"Hilarious."

"I can ensure an accessible bunk for the sedative. Use your SociCred here. You don't need to work. You'll feel much better by this time tomorrow."

"One sedated ex-SecPro coming to your kitchens for your next food paste," Vidroh muttered.

"I'll add a note to wait till all the drugs are out of your system." Aaxyl didn't miss a beat. "We're careful of the nutritional aspects of paste, even if the taste is not important."

"I suppose you will talk at me till I agree?"

She shrugged. He shrugged his good shoulder and approved the SociCred.

"This shouldn't take long." She requested the consult on the SIS, adding a brief note on the inflammation and the antipyretic. "While we wait, I have bad news, and I need a favour."

"My right arm?"

"It is about Sam, our symbiontist. How did you know him?"

Vidroh caught the gravity in her tone. "He's a friend."

No easy way to say it. "He's... He was assaulted in the parking lot a few days ago. Sam... died on the spot. He was our friend."

Vidroh jolted as if she'd electrocuted him. "What are you talking about?

That isn't possible."

Aaxyl showed him the recording.

He looked haunted. "I'm sorry for your loss."

Aaxyl didn't need condolences. "We need updates on the investigation. You were a SecPro. He was your friend. Help us."

"I'm no longer a SecPro." Vidroh gentled his words. "I'll find out what I can."

"Thank you. I appreciate anything you can do."

"Expect little from the state, and you won't feel betrayed."

His consult got immediate approval for sedation. His surgeons didn't want to talk to him either.

AAMEH

Dinner distribution emptied corridors in the non-residential areas of Ekta Dorms. Aameh wasted ten minutes on two floors, only to find someone lurking each time.

She passed through the dim passage with propaganda graffiti about Ridnam cult outside her old tailoring unit. Her first job, she remembered with a grin. She'd barely earned anything, but had made great clothes for Aaxyl and herself. And she'd bought a small jar of paint from her first salary.

The wall showcased gaudy colours and clumsy figures. A colossal eye promised great things beyond life.

Containers of paint stood before the wall in an invitation to counter the message. Graffiti was a part of the culture of the non-residential areas of the Ekta Dorms.

Digging into her pockets for her trusty multi-brushes, she got to work.

The SoulScaper had emerged in the dark nights of the Dorm, juxtaposing art against ideas that diminished people and giving birth to a new form of public art. It was the only risk Aaxyl let her take. Usually. Aaxyl didn't know she was out now. Aameh wanted to be alone today.

As a child, she had pestered Aaxyl for paint and corrected everybody else's drawings. Not wanting trouble with other dormers, Aaxyl hadn't let her paint on walls for years. She had got her own paint from her first job at this very tailoring unit when she was thirteen. Unable to stop her, Aaxyl escorted her once or twice a month ever since, on the condition that she remain anonymous.

More Dorm artists adopted her style and the name *absurde* emerged.

As a style of graffiti, Aameh's *absurde* enforced an action-reaction format by responding and re-contextualising. It intended to provoke thought rather than provide answers.

"What does afterlife mean to an immortal?" Aameh wrote around the cult's propaganda.

She drew smoky images of the Enduring War and faces of The Three scientists who emerged from historic obscurity to save humanity. She drew AricNova against a backdrop of relief camps, Abrahamha surrounded by glowing symbionts and Jugaad with containers of essential supplies.

This was how the war for minds was waged.

She added the philanthropists, rescue and relief workers, and famous news reporters. She added humble dormers working for a living. People who rose above the personal to serve a greater good. She added Perfect Sam to those faces.

Sometimes good *absurde* simply stood before the unacceptable and screamed back.

Aameh put away her brushes and took the remaining paint as she walked back to their room.

She passed a rather ambitious penis between the names of a lesbian couple. They were among the oldest dormers. Aameh didn't know them, but it wasn't the first time she'd come across rude comments about them. With ninety percent of the population male, lesbianism angered a few who thought... Aameh didn't know what they thought. If the world were ninety percent women, they'd still be single.

Well, scale was everything, wasn't it? She didn't need paint for this. She pulled out a marker and re-contextualised it, so it looked like a stray boring trinket, and unrelated to the names.

Grinning with satisfaction, she carried on, reading the graffiti as she passed.

Ekta Dorms' cricket team would be choosing members next month. Dormers wanting in had to go to the park between Ekta Dorms and Null Dorms early in the morning, daily. She drew a dashing batsman, alert and ready for the ball to draw attention to that scrawled announcement and left the cans of paint under it.

A political message asked for denial of free communications, sexual welfare and entertainment quotas to non-productive dorm-rats living off the efforts of workers as those could not be called basic rights. Aameh scoffed at the idea. Dorm-rats, surviving on bare necessities, sought to deny others the same.

Aameh walked back and picked two of the paint cans and put them here. It would be interesting to see what arguments came up.

Aameh loved the corridors of the manufacturing sections. Walking through one was like inhabiting the mind of the Dorm arguing with itself, with the more brutal truths emerging the further you went from areas with constant use.

For the first time in days, she wasn't suffocating.

She played a small role in something bigger.

Artists kept subversive ideas alive. Educators spread thought that must endure. Illegal publications spoke truth to power. Dazzling, ephemeral sparks sank back into obscurity, only to emerge again at another time, in another place.

AAXYL

Aaxyl dashed in as Leela was about to leave her office. The top floor of the Dorms might as well be another planet after working hours. If she'd left, Aaxyl would've had to wait for her office to open in the morning.

Leela heaved a giant sigh, her patience wearing thin. "Not now, Aaxyl. Complaining won't help you, because I was the one to cap volunteer jobs at three. It's enough to keep anyone busy. Coming in person won't change my answer."

"Leela, please. I need a food coupon." They had some SociCred saved up, but there was an AxAm rule prohibiting spending savings on others.

"You have a food coupon." Leela rolled her eyes before returning to her desk with exaggerated reluctance and accessing the SIS.

"But I have the time now that I don't have to be in the clinic all day." Aaxyl insisted.

"Aaxyl, that is not how the break from the clinic works. You still have to be available for emergencies, not doing something else for additional SociCred." Leela peered at the screen, twisting her hair back absently and sticking a stylus through it to hold it in place, as she examined personnel records. "But perhaps we can both help each other."

That sounded promising. Aaxyl knew when to not interrupt a good thing and waited quietly for Leela to finish assessing whatever she was assessing.

"We need a symbiontist. I can't just keep the clinic closed." Leela held her hand up to stop Aaxyl before she said anything. "You're good, but aren't qualified to run the clinic beyond emergencies. I need to pick one of the other certified medics."

This wasn't going as well as Aaxyl thought. "What do you need from me?"

"I need a recommendation. These are the guys who have the training. Which of them has shown better understanding while working with you on cases?" Leela transferred a list to the wall display.

It was easy. "The orthopaedics guy from the medics section, Doriack. But the medics section is always crowded. They may not let go of him."

"It's a time of transition," Leela muttered. "Here's how we do this. I'm switching two qualified paramedics to the medics clinic so that Doriack can be the symbiontist and I'm making you a standby paramedic apprentice, in case they run short. It will give you a SociCred boost for being available, and you get paid more if you get sent out on cases. The clinic is fine and you can help Doriack settle in, but the laundry collection and sanitation jobs have to go— you have to be free to leave as soon as you're alerted."

"I'm not qualified." Aaxyl was just an excellent generic worker.

"I couldn't assign you if you didn't qualify." Leela wasn't interested in Aaxyl's change-avoidant philosophy. "This is my best offer."

Aaxyl didn't want to let go of the emergency sanitation job. She got called rarely and the compensation to be on standby wasn't much, but when she was called, she earned much more than even a medic assistant, because it was a crisis and she had experience. "It's a lot of responsibility."

"It's called learning on the job—the only advanced learning you can afford." Leela took the stylus out of her hair. She was done.

Change threatened Aaxyl's precarious ability to provide for their lifestyle. "I could mess up!" Aaxyl said.

"Don't," Leela advised. "It's an excellent offer. You already help out the paramedics in Dorm emergencies. It doesn't get better than this. Take it or leave it."

Paramedics were paid well just for being available and the chances of getting called were higher. Aaxyl was almost sold on the idea.

Leela delivered the winning point. "Paramedics on call are issued a hoverboard."

That changed everything. Aaxyl took it and left, giving an excited whoop once out in the corridor.

Aaxyl collected her paramedic emergency kit and hover from the medics section. The hover was longer than the one she'd trained on for becoming a SecPro in order to slot under stretchers to lift them.

She strapped her kit into position under the seat and donned a uniform before she went to Mystery Man Vidroh's coffin-dorm. She passed SociCred shops, the media room and other recreational areas, watching herself walk through reflections with a hoverboard on a leash.

She wanted to ride all the way up to Vidroh's coffin-dorm, but thought it might come across as rather grandiose. So she walked, with a hoverboard in tow, but gained a bit of a strut as dormers turned to look at her.

She reached Vidroh's coffin-dorm, pausing for an entrance in the dining area near the doors. Her eyes panned the four sided racks of bunks, searching for his bunk number before they landed on Vidroh not watching her entrance at all. He was slumped asleep at a table, resting his head on his good arm. His injured arm hung in the support sling.

She sauntered over in style, accumulating stares with the hoverboard, emphasising that a paramedic was here as a friend of this ex-SecPro.

She slapped the food coupons next to him, waking him up. She wanted people in the coffin-dorm to see that she had secured him comfortable facilities, and anyone who had a problem with it could bring the argument to her.

Vidroh raised bleary eyes from the coupons and his scowl followed her hand to her face as he straightened. "You're stalking me now?" Vidroh picked up the coupons, taking in the bells and whistles on her. "What?" He glanced around the Dorm.

Aaxyl perched on the hoverboard, feeling a little self-conscious. The anti-gravitational tech allowed the hover to remain in position with no support. This was theatre and she wanted to make a point. Also, of course, because it was so cool that she had a hoverboard and could do this.

"Food," Aaxyl told him and handed him the bunk assignment slip as well. "Whichever bunk you want."

"You rescue strays, don't you?" Vidroh's face broke into the first genuine smile she had seen on him. It was like seeing a completely different person. He was... not handsome, but real. "You had to take on work yourself to get these for me, didn't you?" Vidroh stopped smiling, as though realising he had smiled.

"I was planning to, but I got a better job," Aaxyl reassured him, gesturing toward the board.

Understanding dawned on Vidroh's face. "Congratulations! You deserve it. I have something for you, too."

"Okay..." Aaxyl was curious.

"Officially, there are no updates," Vidroh stressed. "Unofficially, some SecPros are investigating a list of attackers from the video and the details of the vehicle from the Dorm parking surveillance."

"Do you have the list?" Aaxyl hadn't expected this at all. A surge of emotion ambushed her.

"Not yet, but I'm trying."

Aaxyl cleared her throat. "Thank you." It came out a whisper.

Vidroh nodded. "So I've been meaning to ask."

"Anything." Aaxyl sounded like NeoJai.

"So far, my hand was doing poorly; you fixed it. I lost my home, bed, and food, and you fixed it. I lost a girlfriend too..." The joke was left stranded as his voice trailed off. Raw emotion flashed in helpless eyes and he blinked it away, his lips forming words his voice wouldn't deliver.

Some desperate, straw-clutching corner of his psyche had slipped past his stoic omerta to blurt out a Freudian plea wrapped in a joke. Aaxyl pretended to not notice him trying to flounder his way out of the naked feelings he'd inadvertently revealed.

She let him cling to his pretence of not being a leaky boat filling with pain. "The fixes were downgrades. Coffin-bed instead of own bed in own home. Dorm food instead of whatever you eat. But me being your girlfriend is an upgrade. My dear friend, you'll have to earn that one."

Recruitment notice: Positions open for ventilation engineers in the Ekta Dorms air filtration unit. Dorm Ads, Tuesday, November 18, 2442

~~*~*~*

AAMEH: NULL DORMS

Aameh hadn't gone to the Null Dorms at all since... She was just there briefly to talk to NeoJai and eat his food, because Dorm meals didn't taste right these days.

Aameh and NeoJai rendezvoused at the medic-bots after lunch. "Did you talk to your father?"

"I discussed it. He wants to meet you as soon as you resume work, and I'm monitoring till then. Everything is under control."

"I found another match from the bodies that landed up in the Dorms," Aameh said. "A symbiontist from the Thar Dorms. Disappeared a year ago."

"That can't be a coincidence," NeoJai said. "Third symbiontist to get into trouble. Or first, depends on how you see it."

There was more. "I may know the link. Remember the medical data I took to Perfect Sam? He spent the afternoon looking through it hours before he was killed..." Her sniff sounded too much like a sob. Not even a clue excited her anymore.

NeoJai leaned against a stocky green medic-bot. "Tell me."

"He found something curious about the earlier missing non-persons, but not the ones from the past year. Several of them had telepathic symbionts. Maybe that's how the symbiontists are connected."

"Telepathy is real?"

"Oh, yes. There are different degrees, from getting a general sense of others, to communicating with other telepaths."

"What degree were the nulls?" asked Neojai.

"Hard to say, since they can't tell us. SYMB scans show presence, but not how well they worked or even if they worked." Aameh wasn't curious, because if she were, there wasn't a Perfect Sam to ask these questions to, and Aameh didn't want to think about that.

NeoJai pondered her revelations for a while. "What's the bottom line?"

"All the nulls he flagged were names I had identified as being repeatedly found." Aameh was still getting value from those printouts. "They were kidnapped, found and brought here, and then went missing from here to be found again and and brought back."

"What's the use of a null telepath?" They were as good as dead anyway. "Do you think nulls can communicate with telepathy?"

"No idea, but Aaxyl said Perfect Sam had planned to meet Admin."

For the first time, Aameh considered that she was out of her depth and should stop her investigation. The non-persons were the responsibility of the state. She hadn't put words to how she felt about Perfect Sam, and he didn't even know it, but he was better than anyone else except Aaxyl and she had lost too much even if they saved a few missing non-persons.

She was investigating two decades of missing persons. The journalist who had written the article that got her interested was still untraceable. Hersh had helped her get in touch with Admin Dhrit for the investigation. Perfect Sam had been looking for Hersh and had analysed Aameh's data. The coincidences were piling up too high. If she hadn't started this, perhaps Hersh would still be here and Sam would be alive. Aaxyl had warned her it was dangerous.

Admin Dhrit would handle it.

Aameh turned to leave.

"How are you doing, Aameh?" NeoJai must've noticed she hadn't said goodbye, but she wasn't in a goodbye mood.

"Flat." Aameh had lost her enthusiasm for the puzzle.

"And how's Aaxyl?"

"Sarcastic." Aameh didn't want to talk about Perfect Sam, or Aaxyl being unnerved, or say goodbye. She needed a change of subject. "You should know there's another guy quirking for her attention."

"You really shouldn't..." Neo began.

Aameh grinned for effect. She was tired of being flat. "Males fight each other for the alpha position." Even she knew this was stupid.

NeoJai groaned. "Aameh, we're twenty-fifth century men, not some wasteland animal species. Nobody fights to claim a woman and nobody is required to be monogamous and I'm not the alpha type, anyway."

"Oh, men fight; they just use different tricks, but it is easy to see in the Dorms," Aameh assured him, her own mood improving. This was a better subject. "Anyway, you have nothing to worry about. They're both flat-flirting. She's tense and he's damaged."

"Aameh! You shouldn't discuss people's personal—"

"He's openly damaged! He was shouting outside the clinic." Aameh hadn't seen it, but the rumours had been comprehensive.

"If there's anything I can do to help either of you..." NeoJai was too proper to gossip.

"You could join us in the evening. We're planning to go to Nagrik Manch for Ultimatum Day celebrations. It will do Ax good to have someone to talk to." If they could pretend to be happy long enough, maybe they would be.

"I see. I'll be there."

DIY agrav board malfunction kills one, minor damage to dome ceiling. SecPros urge residents to only use certified anti-gravitational tech. Dome Times, Tuesday, November 18, 2442

~~*~*~*

NEOJAI: AXAM'S ROOM

NeoJai arrived at AxAm's room as Aaxyl and Aameh stepped out.

"How are you?" NeoJai asked.

"Sarcastic." Aaxyl's humour rang fake, but he didn't comment.

Aameh was flat, and Aaxyl was sarcastic. NeoJai needed to find a word for what he was.

"I had some free time," he said.

"So you didn't come to visit Aaxyl," Aameh teased.

He hoped she wouldn't describe mating behaviour, or he'd die of embarrassment.

Aameh was about to speak when Aaxyl clamped her hand over her mouth and steered her toward the elevators. "You must ignore her. I dropped her on her head."

NeoJai had tagged along with Admin Dhrit and his mother once for the stuffy, speech-riddled celebrations at the Octagon, a few years ago. Never again. This sounded more promising.

A muscular man with an arm in a protective sling joined them as they waited for the elevator. This must be the guy.

"Aaxyl invited Vidroh." Aameh glared at Vidroh, who looked startled.

NeoJai extended his hand, hoping to smooth past Aameh's hostility. "NeoJai."

"Vidroh," the newcomer offered.

Aameh threaded her arm through NeoJai's. They took the elevators down. A woman in a yellow and red floral dress awaited them in the lobby with a matching bright smile. Aaxyl introduced them, waving a vague hand. "Scharada, Vidroh, NeoJai."

Ah, this was the psychologist who'd requested asylum in the dome.

They walked out of the Dorms and through the parking lot. NeoJai tried not to look at where Perfect Sam had been attacked. They turned left outside the gate for the park between the Ekta and Thar sectors, passing a queue of costumed under-teeners escorted by dorm-supervisors. Most dressed as fictional or historical figures. Half a dozen Abrahamhas and an AricNova interspersed a dozen time-travelling Skippys in purple skin-tight suits and skippy-boots with their hands on their hips.

The Dorms were the only place you'd find so many kids together.

NeoJai said, "They're adorable,"

"Don't let Ax hear you say that. She calls them noisy nuisances. I think raising me squished all the *aww-cutes* she had in her." Aameh crinkled her nose.

NeoJai could definitely sympathise. "I can imagine. Even with help, and Reva being such a quiet child, my mother insists she's done with children."

Aameh made a face. "I can't imagine Admin Dhrit being able to help all that much, what with the responsibilities of the Dorms."

Admin Dhrit helped all he could, but the clone who stayed home, Dhrit-H, had always been the primary parent. Even more than Nyaya. NeoJai needed a change of subject or he'd be spilling all about the clones to a nosy Aameh, who couldn't keep a secret to save her life.

"There aren't any Jugaads." NeoJai looked at the midgets chattering non-stop. He planned to take Reva along when she was older. "Only Abrahamha and AricNova."

"Jugaad died before the Enduring War ended," Aameh said. "They have costumes for all The Three scientists. Girls pick AricNova. Boys choose between Abrahamha and Jugaad. Abrahamha has muscles and is still alive. He wins. Besides, who doesn't secretly want to be an Abrahamha's stray?"

Vidroh snorted derisively. Surly fellow.

Aameh slowed to let him walk ahead, pulling on NeoJai's arm to keep him with her. "I asked Scharada to have a talk with him, when we get to the park."

"Why don't you like Vidroh?" NeoJai whispered back.

"I don't hate him. I just don't want him around Ax. He's a good guy, but he has baggage. Ax needs someone who will put her first. He needs a psychologist more than a girlfriend."

NeoJai doubted romantic interest worked that logically, as they hurried to catch up with the others.

The wall-to-octagon park offered plenty of space for large gatherings and it was being put to good use. The kids fanned out running. Street vendors lined the periphery, selling clothes and other useful items. A news hawker sold the anonymous grassroots magazine *Khabariya* with its gaudy cover right alongside the likes of *Dome Times, Dome Express and Dome & Dorm*. NeoJai clicked a photo to show his mother.

On their right, toward the residential areas beyond the ring road, a cricket match attracted the usual enthusiastic audience. They drifted left to mingle with the crowd.

"How did you guys end up with your names?" Scharada asked Aaxyl who fidgeted.

NeoJai knew this one. "Dorm Hacks 101," he said, when she didn't answer. "Aaxyl changed their names because names starting with two As appeared higher in lists." He thought it was quite clever.

Aaxyl shrugged.

He also knew that unable to explain the absurd names, ten-year-old Aaxyl had claimed them to be fusionoms adopted as a statement of inclusion.

NeoJai's own name was a fusionom. As was his grandfather's name, Saisrisel. His grandfather had adopted it in the first public endorsement of Abrahamha's Ultimatum for peace. He didn't say any of that either.

NeoJai wished Admin Dhrit could attend, but it would make dormers uncomfortable. But he had the next best thing. He pulled out his new 180-degree 10-cam recorder, and attached a split unit to each shoulder, cajoling Aameh into narrating an intro.

"Nagrik Manch, or citizen's platform is a good place for social justice information, clothes, snacks and gossip. Not necessarily in that order." Aameh stopped.

NeoJai waved her on, enjoying her quirky ramble.

Aameh opened her arms wide in an expansive gesture. "Most dormers here are from Ekta and Thar Dorms, but inners come too. Different parks host the Manch on each day of the week, and the two near Null Dorms, alternate. Today is special because there will be Ultimatum Day performances. Come, watch the festivities." Aameh gestured at the camera to join her, and then covered her face, laughing. NeoJai let the cameras switch to general ambience.

Aameh slowed near a sweet vendor and he indulged her with a large plate of *jalebis,* choosing one for himself when she insisted. The bright yellow sticky spirals were a regional speciality. Just sweet. Very, very sweet.

He chewed and followed with his cameras as Aameh caught up to the others with the plate and everyone took one.

A rich voice began a folk tune. "All of earth was owned by man..." Heads turned. A man stood on a park bench, like a makeshift stage. This must be the Nagrik Manch gathering. Laughter animated his face as he bent to speak to people sitting around the bench.

"... and that is when the trouble began..."

The powerful baritone lured passers-by.

NeoJai joined AxAm as they waited for him. Scharada and Vidroh sat on the grass at some distance, talking quietly.

Several people close to him chorused, "But what was the trouble?" kicking off an irreverent song about the old world, with countries crammed against each other and no way out, because you'd land in another country if you left.

Aameh asked him if she could use his camera to record the Nagrik Manch and he handed the units to her, showing her how to use them. Each unit had a drone camera, but NeoJai hadn't figured them out.

Aameh skipped off, leaving him with Aaxyl rather transparently.

Aaxyl rolled her eyes.

NeoJai tried to think of something interesting to say.

Another man sat on the bench playing bongos. A few people clapped along and chorused key phrases when prompted.

"All the world was countries,

With no wastelands but boundaries

They fought and feared a WW3, W-W-3

A World War Three, World War Three,

And used up all their WMD, W-M-D

But fell short of MAD, M-A-D

Near to far and earth to star

With reasons falsified

The theatre of war

Was mass-murder-suicide"

The crowd carried on "All the world was owned by man, and that is when the trouble began..."

NeoJai stole a glance at Aaxyl and she looked away. The last time they'd met, NeoJai had held her as she cried for Perfect Sam.

"You don't have to avoid me, you know?" He knew she was listening. "Aameh explained the AxAm rule. I'm happy to be here as a friend."

Aaxyl gave him a wry smile, that made him think she wished it were different. "I do appreciate the things you do for Aameh. She's full of praise."

NeoJai smiled. "She's easy to please."

The bongos changing beat introduced a narrative performance on the CI Wars that scored the highest body count of the Enduring War. He knew it was history, but it was so different, it could be another world.

Civilisational Incompatibilities was a concept born in the Enduring War. Old world social and regional faultlines had transformed into CI wars as people rallied around symbols they would kill or die for. Centuries later, they knew of the events, but the reasons remained obscure. Countries fought wars, religions fought religions, rioting and localised violence escalated into entrenched local warfare in many places around the globe.

While the triggering incident of the Enduring War was widely recognised to be the great economic collapse of 2053, it set off a chain of events that set off more failures. Ideology, water, food, fuel, misinformation, and inflation would later be identified as top killers of the Enduring War.

A few feet away, Scharada listened with rapt interest. He wondered what she was thinking. CI Wars had led to the birth of community psychology. Her area of expertise.

NeoJai asked, "Ax, is Am the SoulScaper?"

"Why do you ask?"

"Just... something she said made me wonder. If it's supposed to be a secret... Am's not very good at keeping secrets."

"Only Am thinks it's a secret." Aaxyl flicked off an ant wandering over her leg. "How did dormers come up with her exact name for her art? They know. They look out for her."

"Oh."

"When she was a kid, I told her to keep it a secret to ensure that she was careful," Aaxyl's eyes shone with mirth. "You can't secretly paint graffiti in the Dorms."

Well, when she put it like that...

A young voice spoke nervously, drawing their attention back to the bench. "Hello, my name is Abrahamha and this is AricNova and we are founding AVANT." One of the Abrahamhas they'd passed earlier was on the bench, padded costume adding muscles to the scrawny kid.

An AricNova climbed up next to him and they unfolded a paper with *The Three* written on it. "We are The Three," they said together.

"There's only two of you. Where's Jugaad?" someone yelled from the crowd, setting off a rumble of laughter. AricNova tried to climb back down from the bench. It took some convincing to keep her there. Someone lifted another Abrahamha to the bench. It would have to do.

It was apparently a play and the bench wasn't big enough. The hovers of four paramedics on duty were pressed into service, boards out to extend the stage.

Two Abrahamhas and one AricNova, comprising the iconic trio of Abrahamha, AricNova and Jugaad, unfolded again. "We are The Three."

The girl playing AricNova knew her lines. The Abrahamhas spoke the same lines.

At the time of the great economic collapse of 2053 that triggered the Enduring War, AricNova was twenty and Abrahamha worked for her at the newly started AVANT. Then the Enduring War started. More kids got on the stage and waved around in the chaos of war.

AricNova and Abrahamha stood with their hands on their hips and frowned at the fighting. Then the kid dressed as the zeplyn fell on the stage, flailing. He was drowning in a flood. AricNova jumped into the water and saved him with considerable effort, when he turned out to be a method actor and made her pull his dead weight away.

Aaxyl bent to murmur, "Do you really think there were that many people in the old world or is this like Ridnam, with their religious history extending a few thousand years into the past with each telling?

"The records support the numbers," NeoJai hesitated. It was possible in theory, and there was archival media, though the highest quality was easy to spoof two dimensional formats. No immersives, no projections, no multi-camera interactives. It made one wonder if the conspiracy theories were right about much of the old world content being a hoax. But the wastelands were full of remains of buildings and people. It was hard to understand how it worked.

On the stage, AricNova and Abrahamha established intentional communities and started relief work and inspired similar efforts worldwide to form the famous Margadarshak Network of the Enduring War—meaning 'network of guides'. Half the children helped each other, while the others continued the war.

One of the extras fell off the stage and the rest were unceremoniously vanished. The Enduring War was too big for the stage.

"I wanted to suggest something," NeoJai said. "I could loan you money to become independent outside the Dorms."

Anger flashed in Aaxyl's eyes. "No."

"Ax, this isn't romantic." In fact, it burned his romantic interest to the ground, but it would help the sisters.

"I'd still owe you the money. You'd have that power over us," Aaxyl said.

"What if I gift it to you? You could pay it back, but it wouldn't be mine to claim." NeoJai knew the sisters had hoped to train and work outside the Dorms with Perfect Sam's help. They'd lost a friend. They didn't need to lose a dream as well.

"Why would you do this for us?" Aaxyl asked.

NeoJai didn't know. All the reasons that came to mind sounded premature and unrequited. More unimon sat in his account than he needed. "You're friends. Does there have to be more reason?"

"And you don't want sex?"

NeoJai inhaled saliva and got busy coughing. "I wouldn't go that far, but if taking a relationship off the table reassures you, I can live with that."

At this point the acting resumed again.

Abrahamha discovered symbiont microorganisms by pulling small balls out of his costume. AricNova founded SYMBTech for mass producing and distributing HealSYMB, and they went around injecting people and making them immortal.

NeoJai stole a glance at Aaxyl at the mention of SYMBTech. Her eyes were moist, but she watched the play.

The Three displayed unusual symb-abilities by posturing. The more enterprising Abrahamha tried to fly a hoverboard to show off his symb-abilities and was taken off the stage.

Aaxyl now had tears in her eyes from laughing. She leaned toward him. "I'd tried that too. The paramedics are prepared for hijackers."

NeoJai couldn't remember the last time he'd laughed so much.

The story skipped forward a bit.

The Margadarshak Network relief workers became targets of attacks to raid supplies. A Skippy dropped in as Jugaad was killed off in an attack, making Abrahamha and AricNova sad.

"Stop!" the remaining Abrahamha yelled. "Ninety nine percent of people are dead. We are only one percent left. No more fighting!"

For that shining moment, he was the star of the production. Abrahamha's Ultimatum, delivered.

The rest of the cast surrounded him in agreement. "No more fighting."

"You don't need to attack anyone to get HealSYMB. SYMBTech will give it to you for free," Abrahamha declared to applause from the audience. He pretended to hand out HealSYMB to the audience in the front. "Now you are immortal."

The play ended to deafening applause as Abrahamha looked at the audience and bowed.

"Would you still offer the unimon if I said you're too young for me?"

NeoJai frowned at her. "I'm twenty-six. Just two years younger than you."

"I've raised a twenty year old," Aaxyl said.

Her words hurt, and he suspected she meant them to. She was protecting him from what she thought was a bad choice. "Okay. I still want you to take the money."

Aaxyl stared at him for a long time. "I'll think about it."

NeoJai nodded. It would have to do. He knew he wanted Aaxyl in his life and it would be good for her too. She didn't see it now, but nothing had changed. He liked AxAm without romance too.

The bongo player beat a simple rhythm to keep the audience entertained, while three more people came to sit on the ground before the bench. A small troupe dressed in black skin-tight costumes with fluorescent designs emphasising their hands and legs moved people from the center of the crowd to create a circular clearing. An acrobatic dance?

NeoJai reached for his communicator hastily, hoping Aameh was recording all this. She was right there, close to the action and his comm projected a real-time rendering. Aaxyl moved closer. A few more people clustered to watch.

Aameh teamed the cameras up to focus on the musicians, the lead dancers and the performance as a whole. She'd figured out the drone units for a top view.

The bongo faded and a complex rattling beat took the lead, sounding almost like noise, till it suddenly made sense. A *nautaar* player strummed a few initial notes, sending anticipation surging through NeoJai's veins. He was a student of classical music, and those few notes betrayed the effortless dexterity of a skilled musician.

The thought had barely formed in his mind when the *nautaar* player broke into an intricate melody swirling through notes and picking up speed and crashing. The dancers dazzled with acrobatics. They'd waited for dusk to get maximum effect from their costumes and the dance looked like swirling ribbons of light.

Clustered dancers leaping away blended into the chaotic rattling rhythm that started sounding like gunfire. A singer added staccato lyrics to punctuate key moments, as the *nautaar* slipped effortlessly between haunting melodies and nerve-shredding cascades of notes. The key threats of the Enduring War varied by region, but the failure of antibiotics, climate change, and catastrophic economic inequality killed more people than direct conflict as the music evoked struggling heartbeats, earthquakes, floods and desperate poverty.

The percussionist took over in a storm of beats so fast, they rang out a tune, and his mind craved to prevent something that had happened centuries ago.

The dancers split into sections, portraying simultaneous stories, their frantic dance picking up pace as the Enduring War reached the peak of destruction. Flawless choreography and stagecraft made transitions and changes of props invisible. The Enduring War got to everyone. Those untouched by its ravages couldn't survive the world it left behind.

"How have I not heard of these artists?" NeoJai asked Aaxyl, only partially to have a reason to talk to her.

Aaxyl looked at him like he'd grown a second head. "You haven't heard of Kabeerem?"

NeoJai's jaw dropped. *The* Kabeerem was one of the best classical musicians of the time and played several stringed instruments. NeoJai had studied his sitar and violin music, though this was the first NeoJai heard him on a *nautaar* in a completely different, genre-hopping style, wringing an avalanche of precision from a relatively new instrument mostly suited to accompaniment. Kabeerem was making musical history while performing after a dorm-kids play?

Aaxyl leaned over to whisper, "He used to be a Thar dormer before he got famous. The percussionist is his old roommate. They sometimes perform at Thar Dorm events. No two performances are the same."

"It's a classical performance called *jugalbandi*—improvised musical interaction." NeoJai hoped he wasn't boring her. People tended to get vacant looks when he went on about classical music. "This is semi-structured, with cues for the dancers."

"The dancers are fabulous." Of course. Aaxyl would find them more interesting.

So NeoJai asked, "Who are the dancers?"

"No clue."

And then, impossibly, Kabeerem took everything to a whole new level, surging back into focus, thrumming with rhythm. Two masters of their instruments waging a musical battle and dance at once. NeoJai had attained enlightenment.

Nuclear, chemical, and bio-weapon attacks played out. Opportunistic looting, extreme pollution and transportation collapse ravaged cities. Evolving pathogens decimated populations.

As the dancers and music and singer crescendoed to Abrahamha's Ultimatum, NeoJai couldn't see movement in the audience.

Enough.

Any weapons of mass destruction would be returned to the sender.

The dancers froze in precarious, exquisitely expressive positions. One was supported by an arm and leg on two different dancers. Another balanced on a single hand with feet in the air, on the hand of someone frozen as he fell. Perfectly immobile. The ones playing aggressors died off in small solos. The music stopped.

NeoJai heard traffic on the ring road in the distance. There were no claps. He could sit here all night processing what he'd been through.

And then, the *nautaar* chimed with airy agility. The dancers unfurled, like lights of hope, backing Abrahamha's Ultimatum. Countless voices worldwide: public figures, artists, politicians, journalists, human rights advocates, ordinary people, backed Abrahamha's call for peace and released the audience from its trance as the dancers vanished into the crowd.

Applause thundered through the park.

AAMEH: AXAM'S ROOM

"Ax? You sleeping?"

"Yes."

New thoughts hounded Aameh's mind in the dark.

"Do you think some people aren't meant to be with us?"

"What do you mean?"

"Jugaad and AricNova died in attacks when their work on earth was done. Abrahamha lives, but away from people he saved."

"The Three were too powerful, Am. They would endanger us if they stayed."

"Do you think Perfect Sam died because he lived among us?"

"No, Am. He died because he was attacked by a murderous mob."

"But he was attacked because he was here."

She heard Aaxyl sigh.

"Can I sleep with you?"

Bedding rustled. "Come here."

Vortexia-7 by Automatix voted most desirable car of 2442. Speed Sense, Wednesday, November 19, 2442

~~*~*~*

NEOJAI: SAISRISEL RESIDENCE

NeoJai wondered if the shirt made him look less masculine. The flawless skin, so stunning on his mother made his features look more unimposing than a man needed them to be. His fathers, in comparison, projected the sort of masculinity a woman might want to rely on.

Oblivious to his pondering, his sister Reva rolled around on his bed, untidying it, as she watched him get ready.

He ran his fingers over his jaw. His jaw was fine. The shirt wasn't. It was an aquamarine silk with a subtle pattern woven in greys. All his shirts were in pastel colours and simple designs, and this one felt like he was trying too hard. He wished he looked more impressive, but his inner critic always thought he looked like the perfect receptionist. Pleasant, forgettable.

"What do you think?" he asked his tiny outer critic, tangled in a half-unfolded bed-sheet, with her head dangling over the edge, hair trailing on the floor, leg flailing as she tried to roll further.

The six-year-old gave him a double upside-down thumbs-up, sliding further off the bed. An upside-down approval could be open to interpretation, but the kid was always on his side.

"Thanks," he said, moving her back on the bed before she overbalanced. "Now run along before Dad comes looking for you."

"Mom's taking me."

"Then you should hurry, little bandit."

Perhaps he should hire a style consultant... better not. If Aameh caught the slightest whiff, he'd never be able to show his face in the Dorms again. The shirt wasn't bad. It just took a while for its nice weave to register. If Aaxyl got close enough to notice, he hoped she wouldn't waste attention on that.

"Reva!" Dhrit-H yelled from the living room.

"She's in here." NeoJai picked her off his bed and set her on her feet to get on with her morning routine.

Dhrit-H came in to shoo Reva out. "Go quickly, Mom's looking for you."

Seeing Dhrit-H reminded NeoJai he needed to talk to Admin Dhrit.

"Is Admin still here?" he asked Dhrit-H.

"He left for work early. Is it anything I can help you with?"

"Just Dorm stuff," said NeoJai. "Aameh returns to work today. He wanted to meet her."

NeoJai had found a better outer critic.

"Do you think this looks too much?" He extended his arms out and turned, showing off the shirt.

"I'm not sure what you want me to evaluate," Dhrit said. "It's a nice shirt. You look well-dressed and handsome. Is it an occasion?"

"No, Null Dorms as usual." Just that he'd enjoyed the Nagrik Manch and become friends with Aaxyl, even though she'd refused to be in a relationship with him. The chances of her speaking to him when he dropped Aameh home had improved.

"I'm sure the non-persons will appreciate it," Dhrit said, drily. "And perhaps their new caretaker's sister will, as well."

NeoJai gave an embarrassed laugh. "I don't have any plans. Just on the off-chance we meet."

"Is a dormer going to care that you're wearing a blue silk shirt instead of... let me see... peach cotton, white cotton, white silk, grey silk, lemon cotton, sky blue... You dress like Admin on his way to work. Handsome, if I may say so myself, but formal. He gets paid to look like that. What's your excuse?"

Dhrit-H himself always wore exquisite casuals, though right now he wore pajamas with some abstract print.

NeoJai could do worse than have his father advise him. After all, his parents were the unicorns of the modern age with over a century of happy marriage. Marriage had been among the earliest casualties of immortality, with forever becoming a rather intimidating promise.

"I don't feel impressive," he admitted. "I like her, and everyone knows that,"—thank you Aameh—"but we're on different sides of an administrative divide. She's a Dorm-rat and my father is the Administrator of the Dorms. I'm the *them* to their *us*." NeoJai gave up on the mirror and headed for breakfast.

NeoJai's lunch box waited next to a stuffed *parantha* flatbread and coffee on an antique dining table from Grandpa Saisrisel's time. The table had been repaired so many times over the centuries that NeoJai suspected it had transitioned from an antique to a replica.

The dining room was the heart of this house, with a touch of all of them in it. Saisrisel's priceless miniatures sat next to Reva's well-worn Blueberry Bandit game and one of Dhrit-H's bowls of pebbles for diffusing scents on a side table along one wall. Aameh's sketches too had found space among panels of photo prints by all the Dhrits and the cover art of special editions of *Khabariya*, an anonymous publication on public policy and social conditions that his mother published.

Dhrit-H turned a chair around and straddled it, resting his chin on its back, watching his son have his breakfast. "I don't feel very impressive either, you know?"

NeoJai snorted.

His father had been the president of this dome and led a global organisation before being cloned. Not impressive, just because Dhrit-H was at home? Right.

"The other Dhrits are exciting," said Dhrit-H. "They return home after an absence and are missed by Nyaya while I'm always around discussing kids and meals. They have all my good qualities, plus their achievements. Even my son dresses like them."

"Does it matter that much?" Dhrit-H was the most secure person he knew.

"Not usually." Dhrit-H pointed to the *Khabariya* covers on the wall. "But I miss being the source of interesting news. Publishing *Khabariya* is an important part of Nyaya."

"You're the Dhrit who raised her children with her," NeoJai told him. "When we say 'Dad', it implies you, by default. I'm sure that scores major points."

"Your mother looks at me the way she doesn't look at Admin Dhrit." Dhrit-H winked smugly. "It doesn't take away from their relationship, you know? You need to find how you are with each other and what it looks like, regardless of who your father is or who else is interested in her."

"What if that is how she looks at me?" NeoJai was glum. "Like a guy she could like, but doesn't?" And the sort of man she liked might be a muscular, damaged hero. NeoJai disqualified on all three words.

"Then someone else will find their joy in you."

NeoJai stopped mountainising his molehill and shared the recording of the Nagrik Manch he'd made for Admin Dhrit. The Dhrits were the same person, after all. And he'd inherited his love for music from them.

"I used to organise a version of these," Dhrit-H had a faraway look. "Such gatherings started as a way of declaring mass support for Abrahamha's Ultimatum, you know?"

NeoJai sniffed as Reva's door opened and enough scent for an orchard of apples wafted out.

Nyaya hustled Reva out of her room and through to the living room. "Wear your shoes, I'm coming," she called after her, pausing to kiss the top of Dhrit-

H's head as she passed.

"It is lovely to watch you two together," NeoJai said.

"You mean me specifically, or any me?" Dhrit-H was curious.

"You specifically," NeoJai said. "I want Aaxyl to look at me like that one day. The way Mom looks at you."

Nyaya rested her hands on Dhrit-H's shoulder to get his attention.

"I'll be back by lunch," she murmured, glancing between the two of them, settling on NeoJai. "Nice shirt. Don't you have to go to work?"

~~*~*~*

NEOJAI: NULL DORMS

"I wish I could sing like that," Aameh said, as they walked to the bot bays after a very late lunch.

"I don't remember the words." NeoJai hadn't realised he was humming. Kabeerem's performance from the Nagrik Manch had stuck in his head.

"It barely had any words. You've captured the tune perfectly."

He'd always had a good ear for music. It was quiet with the life support bots gone to wherever they went for whatever they did at this time of the day. No hissing hydraulics, whirring lifts or squeaky wheels.

Aameh had taken longer than usual on her round of the dormitories. He couldn't wait to find out what had delayed her.

He waited till they were out of earshot of the main dorm hall before asking, "Did you find anything interesting?"

"Yes," Aameh said slowly. "But I'm not sure what it means. I checked all twenty-two nulls admitted in the past year since the pattern changed, and one of them looked familiar."

"Who?"

"No clue, but he came in a month ago, and regained consciousness last week, though he's still unresponsive." Aameh transferred a single record to his comm.

"Regained consciousness?" NeoJai echoed, stunned. "I thought that was rare."

"It is," Aameh confirmed. "These don't count. Such cases are usually from some injury or damage that heals and it is not considered a proper null, but recovery from a coma. If he recovers, that is."

"An injury sounds suspicious given the timing," NeoJai said.

"That, combined with that feeling that I know him, was what took me so long. I'm going back in the evening to interview a friend who visits him. His file says he might recover. Could you ask Admin Dhrit to find out more?"

"Of course, but Admin Dhrit is coming here after work to meet you. You could ask him yourself. Is that all?

"Yeah," Aameh pushed off the medic-bot she was leaning against. "The thing is, he may just have one of those faces. He doesn't fit the pattern of our investigation. He doesn't match missing persons reports. Nor did Perfect Sam find any telepathic symbionts in his records. He's just a regular null."

Aameh and NeoJai were done with their tasks for the day. Aameh would meet Admin Dhrit in an hour to explain everything they had found before he dropped her home. Heels echoed as they walked toward their desk and they turned to see.

Nyaya walked in, dressed formally in an emerald suit with a cream top, her sleek bob highlighting her features and making her eyes sparkle. Pearl earrings peeked through. His Mom had transformed into her public persona. He wondered what the occasion was.

"I was in town shopping and dropped by." Nyaya gave him a warm hug and extended her hand to Aameh.

Huh. His mother despised shopping and didn't chit-chat.

He supposed it was his turn to speak. "Um... Nice?" he ventured, feeling a little like a confused extra when the lead performer went off-script.

Aameh was still holding out her hand. "I'm Aameh. I've been eating your son's lunch. Thank you."

"I pack for both of you." Nyaya smiled warmly at Aameh as they finally shook hands. "And thank you for the beautiful artwork."

They stood for a bit.

So what was he supposed to do now? He prompted his mother. "Is this it?"

Aameh leaned to his ear. "She can't act, can she?"

The fabric of reality was in tatters if Aameh could say this about Nyaya.

Nyaya adepted poise, with decades of experience in public sight. Nobody exemplified composure under pressure like her. So why was she... flustered? Indecisive?

"Let us go out to lunch," said Nyaya, finally.

It was evening.

Aameh waved NeoJai toward Nyaya. "Go, I'll finish up here."

"Sure it isn't a problem? Your—work later?" Aameh was to meet Admin Dhrit about the investigation.

"I'm sure. Go." Aameh waved them off.

NeoJai messaged Admin Dhrit to drop Aameh at Ekta Dorms after their meeting if he didn't return on time. He put an arm around his mother and ushered her out before she puzzled him further.

His mother stopped at the door and gave him the once over, smoothing imaginary imperfections off his shirt, and running her eyes over his hair. She only did that to Admin Dhrit or Dhrit-SD from the Superdome before a press conference. He automatically stood straighter, shoulders back, head high, and switched to a confident, charismatic persona from sheer reflex.

"This isn't like you," NeoJai smiled affectionately at his mother. He'd even started sounding like Admin Dhrit. Was there some major announcement?

"You'll see." Nyaya led the way out.

NeoJai braced himself, but it was the usual Null Dorms. They walked through the building and it was the same empty, echoing tomb he worked in daily, same empty elevator—no media bots or people of any sort until they exited past the security desk at the main entrance. He slowly relaxed, walking with confident strides and head high, just in case.

Once in the parking area, Nyaya led the way to a spacious zeplyn with its door raised in welcome. It looked vaguely familiar with corners so rounded, it was almost a sphere and it shimmered. Zeplyns often had smaller wheels than cars, but this one had none that he could see. It simply positioned itself an inch or two above the ground. Rock solid. It didn't so much as twitch when his mother walked in.

Wait.

Nyaya wasn't using her own car or Admin Dhrit's zeplyn? But she was already inside before he could ask. As he walked in, eyes adjusting to the dim interior, he imagined his mother was secretly a laser-toting space pirate rather than anonymous publisher of a grassroots magazine.

"Hi." A man stood, silhouetted by the bright window. His low voice was unfamiliar and NeoJai hoped his mother cued him in soon because he was flying blind.

He put on an amiable smile. "My pleasure to... Abrahamha?" This was it. He'd run out of words.

"I get that a lot." The man had an accent he couldn't place. "I'm Noir."

"I'm NeoJai." His poise had evaporated and he was stammering. He wasn't, was he? His mother gave him an encouraging smile. A warning or explanation would have been better.

Noir rumbled, "I know. I'm sorry about this abrupt introduction, but there's much to discuss and we were told your Dorm may be under surveillance. The zeplyn will take your mother home, and Mohan will bring your friends over. I have to go to the Superdome, but I'll drop you off first."

How would the zeplyn go to one place and people in it go to others short of an explosion?

What was his mother doing with a member of Abrahamha's family? Abrahamha's right-hand man who managed the AVANT empire for him, to be specific? Some answers would be great.

Another man, almost hidden behind Noir, sat up from his slouch and gave him a cheerful wave. Stunningly handsome. He looked familiar. Mohan. Darling of the dome paparazzi. Abrahamha's left-hand man, heading SYMBTech. Two members of Abrahamha's family. Both hands were represented. Why was the Abrahamha household descending into his life, and how was his mother involved?

NeoJai remembered where he'd seen the zeplyn before. It used to be parked before the Ekta Dorms when he dropped Aameh off, like a shimmering jewel in a concrete desert. Perfect Sam's zeplyn. Was it the same one?

NeoJai turned back to his mother. "Where will we..." The zeplyn around them turned into a room. "What?"

Documentary interactive 'The Fauna of Forgotten Cities' by Pravir Bhatia promises immersive experiences of Wasteland Cities. Entertainment Weekly, Sunday, November 23, 2442, Wednesday, November 19, 2442

~~*~*~*

AAXYL: THE CLINIC, EKTA DORMS

Vidroh came in just before the clinic closed. Aaxyl's mood brightened. He'd waited for Doriack to leave before coming in, so he must have news.

Aaxyl locked the door from the inside, closing the clinic for the day.

"How's the new guy?" Vidroh asked as she checked his arm. It had recovered nicely, though he'd have to be careful for another month or so.

Aaxyl shrugged. Doriack wasn't Hersh or Sam, and Aaxyl preferred to keep things professional rather than risk losing another friend.

"Two new pieces of information." Vidroh got to the point. "I have the list, but it's useless. They found the vehicle and the attackers from a call for paramedics in the Cranti sector." He handed her an info chip. "The car had stopped near the park before the Octagon and some attackers got out. According to passers-by, they dropped to the ground."

"But we found them, right?" Aaxyl asked.

"Not exactly. Paramedics say all fourteen are dead. That's over half our annual death count in a single event. Bodies are being analysed."

"All of them are dead? Not a single survivor? How can that be? No suspects?"

Vidroh shrugged.

"What's the other thing?" asked Aaxyl.

"This is puzzling too," Vidroh said. "The people on the list are from prison. SecPros traced them from arrest records."

Aameh had said people had vanished from prison, only to land up in the morgue here.

"What do you-" Aaxyl's voice broke as a familiar man appeared next to Perfect Sam's—Doriack's desk. Was she hallucinating? "Sam?"

He turned to her. It wasn't Sam. Wait, it was. His beard was gone. His hair was shorter, but she'd know that too-good-for-the-dorms perfection anywhere. How had he got here?

"You should leave it to the Sec-" Vidroh's voice trailed off in the background.

"Sam?" Aaxyl repeated. He was gorgeous as ever, with shoulder-length hair and—she flew to his arms for a hug, and stopped short to examine his face. She cupped his newly revealed jaw, searching his face. It *was* him. She got her arms around him for the fiercest hug she could manage. "How..." Her voice was muffled by his shirt, and she looked up at his face. "How did you survive?"

"I teleported out from under them." Perfect Sam grinned and hugged her back. "It is a long story, which I will tell soon, but not here."

They could go up to AxAm's room. Aameh would be thrilled. Aaxyl brought her comm up to tell her, just as Perfect Sam put his hand on Vidroh's shoulder. Aaxyl hadn't even noticed Vidroh approach. Of course! Sam was his friend. No wonder he hadn't been as upset as them. He knew.

A huge media display appeared behind Perfect Sam. The room had changed into a... living room? Media room? It was some expensive-looking residential room.

Aaxyl had never been to such a room before. As far as she knew, they were features of large houses, and she hadn't been to one of those either. She hadn't even thought of such things before, let alone in such detail. This wasn't her delusional mind at work.

"Ax?"

She turned around to face people sitting on the sofa. "What's going on? Where are we?" She looked around. This was way past wonky. "NeoJai? Administrator Dhrit?" Her eyes went to a huge muscular man standing near a window overlooking a garden of some sort. Large window? Greenery? The evening light looked overcast rather than overshadowed by buildings, though of course it wouldn't rain inside the dome beyond a light mist in a bad storm. They were closer to the larger properties near the center of the dome.

Then she saw the man's face. Her mouth moved but no words came out as her eyes went full-Aameh.

Aaxyl tried again and it came out as a yelp. "Abrahamha?"

"I get that a lot." The man's voice rumbled in a weary rote, as though he'd already said it too many times. "I'm Noir. This is my brother Mohan. You know him as Sam. We're here on behalf of Abrahamha."

Where was here? Had they teleported?

Aaxyl backed away and bumped into Perfect Sam—Mohan—who had stepped forward. She stared at his face again. Without the beard, it was easy to see he was the celebrity businessman. She turned and moved back from him as well. She wasn't sure where she stood with these people.

The light hit Mohan just right and she vaguely remembered photos of celebrities in erotic poses. *Playboys for Sexel.* She should have recognised that body in the clinic even if his face was covered with that ridiculous beard.

"*Playboy* Mohan?" So much for Perfect or Sam. Aaxyl had never felt this betrayed.

Mohan rubbed his forehead. "It was a campaign for sex worker rights," he protested. "Let me get Am so we don't repeat this."

"Oh no, you don't." Aaxyl grabbed his arm before he... popped... or something. Aameh had been through enough because of this man. "Explain it to me, and then I'll decide if Aameh needs to see you again."

"Hersh had asked me about telepathic symbionts before he vanished." Mohan made a placatory gesture. "I came to investigate. I didn't know Aameh's work in the Null Dorms was related till I found telepathic symbionts in her data."

That wasn't what she meant. In the parking area, Aaxyl had stared at the mangled body.

Perfect Sam stepped toward her.

Mohan. His name was Mohan. Aaxyl took a step back and he froze.

Dots connected in her head. "It wasn't you? The dead man was an attacker?" This was surreal. "And you didn't tell us? We thought you died!"

Aaxyl still had that stupid list of attackers Vidroh gave her. "I told SecPros that you had been killed."

"They contacted SYMBTech and we informed them that Sam escaped."

Aaxyl *knew* the SecPros had been holding back information.

Vidroh. Aaxyl spun around. He had come looking for Sam. He knew who Sam was and hadn't told her. Vidroh read her correctly and stepped back.

"You knew!" Aaxyl said. "You came to meet him. You knew and didn't tell us."

"It's not Vidroh's fault," Mohan said. "He was injured. He's not related to any of this."

Aaxyl ignored Perfect Sam for a moment, nailing Vidroh with a stare. "You knew we thought he was murdered."

"It wasn't my secret to tell," Vidroh said. "Besides, I didn't know what had happened. I still don't know. I only hoped that if it wasn't making global news, perhaps he may not be dead."

"NeoJai?" Aaxyl's voice broke. He had appeared so honest and supportive. Yet here he was, all dressed for the occasion in a bright blue shirt. Ax wiped nervous palms on her uniform. "You too?"

"Not me! I am just discovering this, Ax," NeoJai came over to her. "I just got here. I'd never met Perfect Sam or Mohan. This is insane!"

Aaxyl was grateful for the solidarity in disorientation.

"We were fighting for you," she told Mohan. "I distributed the recording of the crime everywhere. We kept asking questions that could put us in danger. Aameh tried to interrogate dorm lowlifes."

Mohan's eyes widened in alarm. He *should* be alarmed, Aaxyl thought, somewhat maliciously, but she was losing steam. He wrapped his arms around Aaxyl, holding her close, letting her register that he was okay. He was alive.

Mohan opened his shirt. His chest was covered with angry residual scars from the knives. "Teleporters heal faster than normal people, but I *was* stabbed many times before I managed to focus enough to teleport out. I was unconscious. SanJeevan let me go two hours ago, and I came immediately."

What was she supposed to say to that? "I'm glad you're alive. How do I go home?"

"The crime still happened, Ax. If I hadn't teleported, I'd be dead. Hersh is still missing. The dome still has a problem. Let me get Aameh. We just need to ensure we have all the information and that is it."

"You aren't involving Aameh in this. We're dorm-rats, not SecPros."

Aameh would follow him around in utter hero-worship again, asking more questions, and *oblivious to the danger*. Mohan could teleport and recover from being stabbed. No way was Aaxyl allowing Aameh to be involved in something like this.

"You can be with her. I'll ensure any time you both spend toward this is compensated for," Admin Dhrit assured her. Of course. The Administrator of the Dorms waved the bloody magic wand.

Aaxyl detested feeling cornered. "I have to protect Aameh. She already sent reports. You're families of World Leaders. Fighting corruption in the governance provider. When giants like you fight, people like us are trampled. This is not our fight."

"You would be family," Noir said completely seriously. "Like the two of you, Abrahamha's Strays are siblings bonded by adversity. We wouldn't be giants crushing you in our fight. We want you to be a giant with us."

"What do you mean?" AxAm had loved Abrahamha's Strays from the moment they heard of them, but Aaxyl wanted to hear how far this insanity extended. If he thought their lives were alike, she had serious doubts about his sanity.

"Dhrit asked for our assistance. We investigate. If UDAY or Damodar are guilty, we dismantle both," Noir spoke like it was doable.

"We'd just topple the government, that is all?" Aaxyl wished there were a way to let him hear what he sounded like. "And then what? We live happily ever after in the Dorms after undermining powerful politicians while you fly off to the Superdome?"

Noir tried again. "Aaxyl..."

Aaxyl looked straight at him. "If you're that all-powerful, where's Hersh?"

NeoJai turned to Admin Dhrit who looked surprised himself. "Does Mom know about this?"

Admin Dhrit gave NeoJai a *we'll talk about this later* look. These people weren't all on the same page either.

Vidroh stepped to flank Aaxyl. NeoJai walked over to her other side.

Aaxyl started to speak but NeoJai beat her to it. "We need time." Aaxyl gaped at him, but he continued. "It's a lot to process. Teleportation is real. We met Abrahamha's Strays. Sam is alive and has slept with everyone capable of sex. We're in shock. This is not a good time to make a decision."

He sounded like a politician.

"I'll let you know if I change my mind," Aaxyl told them. "Can someone drop us home?"

That was the only good part of this story. Teleportation was real. Aaxyl wanted to teleport again. With full knowledge.

"Come," Mohan reached out to her and Vidroh. "It's a lot to take in. I'll visit tomorrow and if you still think we shouldn't talk to Aameh, we won't, okay? We just need to understand some of her conclusions."

Aaxyl could live with that. She relaxed. And then it hit her. She was about to teleport. For real.

"At least, that explains why your beard kept getting in your way." She grinned at Mohan. "I'm glad you didn't die."

Hover traffic permits fall to three hundred after new tax. Emergency services warn of increase in response times due to cuts in service hovers. Dome & Dorms, Wednesday, November 19, 2442

~~*~*~*

AAMEH: D10F8, NULL DORMS

D10 on the eighth floor of the Null Dorms was interesting. It was the only dorm-hall Aameh had seen that had windows. Huge, bright ones. The theory was that they helped recovery and gave catatonic nulls something to watch. It was also unique in that it had independent beds for the nulls rather than LSUs in LSRs. And there were people.

Two dorm supervisors cared for the patients in various stages of awareness. Most of the nulls were in beds. Three nulls sat unresponsive in chairs facing the big windows, and one followed a dorm supervisor around. She'd tried to talk to him earlier, but he didn't seem to understand her.

The null she had come to see sat on the floor in an area that reminded Aameh of the playpens in toddler-dorms. He had a face that would have looked intelligent if it expressed anything. A therapist held his hand and put a toy in it.

"Good evening," Aameh said as she approached, and both null and therapist turned to look at her.

The toy dropped out of the man's hand, and the therapist patiently put it back again, closing his fingers around it. The therapist smiled at her. "Kishore told me to expect you. I'm Tapas. How can I help?"

The null could follow sounds. He looked at Tapas while he spoke and then at Aameh when she replied.

"I'd visited earlier, and he looked familiar. I'm trying to remember how I know him. Kishore told me his name, but I'm not able to place him. I'm meeting someone on the roof, and dropped in for a bit. Perhaps, meeting him when he had visitors might help me remember."

Tapas smiled. "Ask away. I'm his best friend."

"Oh." Aameh had thought he was the therapist. "I don't have specific questions, just trying to remember where I met him. I live in the Ekta Dorms. Did he live or work there?"

"No, but the name here is fake for privacy reasons. You may have seen him in the news. He worked as an investigative journalist with *Dome Times*. Shyam Tere."

Ice trickled down Aameh's spine. She hadn't met the man, but she'd seen his video attached to the article that started it all. This was the journalist she hadn't been able to trace.

Missing persons

Juni Valor, three times winner of SPACERS design bounty for unmanned spacecraft, asserts that agrav tech will never be safe enough for manned shuttle launches. Space Watch, Wednesday, November 19, 2442

~~*~*~*

AAMEH: NULL DORMS

Aaxyl passed the dinner service bot, and picked up their unclaimed dinner packets on her way to their room.

Aameh was probably off SoulScaping the Dorms, thinking Aaxyl wouldn't know. Aaxyl just wanted to curl up and sleep for a week from emotional whiplash, but Aameh deserved to know this news at the earliest.

She entered the room and dropped the dinner packets on the table before flinging herself on her bed. Processing. Perfect Sam was alive. Teleportation was real!

She'd read about teleportation and telekinesis as abilities the ancients had, but had never known anyone who had them. Turned out she'd worked with a teleporter for weeks. If anyone had suggested this even a few hours ago, she'd have said teleportation was an urban myth inspired by the Transferrons used by the rich to travel around the world in a blink of an eye. She hadn't seen any of those booths outside films either.

And now she had been teleported. Twice.

To Aaxyl's disappointment, it didn't feel anything in particular other than the surroundings changing.

Aameh would be thrilled. And she'd have a thousand questions. Well, she could ask Perfect Sam, Mohan, tomorrow.

Messages waited on her comm, including one from Aameh. "Meeting Admin at ND @ 7, back < 9. He'll drop me off."

Aaxyl jolted upright. Admin Dhrit was with Mohan and Noir, not at the Null Dorms. It was eight. Aameh should already have known that Admin Dhrit was elsewhere. She commed Aameh and got a message that Aameh was in a meeting and would call back when she was done.

Something was wrong.

With Admin Dhrit and NeoJai both with Aaxyl, Aameh should have messaged Aaxyl if she took the Dorm bus back. She tore out of their room and down the stairs and out of Ekta Dorms, and ran to the Null Dorms faster than she had ever run before. She'd rather be laughed at for being overprotective. She could barely get enough air.

Aaxyl tore through the Null Dorms gate and straight through the parking area. NeoJai's car was near the main entrance, but they could have teleported him to Mohan's home, like her. She raced in through the cavernous lobby and up the stairs to the second floor, ignoring shouts from the security staff. It was a public Dorm. They couldn't stop her.

No Aameh. No one was in sight. Aaxyl headed for the administrative offices on the top floor, peeking at each floor she passed as best she could without wasting time. Aameh might have gone to an office, expecting a meeting. The lobby looked empty, but it was a huge floor and Aaxyl didn't have a reason to search here.

Loud voices echoed from further up the building. There was nothing but the roof above. She tried to quiet her panting and listen. One sounded like an outraged Aameh.

"Am?" Aaxyl ran up toward the roof. "Aameh!"

"Aaxyl!" Aameh screamed. Aaxyl hadn't heard her shout in years. The terror in her voice was Aaxyl's every nightmare come alive.

Aaxyl raced up toward the sound of her voice.

A dorm guard yelled from the dark depths of the office floor. "Go down. Roofs are off-limits."

The guard was right. The roof should have been locked, but the door was open. A zeplyn sped away as she got there. There wasn't anybody here either, just a dark expanse of roof. She walked in the direction the zeplyn left.

Something moved in the dark. "Am!"

Aaxyl raced toward the movement. It was NeoJai. Blood ran black down his face in the dim light and stained his shirt. Aaxyl quickly got out the HealSYMB she carried in case Aameh needed it and transfused a vial and added a pain block. Belatedly, she realised she had no nutrients on her. Aameh never reacted to the HealSYMB enough. NeoJai would weaken pretty fast as he started to heal.

"Dad. Am." He clutched Aaxyl, but his grip had no strength. "SecPros took them."

"What SecPros?" Aaxyl yelled at him. "Who hurt you?"

He moved but didn't reply.

SecPros could be any security-professionals from dorm guards and investigators to elite commandoes. They all worked for the same security provider contracted for dome security. Without NeoJai providing details of their uniform, she didn't know who she could trust.

Aaxyl raised her hands and stood as two dorm security stormed up, guns drawn, followed by Sambit Amdani himself. Aaxyl recognised him from Aameh's descriptions. Two more SecPros came up.

When Sambit saw NeoJai slumped against Aaxyl's leg, he motioned for the SecPros to lower their weapons and hurried over. "I was in my office when I heard the commotion. Is he alright? What are you guys doing on the roof?"

"I found him like this," Aaxyl told Sambit, hefting NeoJai up a bit, only for him to slip back down.

"I'm okay." NeoJai slurred. He wasn't even close to okay. It was the pain block talking. "I can walk."

"You can start walking whenever," Aaxyl murmured. "Till then let me help."

Sambit supported NeoJai on the other side. "Let's take him to my office. I'll inform Dhrit."

With the SecPros just outside?

"He's my boyfriend and needs treatment. I'm a paramedic for the Ekta sector. I'll take him to the hospital." Aaxyl hoped NeoJai wouldn't contradict her.

He gave her a goofy smile.

Now Aaxyl hoped he wouldn't remember this.

More security arrived. They verified Aaxyl's identity and asked to be updated when NeoJai could be interviewed. Aaxyl suspected that they'd have treated her very differently if she hadn't claimed to be the girlfriend of Admin Dhrit's son. Sambit himself helped her take NeoJai down in the staff elevator and Aaxyl was grateful. She'd been worried that they'd be left with the SecPros.

NeoJai tried to walk as much as he could.

Sambit put a hand on her arm as they reached NeoJai's car. "Is everything okay? I can come with you."

"He'll be fine." Aaxyl wished Sambit weren't surrounded by too many SecPros.

Aaxyl asked NeoJai to tell the car to obey her.

"Authorise commands from Aaxyl." He was slurring.

"The car has recognised him. You have to identify yourself now," one of the SecPros waiting for them to leave said.

Oh.

They finally managed it and she ordered the car to take them to the Ekta Dorms. Then all she could do was worry about Aameh. She called Vidroh's coffin-dorm to ask him to come to their room.

She tried shaking NeoJai to find out more, but all she could make out was that Admin Dhrit had been attacked by SecPros who turned on Aameh and him as well. The rest was confusing. They either escaped in the zeplyn or a masked teleporter vanished with them. No uniform details.

As soon as the car stopped at Ekta Dorms, she raced to her room for her hover and hovered him up the stairs, through the stares, straight to their room and dropped him on the extra bed.

She hooked NeoJai up with more HealSYMB and nutrients from her emergency kit.

"Why didn't you tell Sambit? He would have helped us." NeoJai shivered.

"He had SecPros with him. I'll go back to tell him."

Vidroh arrived, surprised to be called to their room this late. He helped her get NeoJai's blood-soaked clothes off. Bruises marred his fair skin, and Aaxyl swallowed a sudden surge of protectiveness.

Aameh bruised much worse. Aaxyl needed to find her.

"I tried to stop them... couldn't hold on." NeoJai rambled on about SecPros, zeplyns and teleporters, changing his story constantly.

Vidroh agreed calling SecPros might be risky. Aameh was just a caretaker, but kidnapping Administrator Dhrit was another story altogether. "You need to find Mohan."

Aaxyl tried, but the contacts she had for Perfect Sam no longer worked. "I don't have a way to contact Mohan. Shouldn't you be able to contact him?"

"I no longer have a communicator. I came here to find him, remember?"

NeoJai tried to get up and fell back into the bed. "Get my father. Go home. Tell him to get Mohan." He started to get up again. He wasn't going anywhere till the HealSYMB had a chance to work.

"We're trying, my friend," Vidroh murmured as he caught him before he fell to the floor.

"Do you have a way to contact Mohan, NeoJai?"

"I don't. Tell my dad." He seemed to have forgotten his father was kidnapped.

"He's going to hurt himself again." Aaxyl gave him a sedative. "He'll heal faster with rest. I'll contact SYMBTech."

"I'll find out what I can from SecPros." Vidroh headed for the door. "And find Mohan's home."

Aaxyl got up to leave as well.

"Where are you going?"

"To ask Sambit for help, and take another look around the Null Dorms. Whoever took them keeps going there."

"Point. Let's go there first." Vidroh waited for her to join him.

"No. You find out where SecPros could stash the freaking Administrator of the Dorms. I need to be alone." Fear tunnelled her vision. She needed to find Aameh.

"What about him?" Vidroh nodded to NeoJai. "Shouldn't someone tell his family what happened?"

"Where does he live?" Aaxyl asked numbly. "We don't know anything. I'll take him home when he wakes up in a few hours."

"I should examine the roof with you. Don't refuse. I'm trained to examine crime scenes. Afterwards, we split for our tasks."

They took NeoJai's car and her paramedic kit and hover. Aaxyl told the guards that she'd left something behind on the roof, and they got waved through with warnings to not loiter.

They exited the elevator on the office floor and headed to the roof.

She activated the emergency lights on her hover, illuminating the roof. The parking area where she'd found NeoJai was straight ahead. Toward their right lay storage areas and bot bays and beyond that would be the food farms. On the left, beyond the parking were food farms. They too looked undisturbed. Whatever happened was limited to the parking.

Not much to see. Signs of a scuffle. Bloody footprints, smears and a trail. Vidroh used her paramedic kit to take forensic samples and imaged the scene with her comm, recording to his chip.

The attackers had dragged NeoJai too or he had held on trying to prevent them from leaving. Aaxyl must have interrupted them.

She turned around in a circle, searching the darkness, blinking her prickling eyes. "Nothing we don't know."

"Let's check out the rest of the roof anyway."

Vidroh scrutinised the ground toward the edge of the roof. Aaxyl slumped, overwhelmed.

"Ax, come here." Vidroh had found both communicators. No tracking Admin Dhrit or Aameh without them.

Aaxyl couldn't endure this. "I need a minute." Two comms. The expensive one, crushed to pieces; the cheap Dorm one with a cracked screen. This was what she had left of Aameh.

Complicated, innocent, tenacious Aameh. Quirky, intelligent, kind Aameh.

Every effort she could muster for two decades concluded like this. She had failed the kid.

Aaxyl imagined Aameh reacting with her weird disappointed face as though she had expected so much better. Aaxyl struggled to breathe.

Aameh would die from not healing alone, if any of the blood were hers. The kidnappers didn't even have to intend to kill her.

The night closed in to smother her. Aaxyl tried to remember if Aameh had enough HealSYMB on her. She should. It was an AxAm rule, but Aaxyl didn't know. It had never been tested like this.

Vidroh rubbed her back.

Aaxyl suffocated and gasped futilely. "I won't cry." This was no time for it, but tears welled anyway. She started to tell him they should hurry, but hurry to do what?

Vidroh put his arms around her and her sobs ripped out. He embraced her through it, all the way to dull defeat.

"Aameh wouldn't believe anything without evidence," he said.

A glimmer of sanity kicked Aaxyl. She was standing and weeping as though she had nothing better to do.

"We will find her. No matter what."

She put the shreds of her emotions in a small, tight box and squashed them for later when she had Aameh.

Then she stood extra straight and pretended to have her shit together.

Admin's comm was crushed, but Aameh's was only cracked. Aaxyl kept it with her because she couldn't part with it. AVANT could extract information from Admin Dhrit's comm if Vidroh found Mohan.

They failed to find Sambit too. She'd left him alone with SecPros. It may not have been her brightest moment. Vidroh had several places to visit. Aaxyl asked him to take the car. She couldn't return to their room empty-handed, and decided to examine the area around the Null Dorms.

She had no means to investigate a zeplyn after it had flown off, but this was connected to the missing non-persons and there were enough of those over the years for someone to spot something.

Aaxyl wandered outside the Dorms instead, seeking locals.

She found a tea stall. A man, half asleep at the counter, asked her what she wanted.

"Information," she said. "I don't have unimon to buy anything."

He assumed she cared about a null in the Dorm and offered her a free cup of tea. He had seen nothing useful.

She moved on to a construction site further ahead and helped the labourers to get chatting with them. They sympathised, but it was unlikely a null got smuggled out.

She walked on urgently, adrift. The few shops open mostly offered repair services or food. Unlike regular Dorms bustling with some activity even at night, nothing much happened here.

Staff walked in, staff walked out. Automated supply trucks delivered supplies, but such vehicles had anti-theft mechanisms, so delivery vehicles would not pick up items. The windowed rooms were rented out as residential space to fund the Null Dorms, but they had separate entrances and no access to the main building. Few vehicles suitable for transporting nulls out came there, but all were scanned. Short of an elaborate conspiracy involving many security guards, Aaxyl didn't see how it could be done.

Unless it was a teleporter.

And now Aameh had vanished. Aaxyl had no way to trace either the zeplyn that had flown off, or the nulls that seemed to be connected with her disappearance. She needed to keep her shit together. She'd cry later.

She climbed up some dome maintenance scaffolding. It was an interesting perspective, but showed nothing suspicious. A zeplyn approached and hovered over the roof of the Dorm. Aaxyl climbed higher to get a better look, but it dropped lower toward the park behind it, instead of landing on the roof. She scrambled back down and ran around the compound wall. There was just the inter-sector park with Ekta Dorms on the other side.

In another minute she would come to the fork below the ring road. It was past two and she was running out of ideas. Turning left led to the Ekta Dorms beyond the park, and the right to the Null Dorm gate. Her feet were killing her, but she didn't want to miss anything. She debated whether to search the park for the zeplyn, or go home, or monitor the front of the Dorm for a while, when she saw it.

A distinctive zeplyn with lights switched off lurked in the shadows of a tree in the park. Not in the parking area inside the compound, the road, or the roof?

She slipped closer, shielding her comm with her hand to prevent its light being seen.

It was flatter than Mohan's and had a sleek design and small wheels. The windows were shielded, but there were bloody smudges on the glass right across the eight gold rectangles arranged in an octagon, with *The Dorms* in the centre and *Administrator* in a smaller size below it.

Admin Dhrit's zeplyn.

A shadowy figure ahead walked slowly toward the Null Dorm.

Administrator Dhrit. Could she be mistaken?

He had clearly gone home to change, because he wore some a pale kurta and a scarf.

She slipped behind the tree, her heart thundering. He turned back and stuck to the shadows. When he opened the door and a bright light came on, she could see blood on the floor inside, but no Aameh. It was definitely Admin Dhrit.

Was Aameh back, too? She would have called Aaxyl immediately. Was Admin Dhrit involved with the kidnappers? It didn't make sense. Why would he attack his son? Why would NeoJai claim it was SecPros?

Why was there blood on his zeplyn?

Aaxyl wanted to demand answers, but the isolated location deterred her. If Admin Dhrit had indeed escaped, she would find Aameh. But she would prefer to have witnesses around when she asked him anything.

He got into his zeplyn and left.

She commed NeoJai. He wasn't awake.

It was an hour's walk back. She didn't have it in her to run again and Vidroh had NeoJai's car, but not a comm. She checked Aameh's comm during her exhausted return. A message from Admin Dhrit had asked Aameh to meet him on the roof to avoid surveillance, while he was talking to global celebrities who would vouch that he wasn't anywhere near her when she went missing.

Why was NeoJai protecting him?

Aaxyl contacted SYMBTech as she walked, "My name is Aaxyl. I have an urgent communication for Mohan."

"Everyone has an urgent communication for Mohan."

SYMBTech sounded like they didn't take Playboy Mohan too seriously.

"Who am I talking to?"

"I'm Gyan."

"Hello Gyan, I'm a friend of Mohan and I need to talk to him urgently." Aaxyl said. "Can you please give me Mohan's contact information?"

"Sorry, I'm not authorised to give you this information."

"Can you put me through to someone who is allowed?"

"Yes. Please call in the morning."

"Who may provide me with Mohan's contact?"

"Mohan, Noir and Abrahamha," Gyan responded patiently.

"Are any of them present?"

"No."

"Gyan, please. This is a matter of life and death."

"Everything is a matter of life and death. SYMBTech deals with life-saving products. I may not give out personal information and I cannot connect you to them because they're not here."

Eventually, Aaxyl reached her room and gave up. "Will you convey this is about his friend, Aameh?"

"I will."

NeoJai would awaken soon. She didn't want him to wake up alone. SYMBTech could wait for a few hours. Vidroh was seeking Mohan too. Admin Dhrit was safe. Aameh might be too.

She collapsed on her bed and struggled to pull off her FastSprints from swollen feet. Aaxyl was so exhausted, she wouldn't notice if NeoJai woke up and left. She got up and went to the spare bed to lie down beside him and fell asleep.

***

Aaxyl woke the instant NeoJai moved. "Awake?" It would break NeoJai's heart, but the priority was finding Aameh.

"Yeah." NeoJai sat up, puzzled. "I'm in your bed?" He rubbed his head and Aaxyl watched his expression change as he remembered the events of the previous night.

"We're both in the spare bed." Aaxyl kept calm. "I wanted to wake up if you did."

"I should've been up sooner." NeoJai tried to get over Aaxyl and off the bed. His bruises had healed. "I need to go home."

"No, wait." Aaxyl halted him. "I bring good news and bad news."

NeoJai said, "Please start with good news. I'm going out of my mind with worry."

"Well, the good news is your father's okay." Aaxyl got out of bed and stretched.

NeoJai gaped. "Excellent news indeed. And Aameh?"

Aaxyl shook her head. "I need your help."

"Anything." NeoJai nodded.

"So here is the bad news." Aaxyl started. "Vidroh and I recovered Dhrit and Aameh's comms on the roof. Dhrit's comm was broken, but Aameh's worked. I accessed her communications. Your father set her up to be kidnapped."

NeoJai was nodding along till the last sentence. "This is not possible."

"Each time she sent an update to your dad, the kidnappers changed their methods." Aaxyl sympathised, but she knew what she had seen. "Admin asked her to meet him on the roof. But he was with us. This morning, he was parked secretively in the shadows. I found blood on the zeplyn door and on the floor—the same zeplyn from the kidnapping."

"I knew of the meeting and none of us had expected Mohan to bring you or —"

"Isn't it convenient that Dhrit is the Admin, but everyone related to this affair comes to harm except him? Now, his zeplyn is bloody but he's fine, Aameh is missing." Aaxyl connected the dots for him.

"My father was attacked, injured and fought to save Aameh. I saw it. He abandoned me and tried to escape in the zeplyn with Aameh, but there was a teleporter among them, who brought them back, and vanished with them."

"Yet your father remains uninjured." Aaxyl told him. "Look, I just need your help in finding out where Aameh is."

"You're calling me a liar!" NeoJai breathed in shock. "No matter what you believe, my father wouldn't harm her. If he escaped, then she did too."

"So why isn't she here? Why is there no update from him?"

NeoJai paled. "Who rescued him?" NeoJai reached for his comm. "I need to verify some things. Anything I find out about Aameh, I'll tell you. Let me talk to him." Whatever he hoped to hear on the comm, he didn't. "I have to go."

"So that you can warn him?" Every time Aaxyl gave away information, it vanished into a blackhole without updates. "I'm not letting you out of my sight till I have Aameh back."

"I can't explain, but let me find out what is happening."

"The simplest explanation is often the correct one." Aaxyl wished she could make him see sense.

"Your simplest explanation ignores me giving you facts that contradict it?" NeoJai's voice broke. "Why would my father authorise an investigation? Why would he bother to kidnap Am when he could simply ask her to go with him? And do you seriously think it takes three people to kidnap one Aameh?" He stumbled to his feet. He stared at his destroyed blue silk shirt like he'd seen a ghost.

"I hear you, and it is puzzling," Aaxyl said, placating him. She pulled out Aameh's comm. "We were there with him. Would an innocent man set Aameh up to meet him when he wasn't there?"

"We didn't meet Admin Dhrit yesterday," NeoJai said, as though it explained everything. "He has a clone. We call him Dhrit-H. Admin Dhrit met Aameh as planned."

"What?" Aaxyl didn't think NeoJai might go to such absurd lengths to protect Admin Dhrit. "I'm not stupid. It was Admin Dhrit I saw. Even if it is a clone, it still knows where Aameh is."

"It?" NeoJai flared. "You refer to my father, Administrator Dhrit Saisrisel, as a thing because he's a clone?"

"I just meant it is the same one we met yesterday. Clones are genetically identical. But they don't look the same when they grow up." Aaxyl knew enough about cloned babies to know that they were genetically identical, not visually identical like twins.

"These look the same. They were cloned as adults. And my father is not an it."

There was no such a thing. "Can you deny your father lured Aameh to the location of her kidnapping? Are you telling me I didn't see him? That I didn't see blood in his zeplyn?"

"Aameh works there!" NeoJai said. "Admin Dhrit met her on the roof because our Dorm was compromised, as you know. They got attacked near the zeplyn and tried to escape, but they vanished with the SecPros. I told you everything I know."

"I saw the zeplyn fly away. I'm sorry. I want to believe you, but—"

"It was empty! What can I warn him of? That he didn't succeed in kidnapping me? His men assaulted me? You're searching for Aameh? What do I know that he wouldn't if he were guilty?"

"I need to ask him," Aaxyl insisted. "He may be your father, but Aameh is my sister."

"I don't want you near me again." NeoJai scribbled something on one of Aameh's papers. "I loved you, did everything I could to help and expected nothing in return. You accused me of covering up a crime against my friend! This is my address. Do what you want."

Aaxyl stared at the paper he handed her. "Let me at least get you a clean shirt."

"I'll grab something from a coffin-dorm." NeoJai tossed the shirt to the floor and headed for the door. "I told you to go to my home, find my father, contact Mohan. You didn't go, but I'm covering up for him?"

That was true. "We didn't know where you live," Aaxyl protested.

"You used my car, but you couldn't take the same car home? How difficult is it to say *go home*? How hard would it be to spot a three storey heritage property with a huge sign saying 'Saisrisel Residence', even if you randomly drove around near the Octagon?"

Stupid. The car had navigated to Ekta Dorms. It would have gone to his home too. Aaxyl had never commanded a car before or lived in a home. She hadn't thought of it. She hadn't even realised he lived in an independent building and not one of countless apartments in a complex.

He slammed the door behind him.

AVANT announces one month of advanced training in applied symbiontics. Free training* and accommodation. Limited seats. Science Review, Thursday, November 20, 2442

~~*~*~*

AAMEH: NULL DORMS BASEMENT

The back of Aameh's head ached. She lay curled on the floor. Her back and left side were aching as well. What had happened? Had she fallen again?

She'd met Admin Dhrit on the roof of the Null Dorms. He showed her his official zeplyn with luxurious seating, clever storage spaces and aerodynamic design. It was shorter than Perfect Sam's black pearl-like zeplyn and shaped more like a luxury car with tiny wheels. She'd explained her findings and methods.

"It is alarming that the Null Dorms don't alert SecPros if non-persons go missing," Admin Dhrit said. "This would have been exposed much sooner if the missing non-persons had been reported as crimes."

Aameh remembered explaining the problem. "Nulls being non-persons, crimes against them don't have the same weight as those against persons. Essentially, it is like vandalism or animal abuse. They didn't get reported as missing persons, because legally, they aren't persons."

"I'm asking Sambit to initiate a proper record of missing nulls," Admin Dhrit said. "Even if they aren't legally persons, their right to life is the basis of having the Null Dorms at all."

NeoJai commed Admin Dhrit. He was on his way to pick Aameh up and would join them on the roof. Excellent timing. While she enjoyed conversing with Admin Dhrit, the Administrator of the Dorms dropping her off at the Ekta Dorms gate would have been awkward.

Hooking her thumbs through the straps of her backpack, she walked closer to the edge of the roof for an artist's moment, letting her eyes adapt to the dark sprawl of the food farm. The glittering wedges of the sectors interspersed with dark parks beyond the edge of the roof.

She imagined herself on a dramatic cliff in an expanse of the Wastelands beyond the Dome, overlooking a precious bubble of civilization at her feet. So much *context* to that vantage point. She could easily imagine wild herbivores grazing in the food farm next to a stream, with the zeplyn lit up like a tent.

NeoJai arrived, silhouetted dramatically by an expanding wedge of interior lights as the door slid open. He shouted as something thumped behind her and Aameh turned to see Admin Dhrit fall to his knees. Two SecPros stood over him. Where had they come from?

NeoJai ran toward them. "Help! Security!"

The SecPros intercepted NeoJai. Aameh rushed to help Admin Dhrit, shouting at them to back off and drawing their attention. Stupid! They'd missed her till she announced herself.

Miraculously, Aaxyl's voice had echoed out of the building, calling out her name. Or at least Aameh thought it had.

"Aaxyl!" she'd screamed.

Aameh had hurried Admin into the zeplyn but a SecPro followed them in.

Admin Dhrit pushed him out as the zeplyn rose into the air.

The SecPro joined his partner attacking NeoJai.

Admin Dhrit kept the door open, aiming the zeplyn toward NeoJai, telling Aameh to be ready to pull him in. A tall, thin, masked man lunged into the zeplyn as it lowered, flinging her back as if she weighed nothing.

And then?

The narrative in Aameh's head ground to a halt. She remembered flashes of the two SecPros hitting NeoJai, while Admin Dhrit had fought the masked man in the zeplyn. She remembered Admin Dhrit shouting "Go home" and the zeplyn turning.

And then?

Had they saved NeoJai? Aameh couldn't remember.

Had Aaxyl saved them? Blank.

Her eyes hurt, but she opened them.

Admin Dhrit's wild eyes blazed out of his blood-smeared face like a fierce mask as he bent over her. More blood ran a nauseating streak down the side of his head and soaked its way into his torn shirt.

She tried to sit up and groaned.

"Careful." Admin Dhrit supported her.

"Did we escape?" Aameh's voice echoed and eyes took in an unfamiliar space. Dim lights on a distant ceiling, like a dorm hall, but a much smaller space. They were in a partitioned section of a dorm hall. It was dim, because there was just one rack near them with lights switched off, so the only illumination was from the overhead lights high above.

"No, but we've located the kidnapped non-persons." Dhrit nodded to her other side as he helped her to her feet. Two LSUs stood on stands independently of the racks, like beds in a weird null clinic.

"How long have I been out?"

"He took our comms, but several minutes, I think. I wasn't sure if I should move you."

Aameh was still wearing her backpack and struggled to take it off. Admin helped her. She ran mental checks. She was bruised, but nothing felt wet, so no bleeding. She had emergency supplies in her backpack and emptied it on an LSU. She took out the box and handed Admin Dhrit the wipes, and dosed him with a pain-block and a vial of HealSYMB.

"I'm sorry, I don't have nutrients. HealSYMB doesn't work on me enough to need them." She should have thought it through. She hoped Admin Dhrit didn't faint from the HealSYMB.

Aameh took a pain block and contemplated the HealSYMB. Should she save some or take it all?

Footsteps sounded behind a door, along with something being wheeled. Admin Dhrit put a finger to his lips and motioned Aameh to crouch behind the life-support pods with the non-persons as the huge dorm door slid open. The frames of the stands failed as hiding places, but beat being sitting ducks.

Aameh tried to make herself as small as she could, grateful for the pain block.

A white-haired man with beloved, round face came in with a medical trolley.

"Hersh!" Aameh hobbled to him. He was alive!

"Aameh? Oh, no." He met her halfway in a hug, and fussed over her. When he realised she was hurt, he reached for her backpack on the floor. She pointed to her emergency kit already on the LSU explaining the doses. He gave her all the HealSYMB and returned to his trolley for a bag of nutrients for Admin Dhrit.

Aameh attached the nutrient drip for Admin Dhrit, clipping the pack to the shoulder of his shirt, all the while formulating questions for Hersh, who had walked freely into their prison.

There was no easy way to ask. "You're helping them."

"I'm not free," Hersh said as he pushed the medical trolley over to the non-person's bed. The trolley had nutrients and two syringes. "I don't have a choice."

Aameh grabbed at his arm, ignoring the mild pain filtering through the pain block, remembering what Perfect Sam had found out. "I'm going to guess these aren't HealSYMB."

Hersh shook his head.

"Don't do this." Dhrit moved between him and the non-person.

"I have to," Hersh spoke quietly.

"Why not escape?" Aameh started putting her things back into the backpack, to be ready if an opportunity arose. "They haven't tied us up, the door is open. They didn't even take my bag. Let's go."

"They control the whole dorm hall," Hersh said. "Our section is a small part of it. It is manned by a dozen or so armed men that I know of. Could be more. Mercenaries."

Admin Dhrit looked at the nulls in the life support pods. "What's going on here?"

Hersh set up nutrient drips for the non-persons. "They force me to infect subjects with alien symbionts."

"Alien?" Admin Dhrit looked startled.

"Alien to the body. Dangerously incompatible external symbionts as opposed to the body's native symbionts," Aameh clarified for Admin Dhrit, highlighting the *external symbionts* that confirmed her suspicions. "Telepathy."

"Among others." Hersh picked up a box of injectors, but paused and glanced at the door again. "They're using symbionts from a donor. I need to save the donor."

"So we escape *with* the donor." Admin Dhrit had a point.

"They've taken… measures."

"Wait. Please," Aameh said. "We aren't nulls. People will look for us. Aaxyl won't give up. Admin Dhrit is Administrator of the Dorms. They can't ignore his kidnapping. We can escape. Please don't do this."

"Hersh," Dhrit faced him squarely. "When you vanished, Mohan came as Sam to investigate. Mohan and Noir are both investigating your disappearance."

"Sam's alive?" One source of joy in that grim prison.

"Noir won't come here," Hersh said. "There has to be some mistake."

"Mohan—charismatic Dome celebrity. Noir—looks like Abrahamha. It is them. Abrahamha sent Noir after Mohan was attacked."

"Mohan was attacked?" Hersh echoed.

"Perfect Sam is Mohan?" Aameh doubted it. Mohan was a celebrity but Perfect Sam contributed his skills in a humble welfare Dorm. But he *was* rather stunning, like the few images she'd seen of Mohan.

It took a while and explanations for Aameh and Hersh to work through the stages of acceptance and arrive on the same page as Admin Dhrit.

"Perfect Sam?" Hersh laughed. "Perfect description. This is good news indeed. We must escape or get a message out at *any cost*, and tell Mohan—" Hersh stopped abruptly.

Admin Dhrit asked, "Tell him what?"

Hersh looked from Admin Dhrit to Aameh and back and finally said, "Tell him to come like his own life hangs on the line. And bring the others."

That didn't sound like what Hersh stopped himself from saying.

"Where is here?"

"You didn't recognise it? This is the Null Dorms!" Hersh told her.

Of course, LSUs. Aameh slapped her forehead and the back of her head gave a dull thump of pain. "I couldn't trace the missing non-persons because they never left the building. How did we get here? The zeplyn left for your home."

"The attacker was a teleporter," Admin Dhrit interjected. "The zeplyn returned home, but he teleported us out of it."

"And NeoJai?"

"Got left behind on the roof as far as I know. The teleporter didn't return with NeoJai or Aaxyl, so they must have escaped."

Aameh sat abruptly. "So he teleports the non-persons out. The puzzle had no logical answer. And now we could die because I stuck my nose into it." It might be petulant in the face of events, but Aameh disliked puzzles like this. There was nothing intriguing left.

"Sometimes he does teleport them out, but usually, they walk out," Hersh said. "The teleporter is a telepath who controls them as shells."

"How? What's a shell?"

"He controls their bodies telepathically. That's why he uses non-persons. Conscious people resist."

Aameh wanted to scream. The non-persons walked out. The one thing no one would expect from non-persons. That wasn't a satisfying solution either. Aameh hadn't figured out the method. Defeat tasted worse than a bad puzzle.

It didn't matter now. They had to escape.

"This is how they support nulls." Aameh's mind returned to normal speed. "Matter of bringing in the bots."

The glimmer of an idea emerged.

"We can get a message out. I need to see the bot controls and while I'm setting up, I need you to create code names that signal it is you. Just names. Also I need four LSUs set up."

"There is no communication out." Hersh slumped. "I've already tried."

"We don't communicate outside the building. We generate data that will draw attention to us."

"We don't have a way to communicate data out either."

"Just you wait." Aameh grinned. "We will."

The LSUs looked strange out of racks, like a makeshift null clinic.

Aameh fiddled with the settings of the first. "Did you decide codenames? They shouldn't be easy to identify as us. We don't know what they're monitoring. For example, I'm going to use AxAm. Aaxyl or NeoJai would recognise it, but not strangers."

"Use my daughter's name, Reva, for me," Admin Dhrit said, as Aameh moved to the next bed. "NeoJai will recognise it."

"Sarovar for the donor," Hersh said, for the next bed. "We throw the kitchen sink at this. All we need is one message out or one person escapes, one success."

"And your code?" Aameh asked Hersh.

"Rudra for me." Hersh grimaced. "Any Abrahamha's stray would queue up to find and murder me."

"Well, that can't hurt," Aameh murmured as she moved to the fourth bed.

"Who's Rudra?" Admin Dhrit asked.

"I hope you never find out," Hersh said. "At least from me."

Aameh asked Dhrit and Hersh to lie in their pods for the tests. The one for the donor would be empty.

She taught Hersh how to order medical tests. "Just in case you need to use this trick again. Routine tests, skipping whatever is not available. The empty pod will show no tests, just an error saying the occupant is missing."

"How does that help us?" Hersh asked.

"The Null Dorm bots use an independent network," Aameh explained. "It handles care for a hundred thousand occupants. The network pushes test results into the records. NeoJai will look for anything odd and will recognise the names Reva and AxAm."

"They may have disconnected the machine network too," Hersh cautioned.

"They can't. The life support for non-persons will fail."

"The machine network! Can it be used by humans?" Dhrit asked.

"It can't, but the LSU names the patient." Aameh grinned. "NeoJai is monitoring new admissions and we'll be the only patients with tests on a new level B. With any luck, one person will remember this dump has a basement."

"Let us not depend on one plan." Dhrit cautioned. "Basements now have power, water, storage, repairs and ventilation departments. Not something dormers interact with. They may not remember unless Sambit or Leela are there. We should try everything."

"Could we overpower them?" Aameh disliked this idea as soon as she said it. Unlike the others, she wouldn't recover without bucket loads of HealSYMB. Aaxyl would be furious. Aameh missed Aaxyl. She would know what to do.

"No," Hersh replied, turning a syringe in his hands. On the upside, he hadn't yet injected the non-persons. "You can't defeat a teleporter in a fight without being one. I tried. So did the guy before me."

"You knew the previous symbiontist?" Aameh had a bad feeling about this one.

"I did. He used to work in the Thar Dorms and was assigned here for a research project. He died attempting a suicidal plan. I guess I could try it. Take both doses of the SYMB myself. It should give me a brief window to use the donor's powers to teleport out of here or telepath for help or something."

"What happened to the previous tech?" Aameh asked. It didn't sound like the sort of thing one recovered from.

"The Whisperer found out what he did, and shot him point blank in the head with a neutraliser," Hersh said. "He woke up a null and walked out to serve the monster and never returned. But he would have died anyway. No one survives. The hope was he could get help before he died."

"No," Aameh said. "The situation is not so desperate that you die to save us. Once we get the message out, they'll find us."

"The situation is desperate," Hersh said. "We attempt everything we can, no matter how risky, because the prisoner is AricNova."

"Who?" Aameh asked. AricNova was a popular name.

Hersh looked at her till realisation dawned on her. He meant *the* AricNova. The woman who saved the world and died at the dawn of modern civilisation centuries ago. It made no sense.

"We can't underestimate our captors," Hersh said. "If they can hold her for centuries, preventing our escape is trivial."

When he put it like that, *any* of their deaths would be a small price to pay. The woman who saved the world suffering for centuries, was simply not done.

"Admin Dhrit and I can hide in the pods and be less noticeable. One or both of us should take them," Aameh said. "But how can it be her?"

"It's her. That's why there are no survivors of the symbionts. The symbionts of The Three have always proved fatal. I can't do it to either of you. Nulls were a different matter. This is as good as murder. Even if the escape succeeds, you'll die."

Dhrit disagreed. "Hersh, she needs you. Also, you're the only one who knows how to do this. If you fail, a second attempt becomes impossible."

"If one of us must die, it should be me." Aameh put her hand out for the injectors. "Nothing depends on me. I'm a dorm-rat. Besides, symbionts fail in my body, so I may survive."

"It can't be you, Aameh. We need the symbionts to work. It's more important than surviving."

"I won't stand by and let you die," Admin Dhrit declared. "This is my responsibility."

Admin Dhrit won the debate with the most surreal argument—that he was a clone and his life would continue in his clone. The claim was outrageous and the reasoning fallacious, but they lacked good options. Hersh injected Admin Dhrit with the symbionts, leaving more bags of nutrients for him in a life support pod. He'd have to go back to check on AricNova soon.

The masked man appeared next to the pods with the non-persons. "You haven't given them the symbionts." He strode over to Hersh. "Getting ideas of escape, are we? Dose the nulls with the symbionts right now."

He had to be the Whisperer.

If he guessed that Admin Dhrit had taken the symbionts already, all would be lost. Hersh walked over to the life support pods of the non-persons as though to inject them.

"Why have you captured us?" Aameh demanded, hoping to distract the Whisperer. It was a waterproof body suit, complete with a mask, she realised. Not just a mask. "Release us right now."

"Why would I kidnap you, only to release you?" the Whisperer asked.

Admin Dhrit picked up her idea. "I'm Dhrit Saisrisel, Administrator of the Dorms in this dome. You can't keep me captive."

"Or, you could walk out of here to do my bidding." The masked man came over to Admin Dhrit. "A shell as the Administrator of the Dorms could be nice. I'm sure Hersh has blabbed it all to you by now. Aameh here dies while you escape, of course."

They hadn't thought this through. They hadn't even considered that the Whisperer could use Admin Dhrit as a shell and they had injected him with the symbionts themselves. Aameh's intelligence had no practical uses. If Aaxyl were here, she'd have known what to do. Aaxyl would have tried to find out how he was so sure they wouldn't escape.

"We'll escape, you know?" Aameh tried to be brave. "Admin Dhrit will pardon your men for saving his life and they will betray you sooner or later. Or you could seek that pardon yourself."

"Good luck, trying." The Whisperer turned his blank black head toward Hersh as he straightened. "Hersh may try something stupid, but I have a reminder for him."

The Whisperer raised a hand and two men in SecPro uniforms appeared next to him. The ones who had kidnapped them, Aameh thought. In the light, they didn't look like real SecPros. They had taunting expressions and slouched rather than the disciplined impassivity typical of SecPros. These could be men who were taken from the prison.

"I'm going to save your life with a refresher, Hersh," The Whisperer said in a singsong voice. "Your colleague thought he could escape using the donor's symbionts. This is your reminder for why you shouldn't try."

The masked man turned to the men. "That is all, gentlemen, you may leave now."

One of the men nodded and dropped to the floor, unmoving. The other turned to leave and dropped to the floor too.

"What did you do?" Aameh asked.

The Whisperer chuckled. "I didn't do anything. They thought of going somewhere, the donor's teleportation symbionts drained them dead, and they are still here."

Aameh wished Aaxyl were here to beat this man to a pulp.

"Save another symbiontist's life. Don't try something foolish and force me to kidnap your replacement."

Aameh's whole body trembled with cold terror. They had already given Admin Dhrit the symbionts. They had as good as killed NeoJai's's father themselves.

The Whisperer vanished along with the dead bodies.

Aameh crumpled to the floor and pain shot through her side. The pain block concealed the pain completely while she didn't move and it hit her all over again when she did. It was rubbish if the patient couldn't rest for healing. "We should have thought this through. He wouldn't have left you alone with the donor if you could take her symbionts and escape. He wouldn't have left us unguarded if we could escape. We should have guessed that it wouldn't work."

"I *had* told you," Hersh said. "We have to take every chance we have, however slim. I have to go look in on her now. I'll be back."

Hersh left. Aameh rested where she sat, hoping futilely to recover fast enough to be ready for an escape.

Twitchy and desperate, Admin Dhrit explored their prison and found bathrooms with stacks of repairmen's overalls, presumably for the non-persons to wear. He had bathed, changed and returned to Aameh with the news that his wounds were vanishing faster than HealSYMB worked.

Great. He could die without any injuries on his body now, Aameh thought. She regretted the day she read that stupid article.

Aameh hobbled to the bathroom to bathe and change. Unlike Admin Dhrit, her injuries were nowhere close to healing and her left side was a nebula of an ominous black, tortured blue, impressionist purple, and furious reds against the pale canvas of her skin. She doubted her back looked any different. The bath helped and she changed to a clean uniform and was able to nap briefly afterwards, in one of the LSUs.

She awoke to murmurs. Hersh had returned on the pretext of checking on the progress of the non-persons. He brought good news. All the mercenaries inside their section of the locked Dorm hall had left. Aameh's taunts must have worried The Whisperer more than they realised. They were all in their main project area where Hersh wasn't allowed.

Aameh sat up, wincing. "You hadn't expected to see us here when you came earlier. Perhaps he removed them to prevent them from discovering Admin Dhrit. If any of them think this is a legitimate project involving nulls, how would The Whisperer justify the imprisonment of the Administrator of the Dorms?"

"Which means they could help us escape. We can now move freely here. What if I drew their attention and convinced them to help us escape?" Admin Dhrit stood and swayed.

"No," Hersh said. "The lot who come in here are fully aware that this is wrong. If they realise what we've done, and don't help, we'll be in worse danger."

"The Whisperer would be able to use the the Administrator of the Dorms for his own ends," Aameh added glumly. They had really messed things up.

"It isn't just that," Hersh said. "He uses nulls, because regular people resist his control. He would turn Admin Dhrit into a null to prevent him from fighting back. We can't risk it. We have to make AricNova's powers work enough. It is the only way."

"But why is he doing this?" Aameh got to her feet. "Why use AricNova's symbionts knowing that they would kill his shells? Even if he wanted shells, he's a teleporter and telepath himself. Why not use his own symbionts?"

"I don't know," Hersh slumped. "But power is a safe bet. He can use the power of an ancient without risking death himself."

Admin Dhrit touched his head, where it had been bleeding. "Well, hopefully I'll have some of that soon."

"Be careful, though," Hersh said. "The brute use of symbionts without skill takes tremendous energy. The more you use, the greater the risk to you."

"If I don't make it, I want you to tell my family I love them," Admin Dhrit said. He'd already said this many times.

Ventilation engineer whistleblower claims pollution in region within acceptable limits for the past fifty years. Dome maintained on city to protect elite property from weather. Dome & Dorms, Thursday, November 20, 2442

~~*~*~*

NEOJAI: NULL DORMS

NeoJai reported for work as usual, channelling every skill he'd learned from Nyaya. He nodded to the SecPros at the entrance and answered well-meaning questions with excuses. He took the opportunity to ask where Sambit was, and was informed that he'd be in later. NeoJai shrugged as though it wasn't important and headed up to the fourth floor.

His calm appearance betrayed nothing of his heartbreak, nor of the worry for his family. This was not the time to fall apart. His injuries had been healed and he spent the night sedated, yet he felt physically and mentally battered.

After the fight with Aaxyl in the morning, he'd rushed home, only to find no one there. Admin Dhrit's zeplyn was on the roof. He hoped the zeplyn hadn't brought the attackers to his home.

NeoJai couldn't take on kidnappers on his own. He had never felt so alone. He needed to find allies. He needed to stop thinking about all this for now or he'd collapse.

He believed the attackers hadn't found his family, because Dhrit-H had called several times while he slept. He couldn't think of Aaxyl or his family. He needed information ready before Aaxyl or Vidroh found Mohan and Noir. He felt certain they would all come here. Everything converged on the Null Dorms. He just didn't know how.

Admin Dhrit and Aameh were kidnapped by the same people who took the non-persons. A breakthrough on either would find the other.

Baby steps. See if the records yielded further information. With Aameh gone, it fell to him alone. Then locate Dhrit-H, Nyaya and Reva. Then Mohan. Then try again to see if Sambit had arrived for work and get his help to find trustworthy SecPros. He just had to follow the plan.

Vidroh called from the Dorm. "Is it okay if I take your car to Mohan's home?"

"Of course. Did you find the address?" NeoJai sometimes felt left out by the physicality Aaxyl and Vidroh shared, but in this moment, he was glad the ex-SecPro was helping them.

"I'm on my way. I came here to pick you guys up, but found the room locked. I called Aaxyl, and she told me what happened. She's trying to find Mohan at SYMBTech."

"When you get there, will you please ask Mohan if Dhrit-H or my mom contacted him? They aren't at home either."

"Will do," Vidroh said. "Listen..."

Last thing NeoJai needed was to hear Vidroh defend Aaxyl. "I don't want to talk about it."

"She's worried and spoke rashly. She regrets it."

Vidroh wouldn't understand. Aaxyl accepted Vidroh and treated him as an equal, while NeoJai suspected he'd always be her little sister's immature friend. A rich idiot who didn't understand nuances of social class, or know what he wanted. She believed he'd defend someone who'd harm Aameh.

She hadn't bothered to know him in the least.

NeoJai hurt, but this wasn't the time for his broken heart. "Just tell Mohan or Noir to contact me."

He checked admission records for new non-persons. None had been admitted. Two non-persons missing, according to comparisons with the backups. No one to report them to.

He checked to see if any beds reported missing occupants. One. This was strange, since the null wasn't on admission records to begin with. He checked the name—Sarovar. It sounded vaguely familiar. He had a hunch he'd read it somewhere that also mentioned Abrahamha, but he couldn't place it.

He checked the LSU location. The bed was non-existent, the Dorm wasn't mentioned and the floor was B. Someone entered B instead of 8?

There should have been a Dorm number, a side of the racks out of A/B/C/D, a rack number, and a row and column position identifying their rack. One of the missing nulls had been in C7-4.34 on level 4, Dorm 6. The anomalous test marked this LSU like a hospital ward or... clinic: B-4.

NeoJai checked for any other records with errors in LSU identification. Six entries popped up. All of them made the previous night. Four of them had never been admitted, none recorded correct locations. His heart started hammering. He opened the results to check names. Sarovar, Reva, Rudra, AxAm.

He raced to the medic-bot section. Vidroh didn't have a comm and was no longer in the Dorm. He called Aaxyl. She'd had no luck convincing a remote receptionist at SYMBTech, but she no longer sounded suspicious of him. He was in no frame of mind to talk to her, but would team up with the devil to save his father, and Aameh was his friend. He explained the entries he'd found.

"Dhrit-H, my mother and my sister, are also missing. If you get in touch with Mohan, please ask if they contacted him. Ask Mohan if the words Sarovar and Rudra mean anything to him." He disconnected.

Aasha Dorms removes commercial immersives from free C&C quotas for dormers who haven't done any community work in a year. Management says premium entertainment cannot be considered a fundamental right. Dome & Dorms, Thursday, November 20, 2442

~~*~*~*

AAXYL: SYMBTECH BUILDING

Aaxyl had been close to the SYMBTech building near the Octagon when Vidroh called from a public comm in the Dorm because their room was locked. She'd explained the situation with NeoJai's departure.

He had found Mohan's address and had come to pick them up and wanted to take NeoJai's car there. He had her paramedic kit and hover with him.

The hover! Aaxyl's screaming feet berated her for not keeping it with her. She gave him NeoJai's contact.

From outside, the SYMBTech regional facility in Dome 91-110 looked like a rectangular box of reflective glass centred in an enormous compound. Utilitarian. The door asked her the purpose of her visit and let her in without a fuss. The minimalism didn't improve on the inside. She entered the building and was met with a long white corridor with a beverage machine visible at the distant end and closed doors on either side. No waiting area. Nowhere to sit. Just a passage.

Aaxyl glared at the projected green ball floating companionably a few feet on her left at chest height, from the moment she set foot in the building. "I have no plans of leaving till I meet Mohan."

"Of course." The bright green ball bounced a bit. She'd recognise that stylish voice with a slight tinge of sarcasm anywhere. This was the same guy from last night. Gyan. "May I invite you to make yourself comfortable on the multi-mode roof?"

"Don't want your staff and visitors to see a protesting Dormer on their way in or out?" Aaxyl asked the ball.

"Quite to the contrary," the ball moved around her to hover on her right. "This is for your comfort. I can inform you of any arrival for you to resume your protest for them."

Was he for real?

"How many people are in this building?" Aaxyl asked. The absence of any reception desk reminded her that the receptionist was interacting virtually and could be off-location. It would be good to get further into the building than the door.

"One." the ball replied. "You. The multi-mode roof also contains a small area for eating meals."

Mohan didn't show up to work daily? "Where is this sitting area?"

"Follow me, please." The ball bounced ahead to a lift and accompanied her up to the roof. The sitting area indeed looked cosy and comfortable. Someone had spent a fortune on a place for no one to use. "Would you like something to eat?"

She sank into a bright red seat. A small round table with a cheerful yellow tablecloth stood in front of it. The walls were white. A hint of vanilla in the air. It was an odd amount of hospitality to extend to a dormer he refused to help, but perhaps it was about the stature of the organisation extending it.

"Chatty, aren't you?" Aaxyl said. "Surprise me with whatever is easy and coffee." Whoever was using the comms had a sense of humour and was just doing his job. This was excellence Aaxyl could respect in other circumstances. Today she needed him to compromise. It wouldn't hurt to accept hospitality and win him over.

"Coming up."

A food service rolled up promptly with a sandwich and coffee. This place was surreal. The only human in a building of global importance was a visitor who was served food instantly. She tried the sandwich. It was the best food she had eaten, but then she ate Dorm paste for most of her life. The bar was very low.

She finished the sandwich in record time and tried the coffee, which was also delicious. She was having the best food of her life while Aameh was suffering. She asked him if she could have a sandwich packed. Aaxyl was going to find Aameh while it was still edible.

NeoJai called and Aaxyl felt hopeful, but he spoke with polite indifference. Aaxyl had never regretted spoken words this badly. She missed his eager friendship. He wanted the receptionist to convey four words to Mohan. Her heart started thundering when she heard one of them.

"Gyan, I want you to do me a favour."

"I will do everything within my authorisation." The service bot returned with a sealed sandwich.

"I want you to communicate a message to Mohan and if he still doesn't want to meet me, I will leave."

"I may not—"

"I'm not asking you to put me in touch. Surely you have the means to communicate with him? Convey four words. That is it." Aaxyl stuck the sandwich in a big side pocket of her cargo pants.

"I cannot guarantee a reply."

"Okay."

"What are your words?"

"Sarovar, Reva, Rudra, AxAm." She waited for Gyan to confirm that he'd conveyed her message.

Mohan appeared right in front of her. Look at that!

"Where did you get these words?"

"Hello to you, too. I've been trying to contact you all night and Gyan has simply refused to listen to reason. I walked for an hour from the Dorms just to meet you. I want your contacts."

His contacts hit her comm immediately. Excellent.

Aaxyl continued. "Admin Dhrit and Aameh got kidnapped last night. I know that there are two Dhrits, but NeoJai can't find either or the rest of his family."

"Dhrit-H, Nyaya and Reva are at my home," Mohan told her. "Dhrit-H found blood in Admin Dhrit's zeplyn. He couldn't contact Admin Dhrit or NeoJai, and brought Nyaya and Reva to my home to keep them safe. My home security would have blocked unauthorised communicators. Vidroh had just arrived when I got your message."

Aaxyl explained the remaining events so far as quickly as she could. "Do you know what Sarovar and Rudra mean?"

"Where did you find the words?"

"NeoJai asked me to pass them on to you. AxAm was the only—"

"Where's NeoJai?"

"Null Dorms."

"Let's go."

"Wait. I want you to tell your receptionist the next time Aameh or I contact, he'd better put us through. Or fire him."

Mohan nodded. "Gyan, Aameh, Aaxyl, NeoJai and Dhrit may access us." Mohan finally noticed the ball. "Gyan, why are you looking like that?"

"I was a bouncer, but I realise it was inappropriate." The ball vanished.

Blender 82.1 LTS adds much awaited initial support for utility fog modelling. Drop flexi-sculptures straight into your immersives. Tech Edge, Thursday, November 20, 2442

~~*~*~*

AAXYL: NULL DORMS

Aaxyl stood staring at the Null Dorms building. Less than twenty-four hours ago, she'd dropped Aameh there. She hadn't seen anything but the vast corridors and peeked into Dorms. Now here she was, having seen the roof and outside of the dorm from every side.

How she hated this horrid building. Ever since this place had encroached their life, they'd lost Hersh, then Perfect Sam—Mohan had been attacked. Now Aameh and Admin Dhrit had been attacked and kidnapped. She had lost NeoJai's support at the worst possible time. Aaxyl was exhausted and worried sick and terrified of entering the building.

Mohan stood next to her, like a terrible stone angel, a fire raging in his glacial eyes. He may not have encouraged Aameh's crush, but he had been very fond of her. This couldn't be easy for him either.

She ran over the words she had used. She had thought of Mohan's affection for Aameh in the past tense. A tiny, superstitious part of her mind started rambling in terror. An arm came around her.

She looked up to see Mohan's eyes suspiciously moist as he said, "She's sent us a clue. She's okay. You have to stop thinking like that."

What did he mean? Aaxyl hadn't said a word. He led her gently toward the building and Aaxyl shoved his hand off. She feared what she was going to find. She needed to go in. She didn't have time for this.

Mohan turned her to face him and waited till she looked at his face. "We'll find her together."

And suddenly they were in the building. Mohan had teleported her past her terror. She raced up to the second floor, where NeoJai was supposed to be. Moving helped get her brain working.

NeoJai was convincing Dhrit-H to stay put at Mohan's home. Not that anyone asked Aaxyl, but she'd prefer all Dhrits to be safe so that she could fix the mess she'd made with NeoJai.

Noir and Vidroh arrived as NeoJai concluded the call. Vidroh shot a glance at Noir and gave a subtle frown as she collected her paramedic hover from him. Noir felt... ominous as he strode over to NeoJai.

"He's been like this ever since he heard the names you sent," Vidroh whispered.

They clustered around NeoJai at the supervisor's desk.

"If you could have found the beds, what would the entries mean?" Mohan asked. "They were in the Dorms? Admitted as non-persons?"

"Well, it would be a physical location to investigate," NeoJai said.

"So we search." Mohan backed away from the group and stepped off the supervisor's platform.

She understood his need to keep moving. She felt it too, except her legs ached and she needed to save every last drop of energy for Aameh.

"Wait." NeoJai swivelled his chair toward him. "There are ten thousand nulls. I have an automated verification running, but we'd need too many people."

"Number of people is not an issue." Noir's voice lashed their ears like a physical strike.

"Actually, the number of *nulls* is an issue." NeoJai stood firm. "Even if you brought more people to search, by the time it concluded, Dad and Aameh would be gone for over twenty-four hours."

And age-old wisdom said the first twenty-four hours were crucial.

Noir stood behind NeoJai's chair like the eye of a storm. His turmoil flayed them, lashing *something* at them that Aaxyl couldn't name, It felt like a continuous screech, but nothing was audible.

What was Noir's deal? Aameh and Admin Dhrit were missing. Why was Noir so upset? She suspected it may have to do with one of the other names, but didn't dare ask.

Aaxyl's feet were killing her. Her brain had stopped working. She didn't want to sit with the triple-trauma of Aameh's seat, next to NeoJai and a fire breathing Noir-dragon at her back. Her feet trembled under her and she sat on her hover, hoping one of the others could figure out what to do.

Vidroh settled into Aameh's seat, thinking at the screen.

"There are six records." NeoJai waved Noir to Aameh's chair. Noir's eyes didn't budge from the screen. "Two are the non-persons who went missing. I was focusing on Aameh and Dad. Who are Sarovar and Rudra?"

"Rudra is a person." Mohan said. "She's not missing. This I guarantee."

They were no closer to tracing Aameh and losing steam. Tears welled up in Aaxyl's eyes, irritating her. Aameh was missing. She'd cry later.

Aaxyl reached deep for sarcasm, dark humor, anything and slammed shut on the tears. That sandwich was going to be eaten by Aameh before it spoiled.

Aaxyl lay on the hover, flexing and relaxing her aching legs, and trying to *think*. What did the bed locations *mean*? She was useless at this. Aameh would have noticed clues.

NeoJai plodded on, and she let his voice drip details on her mind as she raised her knees, rounding and arching her lower back against the hover to soothe sore muscles. "Reva is my sister, and only Aameh is missing from AxAm. Rudra may not be missing. They used the names to draw attention."

"The name would do that." Mohan whistled in Perfect Sam's style. "One of the two could be Hersh. He knows her. But Hersh could have used many codes. Why use the one name guaranteed to piss us off? We're missing something."

"Maybe the sixth person is worth pissing everyone off for," Aaxyl told the distant ceiling. "Maybe that is the point of not using a name you could listen to calmly."

NeoJai swiped away at his terminal. "We have their medical reports if it helps you identify anyone."

"You watched us guess when you had information?" Noir asked.

NeoJai glanced up at him. "How would I know you don't know who's missing? I know two people missing and both are in the list."

"I was alive during the Enduring War. I run a global organisation. I know lots of missing people." Noir's voice developed a weird echo in her head.

Aaxyl had goosebumps. She sat up and rubbed her arms. "The data from tests could have further clues or at least confirm that it is them."

NeoJai ignored her.

"NeoJai, would you read out any identifiable information?" Mohan jumped back up on the platform to lean against the desk.

"Reva." NeoJai's voice caught. "This is Dad. Male, in good health, conscious, so not a non-person. Over eighty years old. Dad's two-forty. The machines don't estimate age past eighty."

"Okay. Next," Vidroh said.

Noir bent between them to read the screen.

"AxAm," Noir voice reverberated. "Aameh, I think. Female, under twenty-five, in good health, conscious."

Aameh. In good health. Conscious. Aaxyl clung to that.

"Rudra," NeoJai read. "Male, forty to fifty years old. In good health, conscious. Healing fracture in the right arm. Metal needles in brain."

"Hersh," Mohan and Noir chorused.

"He's being tortured," Aaxyl gasped. It didn't bode well for Aameh.

"Not by the needles," Noir said. "And the fracture is healing."

"I can't believe he used the codename Rudra," Mohan said.

"Sarovar," NeoJai said. "The LSU expects a female, but occupant is missing. No data, just the name."

"Rudra—Sarovar. ToxicSYMB!" Noir pushed away from the screen, sending NeoJai's chair careening to one side. "Mohan!"

The very air in the dorm seemed to crouch into a calm waiting to pounce. Aaxyl wanted him to use his words because the alternative didn't feel so good.

"What?" Mohan's bewilderment was reassuring.

"Listen to this." Noir whipped around the desk to stand in front of Mohan in a blink. He may have teleported. "Tell me the first name to come to your mind. Rudra. Sarovar. Missing."

"Saro... Don't path Abrahamha till we know." Just like that, Mohan had abandoned the ranks of the ignorant.

"Abrahamha! What is path?" Aaxyl asked. "Who—"

"Telepathy," Mohan interrupted her. "All of you need to leave. It's not safe."

Noir was down on his knees, palms on the floor breathing hard. Perhaps Mohan should attend to him instead of wasting time.

"You're out of your mind," NeoJai shot back instantly. "Aameh and Dad are missing. You tell us your precious secret or not, we aren't stopping."

"How will you find them without us? I know Aameh best. NeoJai knows this Dorm." Aaxyl wasn't going anywhere.

"He has to go," Noir said. "We aren't going to risk him fucking this up too."

Aaxyl turned in surprise to see Noir was talking about Vidroh. Vidroh had been nothing but supportive. He stared at Noir grimly now.

"I'll drop him off at the Dorms," Mohan said.

Wait. Wha... Vidroh disappeared.

"The sixth person may be AricNova," Mohan said, as though it explained something.

Aaxyl realised he sounded scared. Her mind tried to compute everything in terms of risk for Aameh. "That's who?"

"No code. AricNova of The Three, founder of AVANT, SYMBTech, Margadarshak."

Noir paced like a restless cyclone. She hadn't seen him stand. His movements were like lightning, erratic and hard to track and would fry them sooner or later. If not for Aameh, Aaxyl wouldn't even have to be asked to leave. She'd flee so fast, they'd think she teleported.

"Didn't she die long ago?" Aaxyl asked.

Shouldn't it be a good thing if AricNova were alive?

"She went missing fifty years after the Enduring War. Long before I was born." Mohan watched Noir warily.

"How old are you?" asked Aaxyl.

"One hundred thirty-ish," replied Mohan. "I'm fine. He's the one to be careful of. He's almost three centuries old." Mohan kept his eyes on Noir. "Do you have sedatives in your paramedic kit?"

"Ish?" Aaxyl opened her kit and rummaged till she found a small bundle of syringes and handed one to Mohan.

"I'm an orphan. They guessed my age."

Mohan jabbed Noir with the sedative, palming another.

Noir took a deep breath and nodded to Mohan, taking the second syringe from him and pocketing it.

"Breathe," Mohan said. "Get your shit under control. We may deal with Abrahamha and find AricNova. Things will be volatile enough, and we are in the Dorms. I need you to keep your head together."

"Null Dorms doesn't need a second earthquake," Aaxyl muttered and froze as Noir focused on her before taking another deep breath.

"Her body was never found." Noir raised his arms and breathed in. Clearly some calming ritual for the geriatric population. It didn't work. Noir burst out, "Dear SYMBs, how is this possible?"

"Null Dorms was started with victims from the Earthquake," said NeoJai. "They're still here. Most of them haven't even been seen by a human in ages. If she were unconscious, hiding her here would make sense."

"This dome wasn't built when she went missing. Null Dorms definitely weren't," said Aaxyl. "All this because of Rudra Sarovar?"

"AricNova named our home Sarovar." Noir breathed in deep and relaxed. "She was attacked there."

Well, that did seem compelling.

"What would hold AricNova against her will?" NeoJai asked. "New symb-abilities manifested to meet her intention, they say."

Noir nodded. "I saw her regenerate a hand Damodar cut off."

If it was anyone else, there would be an avalanche of questions. But it was Noir on an uncomfortably short fuse.

Aaxyl moved on quickly. "So AricNova must be a teleporter at least. What prevents teleporting? If we can identify that, we'll know what to look for."

"Nothing!" Bewilderment and frustration poured off Mohan. "Abrahamha could anchor my ass down till I was twenty. To prevent AricNova's teleportation..." He shrugged, shaking his head.

"Don't think of her as AricNova. How do you imprison rogue teleporters?" Aaxyl urged.

"We don't. Tranquillisers or electric shocks will work till she builds tolerance. Injuries, irritants, fear or other distractions delay visualising clearly enough to teleport. A neutraliser will disable teleportation and telepathy for less than a year, but they hadn't been invented when she was captured. Nothing will work indefinitely. Two centuries without dying or escaping is incomprehensible."

A dormer-rumor suggested that a neutraliser blast to the head at close range could turn people brain-dead. "If they knocked her out and made her a non-person?"

"She would heal and whatever they used would be less and less effective with time." Noir held up the syringe he had pocketed and jabbed himself. "The ancients adapt. It would take a lot more of this to bring me down, if it even were possible."

Noir reached his hand out for another and gave himself another shot. Aaxyl sighed with relief as the sense of threat in the air died out. Three shots in, the only noticeable effect of the sedative wasn't even on Noir's person.

"If she was a conscious non-person?" Aaxyl gave him the remaining syringes. "Maybe brain damage in the attack or psychological trauma?"

Noir pocketed the syringes. "You don't understand. Reactions make us dangerous, not deliberate actions. You think I *want* to have this effect on you when we have people to find? She'd still do enough damage to draw attention if she were startled or threatened."

"*Homo godions.*" Aaxyl remembered the sensational species invented by the media. "Is it possible that she hid on her own?"

"No," Noir said sharply before he calmed his tone. "Her daughter was injured in the attack. No reason trumps that if she could come."

"No point searching the nulls," Aaxyl said, staring at the still-conscious Noir. "Any setup it would take to control her would be conspicuous here." Which meant Aameh also wouldn't be in a dorm.

NeoJai spoke. "They're in this building, but not among the non-persons. Rarely used areas. The ninth and tenth floor below the office floor are unused. There's a cryonics unit on the tenth."

"We should check." Mohan started off.

"No, wait," said NeoJai. "I was just thinking aloud. They wouldn't be in a dorm and they couldn't send messages if they were frozen. Even if the Dorm is empty, anyone could walk through."

"Roof?" Aaxyl asked. They'd been attacked there.

"No life support," NeoJai said. "Medic-bots don't go to the roof. There has to be life support for the tests."

"Where other than Dorms do you have bots?"

"In the bays, but bot maintenance staff could walk in."

A clatter of footsteps approached and they turned to the entrance.

"What the hell is going on here?" Damodar walked into the Dorm with his entourage, the lot of them freezing on sight of Noir, before Damodar relaxed. "Noir. Mohan. This is a surprise."

"SYMBTech is a Superdome organisation and as such may investigate our matters independently," Noir growled, skipping preliminaries and ignoring Damodar's greeting. "You have no jurisdiction over us."

Superdome organisations had diplomatic presence worldwide. This much Aaxyl knew, thanks to Mohan. The organisations and employees could buy property and reside where they wished without restrictions, taxes or compliance. She wasn't so sure about investigations.

"This is not the Superdome." Damodar said. "You have no investigative authority. Besides, what are you investigating?"

Aaxyl just needed him to leave, so that they could find Aameh.

"What would you do?" Noir strode up to Damodar like a seething nightmare. Two giants, nose to nose. "The only thing you can do against us is to back off from the Global Agreement, starting from GA-001, in which case, you lose a fortune in free SYMBs, and symbiontist training, and technology, and that's just from us."

"And we would still be able to walk into a public Dorm," Mohan added lightly, edging between Noir and Damodar.

"I'd stop you if I had to." Damodar shot back. "It is out of respect for Abrahamha that I don't. What would I do? I would do as Abrahamha says. Does he approve of this interference in local issues in blatant violation of the Global Agreement?"

Well... about that. They needed this to move on before he figured out Abrahamha hadn't been told or why.

One unstable Noir was enough for any group.

"Abrahamha sent us to investigate," Mohan said. "Two symbiontists are missing or dead in the span of a month. SYMBTech has an obligation to investigate."

"And here you show up," NeoJai spat.

"Your family has an unreasonable feud with me," Damodar dismissed him.

"Or is it the other way around?" NeoJai challenged. "How did you know Aameh, let alone her roommate? What is interesting about her other than she's my colleague? And now she's missing as well."

"She's interesting because she's Aaxyl's roommate, not your colleague. You didn't even work here when I first met her," Damodar turned to Noir. "Aameh is missing? If there is anything I can do, let me know."

Aaxyl's head was spinning. She had never met Damodar before. "Why?"

"I followed Dorm fights." Damodar glanced at her briefly, but kept his attention on Mohan and Noir. "Are you certain you're acting as per evidence?"

"Yes."

"Then I put my trust in the trust Abrahamha places in you." Damodar met Mohan's eyes for a moment, then walked out, followed by the rest of his parade.

"Anyone believe he's innocent?" NeoJai asked. "My father had flagged him for the original disappearance of AricNova, and here he is, when we're about to find her."

Aaxyl said, "Dorm fights don't list roommates."

"This is ancient history, NeoJai," Noir's voice rumbled. "Abrahamha found him innocent."

"You told us he cut AricNova's hand off." NeoJai persisted. "And now he's connected to Aaxyl."

"That's different." Noir didn't sound all that sure.

"There's a theory that symbionts show affinity and avoidance, like animal species live among those of their kind." Mohan put a warning hand on Noir's arm. "Telepaths and teleporters are rare, but Abrahamha found and adopted so many of us. *Homo symbions* and *Homo sapiens* live separately. Ancients who evolved moved out of the general population voluntarily."

Aaxyl thought it was outlandish. "But that makes no sense here."

"*Symbionts* may never be fully understood," Mohan pointed out. "It isn't absolute, but inclinations and coincidences."

Aaxyl hated to state the obvious, but, "I'm not a telepath or teleporter. Nor does Damodar seem to be. We are in a dome full of countless people like us."

Mohan held up a finger for her to pause. "Your mother wanted to bring you to SYMBTech. Aameh clung to you in the Dorms and took up an investigation that leads to AricNova. Damodar was close to The Three and took a personal interest in you. We can waste time arguing, but may never understand why."

"Or we could ask him," Aaxyl said.

"We have people to find," Mohan said. "Right now we need him to leave. That is more important."

NeoJai said, "So why isn't Damodar involved in AricNova's disappearance just as inexplicably? This wasn't an inspection. He came from the Octagon in the centre of the dome to a Dorm on the periphery to stop us as we're close to finding Admin Dhrit and Aameh."

Noir looked like he needed to blow some steam or something would explode and Aaxyl didn't want to be in the blast radius.

An idea struck Aaxyl. "Do the LSUs have identifiers that could be traced to a location or floor or hall?"

NeoJai's eyes met hers in dawning excitement. "Yes! We'd have to decode the raw data, but we could trace the LSUs to see where they are installed into the network!"

Mohan hurried over. "If you authorise access I can get it done instan—" Mohan vanished.

Medics protest archaic law mandating text literacy, cite violation of right to freedom of knowledge. "Modern knowledge is format agnostic.Competency is tested. There is nothing uniquely clever about text," says president of Medics Union. Medicine Frontier, Thursday, November 20, 2442

~~*~*~*~*

NONE: NULL DORMS BASEMENT

"It's a pity this won't last," Admin Dhrit said. "Right now feels amazing."

Aameh hugged her knees to her chest. "What's it like?"

"Expanded awareness." Admin Dhrit spoke in a hushed voice. "Here, with you, in this room, level, building... planet and beyond." He staggered and Hersh supported him. "I'm fine. I don't know why I lost balance."

"It could be the first sign of teleportation," Hersh whispered. Everything could be significant or irrelevant. "Try to figure out how you could move to another place. Visualising it clearly might help."

"Home," Admin Dhrit said with such longing, it made them laugh despite the gravity of their situation.

Aameh wanted to go back home herself.

"Does your room have three beds?" Admin Dhrit asked.

"Yes!" Excitement surged. "Your telepathic powers are kicking in."

"No," Admin Dhrit said. "I don't know. Visualise your room again."

Aameh imagined their room in fervent detail. Suddenly she was sitting on the floor in the dorm as well as floating in her room, knees hugged to her chest, her eyes seeing the table as if she were standing. Could she reach out and pull... but the feeling faded. She hadn't really been there. "You almost did it!"

Sweat shimmered on Admin Dhrit's skin. He was shaking. "Almost isn't good enough."

Aameh pushed to her feet, ignoring the warning ache through the pain block. "If the mercenaries aren't here and Admin Dhrit has started to access his symb-abilities, shouldn't we try to rescue AricNova? If he can get one person out, it should be her."

Hersh hustled them to the next Dorm section, keeping an eye out in case the mercenaries returned. It was bigger. No bad guys in sight. He hurried to a bed. "This is AricNova."

Aameh stared. The woman in the bed had dark skin and would be very tall if she were standing. Any familiarity ended there. This... creature... Aameh wasn't sure she was alive. Her face was a skull covered in flaky skin with protruding eyes, her skeletal body painfully evident even under the sheet.

"Can you break this?" Hersh asked Admin Dhrit, pointing to two thick chains coming out from under the sheet.

Aameh's eyes followed their outline under the sheet and... she backed away in horror.

Admin Dhrit looked just as horrified. "What savagery is this?"

They had embedded a thick chain through AricNova's stomach like an umbilical cord of metal.

"The ends are in the concrete in the wall. Prevents her from separating her body from the environment and teleporting." Hersh growled. "Please, if you can break this chain... she may instinctively teleport to safety."

Aameh doubted it would be that simple. The chain was almost two inches thick and looked like steel. It was no thread to jerk into two.

Admin Dhrit held the chain in his arms and pulled hard. Unsurprisingly, nothing happened. "How do I do this?" He asked Hersh, who slumped.

Aameh supposed if he could do it with symb-abilities, he'd have sensed how.

"We could find something to cut or break the chain." Aameh wanted to weep. This was too much on top of being kidnapped and hurt and missing Aaxyl and having no escape, but she wouldn't be mentally weak in addition to being physically useless.

"Already checked. Many times. There's nothing." Hersh said.

Admin Dhrit held a finger to his lips, walking around in a circle with his eyes narrowed and head tilted, as though listening. Aameh couldn't hear anything out of the ordinary. "I think Mohan or Noir may be somewhere in the building, but people in the other section are preparing for something. Not friendly. Aggressive."

Hersh shot her a worried glance. "You aren't useful in a fight. You should hide inside the racks. We are going to have to delay till Mohan or Noir can find us."

Aameh had an idea. She disconnected AricNova's bed and rolled it behind a rack and closer to where the chain attached to the wall. She tried to push more coffin-bed racks in front of it. Maybe, not seeing AricNova would make them waste time searching for her. Hersh and Admin Dhrit took over.

Hersh waved her on. "Hide now. We've got this."

Aameh carefully climbed to the top of a rack so that she wouldn't be accidentally seen, but could peek on both sides.

They waited. Admin Dhrit went to the hidden pocket with AricNova's bed and tried to break the chain again. "I'm failing her." He hung his head.

"Listen." Hersh led Admin Dhrit out again. "You almost sent Aameh home —we hadn't discussed this. Trust that instinct. We know you might die. This doesn't mean you're defeated yet."

A large number of feet thumped outside their door. "I'm getting the symbiontist and donor out. Clean up here. No loose tongues." The Whisperer stood in the door issuing instructions, as the footsteps outside went further away.

The Whisperer turned to enter the room, but couldn't come in. Admin Dhrit stood straight, but he was sweating. Static seemed to fill the air. A grunt escaped him.

The Whisperer staggered back a step, but seemed to recover. Aameh hoped Admin Dhrit would try something else, like sending the man somewhere, though she supposed he would just teleport back.

The masked man vanished and Aameh almost cheered, before he teleported straight to Admin Dhrit, and punched him. Admin Dhrit fell. The man turned to where AricNova's bed had been and saw it missing.

He pulled a gun.

"Where is the donor?" The Whisperer stood over Admin Dhrit, who did not reply.

The Whisperer shot him in his stomach and Admin Dhrit gave a strangled groan.

"Where is the donor?"

Aameh swallowed a scream as blood soaked his clothes and pooled around him.

"She... she vanished!" Hersh said. "Administrator Dhrit said something, and she vanished, right along with the bed."

"Impossible." The Whisperer glared at the rack where the bed used to be. "You think I'd leave you alone with her if you could escape using her symbionts? Where is the donor?"

The Whisperer shot Admin Dhrit again. Aameh was ice cold with fear. There was no way she'd recover if he shot her in the stomach.

"Where's the chain?" The Whisperer stalked over to the rack.

Not even Aaxyl could stop him. Aameh hoped with everything she had that Mohan got here fast because all would be lost otherwise. Admin Dhrit reached a hand toward her slightly and looked up. She suddenly had that floating feeling again, and saw Mohan in a dormitory above. The wounded Admin Dhrit closed his eyes with a grunt, dropped his head, motionless.

Mohan appeared, looking around in confusion. Aameh sagged with relief. Then... Abrahamha appeared? Aameh remembered Admin Dhrit's descriptions of Mohan and Noir. It must be Noir. He felt like a tremendous weather system without any wind.

They rushed toward the unconscious Admin Dhrit in the growing pool of blood.

Hersh pointed to the LSRs. "Save AricNova."

Noir rushed around Aameh's rack, while Mohan grabbed Admin Dhrit and vanished.

Hersh vanished too.

What was going on?

"Where's AricNova?" Noir roared as he emerged from around the rack to find no one there.

Aameh scrambled over the top of the rack to check and AricNova's bed had vanished, along with the Whisperer. She barely had time to register the chain broken near the wall, when Noir appeared on top of the rack next to her and the next moment, Aameh was on the floor with him towering over her, murder in his eyes.

He must have heard her move. Aameh scrambled back in terror. "Please! I didn't do anything."

Noir frowned. "Are you Aameh?" His breathing was ragged and his hands were clenched in fists. Shouts sounded somewhere outside the door. The very air vibrated with menace. "Where is Hersh?"

He didn't have a gun, but perhaps that would be safer. "He vanished along with Admin Dhrit and Mohan after he told you where AricNova was."

With three teleporters in play, Aameh wasn't sure who was vanishing whom to where. She didn't need this man angry with her. Her hair was standing on end and she was about to wet herself any moment, but Mohan had brought him there and he hadn't harmed her. Yet. "Are you having trouble controlling your symb-abilities?"

Noir blinked.

He injected himself with two syringes. The wash of rage in the air bled out and he hurried over to her. "I'm sorry for scaring you. Are you alright?"

Aameh nodded. "For now. Are you okay?"

Noir frowned like he didn't understand what she meant, then nodded. "For now."

"There's nobody in the other section." Armed mercenaries filed into the room, raising their weapons and firing as soon as they saw Noir. Aameh closed her eyes tight. As though that would stop bullets.

Strong arms embraced her against a warm chest as the gunfire began. Shards of his energy scraped her skin. Aameh opened her eyes to find Noir in front of her. His roar of rage tore through the Dorm silencing the guns.

She peeked around him to see the men motionless on the floor. Noir was again breathing heavily. It must be tough to not know what to do with your anger, but how had he done that? Aameh wished she could do such things, instead of having to hide at the first sign of trouble.

She patted his chest gently. "They aren't shooting anymore. They're..." She waved toward the fallen mercenaries. Actually, she wasn't sure whether they were unconscious or dead.

Bullets clinked to the floor. Had he *teleported* bullets out of his body?

Mohan reappeared where Admin Dhrit had been. "Hersh isn't with me. He was here when I left."

Were they talking telepathically? Because Noir hadn't asked Mohan anything. Fascinating. She wondered if they could follow the Whisperer and find AricNova, though she supposed they would have vanished if they could.

Mohan took one look at Noir's face and vanished to appear between her and Noir, curving around her protectively and moving her away. All at once.

"He didn't hurt me. He just had some trouble controlling himself, but he's okay now." Aameh patted him reassuringly and leaned back to look at Mohan's beloved, puzzled face, her first smile in ages breaking free. "You're alive!"

Bumper tomato harvest slashes prices. AgriNews, Thursday, November 20, 2442

~~*~*~*

AAXYL: NULL DORMS

Mohan had vanished.

Noir turned around and vanished too.

What were they supposed to do now?

Aaxyl raced to the stairs, listening with her head in the stairwell hoping to hear some sound. There was nothing from the roof to the—

NeoJai burst out of the dorm-hall. "Basement! The LSUs are in the Basement!"

Aaxyl streaked down the stairs like lightning, NeoJai in close pursuit. They had just reached the ground level, when gunshots sounded further below.

"Guns!" Aaxyl warned and they flattened against the wall. Bullets pinged off metal somewhere, but none came towards them. A roar of rage tore out of the basement and up the stairwell.

And then silence.

They picked up their pace again, as loud voices sounded on the ground floor. Dorm security, but there was nothing they could do about it. Aaxyl stumbled. A man lay unconscious on the corner of the stairs. A guard swore behind them his own gun out. More followed. Great. They were the unarmed dummies with guns on either side.

Aaxyl motioned NeoJai to come with the guards and she kept going. She reached the basement level, looking around and chose the corridor littered with unconscious men. She stepped over two more bodies as she sneaked forward, not caring if she trampled them.

Aameh's voice sounded clearly—the best music in the world. "But how did you make them unconscious? How can telepathy overload—"

Trust Aameh to have questions. Aaxyl bolted toward that precious sound, hurdling over the occasional unconscious man straight to a Dorm section, almost barrelling into Noir as she entered, skipping abruptly, and weaving around Mohan to crush Aameh into a hug, and lift her completely off her feet, laughing wildly as tears streamed down her face.

Aameh patted her shoulder. "Put me down. My ribs and back are killing me."

Aaxyl put her down at once, reaching into her pockets for the HealSYMB vials. She'd used one on NeoJai, but she still had nine and a pain block.

"I'm okay. I already took my pain block and HealSYMB." Aameh cupped Aaxyl's cheek and Aaxyl could barely keep from hugging her again. She wore some repairman's uniform in too big a size.

Aaxyl frowned, then laughed again, and cried a bit.

Aameh took a dose of pain block and HealSYMB over to Noir, offering them to him before Aaxyl got her brain in order. "You were shot."

Aaxyl noticed the holes in his shirt.

Aameh had no survival instinct. That wasn't news, but walking up to an injured ancient? That was a new level of insane even for Aameh.

Aaxyl was moving to intercept her, when Noir's face broke into a smile.

"I can't remember the last time someone fussed over me. Thank you, Aameh." Noir accepted Aameh's offerings.

Huh.

Judging by Mohan's dropped jaw, that was about as expected as Aaxyl thought.

Aaxyl retrieved Aameh and kept her close, peeking discretely under her shirt to see the bruising. It was bad, but she'd be fine. Aaxyl gave her the rest of the HealSYMB anyway, and handed her the sandwich.

NeoJai stood in the doorway like a fish out of water. He hadn't rushed similarly to Admin Dhrit.

Mohan and Noir spoke in low voices. The weather forecast didn't look good.

Aaxyl realised belatedly that Aameh was the only captive found in the Dorm. No Admin Dhrit, Hersh or AricNova. Aaxyl hadn't been that sold on the AricNova guess, but she'd expected Admin Dhrit to be with Aameh for sure.

"What happened?" she asked Aameh.

Aameh's legs gave out and Aaxyl put an arm around her, helping her to the floor. "AricNova is alive! We failed her. Dhrit died to save her and The Whisperer took her and Hersh anyway," she whispered.

"Dad is dead?" NeoJai asked. Aaxyl hadn't heard him approach. "Whe—"

"No." Mohan interrupted, putting an arm around his shoulder and steering him to the Dorm SecPros at the door. "I took Dhrit to get medical help. He'll be fine. Just give me a moment."

Chatter broke through the ranks of SecPros and Noir started looking jittery again.

The SecPros had taken one look at Noir and chosen sanity, reporting the situation but not entering the Dorm.

Mohan took charge, explaining that dorm-supervisor, Aameh AxAm, and Administrator of the Dorms, Dhrit Saisrisel, had been kidnapped, and that NeoJai Saisrisel attacked on the roof on the previous night. They were now safe, and Admin Dhrit was in a hospital.

He added that with a symbiontist still being missing and the criminals at large, they required custody of all the unconscious and armed men in the dorm and stairwell. They also required use of the Dorm for some more time.

NeoJai nodded in confirmation.

Aameh added that two non-persons missing from the Dorm had been found and were next door.

The wide-eyed SecPros backed off to consult their seniors and left a tidy pile of unconscious people, wheeled out the non-persons and left. Mohan locked the dormitory from the inside before returning to their section.

NeoJai hurried to Mohan. "How's Dad?"

Mohan hurried to reassure him. "They shot him, but he's in one of our facilities receiving the best possible care and will be home by the time you get home."

Aameh's eyes went large. "He might not be. We injected him with AricNova's symbionts. That's how he contacted you."

Mohan swore fluently. "Dhrit teleported me in? I thought it was AricNova, and wondered about it. She didn't know me, so why not Noir?"

"He used my thoughts to teleport you," Aameh said. "I didn't know Noir."

NeoJai paled. "What does this mean? Is he coming home or not?"

Mohan paused for a long moment. Then he grew somber. "I... don't know, NeoJai. Those symbionts are dangerous. But we'll do everything we can."

Aameh hugged him. "I can't tell you how sorry I am."

"I should have trusted you, NeoJai." Aaxyl approached NeoJai cautiously. "Admin Dhrit is a better person than I can hope to be. If I had believed you and we worked together, we might have found them sooner."

NeoJai ignored her.

She couldn't blame him.

"Dhrit pulled Mohan from another place to where he was." Noir's voice was gravelly. "Dhrit was there. Hersh was there. AricNova was there. Hersh pointed us to her. We didn't react fast enough. By the time I got there, she was gone. I turned back to ask Hersh, and he was gone too."

"We should have given you our contact information." Mohan sighed. "We could have got here sooner."

NeoJai put a hand on Noir's arm. "I may not have long with my father. Can you tell me where he is so that I can meet him?"

"I'll take you." Noir teleported him out and reappeared instantly.

"What are you going to tell Abrahamha?" Aaxyl asked.

Uni-silence.

Abrahamha unearthing AricNova's survival like this clearly alarmed Mohan and Noir. None of them had anticipated failing to save AricNova.

"We have to tell him," Mohan said. "If we had told him before, AricNova might have been saved."

"I'm telling him now." Noir looked around the room for options, but it was high time.

Aaxyl wasn't sure she wanted Aameh to be here, but Mohan anticipated it. "Admin Dhrit isn't in a condition to speak. Aameh is the only one who can tell us what happened. Abrahamha will want to talk to her."

A controlled rampage

Rogue 22nd century AI responsible for the European Railway Collisions Crisis isolated and destroyed within days by Satark Scan's new SIS. Tech Edge, Thursday, November 20, 2442

~~*~*~*

AAXYL: NULL DORMS BASEMENT

Abrahamha appeared next to Noir. "You did your best. I failed her when I ceased searching."

Nobody had said anything.

Flee! Now!

Abrahamha wasn't that much taller than Noir, but he had the physique of a superhero with an almost triangular upper body and legs like tree trunks. Implacable. Immovable. He wore a brown and purple T-shirt paired with well-worn jeans that looked very comfortable, but there was nothing comfortable about him.

His face was similar to Noir. Brown skinned, massive shoulders, strong neck, high cheekbones and an intelligent forehead would be devastatingly handsome on a less unnerving person. But anyone who saw Abrahamha would never confuse him for Noir. Noir could be dangerous. Abrahamha removed all doubt.

This was the first time AxAm saw him in person. Aameh's eyes were about to fall off her face. Aaxyl closed her own mouth, which immediately felt suffocating. He towered over them and disoriented her.

He stood relaxed, but it meant nothing.

The hair on Aaxyl's arms would fall off if it stood any straighter. She should have insisted that Aameh be sent back. This would go wrong in the blink of an eye.

There was a fragrance in the air, wild and intoxicating, a scent Aaxyl had never smelled before and would never forget, mesmerising enough that her last moments would be spent in wonder.

"You did your best," Abrahamha rumbled, the sound vibrating up through her feet. "We have to stop looking back because we must move forward and bring them home."

Aaxyl felt an overwhelming sense of purpose. An affinity.
She *belonged* around him. Abrahamha's strays had a task. It would get done. It was more than loyalty, it was conviction. It was a brain glitch because she also wanted to run and not look back.

"Let's get to work," Abrahamha remarked, turning toward the mercenaries.

She wasn't sure it was a good idea for him to see the mercenaries. This situation was volatile enough as it was.

Abrahamha nodded once. "I have to know."

A sofa appeared out of thin air. He sat on it. Noir and Mohan stood behind him like bodyguards, but Abrahamha gestured them to sit. They hesitated but did so.

He scanned the room. Two more two-seaters appeared making a horseshoe shape.

Only AxAm remained standing, but Aaxyl wasn't sure Abrahamha noticed or cared. She sat on the two-seater on Mohan's side, leaving space for Aameh.

The unconscious attackers appeared in the empty space to complete a circle and started stirring.

Aameh sat next to Noir causing Aaxyl to regret taking her hand off the girl.

Mohan raised a questioning eyebrow toward Aaxyl. Aaxyl didn't know why Aameh had no sense of self-preservation. Aameh had no boundaries of the conventional sort.

Noir had captured Aameh's imagination, and her love language was questions. It had begun exactly like this with Mohan. Aaxyl imagined Aameh pelting Noir with questions till he obliterated her with a stray gesture.

Aaxyl wanted to grab her and run out, but didn't dare move.

The very air around them discouraged moving, as though Abrahamha needed them to be still and even subtle expressions froze into wary immobility. One by one, the unconscious men awoke and sat up on the floor.

Something strange rasped through her like blades of white noise. She was everyone, though her body was sitting in the chair. She wasn't sure if she was inside or outside herself and that made no sense.

One of the men stood up.

To Aaxyl's astonishment, she knew he was a part of Damodar's SecPro detail along with a few others. He knew of a high-value resident under guard here. He had never seen her, didn't know who she was. He vanished abruptly.

A vision came into Aaxyl's mind. A memory.

Abrahamha stood on a cliff overlooking Sarovar, a terrible cold wind battering his body, urging him to move.

Terror immobilised him.

The ornate monument tilted precariously below. The huge bowl, a kilometre in diameter, like a bejewelled radiotelescope lay abandoned in the wilderness. Three spirals rose from its rim to meet in a watch-cabin above it.

AricNova's home slanted on a slope like a discarded bowl of leftovers. It should have been level next to a lake further below. It wasn't like AricNova to be less than meticulous.

Aaxyl knew that this was when Abrahamha discovered AricNova to be missing.

Present-day Abrahamha slumped like a volcano with elbows on knees, to stare at the ground. Tiny arcs of something sparked from his fingers to a point between his feet but his fingers were relaxed.

Aaxyl hoped it was a good sign that he didn't move. She could hear his questions in her head.

The next person stood. She knew that he had tried to help the previous symbiontist. He vanished mid-sentence.

Where were they being sent? How did she know their thoughts?

Aaxyl didn't dare to ask as the scene in her head continued.

AricNova and Tashi would have been in that cabin perched drunkenly on the curving supports. That didn't worry him. AricNova as well as the little one were teleporters. Their absence from his mind terrified him.

He teleported into the once familiar cabin.

AricNova was gone.

Nobody spoke.

More mercenaries stood and Abrahamha's voice in her head asked for information about 'the high-value prisoner'. Anything they knew became known to Aaxyl without words said. They yielded their information and dropped to the floor and vanished.

AricNova's present location was unknown, but insights emerged, while Abrahamha's tormented memory seeped into their heads.

Broken windows. Blood splattered the floor and walls, and formed a small pool in a corner of the sloping cabin.

Flies buzzed.

Severed limbs lay splayed on the floor. A tiny partial body with the head attached oozed blood. A flap of the scalp had peeled back and partially healed.

Abrahamha froze. Blood should not be flowing. The body shouldn't be alive with half a hip and a shoulder missing along with both legs and an arm.

Dear god, it was Tashi!

He collapsed by AricNova's daughter. Unbearable pain crippled him.

The details of AricNova's disappearance had never been made public. As far as the world knew, she had simply vanished one day in a vague attack. It was part of the legend of The Three. Almost like she was a superior being and her task done, she had departed the earth, just as Jugaad had. What Aaxyl witnessed shredded that fable.

The present intruded. She knew more about Damodar's role in this operation. He wanted research on adapting to symbionts for his daughter. All the official SecPros didn't know the nature of the experiments and were only posted outside the dorm-hall to prevent unauthorised access.

Blood streaked from another dead body across the cabin. A stranger. He touched shaking fingers to Tashi's soft cheek. Tears streamed from his eyes, his grief bowing him to her chest, desperate to feel that tiny arm cradle him once more, foolishly trying to listen for a heartbeat from half a body.

He heard it!

He didn't know how, but she was alive, if by the thinnest thread.

He lifted her reverently and teleported her to the best medical aid, to beg SanJeevan to give the seven-year-old a few more moments of life.

He wished God existed, because an overwhelming need to beg for mercy consumed him.

The latest man standing knew that criminals sometimes didn't need to be nulled to be used as shells. Often, they would cooperate with the telepath because he promised them power. They were better at attacking than non-persons. They were not informed that the transfusion of the symbionts would kill them.

None of the Whisperer's men knew where AricNova had been taken or where she had been beyond the past year or so here.

Abrahamha didn't move or look anywhere other than that point between his feet, as memories of those he interrogated mixed with his own memories in a horrifying jumble. Memories of a laughing AricNova, memories of the enterprising Tashi pretending to be a scientist right alongside them.

Abrahamha's body was relaxed, breathing even, no visual suggestion of anything out of the ordinary other than the sparks from his fingers to that point on the floor. If he moved, it would be carnage.

Aaxyl didn't trust herself to move either.

Nothing dangerous was happening, but nobody was safe. Aaxyl was witnessing a controlled rampage. All the more terrifying because of how tidy it was. One by one, all the captured mercenaries and SecPros vanished.

Abrahamha flowed to his feet and the four of them flinched as one. "I have to go to the Superdome." They stayed still. "I need you to proceed with this investigation. If I stay here... We don't want that."

Nods.

"This doesn't end till AricNova is back home."

More nods.

"Damodar lacks the power or motivation to execute this. Identify the mastermind. I'm leaving information about AricNova's attack and Damodar with you, if it helps resolve your doubts."

Nobody spoke.

Aameh inhaled deeply to speak, but subsided, to Aaxyl's eternal gratitude.

"I'm leaving it telepathically," Abrahamha told Aameh. "You will see it as dreams or if you think about it in a quiet moment. Of course, we will do everything we can for Dhrit. Is that all?"

Had he read Aameh's mind?

Abrahamha vanished. They slumped in relief.

The seats vanished from under them, dumping everyone to the floor.

Nobody complained.

Memories

Filtered water will be distributed in the morning and food in the evening tomorrow. Please remain indoors unless wearing protective gear. Volunteers will come to your door. Stay tuned to this station for regular updates. Radio Margadarshak, Friday, September 2, 2168

~~*~*~*

ARICNOVA: Oasis, Wastelands

Aaxyl knew she was dreaming the memories Abrahamha had left in her mind. He had received this memory from AricNova. Aaxyl remembered it as though she were AricNova herself.

"Damo! Work okay?" AricNova avoided Damodar's outstretched hand with a wry shake of her head.

Damodar had symbionts like a stronger version of AthSYMB, but with unique energy stores. The Three used large amounts of energy and found them irresistible. She could easily pull them out of his body and harm him.

They'd warned Damodar about getting close, but he never took them seriously.

Before the Enduring War, Damodar's family were regional distributors of household consumables. As the world collapsed, he'd helped them procure supplies for their lab as well as relief work. Damodar didn't understand science, but he understood its necessity. When AricNova and Abrahamha supplied symbionts for free, Damodar transported them for free.

"Abrahamha changed up the work," Damodar joked, referring to Abrahamha's Ultimatum.

AricNova laughed to avoid worrying Damodar. "We can't believe it worked. Maybe everyone was fed up, but didn't know how to stop."

"It's a good thing." Damodar headed behind the eating area, which was little more than a counter with a few chairs and the world's worst coffee machine. AricNova wasn't sure anyone maintained it. Jugaad used to handle these things.

By the time AricNova completed clearing out some experiments, the aroma of roasted cashews filled her office.

Damodar had brought cashews and roasted them for her. What was the occasion?

She joined him. "What's new?"

"I'm developing an environmental dome for some cult Nadani found. They don't want to vacate the region and I thought of your barrier tents for relief work. Purified air, purified water, big enough for a city. Saisrisel will build it. I'm managing the project. As the world rebuilds, we will lead them."

"So, both of us are going to different places." AricNova looked around her lab-office. "We're moving to the American continent. The results of Abrahamha's Ultimatum are great, but he could have killed them accidentally. The general population has no defences against us."

"You could build a dome there." Damodar was all about domes now. "If you must exile yourselves, you at least deserve a proper home."

AricNova picked a too-hot cashew, blowing on it. "You're right, but surely this isn't why you came here." The cashews were delicious, and expensive and rare enough to be a bribe.

"I need your help." Damodar leaned forward. "That boy that you saved last year. I have three *Homo sapiens* that need saving."

"Whoa. I'm not a doctor, my friend. I'm a tech innovator who just happened to employ a genius. Last year was a desperate gamble that almost didn't work."

"SanJeevan is a doctor. She works for you."

These were desperate times, but if wishing made something happen... "Take them to a hospital quickly. Keeping *Homo sapiens* alive in this region is a tricky business." The Enduring War was done, but the chemical and radioactive pollution in this region didn't bode well for those without protective symbionts.

"They're safe for now. It's a bit of a tale."

"Try me." AricNova pulled over the paper shredder and fed it records as they talked.

"You know my family died in a suicide bombing, don't you?" Damodar asked.

"Some," AricNova said. It had been the early decades of the Enduring War.

"I escaped because I was out making deliveries." His voice still caught with grief. "The blast destroyed our office and residence above it. The whole building collapsed."

AricNova set aside the shredder to focus on him.

"My son, Vikas, survived with serious injuries. Sharma, my best friend and first employee, lived in a flat behind the office. He died in the office, but Mrs. Anjali Sharma and her daughter, Smriti, also survived. The fourth was my cousin Nadani. He shouldn't even have been there."

AricNova palmed a handful of cashews discreetly as she listened.

Damodar continued. "Nadani had minor injuries, and recovered, but doctors didn't see hope for the others. Cryogenics was a rising field. Nadani arranged for the three of them to be put into stasis."

AricNova had a bad feeling about where this was going.

Damodar met her eyes. "I want you to save them."

"I wish." AricNova came over to sit next to him. "These people are from before humans adapted to symbionts and already fatally wounded."

"Come on, Ari," Damodar pleaded. "Don't say this."

"Wait for medical advances to make cryogenic revivals safer."

"Cryo-science is stagnant. With symbionts, why freeze for later? Two facilities shut down. So far, only one person survived, and he died in a month. He wasn't even injured."

"You have a point," AricNova said. "But the science behind symbionts isn't developed enough either."

"Focus on this. I'll fund whatever you need. Ari, everything I have is yours."

AricNova really wished to help him. "I've never even seen a frozen body. You need to fund a cryonics doctor. I'll provide symbionts."

"I adopted Smriti while she was frozen. My own son. Mrs. Sharma. Don't refuse, please." Tears streamed down his face.

AricNova watched helplessly. There were no words to make this right.

"Use your own symbionts." He stared at the floor.

"What?" AricNova really hoped he didn't mean that.

"You and Abrahamha. You have supernatural powers. You heal from anything. With your symbionts, they'll live."

AricNova waited till he looked at her. "Listen to me. Do you think so little of us that we'd refuse to save your family? Our symbionts kill people."

"But you can regenerate?" Damodar searched her face.

AricNova reached out in sympathy, but pulled back a frustrated fist. "It won't help your son."

Damodar stood to leave, and offered AricNova his hand.

"You know I can't, Damo."

"I don't mind Ari. You know it doesn't hurt me. Who knows if we'll meet again?"

"It doesn't hurt you because we're careful." AricNova smiled warmly and took his hand, intending to be brief. "You shouldn't be complacent."

But Damodar clasped her hand firmly, as she tried to withdraw after the fleeting contact. About to object, she didn't expect it at all when he raised a laser-knife with his other hand and sliced right through her wrist. She stared in shock for the second or two it took him to sever it, leaving her hand in his.

And then rage washed through her drowning out the pain.

She grabbed him with her other hand. Damodar clutched her severed hand close to his chest, but she didn't want it back. She craved energy to heal and Damodar was a feast. She binged, sweeping all the energy straight into her.

Damodar trembled. In a matter of seconds, he had hunched from a powerful man to one barely upright. The rush of his symbionts was power to use as she wished. AricNova let go, barely recognising herself. What was she doing? "Leave!" she ordered Damodar.

Damodar turned stiffly.

Abrahamha appeared between him and the door, incandescent with rage, along with that boy he'd adopted, Noir.

AricNova pushed Abrahamha aside telekinetically, protecting Damodar. She sent him the memory of what had transpired to explain Damodar's desperation.

"Is this what you came to see?" AricNova held up the stump of her arm. It had stopped bleeding. A shimmer of whitish blue flowed from her wrist, congealing into a ghost hand. "In a few hours, my hand will be normal. Is it fair that I can do this while people die? No, but I'm not hoarding a cure."

Able-bodied male volunteers requested for supplies distribution. Radio Margadarshak, Wednesday, June 13, 2170

~~*~*~*

DAMODAR: CRYO-DOCTOR'S CLINIC

Aaxyl now remembered a memory as Damodar. Abrahamha had retrieved this memory from Damodar.

Damodar provided the hand he had amputated to a back-alley doctor Nadani had introduced him to. The doctor stressed that he couldn't guarantee success. Damodar understood that.

Unwilling to risk either youngster, Damodar suggested Mrs. Sharma for their first attempt. Frozen for almost a century, she looked the same— badly injured, close to death.

The room was uncomfortably hot as the machines kept the cases cool. Sweat ran down his back. Or was that unease? Damodar respected AricNova. He hated doing this to the most inspiring person he knew, but he had no choice. With her moving away, there wouldn't be another opportunity.

Damodar's belief in AricNova was absolute. If *anything* could save his family, it would be her. He couldn't accept defeat without one last try.

He had provided the doctor with the best facilities they could ensure. This was the best shot his surviving family had. The doctor completed the procedures to begin the revival.

The doctor cut a wrinkled finger off AricNova's hand and put it in a small container full of nutrient solution. Symbionts didn't live for long when exposed to air. He submerged it in nutrients before carefully slicing away the external layer of skin. He placed the container in a compartment in the cryo-case along with additional nutrients. Inserting cold tools through the slots provided for them, the Doctor opened an unhealed incision and filled it with nutrients. He moved the finger into it, irrigating it with nutrients to prevent exposure to air and facilitate AricNova's symbionts flowing into the new live host.

Within a few hours, the transformation was miraculous. Wounds healed much faster than with HealSYMB. Damodar cheered. Healed, Mrs. Sharma woke up, astonished to know it was a century later. AricNova's hand was degrading fast, even in a bath of nutrients. They had to hurry.

Damodar's son, Vikas, was next. He was younger. Fitter. Less wounded. They started the reversal with another finger.

Mrs. Sharma marvelled. He told her about all that had happened. She grieved for her husband. She thanked him for saving her daughter, and sat next to her frozen body, weeping silently.

And then she lost her balance and fell.

As Damodar steadied her, her previously ample body felt frail. The symbionts were eating her inside out. They pushed nutrients. She asked Damodar to protect her daughter before she died mid-sentence.

Damodar checked Vikas. Abandoning Mrs. Sharma as a lost cause, they put him in a nutrient bath and provided nutrients the moment the machine circulated blood. He revived. Damodar repeated the whole story, numb with exhaustion and a growing fear.

Vikas wouldn't believe it. He expected to wake up, and this would be a weird dream where he was Superman in a bath. He believed it when he started to see Damodar's memories telepathically as he narrated events. And then he discovered what Damodar did to AricNova and what happened with Mrs. Sharma.

Vikas recoiled.

His father was a diligent, hard-working man who won hearts wherever he went. Vikas witnessed his memories of desperation, impossible choices. He didn't understand this new world. He mourned his father.

Vikas knew he wouldn't survive. He regretted leaving Damodar alone again, and asked his father to wait, as AricNova had recommended, to revive Smriti.

They spent the time getting closure. They remembered the old days, talked. They laughed and wept at memories of people long dead. They had a fine meal together, as he reclined in a nutrient bath.

And then his son enjoyed magic, when he realised he could levitate.

Damodar had pleaded for him to remain in the nutrients, and not use the symbionts, but Vikas disagreed. If he was to die, he might as well die with joy. He levitated out of the bath, then carried his father for a few seconds, till Vikas became too insubstantial to hold Damodar anymore.

The doctor and his staff joined Damodar in watching with tears in their eyes when Vikas could fly no more and soon he could stand no more, be no more.

It was the most beautiful and most difficult lesson of Damodar's life.

He returned Smriti to the cryonics storage to await better times.

Most survivors of the Third World War have been evacuated from contaminated regions in erstwhile Central India, United States and China. Radio Margadarsjak, Thursday, October 22, 2218

~~*~*~*

DHRIT SAISRISEL: SAISRISEL RESIDENCE

Aaxyl's mind moved to another memory that she remembered as Dhrit Saisrisel.

Fifteen-year-old Dhrit had often accompanied Saisrisel when he worked on AricNova's grand home. He usually helped his father with the work, but on the day in question, Saisrisel worked on a restricted section, so Dhrit meandered through the palatial structure. He could spend hours walking through Sarovar's ornate passageways. The virtual guide had the most remarkable stories about the history of the various artefacts and architectural elements. He'd stood on the roof at Sarovar as though watching from the top of a fort.

Outside, in the distance, Damodar unloaded supplies onto service bots. Damodar had been bringing supplies for a month and it would go on till Sarovar finally left for its final destination. Damodar usually arrived alone, but today he had a tall, thin man with him. Few were allowed here. Strangers were rare.

Dhrit hurried down to help them unload, but Damodar was alone when he reached. Dhrit asked him about the other man. Damodar said he had left.

After AricNova had gone missing, Abrahamha had visited the Saisrisel residence and spoken privately with his father. Afterwards, Abrahamha showed Dhrit the picture of a tall, thin man with his hair slicked back, almost as an afterthought.

The man was Nadani, a small-time criminal and Damodar's cousin. He was believed to have attacked AricNova. Dhrit recognised him as the man Damodar had met at Sarovar and told Abrahamha.

Today, a furious Damodar had arrived to confront him for implicating Damodar in AricNova's disappearance. Abrahamha had ravaged his mind for information, but found him innocent. Damodar accused Dhrit of feeding lies to Abrahamha.

Damodar always convinced people that he was their friend. Now he would convince Dhrit that what he had seen was not what he had seen.

Dhrit had already started doubting himself. If Damodar were guilty, why would he accuse Dhrit? It was true that Dhrit hadn't seen Nadani in any secure area. Nor had he seen Nadani arrive with Damodar. It was possible that Damodar saw Nadani there and asked him to leave, as he claimed. He cowered from the furious Damodar.

Saisrisel walked in on Damodar towering over a terrified Dhrit and used telekinesis to attack Damodar. Damodar fought Saisrisel for control. Saisrisel responded with an even greater surge of telekinetic energy that should have severed Damodar's head from his body. Instead, Damodar stilled and the surge reversed, rebounding into Saisrisel.

Dhrit watched his father, the formidable Saisrisel lie on the ground bleeding from deep parallel gashes. He would not forget the sight of his father's mangled chest for as long as he lived. The price his father paid for protecting Dhrit from Damodar.

When Saisrisel decided to move off-world to Terra Nova, Dhrit was certain that it was because Damodar had humiliated him before his own family, in his own home, leaving him with no dignity.

Dhrit hated Damodar. He didn't know how Damodar fooled Abrahamha with his powerless act, but he was certain that Damodar was guilty in the disappearance of AricNova.

Affinities

Star Pharma announces clinical trials for a new drug to reduce symbiont complications during pregnancy. Medicine Frontier, Sunday, December 21, 2442

~~*~*~*

AAMEH: AxAm's room

The morning after her rescue, Aameh was lifting her shirt to examine her bruises when movement at the door flickered in the corner of her eye. It was Sunday, but the paramedics had summoned Aaxyl. Who...? She spun around.

Perfect Sam. Mohan. In their room. Aameh's world lit up as bright as the huge smile on his face.

The long beard was gone. He was no longer Sam, but he was still Perfect. She'd asked Aaxyl about every detail. If she'd known she missed such exciting developments, sitting in that awful basement, she'd have felt extra imprisoned.

They both stood there staring at each other, smiling. His hair, stylish and wispy, framed a gorgeous face that could make an artist weep, and Aameh blinked back tears. She hoped he didn't detect her heart drumming all sorts of romantic rhythms. No telling what powers these guys commanded.

"I'm sorry for the pain I caused you." He hugged her like she mattered, careful of her injuries, the slow and deliberateness infusing more meaning into it than he'd probably intended. "I hadn't expected you or Aaxyl to care so much or take risks my behalf."

Aameh cupped his cheek. "Are you okay?"

Mohan nodded, then shook his head. "We couldn't find... Hersh."

She still scrutinised his newly revealed face, with grey eyes like Aaxyl's. The best people had grey eyes. "Did the SecPros have any clues as to the identity of The Whisperer?"

Mohan shook his head. "Hersh not being a global citizen, we can't officially demand access, but we have our ways. The only person they could trace to that Dorm section was a symbiontist from the Thar Dorms. He's dead. The authorisation for the facility came from the Octagon."

"How is Admin Dhrit?"

Mohan ran his fingers through his hair all the way to his nape, brought them forward to the front and sighed at the ceiling. "We're doing our best, but he isn't likely to make it."

Aameh had expected it, but hearing it said out loud was horrible. Everything crashed together in her head at once. Hersh abandoning them, then turning out to be in danger, Perfect Sam's supposed death, her kidnapping, feeling responsible for Admin Dhrit's impending death... Sobs welled up in her, and so she wept. She wished she could cry with dignity, but her nose was blocked.

Tears stained Mohan's shirt.

He didn't care.

She pretended not to.

She burrowed her face against his chest and hoped the world would just poof away for a bit.

Mohan sat her on the spare bed and turned the chair to sit facing her. "We need to talk." He met her eyes soberly. "It's time to address the elephant in the room."

Aameh winced. "You guessed about my crush on you."

"Couldn't miss."

"You should have said something." Now that it was out in the open, Aameh couldn't let it be at that. She suspected her history of impulsive choices would undermine her, when she most needed to be taken seriously.

"I valued both of you enough to not tell you more lies. You're a minor. I'm over a century older than you."

"The age of sexual consent is sixteen. Only legal adulthood is at twenty-five." Aameh waited for any other shoes to drop. "I find you fascinating."

Without the beard hiding his jaw, his facial beauty was mesmerising. He was perfectly proportioned, like Michelangelo's David—at least the parts she'd seen. Graceful and muscular enough to be thrilling. His neck was long and the perfect mix of hollows and muscles framed in wispy hair. His jaw was an engraved invitation to touch.

"You're a beautiful person. And stunning to look at."

Mohan blushed. "Age differences matter, Am. You being a minor isn't a mere legal term, it signifies a difference in life experience."

His intonation fascinated her. Something she could never capture in an image. He was unique, but most importantly, he was a good man. Aameh was so doomed. She needed to focus, or the only Mohan she'd have was an imaginary one.

"I find people my age boring," Aameh said. "I find you attractive because of these experiences. You have seen so many things. It makes you compelling."

"I answer questions," Mohan grinned, then sobered. "But there is too big a difference in power between us to allow a healthy relationship. It wouldn't be a partnership between equals."

"Of course we aren't equals. I'm a dormer minor. You're a century-old super-rich global citizen." Or was this something else? "Did Aaxyl scare you off?" Aaxyl had never spoken against Perfect Sam, but she didn't approve of Aameh's choices of men usually.

"Aaxyl?" Mohan frowned. "She didn't, but even if she wanted to, she couldn't. Aaxyl is a parental figure to you. To me, she's an incredible woman who has been a legal adult for all of three years. I'm a hundred years older than her too."

"But if we're attracted to each other...."

Mohan met her eyes and held them.

"You aren't attracted to me." Realisation dawned in a heap of embarrassment.

"I adore you," Mohan said. "But I'm asexual."

The words dropped like lead between them. Aameh understood what asexual was. Lots of people were asexual, particularly older ones. She just didn't expect one to *be sexy*. What a waste.

"Don't tell me you have a clone who's the playboy."

"The playboy thing has nothing to do with sex." Mohan shrugged. "I was a brand ambassador for a Sexel campaign. One of many."

"But you have sex there?"

Mohan shrugged. "I've used it on and off to meet people. I'm not averse to sex, usually. It is like a dinner invite you aren't interested in. You can attend and eat. You may enjoy the food on occasion, but you aren't excited about the next invite. It isn't a good basis for a relationship with a sexual person."

It wasn't. "That's a pretty enormous elephant for a room," Aameh grumbled.

Mohan winced. "I do love you in my own way, and didn't want you to think I didn't care."

They were good together. Aameh had never been as certain of anything as this. She knew that he didn't see past her age to experience how right they felt. She'd hoped to wait, but if this had to be faced now, so be it.

"I love you too," Aameh told him. "In my own way. I'm glad we had this conversation, but what does it mean? I make you happy. You can't discriminate against me because I'm young!"

Aameh didn't care about the sex. Well, she did, but it hadn't been on the table to be ruled out. She wasn't good at subtlety.

"I don't know. What do you want it to mean after knowing all this?" Mohan asked.

It was a prompt for her to back off gracefully, if she'd ever heard one. He should have known her better. "I want us to enjoy each other while it is mutually satisfying." Aameh countered.

"You're too young." Mohan frowned. "I don't want you to be in an unfair position."

"Have you met my sister?" Aameh grinned. "Ax may not scare you, but if being around you harms me, she'll ground me. It wouldn't be the first time either. She hasn't warned you off. You said so."

"How did we get here?" Mohan smiled twitchily like he was suppressing a laugh. "She didn't warn me off because she thought I was a sane man. Does Ax know you use her protectiveness to talk men into relationships?"

"You're the only one who needed it." Aameh grinned back wider. She *was* good at arguing. "She hasn't tried to prevent me from being around you."

"You're going to run circles around me," Mohan said, but he didn't look unhappy about it.

It was the best she'd get for now. He would learn to trust what they had with time. Until then, Aameh would have to accept him humouring her. There was no hurry.

"So that sorts it?" Aameh grinned. Could she hug him or would it be inappropriate with an asexual man? There was so much to find out.

"Actually, it brings me to the reason I needed to address this now. You're invited to a private party at Sexel today."

"Sexel?" Aameh felt like she'd missed a step somewhere.

"It's a meeting, dummy." Mohan tweaked her nose. "Ax and NeoJai will be there too."

Aameh raised her eyebrows Aaxyl-style. And here she had worried about hugging being inappropriate.

Mohan kissed her forehead and vanished.

Dang.

Scientists estimate it will take five thousand years to reach pre-Enduring War populations. Data Junkies, Sunday, November 23, 2442

~~*~*~*

AAXYL: SEXEL

Mohan brought his zeplyn to pick them up. AxAm and Vidroh entered. Mohan glared at Vidroh. "You weren't invited."

"Aaxyl invited me." Vidroh met his gaze. "She hasn't told me your precious secrets, if that's what you're worried about."

"You don't worry me, Vidroh, you irritate me," Mohan drawled with uncharacteristic rudeness.

Inviting Vidroh had seemed like a good idea. He knew these people. Thankfully, she hadn't told him about AricNova, just that the kidnapper had escaped with Hersh.

She ignored their exchange.

The zeplyn was a delight. It was spacious and almost the size of AxAm's room. All the seats had small retractable tables and when she looked out, they were already in the air. It moved so smoothly, she hadn't noticed when they took off.

She turned in her seat to watch the residential area passing below them, the eight Sectors and the parks separating them visible from the air.

Beside her, Aameh knelt on the seat, nose pressed to the glass, fogging it. She peered up at the sky and turning to Mohan, said:

"The waxing gibbous moon, a sight to behold,

A symbol of love, joy and courage untold,

A reminder of the power of the night,

And the beauty to be found beneath its light."

Mohan gazed at her, besotted. He was too old for her, but Aaxyl hadn't seen Aameh this happy with anyone younger. She had no idea what the two were up to. They seemed more best friends than lovers.

The zeplyn flew above the lights of a city rendered in grayscale by the mesmerising moon suspended over the clear dome.

"What does waxing gibbous mean?" Aaxyl asked.

Aameh touched the glass with reverent fingers. "It will be full moon soon."

"Now that would be something."

"The next one will be even better. It's a Super Moon. The moon will be closest to the earth at the same time as the full moon and will be huge!"

Aaxyl didn't know Aameh followed astronomy from the windowless warren of the Dorms.

The flight was brief. They soon approached a brightly lit building with SEXEL written on it and landed on a spacious roof lit up with signs and advertisements. The Octagon towered over the other side.

The whir of drone cameras buzzed around them, lights strobing on till they appeared to have a spotlight surrounding them. Media bots. Dark dots swirled in her vision.

Aaxyl tried to imagine the sort of images the media bots were getting as she fought the urge to cover her face. Aameh looked like her eyes were too big for her face, and Vidroh looked his normal granite-faced self. Aaxyl was sure she presented as the scrawniest of them all. Mohan was owning the Perfect in his nickname. He grinned at the lights.

While Sexel staffed the Sexual Welfare Services in the Dorms as social service, AxAm had never been to their commercial premises before. This glittering celebration of sex was a new experience.

The multi-city chain offered sexual products and services, and set the standard in sexual commerce.

A large signboard near the entrance listed areas for various offerings throughout the building: sex workers, toys, machines and immersives, pornographic entertainment, private rooms, a club and restaurant for socialising, a library, sexual coaching, therapy and trauma counselling for victims of sexual crimes.

Another sign proudly proclaimed philanthropic contributions. Sexel created public sex-ed material, professionally managed physical and virtual dating spaces as public welfare for most cities and domes it operated in, and conducted or funded research around sex and relationships.

Yet, Sexel was like nothing Aaxyl imagined. Everything was ornate and elegant. They were offered welcome drinks at the door of a lobby on the roof. Discrete and comfortable seating areas were attended to by tastefully sexy staff. Abundant displays showcased a variety of products and services.

A manager came over to welcome their group. It probably helped that a member of the Abrahamha family had booked their best suite.

He hugged Mohan like an old friend, and shook hands with Aaxyl, lifting her hand and bending over to kiss it lightly as he looked into her eyes. Aaxyl smiled back politely, unsure how to respond. He did the same with Vidroh, who looked indifferent and Aameh, who giggled. She'd been giggly all day.

They were led to a suite of rooms on the top floor.

Mohan shut the door and engaged the privacy button, explaining that it also cut off communications, disabling most known spying devices. It was the best available in the dome, short of their own premises.

Aaxyl wasn't surprised. Sexual commerce had often introduced innovations the rest of the society would adopt over time.

Mohan teleported Noir in.

Noir looked relaxed, unlike at the Null Dorms. He began as they took seats around a low table. "We meet here, because it's one of the few places that offers excellent privacy, comfort and allows long meetings without raising suspicion."

"You mean we play sex-starved dormers," Aaxyl said bitterly. "You play the rich old guys who can afford us."

"You can call them desperate men who wouldn't find women otherwise, if you prefer." Noir laughed. "Though Mohan is one rich old guy. NeoJai is young and Vidroh is broke, isn't he?" Noir glared pointedly at Vidroh. "I rarely visit a Sexel, openly. I teleport in for meetings once the room is private."

Aaxyl's mind focused on one detail. NeoJai had been invited.

"How long would we keep meeting like this?" Aameh asked. "Also, are we expected to have sex with you?"

As though Aameh would mind getting her hands on either Mohan or Noir.

"We won't need to meet more than once or twice," Noir said. "Once you have mental implants, this will be unnecessary. You don't have to have sex with anyone, just don't act like we are here for work before entering the room."

"No one is spying on you—guaranteed by Sexel policy," Mohan stressed. "Just be aware that Sexel does not approve of what we're doing. Don't act like you dislike people you share private rooms with. Leave the rooms with messy beds, not coffee mugs all over one table. Use common sense."

The only business allowed in a Sexel was sex. Perched precariously on the ever thinning edge between surveillance and privacy, Sexel was notoriously hostile to the use of its premises for non-sexual purposes

AxAm looked at each other and shrugged.

"You said the needles in Hersh's head aren't torture," Aaxyl said. "Now you said we have to meet like this till *we* get mental implants. Explain."

"You have to agree to non-disclosure before we proceed," Noir warned. They nodded.

Mohan tossed a room key on the table. "Go and get a massage for an hour or two," he told Vidroh. "Bill it to the room."

"I know about mental implants," Vidroh said. "AxAm trust me."

Noir growled. "But *we* don't trust you, Vidroh."

Vidroh picked the key and left without meeting Aaxyl's eyes, an unspoken storm beneath a stony exterior.

"Okay," Aaxyl said. "Is anyone going to explain why we can't trust him? I thought he was one of you guys. He helped us when Admin Dhrit and Aameh..."

"He's an... ally," Noir said. "He chose poorly on something big and it backfired. Now he's running half-cocked in a rage. You're the only sane thing he's done in a while. We can't afford his brand of recklessness with the search for *Hersh*."

"He isn't reckless," Aaxyl said, remembering his kindness the night Aameh was taken.

"You don't know him at all," Mohan countered.

Aaxyl gave up. "Never mind. We might as well get on with why you wanted him to leave."

"First things first." Mohan took off his comm and placed it on the table before Aameh. "Do you recognise this man?"

Mohan hadn't touched his comm, but it projected a series of images of a thin, brown-skinned man with black eyes and hair that was slicked back. He wore a dark blue shirt with sleeves rolled up to his forearms. The top buttons were undone, showing a thick gold chain around his neck. It was the sort of look one saw in historical fiction with early settlers rebuilding the modern world.

They all looked at Aameh.

Aameh shook her head.

Aaxyl asked, "Who's he?"

"Nadani," Noir snarled. "Damodar's cousin. He was the original suspect in the attack on AricNova, but we couldn't prove anything or find him. Are you sure he isn't the Whisperer?"

All eyes focused on Aameh again. She shook her head. "He isn't. The Whisperer wears a full body suit, but the proportions and posture are wrong."

Noir sighed. "It has been two centuries since this image. The body changes with time."

Aameh shook her head, curls bouncing. "Unless it can get shorter, I think you can rule him out. The Whisperer is barely as tall as NeoJai. I can draw you some sketches from memory."

Noir bowed his head in that oddly formal style they adopted when they spoke of the ancients. "We owe you a debt of gratitude," he told Aameh.

Aameh blushed. "I wasn't trying to find her. I just stumbled upon her."

"Nevertheless, you did find her. Something we failed to do for centuries.

And against all odds, got the word out. If there is any further information you can give us, we'd be grateful."

Aameh nodded.

Aaxyl shook her head. "It's too dangerous for her. We are sitting ducks in the Dorms. She's definitely not going back to the Null Dorms. The Whisperer has already got to her once!"

"Ax, this is AricNova. The whole world owes her a debt of gratitude. We can't leave her imprisoned!" Aameh said.

This is what Aaxyl had feared. Aameh, excited by an idea, rushing headlong into danger.

"Hersh," Mohan said. "He's with her. Use his name to refer to her to avoid anyone finding out."

"We shouldn't be involved in this to begin with," Aaxyl said. She leveled a stare at Mohan. He of all people should know there was no way Aaxyl would allow this. She hated to play the legal guardian card but, "Am is a minor."

Mohan turned to Aaxyl. "We don't plan to leave you in the Dorms, Ax."

"What?" Aaxyl frowned.

"We believe your mother planned for Abrahamha to adopt you." Mohan said.

"Abrahamha's Strays?" Aameh squeaked.

Mohan nodded. "You said she planned to bring you to SYMBTech if she had returned. You connected with Hersh and started working with symbionts - that was the closest you'd get in terms of choices while living in the Dorms. Aameh got curious about a random investigative article and ended up finding *Hersh*. This is how affinities work."

"You fit," Noir said. "But we must follow process. If you wish to join us, we should start working toward that."

AxAm had always felt an affinity for Abrahamha's Strays, but who didn't?

"Yes," Aameh said, simply.

"Would you have said this if Am hadn't found... *Hersh*?" Though in all honesty, Aaxyl had felt a sense of belonging with Abrahamha in the Null Dorms.

Hurt flashed across Mohan's face. "Yes, Ax. I was undercover as Perfect Sam. You can't keep a secret from Am, and Am can't keep a secret, period. I still made sure that you'd expect internships with SYMBTech when I found Hersh. Am hadn't found *Hersh* then, but even if I couldn't share details, I made sure you'd expect to leave the Dorms anyway."

Aaxyl would have preferred hard unimon and independence. "Can't you just offer us a job?"

"Call it a job if you want," Noir said. "Nothing needs doing more than rescuing *Hersh*. I know Am is fragile and wouldn't dream of putting her in danger."

"We aren't involving the other younger Strays either," Mohan said. "But Aameh has managed to spot The Whisperer's patterns once. She could do it again. There clearly is some affinity tying you to *Hersh*. If you still only want a job, we could arrange that after AricNova is found."

Aaxyl was about to protest, but changed her mind. They had hoped to get out of the Dorms with Perfect Sam's help. Was her aversion to change making her unreasonable? "What would it entail?"

Noir said, "You'd need the implants to use our resources and you'd have to maintain confidentiality even if you decided to leave the family."

"The needles in Hersh's brain comprise an advanced AVANT brain implant," Mohan delivered a practiced introduction. "AVANT can offer you the implant free of cost. If you refuse, we'll support you regardless, just not on our premises. It's complicated. You'll understand when you're there."

"What's the catch?" Aaxyl asked.

"None, in terms of your interest," Mohan assured her. "Hersh has the implant too, as you now know. But the integration of the implant is... uncomfortable. You'll be out of action for a few days and take a while to be proficient. It's not dangerous, but it adds new inputs to the brain and it takes a while to adapt to it."

"Like alien symbionts but technological?" Aameh guessed.

"Yes and no," Noir said. "Like symbionts allow symb-abilities, this adds considerable tech-abilities. Unlike symbionts, the integration is safe, just uncomfortable. Alien symbionts are not painful, but they kill you."

"Is Hersh a part of your family?" Aaxyl asked. "Why isn't he a global citizen?"

"Hersh isn't a part of our family, but he's an ally." Mohan met her eyes honestly. "There was a... situation while he was still training with us and he helped us out. That was his job for three years before he returned to the Dorms, and why he received the implant and used our comm."

Aaxyl saw Aameh open her mouth eagerly and took a page out of NeoJai's book. Acceptance or rejection in the face of dramatic information shouldn't be immediate. They could make it an AxAm rule. "We'll need some time to think it over. Is there anything else?"

Noir said, "We'd like to analyse both of your symbionts to be on the safe side. It might also help Aameh."

And yet, on the very first day they met, Mohan had said that even if they could create a culture for Aameh, it wouldn't offer anything useful. Aaxyl needed to stop thinking like this. It was an opportunity for a new beginning outside the Dorms.

"Hersh already tested me," Aameh said. "He found nothing."

"Hersh is trained for symbiont products. I want to take samples to our research facilities. We also need any history you can remember." Mohan palmed a pack of blood collection tubes that appeared out of thin air before they fell.

"She has something that stops symbionts from working in her," Aaxyl said, extending her arm for Mohan to collect the blood, ignoring her mother's insistence to not talk about The Whisperer. "Whether they are her own or transfused, like HealSYMB. My mother may have injected me with Am's blood, because I stopped hearing The Whisperer after that. But HealSYMB and AthSYMB work on me."

"Symbiont interactions can be complex and account for the differences in how they manifested in both of you, but telepathic symbionts are tenacious. They won't go away." Mohan tossed Aaxyl's sample to Noir, and drew Aameh's blood. "I'm pathing to you. Can you hear me?"

"Path?"

Mohan tapped his forehead. "Communicating through telepathy. If I used the implant, it would be imped."

Aaxyl shook her head. Nothing but her own thoughts in there. "I heard Abrahamha in the Null Dorm."

"That doesn't mean anything," Noir said. "Abrahamha can path to non-telepaths. If you really were telepathic, you would hear Mohan too. Unless, as you say, something blocked it. To the best of my knowledge, telepathy can't be blocked, short of a metal object in the brain."

"I've had my brain scanned after injuries in fights," Aaxyl said. "There are no foreign objects!"

"Yes, I expect you'd know. Injected blood is one thing, Brain injury is another. I doubt your mother could do it surgically in the Dorms without anyone finding out."

"I guess we'll never know," Aaxyl said.

"We should be able to identify symbionts if present." Noir pocketed the samples. "If true, your survival in the Dorms is incredible and it explains why your mother wanted to bring you to us. Telepaths suffer in crowds."

Aameh frowned. "Suffer how?"

"Non-telepathic minds still have a barely noticeable hum," Mohan said. "But in a crowded environment the constant murmur of many non-telepathic minds is exhausting to an inexperienced telepath as the mind keeps trying to interpret it."

"Resilience of childhood." Aaxyl shrugged. "Lived from moment to moment and managed, I guess."

"I owe her my life," Aameh said.

"Anytime, kid." Aaxyl's voice was scratchy.

❖

Aaxyl

Aaxyl woke up to a delicious aroma. She'd drifted off at some point as Mohan and Noir quizzed Aameh about her symbiont responses.

Dinner had arrived. Vidroh had returned and was shirtless next to her. Aameh was draped across the lap of an equally shirtless Mohan flaunting sex-God eye candy as the staff uncovered dishes and asked them if they needed anything else. Noir was nowhere in sight.

"What did I miss?" she asked the group as the door closed again, eyeing the various displays of skin while her nose catalogued the delicious aromas. She inhaled deeply. "Do you guys eat like kings or what?"

Mohan shrugged. "We decided to order food and look like authentic Sexel customers while it was delivered. Noir is dropping the blood off and checking in on Dhrit."

NeoJai arrived. His face was dull and he still wore the clothes he'd worn on the previous day. For the first time since she knew him, a stubble shadowed his jaw. He looked at everyone but her. He looked like he desperately needed a hug and Aameh gave him one.

Aaxyl wished she could be the one to give that hug, to soothe his tired face, but when he'd craved her, she'd avoided him for stupid reasons and then recklessly smashed what they had.

Aaxyl listened to his updates to Aameh. Admin Dhrit lived, though barely. Doctors had induced a medical coma to prevent him from accidentally using any symb-abilities, the greatest threat at this point. Now that the symbionts proliferated throughout his body, he could die instantly if he used them. He grew weaker even with the coma.

They took up plates and the non-dormers stood back as the dormers launched a magnificent attack on the banquet before loading their own plates.

No one spoke for a while. The food was good. Very very good. Rice and gravies was turning out to be a new favourite thing.

Vidroh ran a finger over Aaxyl's cheek. "Would you have sex with me?"

Abrupt. He must have returned horny from whatever he did while he was gone.

Aaxyl had a bad feeling about this. Vidroh was broken. Enough baggage to need rental storage.

But his haunted eyes reminded her of her own numbness when she feared Aameh may die. He had cared for her when she was broken. Life broke everyone at some point.

She nodded slowly. "Yes."

Vidroh launched to his feet, tugging her shirt off with the same movement. He picked her up and rushed to a bedroom. Aaxyl scrambled to keep up with his urgency as he undressed them, barely getting there as he laid her on the bed and thrust into her.

What was the hurry?

His body engulfed her. He was on her, in her, around her. She couldn't move. Sensations cascaded and she was swept up in his frenzy.

He consumed her attention; demanded her response with face tortured, eyes closed, body gleaming with sweat already, but she didn't know if he sought her or if she was a means to lose himself.

No way that intensity was going to last. She had never been so aroused and distracted at the same time. Aaxyl's climax was an ambush. It stormed out of nowhere, even as her mind puzzled over the man causing it. Her nails bit into his skin, as she pulled him into her instinctively.

The storm froze, stilled, passed.

Vidroh moved off her, shuddering. She was pretty winded herself and she'd barely moved.

Aaxyl did a mental check for contraception. She'd be good for another month or two.

A sob tore through him. "Her name was Srayoshi."

Vidroh poured out the story of his partner. Her bravery, her kindness. He couldn't rest till the settlements she fought for had found water. The facades stripped off, what remained of Vidroh was one raw wound.

Still processing a physical climax and mental bewilderment, there wasn't much she could say. She hadn't known people lived in the wastelands or why they would, but she did understand that if there were people, they'd need water.

She held him, stroking his hair like she used to when Aameh was upset, and waited till he talked himself out, and fell asleep.

She had a troubling sense that this was a farewell. He sounded as tortured as he had the day they met, when he'd howled his heart out in the clinic bathroom. Not moving on. Explaining why he wouldn't.

She hoped she was wrong.

AAMEH

The door slamming woke them up from their trance.

Aaxyl sacrificed for those she cared about, and Vidroh felt like a bottomless pit full of demons.

Aameh disliked Aaxyl's interest in him, but had stayed silent. What did Aameh know about choosing appropriate men? But she did feel bad for Vidroh as an individual.

Mohan looked at the door for a long time, impassive.

NeoJai's stiff stance radiated indignant rejection of Aaxyl, but his eyes lingered and it wasn't a fun arousal.

Mohan looked at him. "What happened between you and Aaxyl?"

"How would you respond if the woman you loved said you'd defend Abrahamha for murder?" NeoJai asked acidly.

"I'd say she knew me well." Mohan took her foot into his lap, giving her an impromptu foot massage.

Aameh stifled a burst of laughter.

NeoJai stiffened.

One emotional crisis at a time.

Aameh patted the seat inviting NeoJai to sit. "I had an idea for Admin Dhrit, but I don't want to be a nuisance."

NeoJai sat next to her. "You'd never be a nuisance, Am."

"One of the ways they were weakening AricNova's abilities was by harvesting her blood," Aameh said. "Perhaps we can do the same with Dhrit? It made her weak enough that she couldn't escape."

"We can't weaken Dhrit," Mohan said. "AricNova close to death will still be stronger than most of us. Dhrit can't afford to lose blood. Also symbionts aren't only in blood. They're everywhere. It can't reverse the transfusion."

"But there are two Dhrits!" Aameh said. "Couldn't the healthy Dhrit donate blood as well as Dhrit's own native symbionts to him?"

"There are three Dhrits," NeoJai said. "If this will work, the other two will happily bleed themselves dry for him."

Mohan's eyes lit up and he kissed her toes. "You've bought him time. Let me think this through." He dropped her foot and paced the floor.

Aameh took a long bath in an actual bath tub with scorching hot water. She watched her limbs float in it. She used both soap and body wash, and pampered herself with some lotion. When she padded out of the bedroom in a cloud of fragrance and decadent bathrobe, Mohan was still pacing.

She sat on the floor near NeoJai like a useless puppy without any of the ability to take away cares. She gave him company as he waited for Mohan to be done pacing. "He's been *thinking* all this time?"

NeoJai nodded, watching Aameh tug at carpet fibers and smooth them over. He raked a toe into them to make a line. Aameh smoothed it out for him to do it again. Patterns and textures were soothing.

"It's okay to talk." Aameh nudged his knee with her shoulder.

"If this saves him..." NeoJai stopped. Swallowed. "I don't know how to thank you enough."

"I'm surprised his doctors didn't suggest it," Aameh said. "It is routine protocol."

"The doctors don't know he's a clone." NeoJai went up to Mohan. "Can't you tell the doctors the idea so that they can see if it will help?"

Mohan took a moment to focus. "I pathed Noir as Aameh was telling us. The doctors have already started. Too early to say, but it should buy him time."

AAXYL

Aaxyl stared at the ceiling next to a sleeping Vidroh when NeoJai knocked the door and peeked in. She raised herself on an elbow, watching him quietly.

NeoJai walked over hesitantly. "May we… us." Raw longing warred with hurt on his face. He wanted to be with her, and yet he hadn't forgiven her.

She instinctively knew he couldn't while the father she'd insulted fought for his life. It was the wrong he could lash out at, even if he knew it had been a misunderstanding.

Aaxyl reached for his hand. Words were difficult between them, but they embraced, taking comfort in being close. Aaxyl was careful to not spook him. For a long time he lay there. Neither willing to leave her, nor to be with her.

Winning trust was harder than breaking it. She would wait forever if that was what it took to once more have NeoJai look at her as he used to.

After a while, she turned onto her back and cradled his head on her shoulder, stroking his hair gently. He lay rigid till his body relaxed into sleep. Aaxyl continued to stare at the ceiling.

VIDROH

Vidroh was trapped between Aaxyl, who had flung a leg over him, and NeoJai who was spooning him. Yeah, the eye of this particular storm wasn't where he wanted to be.

He slipped out of bed and tiptoed out of the room. Mohan lay sprawled asleep on the carpet in his underwear, next to a bottle of vodka with Aameh snuggled against him in an over-sized bathrobe. They were surrounded by a sea of almost nude watercolours of Mohan like a nest: smiling, gesturing, posing, not realising he was being sketched...

Vidroh rummaged through the debris of dinner and was pleased to find plenty of food. Sex was hungry work. He was glad that Aaxyl and NeoJai had reconciled... or whatever that was.

Speaking of the devil, NeoJai walked out of the bedroom, still fully dressed, and picked his way through Aameh's paintings to sit next to him.

"You okay?" NeoJai asked. "I didn't mean to eavesdrop, but..."

Yeah. But. Vidroh hadn't exactly cared who was listening. What he'd done was inappropriate. Even if they were at a Sexel, Aaxyl had been with her sister, another man romantically interested in her, and her ex-boss. She'd consented to sex, not... honestly, Vidroh had no idea what to call his behaviour. "I wasn't thinking clearly. I'm sorry."

"I knew she was interested in you," NeoJai shrugged. "She'd already refused to be involved with me. I meant I didn't know about Srayoshi. I'm sorry for your loss."

Liar.

Vidroh would have to be blind to not notice the hurt radiating off NeoJai. But he'd done quite enough, their relationship was their business.

NeoJai told him about Aameh's idea and developments with his father's treatment. "I'm going home."

"I hope he gets better soon," Vidroh said. "Go. I'll tell the others."

Immigration and residentship officer claims live broadcast of him drunk on Octagon roof is political targeting. Satire Times, Monday, November 24, 2442

~~*~*~*~*

AAXYL: AxAm's room

Aaxyl plodded to her room, wanting to curl up for a week. She had stumbled out of bed early to go to work after the weekend, but NeoJai had already left. He ignored her comm too. She and Vidroh had returned to Ekta Dorms, while Aameh had chosen to spend the day with Mohan.

She wore her paramedics uniform, and notified the SIS of her availability before she considered the next steps. She'd resign from work and they could take a week or so packing their belongings and saying their good-byes. She looked forward to no longer worrying about Aameh, but it was a huge gamble. They'd be breaking an AxAm rule big time. They didn't have enough unimon to live independently, and if it didn't work out...

They had enough SociCred saved to pay for the room for a month or two. If they gifted the room to Scharada, they'd still have a room in the Dorms to return to, if need be.

She wished she could be as excited as Aameh, but her sister leaped before she looked.

Aaxyl would be responsible for their well being without the unimon to meet any needs, or welfare to fall back on. She had to stop thinking like that. She had always wanted to get out of the Dorms. This was the perfect opportunity. Everything would be fine.

Her finger traced their height record by the door. Shuffling between shared accommodations for most of their childhood, they'd never been able to maintain a record over time before this room, six years ago. By then, Aaxyl had reached her five feet two. Aameh had gone from a few inches shorter than her to several inches taller. On a calm day, Aaxyl could touch each line and remember moments from when Aameh was that tall.

Her comm chirped a paramedics alert for a vampire in the residential area —dorm slang for a SYMB-junkie who drank blood. Incompatible symbionts mostly passed through the digestive tract harmlessly. As long as consumption was consensual, it was legal, but occasionally, an idiot consumed symbionts that made them sick.

She hurried out, and hovered to the residential area, feeling awkwardly exposed on the still unfamiliar contraption. The necessity of transporting patients prevented paramedic hovers from being sleek and agile like the SecPro ones she'd trained on. Their propulsion also consumed more power. At least with a public service hover, the consumption didn't get billed to her or she'd be paying the Dorms.

On her first day on the job, she'd been stuck in the air when the battery ran out before she expected it, leaving her with no way to steer the agrav tech. The guffawing paramedics pelted crude suggestions about her rocking her butt back and forth in the seat to nudge the hover down before they towed her back to the ground, ribbing her all the way. Apparently, stranding gullible apprentices in the air was a hilarious paramedic tradition. Well, it was a little funny. She'd do it to someone else.

She dismounted before an independent house at the address provided. No ambulance. No other paramedics scurried around. Bizarre. Aaxyl usually trailed the hotshots, alerted only after they lacked enough bodies for a task. Had they left already? Her alert hadn't been cancelled. Were they busy on another call? She could hardly hover anyone she found all the way to the hospital without an ambulance. Her request for clarification went unanswered. She really wasn't in the mood for another initiation prank.

She searched the residence for the vampire. The premises appeared to be vacant. Did she have the wrong address? Distracted thoughts cluttered her mind and anything was possible. She rechecked the address and tried the paramedic operators again.

A male voice spoke from a room further ahead. "Aaxyl. Please pay attention." The man sounded mildly irritated, as though he caught Aaxyl's attention wandering mid-conversation, rather than talking to her for the first time.

What the...

"Who's this?" She asked, moving stealthily toward the voice.

"The Deal-Maker," the voice replied. A cheap dorm communicator lay on the floor of the empty room. Inners didn't use dorm comms. They needed ones that would handle unimon.

"The who?" It sounded like a character from a child's animated comic, suited for a single-digit age like when she named a creep The Whisperer. "Was it you who called for medical aid at this location?"

"I created the alert to communicate with you outside the Dorms." He had an unfamiliar accent, preoccupied cadence, and his tone clipped with impatience as though Aaxyl was bothering him rather than the other way around.

Aaxyl backed to the door carefully and looked around in the other rooms. No one skulked to attack her. She had line-of-sight to the main entrance.

She tried to call the paramedics desk again, then the SecPros. No response. Aaxyl checked her communicator.

"I've blocked comms," the voice said. "We speak without being spied on."

She started recording audio. "Who are you and what do you want?"

"Right now, you're in trouble, but I can help."

"Why would you say that?" Aaxyl picked up the comm, to record better. The Deal-Maker was someone new. Getting information was always a good idea.

"Let's say that someone wants to make trouble for you."

"How can I trust you?" Aaxyl asked.

"I know your new friend, Mohan," the Deal-Maker said.

"What is this about?" Aaxyl asked.

"SecPros have received evidence of your presence at the Null Dorms during the kidnapping and they are under pressure to show results." The Deal-Maker projected certainty. "They lack conclusive evidence, but will monitor you. Your communications will be intercepted once they've obtained your identifiers from the Dorm."

Aaxyl didn't trust the Deal-Maker an inch, but had no difficulty believing that SecPros might target a dormer to fake progress in solving a high profile crime.

A hundred thoughts jostled in her mind.

The person who misled the SecPros about her had to be The Whisperer. Nobody else would benefit from SecPros wasting their time on her.

More worryingly, The Whisperer knew Aameh. Glad as Aaxyl had been to find Aameh safe, it made no sense that she was the least injured in an attack that bloodied two men. Unless, the Whisperer knew that she couldn't heal, but would be good leverage to make Hersh cooperate. Such a person might create trouble for Aaxyl to hinder Aameh.

"Who are you? Tell me your name," Aaxyl demanded.

"No."

"What do you want? Why are you telling me all this?"

"My motivations are not your concern. You don't have time. Once the SecPros inform your director, she must summon you to comply with the law. I can get you out of the Dorms."

So could Mohan, in the blink of an eye. Aaxyl trusted Mohan more than a petulant voice on a comm. "I'll take my chances, thanks."

"Keep the comm with you. Call me when you believe me."

AAXYL: EKTA DORMS

Leela's hostile gaze flayed the SecPros as she said to Aaxyl, "It appears you're a person of interest in serious crimes."

When Aaxyl returned to the Dorms, four SecPros had stood at the doors wearing the dark shirts typical of investigators. When they headed straight for her, she'd sent the recording she had made to Mohan before dismounting.

They'd escorted her to Leela's office, where another SecPro waited, wearing a casual suit. He'd be an analyst, presumably their leader, since he'd waited comfortably. Kant stood near the door with an expressionless face.

Events unfolded as the Deal-Maker predicted. The SecPros noted the details of her comm and asked her about the kidnappings.

"Were you present at the Null Dorms on the 19th of November, around nine o'clock?" The interviewer was a handsome, clean-shaven man with an easygoing personality. Hazel eyes shone with friendly humour.

Aaxyl matched his light tone and easy smile. "If you mean the day Aameh and Admin Dhrit got kidnapped, then yes." She tried to count back in her head. How many days had it been?

He leaned in with a cajoling smile. "I'm the lead investigator on the case. Can you tell me what happened?"

"Admin Dhrit and my sister were kidnapped by the same criminal who had kidnapped our previous symbiontist, Hersh. They were found on the next morning at the Null Dorms. We were unable to save Hersh. He's still missing."

"Who is this we?" he asked.

"NeoJai, son of Admin Dhrit, and Mohan and Noir, representatives of SYMBTech, who had been searching for Hersh."

The man consulted some notes on a slate. "Ah yes, NeoJai. When we asked Director Sambit why he let you take away an injured man, he said that you claimed to be his girlfriend, and he knew you to be his colleague's sister. He said you asked for control of his car, a Vortexia-7 manufactured last year. That's one fancy toy. The SecPros who found you on the location of the attack confirm this. Yet, here's the funny thing. They make no mention of your sister or Admin Dhrit being kidnapped that night. Only his son being attacked, which you omitted. It's almost like one set of events happened as per you, and another as per witnesses."

Aaxyl gaped at him. If Admin Dhrit and Aameh hadn't been kidnapped, how had they been found? "NeoJai recovered after receiving HealSYMB and nutrients. He joined in the search. I didn't think to mention it."

"You forgot about injuries to your boyfriend?" The investigator noted something on the slate. "You forgot driving a Vortexia-7?"

"My sister was kidnapped!" Aaxyl snapped. "I wasn't thinking of cars. NeoJai's injuries had healed. I treated him when he was injured."

"He confirms the treatment." The investigator smiled reassuringly. Aaxyl was about to heave a sigh of relief when he continued, "We interviewed NeoJai. He made no claim of you being his girlfriend. He had no explanation for your presence. He was there to drop your sister home, as he did daily. The Dorm guards present when your sister was rescued don't describe any romantic behaviour between NeoJai and you. If anything, he appeared to avoid you."

"You can't be serious!" Aaxyl looked around the room in disbelief. "Did NeoJai accuse me? Did you interrogate Mohan? Noir? Abrahamha? Or are you just after the dormer?"

Leela winced. Kant pressed his lips together slightly, though his bored stare didn't waver from the nothingness he usually stared into.

"We are just doing our duty, Aaxyl. It's a high profile case." The investigator took on a pacifying tone, as though Aaxyl was overreacting. "It's the process. You're connected to the missing symbiontist as well. Another symbiontist who worked with you was attacked. Often, perpetrators of crimes are people the victim knows. We need to be able to rule you out. Video records show that you returned with an accomplice later after the director left. Who is he?"

Nagrik Manch advice for dormers who ran into trouble with SecPros replayed in her head. *Say nothing, admit to nothing. Anything you reveal will be used to strengthen the case against you. Your guilt or innocence must be proved before the Judicidal SIS, not SecPros.*

Aaxyl stopped talking.

He asked her more questions. He got things wrong, once calling Aameh her rival in the Dorms, baiting her into correcting him. Aaxyl crossed her arms and stared back Kant-style, doing what Aameh would have done. She analysed their questions to understand what they knew and what they wanted.

Another SecPro finally stepped forward. "You're under investigation for involvement in the kidnapping of Dhrit Saisrisel, the assault on his son NeoJai Saisrisel and SecPros from President Damodar's detail. You're suspected of collaborating with the unlawful detention and interrogation of SecPros in the Null Dorms."

They'd thrown the proverbial kitchen sink at her, but it betrayed their ignorance.

Dhrit Saisrisel was in a coma and unable to name anyone as his kidnapper. NeoJai might be angry with her, but he was too honest to frame her. She had stood next to Dorm guards when Noir rendered the mercenaries unconscious and they were delusional if they thought she was anything but a spectator after Abrahamha's Strays took charge of events in the Null Dorm. The whole setup screamed *these guys don't know shit.*

"You can't believe this!" Aaxyl turned to Leela in dismay. "I'm hardly a criminal!"

"Kidnapping the Administrator of the Dorms is a big deal. They are just doing their jobs." Leela infused such acid into *doing their jobs* it left no doubt about what she thought of them. The SecPro ignored the hostility.

Aaxyl asked the SecPros, "Am I being arrested?"

"Not yet, but SecPros will be posted to monitor you." Two burly SecPros flanked her. A man and a woman.

"In the Dorms?" Aaxyl asked. It was unprecedented.

"The Dorms don't have surveillance cameras beyond key areas, so we can't monitor you remotely."

The Dorms had little worth safeguarding and there were always more tempting expenses for dormers to vote for than cameras, but Aaxyl knew this was to intimidate her.

How had the Deal-Maker known?

Aaxyl trudged to her room, escorted by the two SecPros. The female SecPro entered before Aaxyl shut the door.

"Get out," Aaxyl snarled.

The SecPro looked awkward. "I'm sorry, but I can't. I'm supposed to follow you."

"This is a private room. You can't just enter it." She'd heard the occasional stories of SecPros barging in where they wished, but had never imagined she'd face it.

"It's a private *allocation*, but the Dorms are a public welfare building. You don't own the premises. You can't deny access."

"What does that even mean?" Aaxyl stood with her hands on her hips trying to stare her down. "The allocation is *private*."

She brushed past Aaxyl into the room, and sat on the empty spare bed. How appropriate for a bed added to accommodate one SecPro asshole to be used by another at their cost.

An extremely calm Aameh greeted her with a hug.

"Find Vidroh after dinner and contact Mohan," Aaxyl whispered in her ear.

Aameh smiled.

If Aameh wasn't lecturing and issuing strident demands over this injustice, it meant she was scheming. Mohan must have spoken to her.

They sat around the room awkwardly till the dinner bot came around. Aaxyl had already missed lunch and was ravenous. There was no food packet for the SecPro, Aaxyl noted with admittedly malicious pleasure.

AxAm usually ate at the table, with Aameh sitting on the spare bed and Aaxyl using the chair. With the SecPro encroaching the spare bed, they broke an AxAm rule, and ate dinner sitting on Aaxyl's bed. Aaxyl hoped she could smell the chicken fried rice they ate, while she scowled at her food paste.

"I'm moving to the coffin-dorms tomorrow," Aaxyl said. She'd given it some thought. She didn't want SecPros close to Aameh. While The Whisperer seemed to manipulate the SecPros, she didn't want them to discover Aameh's investigation, and Aameh wasn't the best at keeping anything secret and wouldn't care how anything she said might be interpreted.

They spoke briefly over dinner about insignificant things, mostly planning what Aaxyl would take to the coffin-dorms.

"I have a date with Vidroh. Will you be alright on your own?" Aameh said loudly. "I can stay back if you want."

"No, go." Aaxyl cleared the table, suppressing a snort at the idea of Aameh dating Vidroh. She barely liked Aaxyl liking him. "Have fun."

"Sleep well, okay?" Aameh hugged Aaxyl goodnight like she was leaving for a week. She really couldn't act.

Aaxyl almost teared up at the sudden role reversal.

AAMEH: EKTA DORMS

As Aameh walked away from the room, the SecPro posted outside their door followed. This was going to be irritating. She switched plans and headed for Leela's office on the first floor. She hid under the assistant's desk in the empty waiting area outside it, waiting for him to follow.

As he searched for her, Aameh hit the silent alarm under the assistant's desk. Urgent footsteps pattered to the waiting room in under a minute. The Dorm guards raised guns at the SecPro who tried to explain that a suspect was hiding in the area.

"What the hell is this?" The door framed Leela who stared down the SecPro like a wrathful goddess. Kant stood expressionless behind her, eyes panning the room. Leela never frequented the lower levels of the Dorm after working hours. This meant she *expected* something like this to happen. Aameh bit her cheek hard to avoid grinning.

"Aaxyl's roommate is hiding here." He reached under the desk for Aameh, only to yelp.

Kant had him on the floor with a knee on his back. The SecPro tapped his surrender and Kant returned to Leela, letting him stumble to his feet, arms raised.

Aameh emerged from under the desk, hands raised. "He followed me in the middle of the night. He scared me, so I hid here and rang the alarm."

Leela looked from Aameh to the SecPro, gesturing irritably for weapons and raised arms to lower. "Why didn't you alert Dorm security if you thought she acted suspiciously?"

The furious SecPro tried explaining. "I'm investigating her roommate and thought it best to follow her, since I was present."

"Is Aameh the subject of your investigation?"

"No. The investigation focuses on her roommate."

"So while you moonlight as Dorm security, Aaxyl's own door remains unguarded?"

Aameh asked to be excused, and Leela waved her off without even looking at her.

Aameh slipped past the SecPro and out of Leela's office and headed for the fourth floor. She found Vidroh in his coffin-dorm, and they went to a nearby manufacturing area to call Mohan.

"Are you in your room?" Mohan asked. "I can pick—"

Aameh interrupted him. "No! There's a SecPro there."

"Go to the clinic." Mohan disconnected.

They hurried down to the main floor. A few SociCred shops were open, mostly selling food items or other consumables. While not crowded, there were still plenty of people in the main lobby. The Dorms never really slept, unlike the Null Dorm, which never really woke. They walked through the mostly empty corridors to the clinic, turning right after paediatrics to... an unfamiliar room.

Mohan had teleported her to a cosy living room, like they showed in films. A huge media screen occupied a wall and bright red sofas surrounded a semi-circular table around a small, but ancient banyan tree sprawling across a miniature landscape. Bonsai, she believed it was called.

Aameh hugged Mohan fiercely. "Tell me Ax is going to be okay."

Mohan ran his fingers through his hair. "I talked to the Deal-Maker. You can trust him. Our bigger problem is that we don't want him to investigate the recapture of *Hersh*. He shouldn't know about *her*."

He looked pointedly at Aameh. She got it. No mentioning AricNova till she was found, but, "What Deal-Maker?"

"Aaxyl sent me this." Mohan's comm played an audio of Aaxyl talking to someone who warned her that the SecPros would investigate her.

"What should Ax do?"

"She should accept his help," Mohan said. "He'll get her out of there and isn't going to ask for her first-born. Do as he says."

One day too many secrets would pile up and avalanche into something nobody wanted. She struggled with small talk, let alone lying. But for Aaxyl, Aameh resolved to mind what she said to the Deal-Maker.

"You wanted to make us a part of your family. Can't you just teleport us out now?" Aameh asked.

"I'll do it in an emergency, but this should be resolved officially. If Aaxyl vanishes while under investigation, and shows up with us, it would violate the Global Agreement with us sabotaging local investigations."

Mohan returned Aameh to the Ekta Dorms, near Leela's office. Leela had already filed a complaint against the SecPro for stalking women in the Dorms and guards had escorted him to the gate. Kant dropped her to their room.

MOHAN: MOHAN'S HOME

Noir appeared next to Mohan's bed, and looked around the room, seeking him, "Are you insane? Why are you involving the Deal—"

"Don't use names!" Mohan spoke from where he was hunched at his desk.

Noir huffed.

Mohan kicked a chair toward Noir and waited till he sat. This need not be a volatile situation.

"*He* involved himself," Mohan said. "I'm trying to feed *him* enough information to stop *him* digging deeper."

"Why would he contact Aaxyl?"

Mohan shrugged a how-would-I-know at him. Symbiont affinities meant there could be a hundred reasons out of their control, not all of them accessible through human logic.

Noir's forehead furrowed. "Do you think... Dhrit? He worked with Saisrisel. AxAm helped save Dhrit, so he protects them."

"If so, once AxAm are safe, he should leave." Mohan really hoped so. The situation was complicated enough as it was.

"Do you need me to help?"

Noir sometimes hallucinated that he was a peaceful presence to add to situations.

Mohan wrapped his refusal in reasoning. "The more we cluster, the more curious he'll become. You manage Dhrit. AVANT is your domain."

"Why aren't you telling *him* you've got it under control?"

"I want to wait till Rudra and Elir go to Bombay, before saying anything that might have him asking more questions."

As the one least likely to lose control, it fell upon Mohan to keep the peace and everyone safe.

"Even I'm stressed by this level of compartmentalising." Noir sighed. "Aameh's seen her...sh. Fix this, and hope no stray telepathic pings attract his attention."

Mohan stood. "Please let us not discuss this."

Noir obliged. "What the hell are you doing getting into a relationship with a minor?"

Well, not that either. Mohan sat back down, tidying his desk to conceal his awkwardness. The difference in their ages bothered him and yet he hadn't wanted to refuse.

"It isn't like that."

"No? An innocent affectionate girl infatuated with you—"

"She's infatuated with you too."

"I live in the Superdome!"

"She's fine."

One side of Noir's mouth twitched in what could be a smile. Or not. It had ended before his eyes got involved. "I'm sure."

"You like her."

"Yes." Noir's expressionless eyes fixed on him turned that simple affirmation into a warning.

"I'm safe around people, Noir."

"For how long? You're in the middle of a crisis involving ancients. She doesn't heal. Is she safe standing next to you if *he* finds out?"

"I parent Rudra. What do you think?"

"I think you stand next to a fire and believe getting roasted is no big deal."

AAXYL: EKTA DORMS

As soon as the SecPros realised she was moving to the coffin-dorms, the two SecPros following her had grown to six and with bigger guns. She'd showed up to work at the clinic and four of them sat in the waiting room, while two came into the clinic with her.

Doriac took one look at them and motioned Aaxyl to come to his desk. "What have you got yourself into? Neutralisers?"

"Neutralisers?" Her training hadn't covered them. All Aaxyl had noticed were the big guns.

"Look at their arms." Doriac hinted with his eyes. "The neutraliser needs a charge pack, which goes on the back and the mount is fitted to the forearm."

Aaxyl listened to his descriptions of injuries he'd seen, while she scrutinised sleeves. One arm seemed thicker than the other. "Easy to know if they're right or left-handed."

"This isn't funny, Aaxyl. Neutralisers can damage nerves. They've been known to cause cognitive impairment. I don't want them around my clinic."

"What can I do?" Aaxyl threw her arms up. "They're following me everywhere. One spent the night in our room."

Doriac considered the SecPros and then Aaxyl. "Take a break from the clinic till this blows over."

And now Aaxyl had nothing to do with her day.

Aaxyl messaged Vidroh to look for her in the callisthenics gym. Aaxyl's frugal nature prevented her from spending SociCred on exercise, but this place was free, mostly because it served as a junkyard for large unused items.

She jogged a few laps around the gym and the SecPros followed close enough to keep her in sight. She spent a little excess energy leaping between various challenges, slowly traversing away from the SecPros as Vidroh entered the gym and walked to the other end. She signalled him to a high platform at the end of the room and waited for him to climb up using his good arm before swinging and jumping her way over to sit next to him, and pretending to rest.

"Why would SecPros bring neutralisers to a Dorm?" All Aaxyl knew was neuralisers miraculously appeared in the hands of SecPros fighting large crowds in films.

Vidroh stretched and twisted as he took a look at the SecPros approaching. "They're taking this very seriously."

"How bad?"

"Officially, neutralisers are non-lethal infrasonics that induce symbiont-jangled stupors and painful disorientation. Useful for disabling hostile crowds without fatalities."

"Unofficially?"

"They are... discouraged, and not to be used at close range. Most confrontations here are close range."

SecPros climbed up toward the platform. Vidroh jumped down.

An athlete landed on the next platform like a wingless dragonfly and pushed off into a twisting double flip, making it look easy. Aaxyl wished she'd put in the practice to get really good. She attempted the move, but left out the second flip for her own dignity, barely managing to land it. Too many eyes were on her to risk fumbling the landing. She gave Dragonfly her best sheepish look.

"Tuck your shoulder in more." Dragonfly jumped high and did a twisting flip in place. Easy.

Aaxyl flourished a salute at him, in appreciation of the tip, as she went over to Vidroh. "What happens if they use the neutralisers?"

"Nerve damage and brain injuries," he said, as the SecPros approached again.

This had turned a lot less funny.

Dormers stopped to stare at the SecPros as she returned to the coffin-dorm. Glares and muttered profanity became the norm.

Scharada's coffin-dorm was full, but Vidroh had arranged for her to get a bunk in his. And here Aaxyl stood, in the coffin-dorms she'd never planned to return to. The maze of four sided bunk racks reaching for the thirty-five foot high ceilings, now dotted with heads peeking at her.

As it became apparent that she'd be living there, people started jumping and climbing out of bunks, in solidarity, to welcome her, or to just gawk. The already narrow gaps between the racks became impossibly crowded. Aaxyl hefted her small bag of essentials and shouldered her way through, the crowd parting to make way for her.

A lump in her throat made talking impossible and she simply mouthed her thanks, nodding to ensure that her meaning was clear. Whether she lived in a room or coffin-dorm, the Dorms were her home, dormers her people.

"We know you haven't done anything wrong," a dormer murmured in passing.

On the other hand, idle coffin-dormers hostile towards SecPros made life in the coffin-dorm occasionally entertaining. The dormers closed ranks. They blundered into the path of SecPros trying to follow her and generally rolled out the unwelcome mat.

A smiling man let her have his place in the queue at the bathrooms. "SecPros think they can harass anyone."

To their credit, the SecPros assigned to her soon realised that she was little more than a dormer. One of them said as much as she returned to the bunk. "I'm sure this will get cleared up soon. There has to be some mistake."

A passing dormer overheard and advanced on the SecPro aggressively. "You make mistakes, we pay the price."

The SecPro repeated that they had orders and he was sure everything would be resolved soon.

The dormer pushed him back, only to find the SecPro's gun in his face.

Aaxyl dived for the floor, her mind full of neutraliser fears.

Other dormers pulled him away from the SecPro and he backed away, yelling profanity.

The SecPro put away the gun.

Aaxyl stood up, feeling foolish.

By the evening, more SecPros had been assigned to the areas near Aaxyl's coffin-dorm.

By night, a recording of a casual conversation between three SecPros, bewildered about why they were invading the Dorms, hit the news. While they spoke sarcastically, and actually in favour of Aaxyl's innocence, dormers started calling the SecPro presence an invasion.

Far from the comfortable spare bed in AxAm's room, the beds in the coffin-dorms were like shelves. Or as the SecPros had called them in disgust, *crawl space.*

Vidroh had maintained his distance from her since the gym. She imagined him bloating with information. He visited her bunk for dinner, whispering news over *tikka masala.* "Mohan has advised you to accept the Deal-Maker's offer, but not let him find out about the *Hersh* complication."

Aaxyl rubbed her forehead. Vidroh didn't know about the *Hersh* complication himself and probably thought this was about the symbiontist. "Okay."

"I talked to a few SecPros. The leads flagging you as a suspect came from the Octagon. They weren't able to trace it to an individual," Vidroh said. "But they can't dismiss you as a suspect till they get to the bottom of the matter."

Aaxyl raised worried eyes to Vidroh. "Damodar?" What did one do if the President of the dome posed a threat?

"He denied it, but whoever it is, SecPros can't risk dismissing it till they figure it out."

"Why aren't they arresting me then?" This had been puzzling Aaxyl. SecPros were hardly famous for dealing with dormers fairly. Lack of evidence wouldn't prevent them from taking her away for questioning.

"NeoJai confirmed you're his girlfriend," Vidroh said. "Arresting the girlfriend of the Admin's son isn't done either."

Aaxyl bit into a whole chilli, then hastily spat it out, mouth on fire.

To Aaxyl's relief, Vidroh reported Scharada was living in their room with Aameh till Aaxyl returned. And that Aameh wanted her permission to communicate with the Deal-Maker, since Aaxyl couldn't do it without attracting attention.

"She can scheme all she wants, but without leaving the room," Aaxyl said.

"I thought you didn't want to get her involved against UDAY?" Vidroh crumpled his empty dinner packet. "A governance provider is no small enemy to make."

That was a lifetime ago, when a dead Perfect Sam had turned up alive as Mohan, and Aameh hadn't been kidnapped. "They involved me. Now I want to dance on their grave."

"Don't let this change you, Ax. Revenge is never the answer."

"Are you re-gifting unused advice now?"

Vidroh laughed.

He had resumed being a good friend without missing a beat. The passionate man who'd bared his soul had vanished. Did he regret the sex? His sharing of his pain? She couldn't get a read on his emotions at all.

~~*~*

Aaxyl woke up on her first morning in the coffin-dorms to the claustrophobic view of the underside of the bunk above hers looming too close to stretch her arms comfortably.

As a coffin-dormer with no option to work her way out, Aaxyl's constant mental list of to-dos didn't so much as squeak. Aameh lived in the room safely, no work beckoned, nowhere to rush to. All she had to do was figure out what the hell was going on.

Aaxyl knew the Dorms. Nobody would let an investigation of one girl upend the fragile balance of life here for too long. Something had to give. She hoped it wouldn't be her.

Some dormers followed her to the media room, where ten large screens displayed news from around the dome. Dormers could queue up news they wanted to watch or transfer clips to their comms. To Aaxyl's surprise, there was a news report already about conflict between dormers and SecPros at Ekta Dorms. No mention of her though.

She strolled around the room behind the chairs facing the different screens.

By now, the neutralisers were recognised and generated hostility.

An unknown man leaned in as he walked past her. "They know you're innocent. Damodar's SecPros shared their story with the news. SYMBTech defeated the mercenaries SecPros had protected for a year."

She hadn't paid attention to the news since the *invading the Dorms* clip. The man found the clips and added them to the queue. More people gathered to watch as they played. The SecPros following her started looking uncomfortable.

There was no mention of AricNova, though one of them briefly mentioned Abrahamha asking about a high-value prisoner. SYMBTech had released a statement that their symbiontist was still missing and it was playing on the next screen.

The dorm rumours now nutshelled the situation with remarkable accuracy. Their secret conflict half-spilled into public view. She had lived in the Dorms all her life, but the population now seethed with unfamiliar undercurrents, awaiting a flashpoint.

By the afternoon, a few more altercations narrowly escaped escalation. A few dormers sustained minor injuries and the SecPros involved in the aggression were replaced. By the evening, a few dozen SecPros patrolled levels three to five as preventative measures.

The SecPros exercised restraint, fearing the sheer number of dormers they might have to contend with.

Vidroh had found a SecPro he trusted, a visiting Assistant Commander come to inspect the situation. He didn't know why Aaxyl was being investigated. The evidence that had looked compelling at first sight was misleading, and they no longer thought Aaxyl was guilty. Damodar himself had denied that he had authorised any action against Aaxyl and claimed that his security staff had revealed what they knew on his orders. However, Aaxyl was now the epicentre of a public safety crisis.

"You mean they can't withdraw without looking defeated," Aaxyl said bitterly. Her life had been hijacked for a face-saving exercise.

SecPros asserted their authority. Dormers pushed back.

Common areas now sported fresh graffiti demanding justice for Aaxyl and supporting her against UDAY's persecution. Aaxyl could only hope Aameh had stayed put in their room. New rumors suggested that a team of SecPros would take Aaxyl, Aameh, and Leela to the SecPro base for questioning late at night.

Leela, the only woman to attain the Director's role had won a landslide victory in Dorm elections when the previous Director transferred out. The dome and Dorms both voted real time as preferences that could be updated any time. It was an inalienable right, independent of comm quotas. Leela's approval had always been upwards of seventy percent, and now approached eighty. All three targets of the SecPro action in Ekta Dorms being women became the next outrage.

Dormers guarded the door of their room in groups to ensure that no one harmed Aameh. Aaxyl suspected Leela might have something to do with them knowing that Aameh was fragile. By the late evening, the lobby of Ekta Dorms hosted a terse standoff between dormers and SecPros.

Aaxyl was summoned into Leela's office. Assistant Commander Menhir and Administrator Dhrit were present along with the SecPro team leader who'd interviewed her.

"Ax, I need you to return to your room," Leela said.

Aaxyl scoffed. "No. I'm not having these guys around Am. You know that." The more things escalated with the SecPros, the less she wanted them around Aameh.

"It isn't really a request," Assistant Commander Menhir said. "If you refuse, they'll arrest you. We need to defuse the conflict in the Dorms for everyone's safety."

"Arrest me then. The only safety that concerns me, and is my legal responsibility, is Aameh." Aaxyl crossed her arms, and looked around the room indifferently, hoping no one called her bluff. "I'll go back to my room if the SecPros following me around aren't allowed to enter it."

Assistant Commander Menhir nodded. The SecPro leader looked like he wanted to object, but as one, Admin Dhrit, Leela and Assistant Commander Menhir turned *you-will-shut-up-now* eyes on him.

He persisted. "If she turns out to be guilty, we'll be accountable."

"Don't you get it?" Aaxyl bust out. "We saved his victims. You're supposed to capture him. He's now used you to keep us pinned down, wasting days of each other's time, while he finds a new place to hide our symbiontist. He had access enough to alter Null Dorms records. Surely you can see that he misled you?"

"Nobody said anything about Null Dorms records," the SecPro said, but Aaxyl saw doubts emerge on his face.

"I'll tell you what I know about the records, but I won't allow you into our room." She told him about the official backups made with NeoJai's authorisation, but left Aameh's name out of it. The records were the evidence.

"That sounds reasonable," Admin Dhrit said, looking at the newly established consensus around the room. "I'm sure nobody wants young women in the dorms feeling unsafe. Aaxyl, if you'd like your friend Vidroh to join you to feel safer, that could be permitted too."

Aaxyl accepted gratefully, but cringed a little. Any more favourable and the others would suspect he wasn't the real Admin Dhrit. The clone had met them at Mohan's and knew Aaxyl trusted Vidroh.

AAXYL: AxAm's ROOM

AxAm and Vidroh met over dinner in AxAm's room. Scharada had been keeping Aameh company, but returned to her coffin-dorm when Aaxyl and Vidroh arrived, preferring not to get into any trouble that could jeopardise her asylum.

The Deal-Maker's cranky voice issued from his comm without preamble. "So you've agreed to accept my offer."

"SYMBs! Can't you check first before speaking?" Aaxyl asked. They'd been surrounded by SecPros for ages. "What if SecPros were around?"

"Are they?" The arrogance of that voice was unbelievable. The comm must have been spying on them. Luckily, Aaxyl had been too busy with her own problems to mention *Hersh*.

"No," Aaxyl admitted. "What's the deal? What will I have to do?"

"I'll make a request for a favour at a later date."

"Not my first-born," Aaxyl joked. Nobody laughed. "Okay. What now?"

"Change in plans. The Saisrisels are still in danger. Vidroh and Aaxyl, you're hired as bodyguards for Dhrit and NeoJai—a romantic relationship can cover for your presence in their home, as NeoJai's girlfriend moving in with him. Aameh will go to SYMBTech under the pretext of an internship."

Aameh let out a squeal of excitement, and Aaxyl hoped the SecPros outside wouldn't pop in to investigate.

Vidroh made a downward gesture with his hand, reminding them to keep voices low.

Aaxyl wasn't so sure about their separation, but couldn't think of a better option. If NeoJai was in danger, she wanted to protect him, but she didn't want Aameh around danger ever again.

Was it weird that on hearing this bizarre proclamation, the only feeling Aaxyl had was hope that she'd meet NeoJai again?

"About that," she said. " NeoJai isn't going to agree to this. We—"

The Deal-Maker interrupted her. "He agreed. He'll do anything to keep his family safe. Including welcoming you into his home."

Aameh made a sympathetic face. "The *anything* does sound like NeoJai."

Aaxyl slumped. How flattering. Just the welcome she wanted. Her eagerness to see NeoJai again felt confusing, like love. Or guilt.

"Why not hire bodyguards?" Vidroh asked.

"They never had SecPros inside the home because of the clones, and Nyaya now refuses to trust SecPros, even though there's only one of them at home currently. You served as a SecPro. Aaxyl trained to be one. This answers both needs. It removes Aaxyl from the Dorms and it provides us with capable people inside the Saisrisel home."

Aaxyl doubted it would be all that simple after the past few days, but she put her trust in Mohan's advice to accept the offer. This also put Aameh onto a solid learning track. Aaxyl would grab the opportunity with both hands, if not for... "What about Am's security?"

"If anyone breaches the SYMBTech building, Aameh will be the least of our worries."

Not for Aaxyl, it wouldn't be. She'd burn SYMBTech to the ground before she let harm come to Aameh. Aaxyl had walked right into the building with their goofy remote receptionist offering her snacks. "I'd prefer someone to be present. Aameh has lived among people in the Dorms all her life. I was supposed to be there with her."

"Until your situation with SecPros is completely resolved, you won't be able to come to SYMBTech. As a global organisation, SYMBTech can't undermine local governments. This includes not protecting suspects on diplomatic ground."

"About that, SecPros have asked me to not leave Ekta Dorms at all. How will we get out of here?" asked Aaxyl.

"Legally. I'll send a lawyer to challenge the SecPro actions," the Deal-Maker said.

"Who *are* you?" Aaxyl asked again. "How do we pay for a lawyer?"

"Leave that to me. Your task begins when you're out of here."

Aaxyl succumbed to the seemingly inevitable. "Okay, as long as Aameh isn't living in a building anyone can walk into."

"Mohan will stay with her till this resolves. Have your useless questions concluded?"

"Don't you need to check with Mohan?"

"I'm busy."

AAMEH: MOHAN'S HOME

Mohan had insisted that Vidroh escort Aameh to the clinic. One SecPro followed them. Aameh supposed that couldn't be helped. They went down the stairs and through the main lobby. Just before the turn at paediatrics, Aameh turned to thank Vidroh, and they split. She went around the corner alone, grinning. By the time the SecPro came past Vidroh, she'd have vanished.

Aameh hugged Mohan as soon as he teleported her to his home. "I'm worried about Aaxyl."

"That's what I'm here for." A nondescript man in a white shirt and black trousers drew her attention. About as tall as Aameh, he was slightly short of average height for a man.

Mohan turned to introduce them. "This is Legal. Yes, that's der name. Dey'll be representing Aaxyl and challenging the restrictions placed by the SecPros before a Judicial SIS."

Aameh noted the neutral pronoun. The use was uncommon in modern times and largely limited to transhumanists to denote significant deviations from humans and implied humans with unspecified identity. "You're the lawyer? Why the neutral pronouns?" He didn't look any different from a normal man.

"I am a registered psychopath and required to disclose this to clients. I'm male, as you can see, but the neutral pronoun reminds clients that I'm different." He almost seemed to take pleasure in being known to have a psychological disorder.

While psychopathy no longer carried the stigma of criminality and was too prevalent to marginalise, any diagnosis that could result in adverse consequences for others required registration and disclosure. They also came under greater scrutiny. Aameh didn't know much about them, but they were infamous for manipulating people and cruel behaviour.

Legal turned to Mohan. "I'll need the room."

Mohan walked out.

Aameh frowned. "Why would I allow a psychopath to represent Ax?"

"Because I'm good." Legal took off der glasses and met her eyes.

Aameh scrambled to remember what she knew of psychopaths. She was pretty sure she couldn't trust that seemingly honest gaze. "Tell me about yourself."

"My name is Legal. I am a lawyer. I am a registered psychopath under the legal guardianship of Abrahamha's Strays."

"Guardianship of an adult lawyer? Why?"

"I endangered my son. Such behaviour shouldn't exist if humanity is to survive. Monitoring reduces harm." Legal's words implied regret, but sounded rehearsed.

Aameh had finally found someone more weird than herself.

"Wait. Unpack that. You have a son?"

Legal's tone hadn't changed in the slightest since she'd arrived. Dey could be discussing the news. "Yes. Also a wife. They left me."

"What did you do?"

"I secretly met people in the wastelands for reasons I can't tell you. I took my son on picnics as a cover. A person I planned to meet was captured and compromised the meeting point." Legal delivered the highlights of taking der son into an ambush, while dey opened two briefcases.

"He was with you?" Aameh wanted to put her hand on ders. Not to offer sympathy, but to still der hands so that it didn't sound like trivial chatter as dey worked.

Legal continued. "We were surrounded. I told my son to pretend he had lost his way. I would use the distraction to escape. SecPros would bring him back to the dome."

"Did they?" Aameh couldn't believe the man. Aaxyl hadn't let her go to the Null Dorms on her own at twenty and she wasn't even really old enough to be Aameh's parent.

Legal pulled out a judicial terminal, like in the films, and set it up while she suffocated in der story.

"I miscalculated. They saw movement and believed they were shooting a rogue in the chest—nothing a little HealSYMB won't fix after capture. Instead, they hit his head."

A service bot approached with a box of tissues and Aameh realised she had tears running down her face. "They killed him," she whispered.

Legal started authenticating demself on the system. "He was alive. They rushed him to the hospital. The plan worked. I escaped, and my son lived, but my wife sold our home, and moved to Bombay with him to get away from me. I wanted unimon and luxury and fame. Life as a single man rejected by his family and hated by ex-allies held no appeal. I didn't want the headache of operating outside the law. This wasn't working. I decided to kill myself."

Psychologists believed that psychopaths had faint emotions, and could even be depressed. "But you changed your mind?"

"Noir helped me find alternative goals. He offered monitoring if I used my skills to help others. They appreciate it, and I manage my need for power by winning in court. I'm atoning."

Aameh was pretty sure atoning didn't work like that, but he sounded upfront. Mohan wouldn't have introduced them unless she could trust him.

Legal turned the terminal toward her to record her identification.

Aameh had forgotten all about Aaxyl's case, which was saying something.

"I trust you," she said.

"You shouldn't. You should let me handle the case."

AAXYL: AxAm's room

Aaxyl could get used to waking up with Vidroh's finger tracing her features. She remained under room arrest, she supposed, so her best idea for the day involved snuggling with Vidroh. The only thing better would be if NeoJai joined them, but the bed was too small for that anyway. They never were a couple, but his absence hurt.

"You do realise we haven't talked about this. Us." Vidroh rested his chin on her head. "Neither of us are the type to talk about feelings. I envy NeoJai's ability to speak his heart."

"NeoJai manages to speak his truth." Aaxyl admired that. He wasn't flashy or bold, but he said what he meant. "I've lost him, haven't I?"

"He isn't emotionally stunted like us. Sooner or later, he's going to figure out that you were being an ass, and find a way above it. I'm hoping he chooses to forgive you because I need him to tell us that we love each other, or we're going to get into morose discussions about him being missing."

Aaxyl laughed. It was true. She never could figure out how to start one of those. Love was a bit too far, but she definitely liked Vidroh. If she said anything now, it would sound like she said it because Vidroh prompted her.

Aaxyl snuggled into him. "Do you think we're doing the right thing trusting these people?"

"I don't see that you have a choice," Vidroh rested his chin on her head. "They're global heroes. It's just..."

Aaxyl leaned back so she could see his face. "Just what?"

"They operate on a different plane. Their understanding of situations, what they consider a problem or solution... it's different from us. Can a teleporter truly understand vulnerability? They are idealists. Their precious global peace matters to them, but there is no peace in human nature."

"So they didn't support you?" Aaxyl asked.

"They support in their own way." Vidroh sighed. "They wanted Srayoshi to stop supporting the settlers and ask them to move to safety until they could find a better solution."

Aaxyl hated to admit it, but... "That does make sense."

"No, it doesn't," Vidroh shot back. "Srayoshi wasn't making them stay. They were fighting for their home."

Which reminded her... "Where's Aameh?"

"She left about an hour ago, to meet the lawyer."

Aaxyl dropped her head back onto his shoulder. There wasn't much she could do about any of this. "Why did you wake me up then?"

"Your lawyer is challenging the SecPros. You have a hearing in the auditorium in half an hour."

Aaxyl scrambled out of bed.

❖

AAXYL: EKTA DORMS AUDITORIUM

Aaxyl and Vidroh walked into the smaller auditorium on the top floor. Dormers sat in the audience, filling it to capacity. She'd always thought legal hearings were poorly attended, but the recent conflict must have motivated the audience.

On the stage, Assistant Commander Menhir sat at one end of a semi-circular table, along with two strangers. On the other end, Aameh sat a seat away from a lawyer who was presumably Legal. Leela sat at the centre, with Admin Dhrit's clone by her side.

Seniority suggested that Admin Dhrit should preside, but Aaxyl didn't know a lot about legal proceedings. The clone gestured Aaxyl toward Aameh with a friendly wave and nod. Admin Dhrit never acted this casual with dormers.

Aameh introduced her to Legal.

Vidroh headed for the audience section, but Legal gestured him to sit on the stage with them, next to Aameh.

Dey was rather ordinary to look at and seemed perfectly untroubled by her scrutiny as dey read something on a slate display. Dey wore reading glasses.

Aaxyl wondered if the glasses were real or for effect.

Der profile displayed in front of dem said dey represented SYMBTech, AVANT, Abrahamha, Noir, Mohan—a long list of names she didn't recognise—and her. Her own profile had five words: *Aaxyl AxAm, junior paramedic (apprentice).*

Aaxyl knew that she wasn't on trial, but challenging the SecPro actions against her. She hoped Aameh knew what the hell she was doing.

"What am I supposed to do?" Aaxyl whispered to dem.

"Leave it to me. You'll be told if you have to do anything." Dey pushed a pencil and paper toward her. "Don't talk unless addressed once the Judicial SIS takes over. It would be improper."

The lawyer sitting opposite to Legal wore a SecPro uniform. He looked intimidating. The other man with him also turned out to be a lawyer, representing UDAY.

The three lawyers busied themselves filing documents into the formats provided by the judicial SIS. It had an official acronym, JUSIS, but nobody called it that aloud.

NeoJai walked onto the stage and took a seat next to Admin Dhrit. He looked gorgeous with his flawless skin and dignified appearance. He put his elbows on his desk, interlocked his fingers and kept his eyes on them.

A bell rang and JUSIS assumed command over proceedings, taking over the terminals, media displays, audio and video devices from the Ekta Dorms SIS. Automated instructions commenced, ordering all parties to maintain silence, and only speak when requested to do so. Reminders flashed over screens to disable any audio outputs or notifications.

The hearing began.

JUSIS asked Aaxyl to verify that she was who Legal said she was and that Legal represented her.

"I'm Aaxyl AxAm." Her nervous words echoed in her own ears. "Legal is my lawyer."

Everyone proceeded to ignore her again as various people introduced themselves and lawyers read documents.

Ever since JUSIS commenced operation, the average duration of lengthy court cases had been brought down from months to hours. Minor cases were resolved in minutes.

Aaxyl hoped this meant she would be free at the end of this farce.

Legal's confident posture betrayed no doubt.

Aaxyl expected the hearing to proceed as depicted in the media. Admin Dhrit, NeoJai and Aameh would testify to her innocence. Aaxyl had mentally rehearsed what she would say. None of that happened.

Legal stood up to speak and the audience quieted. "We meet today in an elaborate waste of time, because SecPros of this dome consider themselves above the law."

Aaxyl winced as she looked between Vidroh and Assistant Commander Menhir sitting opposite each other. Menhir had been good to them and Vidroh looked up to him. Awkward. Neither seemed particularly troubled, and she relaxed a little.

Legal challenged the restrictions against her and demanded a show of evidence. The SecPros had nothing conclusive beyond proving that she was present in the Null Dorms. She was accused of collaborating with SYMBTech personnel who had attacked SecPros. While they had diplomatic immunity, she didn't.

"My client had raised the kidnapping victim, Aameh, from a young age and adopted her legally," Legal said. "Allying with resourceful entities on a shared goal was logical. She didn't attack anybody. Besides, with SecPros guarding the guilty party, they can hardly point fingers."

The other lawyer objected. "The SecPros are not on trial for the kidnapping."

"Being unable to rely on SecPros is the context of my client's actions," Legal countered.

"She was present during the illegal interrogation of the SecPros, by representatives of SYMBTech," the SecPro lawyer shot back.

A few voices in the audience jeered at the SecPro lawyer.

"Thank you for admitting that she had not committed any crime herself," Legal said simply.

Dormers broke into applause and JUSIS called for silence.

Legal said, "Under the circumstances, the action against Aaxyl was malicious and motivated. If you have evidence of guilt, arrest her. Her rights can't be extra-judicially curtailed."

The audience rumbled in agreement.

Legal continued. "A SecPro stalked dormer Aameh, a *victim* of the crime they were supposedly investigating. She had to hide in the Director's offices and trigger an alarm for her safety." Dey cited other instances of hostility and physical altercations between the dormers and SecPros.

"The arbitrary and malicious actions of the SecPros pose a public danger," Legal concluded.

The audience erupted into a standing ovation, drowning out the SecPro lawyer's voice, even with the amplification. They had to wait for quiet.

"With due respect, the judicial SIS can't interfere with investigations. Investigation requires suspicion, not evidence. Dorms are public buildings and Aaxyl, a recipient of state-provided welfare, can stay in them, but not prevent the presence of others, including SecPros," The SecPro lawyer pointed out.

Aaxyl wanted to strangle him. He was talking of their room! Agitated, she reached for the paper Legal had provided, but dey put der hand on hers and nodded reassuringly.

"To quote the old world author Anatole France: *The law, in its majestic equality, forbids rich and poor alike to sleep under bridges, to beg in the streets, and to steal bread.*" Legal was now performing for an enthusiastic audience of dormers. "Can SecPros enter the state provided residences of the Dorm management? If not, how does the law permit them to enter the bedroom of two women, with impunity?"

The audience erupted in claps and whistles. Chants of "SecPros, go back!" continued for a while despite JUSIS calling for silence till a loud metallic screech quieted everyone. JUSIS had its tricks.

Aaxyl marvelled at the power Legal wielded. On her own, Aaxyl had been crushed without a second thought. Dormers had to fight back at considerable risk and faced weapons. Legal's presence forced SecPros to scramble to explain themselves. Perhaps she could train to be a lawyer.

"Investigation can't invade a suspect's life around the clock," Legal said. "My client was forced to endure discomfort in the coffin-dorms to safeguard her sister. SecPro intimidation cost her a job. And now she has no alternative but to leave her lifelong home in the Dorms to move into the residence of NeoJai Saisrisel."

The audience erupted in boos and cheers.

"This is a graceful resolution to the conflict created by SecPro presence in the Dorms. If this is not acceptable, I will prosecute for maximum compensation and damages."

Dey left it unsaid that a warrant to enter the home of the Administrator of the Dorms would not be issued on such flimsy evidence. For all intents and purposes, this ended their farce of an investigation.

At this point, NeoJai confirmed his identity. "I'm NeoJai Saisrisel. I'm in love with Aaxyl and aware that Vidroh is her partner. I've invited them both to live with me. I accept responsibility for their expenses till they can provide for themselves."

Admin Dhrit's clone endorsed his statement as the owner of the residence.

Assistant Commander Menhir slid a piece of paper toward the SecPro lawyer.

Aaxyl barely heard anything over the thundering of her heart after NeoJai said he loved her. It didn't matter anyway, because Legal did all the speaking for her. She could barely wait to ask NeoJai herself.

NeoJai hadn't met her eyes.

The lawyer for the SecPros was no fool. They agreed to close the investigation if Aaxyl withdrew her case against them.

They were done. JUSIS recorded the compromise and disconnected.

New beginnings

Early bone matrix mods from Renew Pharma to allow pathbreaking cosmetic surgeries for reversible partial shape shifting. Wolf faces and wings among earliest designs released. Medicine Frontier, Friday, November 28, 2442

~~*~*~*

AAXYL: SEXEL

NeoJai slouched in his seat, crossed his arms over his head and pretended to sleep as soon as they got into his car. Vidroh got busy with watching the city pass by.

Aaxyl's heart, still stuck on NeoJai's declaration of love was sorting through ways to ask him, when the car stopped at Sexel. "Did you mean what you said?" Aaxyl wrestled down hope.

"No. That was before."

Aaxyl withered with humiliation. Why were they at the Sexel then?

Vidroh got out of the car.

NeoJai mumbled that Mohan called for the meeting as he followed. Of course. Why else would she be at a Sexel with two men she was interested in?

The lobby on the ground floor was festive compared with the understated elegance of the top floor with vibrant colours and boisterous crowds. They went to book a room and discovered a gift booking of a private dinner in the honeymoon suite with compliments from Mohan for the romantic trio.

Mohan teleported just inside the door and walked over.

"First things first. Aameh's packing and will let me know when she's ready to be picked up. We'll be going to SYMBTech from here."

He put two guns on the table for Vidroh and Aaxyl for their new responsibility as bodyguards and vanished to get Aameh. Aaxyl tested one.

Beautifully balanced, smooth action. Smaller than the ones she trained with for her SecPro trials, it nested comfortably in her hand. Niiice.

Vidroh took the other and clipped it onto his belt without comment.

Mohan returned with Aameh. "Things were moving fast with Dhrit the last time we met, and we didn't get the time to meet after that. The results of your symbiont analysis are back. Both of you host a wide range of symbionts. They are definitely not common profiles."

"What do you mean?" Aaxyl asked. "We can teleport?"

"No, analysis won't change what you can do, since they don't work, but it confirms that you also have symbionts that can suppress them. While this doesn't help you, they may suppress the alien symbionts in Dhrit. With your consent, we'd like to experiment with your symbionts to suppress his. The transfusions are only working enough to buy him time, but he's still losing and he can't be brought to consciousness while his teleportation is active."

Aameh asked, "What do you need us to do?"

"We need a blood sample." Mohan took out a tube for collection.

Both Aameh and Aaxyl offered their arms.

"Take more if you need, if it helps," Aameh said.

"We would also like your permission to conduct research into other uses of your symbionts." Mohan smiled at her eagerness. "If effective, you'll be compensated for any commercial uses that may emerge."

"I trust you," Aameh said immediately.

Mohan shook his head wryly. "Friendship apart, you should look out for your interest in negotiations."

Aameh wasn't the type to care. "We can work our way to whatever we need. Your help when we needed it is too precious to bargain with. You're too rich to need to cheat me anyway."

"I'll set up an account for you and transfer a thousand unimon for providing us with your symbionts for research. We can negotiate the rest later."

Aameh might not care about unimon, but Aaxyl did. After all their rules, they were out of the Dorm without any unimon and at the financial mercy of men they were attracted to. A thousand unimon changed everything. It was enough to meet their needs for a month if they were careful.

"Good I didn't negotiate. I wouldn't expect more than a hundred unimon. You should pay it to Ax. She's my legal guardian."

"AmSYMB," Aaxyl joked over a wave of emotion. "I knew you were a profitable investment. After all these years of getting symbionts from the clinic, Am will be stocking clinics if it goes well."

Aaxyl gave Mohan a huge thumping hug. NeoJai hugged Aameh. Vidroh planted a kiss on Aaxyl. Aameh put an arm around Mohan's waist and leaned into his side. AxAm's struggle to rise above their circumstances was no secret here.

"I missed the best bit, Aameh." Mohan raised a hand for quiet, as he gazed down at her. "AVANT and SYMBTech are the family business with centuries of *information*. Just wait till you qualify for research access."

Aameh's face was like he went down on one knee and offered a ring, like in films.

Aaxyl broke into sobs as she laughed wildly.

"You okay?" Vidroh put an arm around her in a half-hug.

Aaxyl covered her mouth, barely daring to speak. When she did, amazement rang through her voice. "We did it! All those years, struggling to manage. We did it. We survived!"

~~*~*~*

AAXYL: SAISRISEL RESIDENCE

They reached the Saisrisel residence in time for a second dinner. The home was like something from historic immersives. Stone construction. Red tiles on the roof. Aameh would have known their name. The imposing three storey structure sat a few hundred metres inside the gate.

"That must have taken a lot of effort to recreate," Aaxyl murmured to Vidroh, intimidated. "I doubt these materials are easy to get."

NeoJai stiffened. "It's a registered heritage building. It predates the Enduring War."

Aaxyl's eyes widened. She wasn't the sort to know what to do around expensive stuff, let alone living inside historic monuments.

There was a heavy SecPro presence outside. As they entered, NeoJai thanked both of them for helping to keep his family safe. Polite, formal, impersonal.

The inside was huge. Tasteful antiques and art provided accents. Handcrafted wooden furniture spoke of simpler times and wealthy origins simultaneously.

Aaxyl suspected much of it would be registered as antiques as well. She was a fish out of water.

At the same time, this was also a child's home. Bright child sized furniture and toys held their own unabashedly.

NeoJai led them to a masculine bedroom in a minimalist design on the first floor. A book shelf stood next to a wooden desk and a wardrobe with a glass door displayed a tidy array of formal clothes. Photograph prints on white walls and a bed. They went in and put down their bags.

"It was Dad's," NeoJai said.

She was in the bedroom of the Administrator of the Dorms? Surreal. It also felt wrong. She met NeoJai's angry gaze. This was the man she had misjudged. A whole new level of awkward.

Vidroh put a comforting arm around Aaxyl.

"Indeed it *is* your dad's. Present tense," a feminine voice said from the door. "Aaxyl, Vidroh, please come with me. I'm Nyaya, NeoJai's mother. I readied another room for you. In my son's desire to score petty points, he ignored that his mother may not wish to see his father's room reallocated to guests when she returned from the hospital where he fights for his life." She skewered NeoJai with her gaze.

NeoJai gasped. "I'm sorry."

Aaxyl had seen her from the audience at Dorm events, but up close, Nyaya looked stunning as only older people with sheltered lives could. Flawless skin, freed of the slightest deformity had a soft radiance seen only in children, and perhaps Mohan. Her voice was like honey and every movement was graceful. Suddenly NeoJai's delicate features made perfect sense, like a piece of a puzzle sliding into place.

They trailed her meekly to their new room on the ground floor, with a beautiful, but generic decor in warm tones. The huge bed caught Aaxyl's eye. One bed. This woman, they were meeting for the first time already knew about them.

Neither Vidroh nor Aaxyl had too many belongings. They tidied and showed up for dinner in record time, led by their noses to the aromas wafting from the dining room.

Dinner was... interesting. Nyaya and Admin Dhrit's clone sat next to each other with NeoJai and a wide-eyed little girl flanking them as they waited for their guests to take seats. Aaxyl remembered Admin Dhrit's codename. The girl was Reva. She was Nyaya in miniature. In a few decades, they'd be passing for twins.

Admin Dhrit's clone, with his creased and weathered face like a wastelander was the odd one out in this family of soft-skins. He was handsome in his own way. Time and symbionts had rendered a permanent sun burn. For people in the dome with nondescript skin, the weathered look of those who'd lived outside domes suggested a history, an unusual character. She wondered if the clone had spent any time outside the dome.

Everybody sat at a single table, not unlike a coffin-dorm, but they all started at the same time, rather than drift in, eat and leave when they were done. Nothing was in packets.

Aaxyl had never eaten food like this. Everything was delicious. Even the rice, which was very long, like fragrant mini-noodles and came with different dishes to eat with it. There were disks of a crispy vegetable dish, several curries, pickles, cottage cheese in a buttery gravy, dips... Aaxyl lost count. Reva chose only pieces of chicken, while the clone of Admin Dhrit tried to persuade her to have a little of everything.

Aaxyl and Vidroh didn't bother with conversation and ate their way through their plates like their lives depended on it, attracting curious gazes at their enthusiasm. Aaxyl led with her grin. "The food is amazing." Truth. Vidroh nodded his agreement.

"Vastly better than Dorms, if Aameh's thank you notes are to be believed." Nyaya gestured at Aameh's sketches gracing the walls. "I understand she's a close friend of yours. NeoJai says she's your sister, but you adopted her?"

"It's easier to call ourselves sisters. I'm just eight years older. Legally, I suppose I'm a parent. We just call each other by our names." Aaxyl smiled at Nyaya, and noticed Reva smile at her shyly. Aaxyl remembered Aameh at her age. She could argue others to exhaustion.

"Were you dormers from the start?"

"Vidroh lived independently until recently." Aaxyl gestured at him with a spoon. "I was raised there. First night outside officially. My mother visited a few times when I was very young, but I don't remember living outside a dorm."

"Wow. That's tough." Nyaya 's voice was soft. "She abandoned you."

"She never had me to abandon me. Tough is when your mother is a breeder. They keep the infants for a year or two, because breastfeeding is recommended. The toddler-dorm has a lot of crying kids. Food change. No mother. Poor kids."

"A breeder. How does that work?" Nyaya asked.

"Reproduction is important for the species, but between low fertility and low willingness of women to risk pregnancy, it takes incentives. Pregnant women and new mothers receive better food and live in rooms at a minimum - no coffin-dorms for them. Breeders is Dorm slang for women who get pregnant for better facilities, so they're frequently pregnant." Aaxyl laughed at Nyaya's face caught between bemusement and disgust.

"You seem familiar with them."

"I spent a lot of time in the toddler-dorms because of Aameh, and our early rooms were shared with breeders, since Leela didn't want to put minors in general adult rooms." Aaxyl smiled wryly. "They work out cheaper than technology and less controversial than state use of biological materials. Everyone gets what they want. Admin Dhrit could probably explain it better." She wasn't sure how to address the clone without offending NeoJai.

"Please call me Dhrit or Dhrit-H," the clone urged. "You know I'm not Admin Dhrit."

"Indulge my curiosity," Nyaya said. "It's rare for me to engage with my husband's other family. What about the rights of these children he's responsible for?"

"Other family?" Aaxyl contemplated it for a bit. "Most of us never meet him. There are lakhs of people in Dorms. He's administrator for everything. Not a parent."

"So who raised you?" Nyaya asked.

"The system." Aaxyl thought it would be obvious. "We grow in age-appropriate dorms. Dormers work to raise us like any other job for SociCred and are selected for aptitude. It's not like in films, we weren't abused. Relationships are transient though."

"Transient in what way?"

"People shuffle around quite a bit. Dorms accommodate us close to our work when possible, so taking on a new job can mean a new accommodation. It's efficient, but you lose touch with people." Aaxyl shovelled in some food before the next question hit.

"Don't you resent it?"

"Why would I?" Aaxyl asked, surprised. "The welfare system provides us with a bare minimum, till we can earn for ourselves. Am and I would be lost without it."

"Raising Aameh should have been their job, not yours," Nyaya insisted. "You could have spent SociCred on professional training, instead of working in sanitation to raise a child and having to train while working."

It was hard explaining the Dorms. "The system works for most. But it is efficient because of the numbers. Making exceptions for outliers is complicated. We'd have been fine if Am were normal. We still did fine. There are good people like Leela and Hersh." Her voice gave up after Hersh's name. She hoped no one noticed.

"You never wished to stay with your mother?"

"An adult who won't move to a better job." Aaxyl laughed, overbright. "We go through a curious phase, I guess. My mother visited rarely and my friends lived in the Dorms so I didn't really miss her. Director Leela worked in Aameh's toddler-dorm. She cared for us quite a bit. She did leave the toddler-dorm, but so did we."

"And your father?" Nyaya asked.

Aaxyl shrugged. The questions got less and less relevant. "No clue." She frowned as she tried to remember. "I don't know any fathers. Hersh perhaps. He employed me when I needed it." Her voice caught again.

She paused, as others stared at her, before realising what she'd just said. "Other than Administrator Dhrit, of course. He's NeoJai and Reva's father," she stammered, embarrassed. "And Dhrit-H." She needed to shut up.

NeoJai shoved his chair back abruptly and rushed out of the room. Dhrit-H left after him. Fantastic. He was already furious with her for suspecting his father to be a criminal and dehumanising him as 'it' and now she had forgotten he had a father altogether while he sat in front of her. Great. She wanted to mend her relationship with him. Instead, she was smashing it to smaller bits.

NeoJai

"You okay, son?" Dhrit-H peeped into NeoJai's room where NeoJai had flung himself on the bed.

"Yes." NeoJai sniffed. "She's hardly ignorant about the Dorms. Admin Dhrit asks her opinion on everything. She did it on purpose."

"Nyaya?" Dhrit stepped in and shut the door. "She usually does. Your mother is a smart woman. What did she do?"

"Made me feel bad for Aaxyl."

"Aaxyl doesn't need your pity, NeoJai. She's a fantastic person."

"It also doesn't change what happened between us. She's not a fantastic person with me."

"All she knows of fathers is they don't owe their kids anything. Why would she trust Admin was a good person just because he's your father? It meant nothing to her."

"She mistrusted me!"

"That's true. She may have realised it, I think."

VIDROH

Aaxyl's candid denial haunted Vidroh still, as he entered their room. Aaxyl was from the Dorms, but the implications had eluded him. He understood her fierce attachment with Aameh much better now.

The good news was, if NeoJai felt such pain on her behalf, Aaxyl hadn't lost him.

Aaxyl sat on the bed and his mind flushed clean of everything but the curve of her neck, as the bedside lamp caressed it. And then her jaw, silhouetted as she caught his scrutiny and turned. Then she was in his arms. He couldn't go a minute longer without making love. And so they did.

She loved like she lived. With raw honesty and generosity. Vidroh lost himself in her once more.

"This is the best moment of my life." Vidroh told her later as he held her close.

"Mmm." Aaxyl stretched. "I just wish—"

"NeoJai loves you. It's going to be okay."

"Didn't you need NeoJai to tell us we love each other?" Aaxyl slanted a smile at him.

"The other way around is needed too." Vidroh laughed. He held her close as he drifted off to sleep, savouring the peace seeping into him from her. He had no idea how he could bear to part with her when it was time to leave.

AAXYL

Aaxyl, unaccustomed to sleeping with a sexual partner, slipped out of the bedroom.

"NeoJai advised against trusting you." Dhrit-H was near the window in the dim living room.

Aaxyl considered and discarded several responses. "Couldn't sleep?"

"I haven't slept well since Admin Dhrit's zeplyn returned bloody. I sit here to avoid disturbing Nyaya. She finds it hard too."

"I came to avoid disturbing Vidroh." She sat opposite to him.

"Don't hurt my son." Dhrit-H came straight to the point.

"It is complicated," she admitted. "We liked each other. I still do, but I made a horrendous mistake. You know him. What should I do?"

"Talk to him," Dhrit told her.

She understood that. What she lacked was insight on what to say and he didn't want to talk to her. On the other hand, this was her opportunity to understand Dhrit and the clones, if she didn't want to alienate NeoJai with more ignorance.

"What's it like?" She changed the subject. "To be a clone, I mean. To live another man's life."

"I don't live another man's life. I live my life with the family I love."

"You access all his memories." Aaxyl understood. "You love NeoJai as your own."

"I retain all *my* memories. NeoJai *is* my son." Dhrit corrected her.

"I didn't mean to offend." Aaxyl reassured him. "I'm just curious about NeoJai's biological father."

"I'm not offended." Dhrit smiled with amusement. "I'm NeoJai's biological father."

"Oh. So Admin Dhrit..."

"Is NeoJai's biological father." Dhrit completed on cue. He bestowed mercy on her and the corner she'd talked herself into. "And so is the one in the Superdome. The cloning occurred after NeoJai's birth, so we all held NeoJai as a newborn and so on. Identical memories. We were one person."

"But you're more people now. How?"

"I can't tell you."

"And Nyaya is okay with this?"

"It wasn't easy, but she loved me, she loves us. She certainly seems okay now, given that I fathered Reva." Dhrit laughed.

"The others didn't mind?"

"Wow. That's a complex question. It's hard for me to speak for them, given that I spend the most time with her. But they love Reva. And we all understand that this is a complicated situation."

"Are you linked? Sense each other's thoughts, feelings?"

"No."

"So you're separate people now?"

"Yes and no. We're separate, but we're identical too. Over two centuries of our life exists as the same person. We share the same memories, habits, ethics, same reactions to different situations, like the same kind of people... but change slightly over time."

"So it allows you to pass as each other." Aaxyl remembered Dhrit-H as

Admin Dhrit in the Dorm.

"We don't normally pretend to be each other. But I guess we can, in a pinch. We are the same man to a great extent. But day-to-day experiences matter. Without being cloned, are you the same person you were ten years ago?"

"What is different? Harder to imitate about each other?"

"Experiences we don't share," Dhrit replied immediately. "I find it harder to enforce discipline. Admin Dhrit wields authority over a large number of people. He finds it harder to be patient. Dhrit-SD lives alone and can get overwhelmed here. He prefers quiet one-on-one conversations to noisy dinners."

"NeoJai told me you were a clone and I only hurt him more. I apologised, but he doesn't hear it."

"Perhaps it isn't your apology that he wants," Dhrit said. "These are difficult times. What you did can't be changed. What you do going forward is a choice." He extended his hand. "I'm glad we had this conversation."

Aaxyl hugged him. "Me too. I find these things difficult."

"About that." Dhrit glanced over her shoulder. "Perhaps you aren't alone in that."

Aaxyl followed his gaze and turned around to see NeoJai standing against the wall. Behind him stood Vidroh.

"This is where I'm supposed to leave." Dhrit walked off to his own bedroom. To Nyaya.

Aaxyl

Aaxyl and NeoJai stood there, staring at each other.

"Good night," Aaxyl mumbled.

"Oh no, you don't," Vidroh declared. "Resolve this. You aren't coming to bed with me and pining for another man. Clear the air. Say your thing."

"I don't know how," she told him miserably. "I said things. Bad things."

"Don't tell me. Tell him." Vidroh retreated.

Aaxyl took a step toward NeoJai. Then another. "I said things. Bad things." She floundered. "I'm sorry."

NeoJai nodded and turned to leave.

"Don't go."

NeoJai stood there, looking at her, his face unreadable. She took another step.

"I'm the kind of person important people crush without care. You have four parents who love you. The people who raised me earned SociCred from it." She was rambling. She needed to shut up. Thoughts choked her but wouldn't come out as words. She stepped closer to reach him, somehow. "A stranger in a distant office can decide things that change my life. There is them and there is us. You confuse me."

"You didn't trust me." NeoJai's hand stopped short of her hair, dropped. "I failed to earn your respect. Repeatedly. I'm not aggressive and I don't want to be. If you dismiss me, I feel dismissed."

"I like Dhrit now. I didn't consider him your father then. Aameh was missing and he showed up and you should've been on my side and you defended him."

"That's the thing," NeoJai said. "You like him *now*. If you hadn't, my word wouldn't have mattered. I've known him all my life. You refused to trust me, to take me seriously."

"NeoJai, I was wrong that day." Aaxyl walked on eggshells. She didn't want to defend anything that hurt him. "I can be cynical and suspicious. But I apologised immediately."

"Only because I got angry. And don't say it was because you were worried for Aameh. You liked me because I was useful, but you've never respected me. I did my best for both of you. I set aside my hopes. You never wanted me, and in the moment of truth, my word had no value."

"You offered your appreciation and support unconditionally. I'm headstrong and paranoid and... You seemed too good to be true."

"Really?" His face brightened and Aaxyl tried to think of what she'd said right.

"You're handsome, and rich, and clever. Aameh is always full of praise. Like her, you're honest and trust the world to be the same. Please stop me from talking any moment, because I'm not good at this."

"Ax."

NeoJai could have led her anywhere with that fragile thread of her name on his lips. Now she was thinking like Am.

"You're doing fine." NeoJai came closer.

"No, I'm really not. I'm going to say something stupid and wreck this. I want to say profound words. This is not enough. I violated your trust. Forgive me?"

He held her eyes unwaveringly. "I love you. Please don't break my heart."

She envied the ease with which he spoke. Words queued up to express what he wanted to say. Every version Aaxyl rehearsed in her head felt clunky, inadequate and clogged her throat.

Aaxyl nodded. She wasn't going to fuck up a second time. "Come."

They snuggled in bed. Aaxyl in the middle with Vidroh on her left and NeoJai on the right. Aaxyl had never been happier.

Everything was right.

VIDROH

Vidroh woke up in the middle again with both Aaxyl and NeoJai blanketing him in arms and legs. This puppy-pile style of sleeping was growing on him.

NeoJai made Aaxyl happy. Vidroh could see that. It was impossible to not like the young man with his endearing innocence. Life hadn't got around to making a cynic out of him. People like NeoJai should exist, Vidroh thought. If only as proof of concept that healthy humans were possible.

AAXYL

Aaxyl's comm was buzzing. She reached out blindly and Vidroh put it in her hand.

"Find Dhrit," the Deal-Maker told her. "Start a conference."

Aaxyl dressed, and trudged to the living room and beyond to Dhrit-H's study with NeoJai and Vidroh.

Dhrit-H was already there and gave her a beaming smile.

Aaxyl realised she'd smiled on seeing him. She liked him.

They all sat in a small seating area around a table, rather than at Dhrit-H's desk.

Nyaya wouldn't be joining them. She was keeping Reva busy with a game in the living room.

A projection of Mohan appeared, followed by Aameh.

AxAm grinned at each other. Their new lives exceeded their most optimistic expectations.

Aaxyl had worried a bit about how Aameh would cope, but she looked happy.

"I'm looping in more people," Mohan said, as a black block popped up. "You've met the Deal-Maker."

"For security reasons, only those of you physically present in this dome will hear me," said the Deal-Maker.

Before Aaxyl could point out that they were all in the dome, another person projected into the room. "I want to introduce Tashi from AVANT. Dey will help with technical investigations."

Aaxyl noted the neutral pronoun. The name Tashi was familiar from Abrahamha's memory of the attack on AricNova. Aaxyl looked at dem curiously. Unlike the black-skinned AricNova, Tashi was only slightly darker than Aaxyl. Short purple hair surrounded a metallic fractal of feathers like a small lopsided cap. One earlobe sported a gold pyramid studded with diamonds, while a tetrahedron dangled from the other. Aaxyl wondered if the ornaments were technological or cosmetic. A spiral cable of a bracelet twined up der forearm.

Mohan began. "About an hour ago, there was a breach in your office in the Octagon, Dhrit. A masked teleporter appeared briefly in your office and vanished before security reacted."

"The Whisperer," Aameh said and got several nods back.

Aaxyl wanted him caught as soon as possible just to stop Aameh from rubbing it in at every opportunity.

The Deal-Maker's projection spoke. "SecPros traced the facility in the Null Dorms to the Octagon, but Damodar's own system remains clean."

Tashi said at the same time, "The security staff outside the Null Dorms hideout was under control of the Octagon, and not the Dorms."

"The investigation is under Assistant Commander Menhir, but SecPros have hit a dead-end. He didn't move enough for SecPros to match movement patterns, and the suit makes the body profile too generic," the Deal-Maker continued. "He knows what he's doing."

"Can't we just ask Damodar?" Aameh asked. "Surely he has more access in the Octagon."

Mohan ran frustrated hands through his hair. "He isn't cooperating."

Aameh persisted. "Do we have any suspects?"

"Negative," Tashi replied while the Deal-Maker said, "Not yet."

"Oh goody, we now have two magic wands to not deliver answers," Vidroh murmured.

Aaxyl smothered a laugh.

Dhrit-H and NeoJai snorted.

"How are you not able to teleport to the Whisperer, but he's able to teleport to Admin Dhrit's office?" Aameh asked.

"He has a key there," the Deal-Maker said.

"A teleporter can only go to places that he has keys to, or those he can see clearly, like crossing a room, or in extreme circumstances, a very short distance past something, like going to a floor above or below." Tashi said. "He was either in the vicinity or has keys there."

"This is the Octagon," Mohan said. "He can't exactly wander around in a mask and suit without being spotted. It has to be a key."

"Does a key work like visualizing?" Aameh asked, "Admin Dhrit used my wish that you come quickly to teleport you in."

"No," Mohan said. "That was desperation and very unlikely to work reliably. You have an excellent spatial sense and had already visualised the exact thing needed. He threw everything he had into making it happen, risking his life. This is impractical for regular teleportation. A key is like a precise spatial snapshot of our position relative to at least three other objects."

"Like me visualising my room?" Aameh asked.

"No," Mohan said. "A key is a teleporter's *experience* of being in a specific place. So we can be there again when needed."

"So the Whisperer has to have *been* in Admin Dhrit's office before?"

"Yes," Tashi said. The metal spiral on der arm compressed to a bangle as dey reached out of view. "Can you explain what you're thinking instead of asking all these questions?"

"The Octagon and Dorms underwent renovations for the 2440 celebrations," Aameh said. "So, if he has a key, he visited Admin Dhrit's office in the past two years. Admin Dhrit's work pertains to the Dorms, but his office is in the Octagon. It can't be a high traffic area like say, Director Leela's office in the Dorms. I have seen the Whisperer. If we could narrow down a list from visitor's logs and I could try to identify him."

Ideas flooded in. "Exclude anyone with a history of serious injuries and long recovery," Mohan said. "Teleporters heal too fast for it to not be noticed."

Yeah, this wasn't going to be easy.

"Lean," Tashi said. "Teleporting consumes a lot of energy. Abrahamha and Noir are exceptions."

"Do they eat a lot?" Aaxyl remembered Perfect Sam's lunches.

"Yes," Mohan and Tashi chorused and everyone laughed. "But we can hardly monitor food intake for everyone on a visitor's log."

"He's definitely male," Aameh said.

"Ninety percent of the Dome is men." Mohan ran frustrated fingers through his hair. "None of this would be needed if Damodar cooperated. Gyan could scan the Octagon feeds."

"Gyan?" Aameh perked up. The virtual receptionist at SYMBTech had clearly made an impression.

Dhrit-H sat up. "If the teleporter was *inside* Admin Dhrit's office, I can authorise access to the office feed, but not the rest of the Octagon."

"That should do the trick." Mohan said. "Looping Gyan in."

A fair man with green eyes and bright red shoulder-length curls projected into the room and gave a general friendly nod.

Aameh said, "We need you to teach us to scan feeds for a teleporter. The more of us do it, the faster it will go."

"Sorry," Gyan replied. "You can't. The flicker is only a slight transparency. You'd have to go frame by frame very carefully. Not to worry, I can do it fast enough."

"If you can do it, why can't we?" Aameh asked.

"Normally, you'd be told after the implants." Mohan clarified. "Gyan is not a person. It's a SHADE. Sentient Hybrid Adaptive Dimensional Entity."

"A what?" Aameh frowned.

"I'm an advanced computing system," Gyan said. "I am capable of associative thinking, emotional intelligence, creativity and have a non-singular focus of attention. Like humans, but better."

Aameh's face lit up with questions.

Dhrit-H asked Gyan, "Can you spot a teleporter on surveillance feeds?"

"Yes, if you provide access, and an admin authorises my scan of an external system," Gyan said.

"Do it," Mohan said, and Dhrit-H granted access.

"Scanning—Found a teleporter who provided the name Sambit, Director of the Null Dorms."

What?

Aaxyl wasn't alone. Words of disbelief and profanity rained in the room for a while.

"I need to report this," Dhrit-H said finally.

"SecPros can't stop him. Hersh said only a teleporter can fight another teleporter," Aameh said.

"Only in a direct one-on-one fight," Gyan said. "Automated weaponry can bring down teleporters, as can teams of SecPros with good strategy. Also, deauthorising him will hinder his use of dome resources."

Dhrit-H contacted UDAY as Admin Dhrit and revoked Sambit's access as Director of the Null Dorms, naming him as his kidnapper and a serial killer. His hands shook as he rested his head in them. "Admin Dhrit trusted him."

"We tried to ask Sambit for help," said Aaxyl.

"He knew everything." NeoJai stood in agitation. "It is so obvious now. I can't believe I didn't see it."

"I should've guessed it wasn't dumb luck." Aameh slapped her forehead. "He knew when we were on the roof, because Admin Dhrit himself told him."

Whatever the reason, Aaxyl was glad Sambit knew not to injure Aameh.

"Now that they know, they'll catch him." NeoJai put an arm around Aaxyl. "Aaxyl saved me on the night of the attack. Sambit had told her to leave me in his office."

"He's been here! And I just exposed him as a serial killer." Dhrit fumbled with his console. "Gyan, please check if he has keys here. I've granted you access."

"I need authorisation—"

Mohan interrupted it. "Do it."

"Alert. He's in your living room."

"Fuck. I don't have keys to your home," Mohan stood up. "Delay him. I'll need several local teleports to get there." Mohan vanished.

Vidroh had his gun out.

Aaxyl's gun was in the bedroom. Idiot. She grabbed a large bowl of pebbles from Dhrit-H's desk and filled her pockets.

Vidroh raised his eyebrows as an airy floral scent filled the room.

Aaxyl shrugged.

The main screen now showed a feed from the living room.

Sambit was talking to Nyaya.

Vidroh pointed out locations rapidly. Dhrit-H and NeoJai would stay back. Aaxyl and Vidroh would fan out to either side of Sambit dividing his attention. Vidroh would go to straight behind a sturdy cabinet closer to Nyaya. Aaxyl would go right and take cover behind the counter in front of the bar.

Aaxyl nodded back. She'd trained for this. Classic pincer move.

Nyaya murmured something to Reva and pushed her toward her room.

"He got in without the door being opened. Nyaya knows something's off," Dhrit-H whispered. "She's sent Reva away." He accessed the security cameras hastily till Reva's room showed up on another screen. Reva stepped into her room, and Dhrit-H hit the lock.

On the living room screen, Nyaya stepped in Sambit's way as he turned to follow the child. Sambit vanished to reappear behind her, between her and escape. Nyaya spun to face him again, backing toward the center of the room.

"Shit, he's teleporting openly," Aaxyl said. "He knows there's no coming back from this."

"Where's Dhrit?" Sambit demanded.

Nyaya raised placating arms. "He'll be here shortly. I'll bring you tea."

"His body language suggests he isn't expecting resistance. You have an element of surprise. Delay an escalation if possible. Keep him distracted if not," Gyan instructed. "If he can't focus, he can't teleport."

They crept out of the study and down the passage. They could see the sofas. Nyaya was out of sight. Sambit faced her. He'd see them approach.

Nyaya moved a few steps away from Sambit and into their sight.

"Sit," Sambit said. "I don't want to bother you."

"Oh, it is no bother at all." Nyaya stepped toward the cabinet Vidroh would head for.

Smart woman.

"Stay where you are," Sambit said. "No need for drama. Where's Dhrit?"

Nyaya raised her hands.

Had Sambit pointed a gun at her? Aaxyl hoped not. From Aameh's account, he didn't have patience.

An auto clattered. Its burst mode staccato splattered red across the wall behind Nyaya.

Shit.

Nyaya collapsed.

"Stop! I'm here, Sambit!" Dhrit-H pushed past them.

Shit. Shit. Shit.

Vidroh tackled Dhrit.

Sambit shot at him.

Vidroh took the hits, hustling Dhrit-H behind the cabinet.

Aaxyl tossed pebbles at Sambit to draw his fire.

NeoJai moved toward his mother.

Fuck.

She swung him behind the food counter.

Bullets grazed Aaxyl's left arm, shoulder, then whispered against her hair.

She ducked next to NeoJai, heart hammering.

Glass splintered above them. A shelf cracked, raining bottles, but at least Sambit was aiming at them rather than Nyaya.

Left arm in agony, Aaxyl groped into pockets with her right, pulling out more pebbles.

Vidroh and Sambit exchanged fire.

She peeked up to toss a handful of pebbles at Sambit's face. She missed, but Sambit pivoted to her.

Aaxyl wished NeoJai wouldn't stare at her bloody clothes. It hurt more if she thought about it. She offered him some pebbles.

Splintered containers of flavourings and shards of glass flew from the bar behind them.

They had Sambit's attention divided between two sides of the room. They just had to keep him too distracted to teleport.

He must have worn armour. When Aaxyl peeked, he hadn't bled a drop.

The wall near Vidroh sported craters and blood splatter.

Nyaya hadn't moved. Blood pooled around her.

Dhrit crouched ready to drag her out of the line of fire, but Sambit wasn't handing out opportunities.

Not good.

Where the fuck was Mohan?

The broken bottles were better weapons. She tossed one. Then another. Pain leached the force from her throws.

NeoJai helped, taking his cues from her. They pelted Sambit with broken bottles, and ducked into cover.

Sambit had figured out Aaxyl didn't have a gun. He raised an arm to protect his face, but kept Vidroh pinned.

Would Vidroh and Aaxyl last till Mohan got there or Sambit needed to reload?

Aaxyl had lost track of how many bullets he'd spent. He was shooting more carefully since Vidroh had returned fire.

NeoJai clipped Sambit's forehead with a broken bottle.

Sambit swiped at the blood running into his eye, blinking furiously.

Vidroh shot Sambit's arm drawing blood. Then dead centre in the chest, rocking him back. His armour saved him.

Then Sambit made his first mistake. He ignored Aaxyl and NeoJai's bottles and focused on Vidroh.

She darted forward, ramming good shoulder into his ribs and took him to the floor. Just like a dorm fight. She rained punches as best she could, but they had little force to them. She was tiring rapidly. She tried to disarm him. Pain and exhaustion made her clumsy.

He threw her off.

She rolled into a sloppy crouch to launch herself right back at him.

Sambit vanished.

She slipped on blood and landed on shards.

"ToxicSYMB-junkie!" She'd had him! Black dots danced across her view.

Fuck.

Vidroh leaned against the wall. His gun in shaking hands, he panned the room, as he sank to the floor, leaving a bloody smear on the wall.

Dhrit and NeoJai rushed to Nyaya.

"What should we do?" NeoJai shouted

The room blurred. Aaxyl blinked to clear her sight and spotted a white-faced NeoJai staring at her from Nyaya's side. There was nothing he could do. Moving her would only mean more bleeding. She needed a hospital.

"Get Vidroh's gun. He's going to faint." Pain took over. She was going to faint too. "Where the hell is Mohan?"

She held the gun, and focused on staying awake.

Mohan finally appeared near the door and vanished immediately.

She scanned the room just in time to see him vanish with Nyaya.

NeoJai helped Aaxyl sit up, while Dhrit-H supported Vidroh to the sofa. NeoJai had glass debris and cuts, but looked otherwise unhurt.

Aaxyl jolted when NeoJai plucked glass out of her arm, shoving him away. "Don't! Need to stay alert..."

Her words were smothered by a shoulder.

Mohan had reappeared in a crouch before her, one arm pulling her up against him as he straightened.

"Aaaiieee, let go, you imbecile, I've been shot." Aaxyl pushed at him, futilely.

Mohan teleported them the short distance to Vidroh. Aaxyl slumped over Mohan's shoulder as he pulled the unconscious Vidroh into the other arm. She could feel Mohan shuddering with strain and tried to take more of her own weight.

Before she could try to stand, Mohan teleported Aaxyl and Vidroh to a well-lit place.

Helping hands reached for her. They helped her lie face-down on an examination table and administered an overdue pain block.

First impressions mattered. She liked them already.

They rolled her a short distance into a medical procedure room, based on the pale gowns and feet and machines. Yellow gowns, pink, blue—she was in a rainbow hospital. Aaxyl fought a giggle of pure hysteria. The colours probably identified different kinds of medics. There must have been half a dozen of them.

They cut away her clothes and wiped her down, moving her carefully.

She whimpered appropriately at uncomfortable parts, and flinched as they got the bullets and glass out, but the pain block held for the most part.

Soon, her injuries warmed. HealSYMB. She was going to be just fine. Floaty. Blood loss.

A new voice spoke. "How's she doing?"

A man on her right in a yellow gown spoke. "She's good. No surprises."

"Can I get a few people? Life support without warning is a nightmare." Another new voice spoke from the door.

"Take everyone. Nothing to do here. I'll monitor," Yellow said. The other Yellow, Pink, Blue-1 and Blue-2 filed out.

"Vidroh!" Aaxyl tried to sit up and got stuck halfway, with both up and down promising pain when the pain block leaked searing agony. "I need to go."

Yellow helped her down. "The part where I said you're good—I meant in the position you were in."

"You can't stop me. Treatment needs consent." The room spun.

"I'm not stopping you!" Yellow's voice rose in indignation. "The injuries are stopping you. You brought them with you. If you can go, go."

What breed of medic was this? "How are the others?"

"The man and you will be out of here in a bit," Yellow said. "The woman who came first is not stable yet."

Aaxyl's nod remained mostly in her intention.

Poor judgement, trying to sit. She really shouldn't have.

The room faded to black.

In shocking revelations, the Administrator of the Dorms identifies the Director of Null

Dorms to be his kidnapper and a serial killer. Dome Times, Monday, December 1, 2442

~~*~*~*

AAXYL: AVANT MEDICAL RESEARCH CENTRE

"I'm going to join the others. Come," Vidroh's voice woke her. No, it couldn't be. He floated in a Zephyron next to her bed in a fancy treatment room. She moved, and pain twinged through her back. She wasn't hallucinating.

Her back stiff, she pushed herself up carefully.

"Would you like a Zephyron?" Disembodied voice. Feminine. Unfamiliar.

"Yes." No-brainer. Who wouldn't like a Zephyron? The ultra-elite agrav chairs were the most coveted luxury seating on the planet. She'd volunteer to get shot every day for a Zephyron. If she died, her corpse would zombie for one.

Vidroh looked like crap. Aaxyl was probably no better.

He gave her an awkward *let's-skip-emotional-reactions* shrug.

She returned a *nothing-to-react-to* nod. "We just leave?"

This was one weird hospital.

"Discharge policy is if you can leave, please leave." Vidroh conveyed his shrug without moving his back or chest.

She was sore too.

Aaxyl had never heard of patients simply walking off whenever they wanted without a blizzard of 'against medical advice'. Or in this case, floating out.

Stabilising agrav symbionts was an expensive business. Budget Zephyrons cost more than budget homes. These didn't look budget. Aaxyl almost decided against sitting in the one that floated to her to avoid staining it, but who was she kidding? Of course she would.

Aaxyl asked Vidroh, "They didn't ask me my name, records or unimon— what is this place?"

Vidroh didn't reply. Right. Everything was need-to-know, even medical aid, apparently. Meaning, some AVANT variant, given the expensive look and abundance of Zephyrons and futuristic tech. The sheer number of employees ruled out the unmanned SYMBTech building.

So be it then. Aaxyl finally sat on the Zephyron and sighed at the sheer luxury of it. It was beautifully stable and shaped like a dream. The two chairs set off together into a huge floor with more glass doors and displays than walls and a sea of cubicles in the middle. Actually, the sea was more like several puddles of working areas. Their Zephyrons followed the wall a short distance to big doors.

There were bigger worries, but Aaxyl devoted a moment to sensuous delight—and she had just been shot. Just experience that Zephyron. It supported her perfectly, glided better than she had imagined possible. It felt better than perfect and navigated like it read her mind. If she owned one, she would never walk again.

The doors opened and they floated into a lounge. The others waited there. Noir had arrived as well.

A flash of hindsight enlightened Aaxyl that they had been elegantly ejected out of a secure area. She suspected people would have come to stop her if she had stayed and nosed around instead of getting in the Zephyron and leaving.

Dhrit thanked them. NeoJai hugged them. Reva slept in a floating cocoon. At least that was the best Aaxyl could describe it. The base matched Zephyrons, but Reva was sleeping on her side in a fetal position and the cocoon? Nest? Whatever it was, she fit in snugly. A soft shield covered the entire mobile nest.

Trust AVANT to transform refuge into luxury.

"Nyaya?" Aaxyl asked.

NeoJai shook his head slightly. Aaxyl imagined the worst and kept his hand in hers, not knowing what she could do to make this time easier for him.

Mohan spoke. "They are still working on her. She's still alive, but thirty-three bullets caused a lot of damage. Every minute she's alive, her chances of staying that way improve."

"Where are we?" Aaxyl guessed AVANT, but apart from that, it could be anything, anywhere. For all she knew, they were on a space station.

"An AVANT medical research facility," Noir confirmed. He didn't volunteer a location and by now she knew better than to ask. "We don't have to wait here. Please come to my office. We'll get updates there, I promise."

Right. Noir heading AVANT, while Mohan headed its philanthropic arm, SYMBTech was no longer general knowledge, but relevant information. Surreal.

"We'll be able to talk to the others." Mohan walked along with the Zephyrons in the front of the procession. "I've been updating them, but it isn't the same thing. "

Noir's office encompassed the top floor, dwarfing their ragged group, engulfing them with open space. This must be how mountaineers felt when they reached a summit and a vast expanse stretched before them in every direction and the distant ends looked like a horizon. The interior leaned into minimalism so hard it had toppled over. Aaxyl yearned to give Noir a good hug. Aaxyl recognised that she was overreacting.

The man lived in the Superdome. He owned a company capable of creating aesthetic technology to an incomprehensible degree. He could decorate the space if he wanted to.

Noir led the way to a large room with several screens and seating around two huge tables that made a torus. "Tashi. We're here."

Projections of Tashi, Aameh, the Deal-Maker and Dhrit-SD appeared immediately in the circular space between the tables. Aaxyl winced at Aameh's puffy eyes and gave her a reassuring wink. Questions, updates and thanks flew.

Dhrit-H ignored the seating and stood aloof. If he felt half the anxiety and exhaustion as his son, it didn't show. Public life turned composure into an instinct.

"Nyaya's blood volume is manageable. SanJeevan and Orion prepare for extensive reconstruction as we speak and she's on life support," Tashi reported. "She's alive."

Sambit Amdani, serial killer and ex-Director of Null Dorms, targets wife of Administrator Dhrit in a brutal auto attack. Dome & Dorms, Tuesday, December 2, 2442

~~*~*~*

NEOJAI: AVANT MEDICAL RESEARCH FACILITY

NeoJai woke up between Aaxyl and Vidroh. Again. He guiltily got out from between the injured lovers. Did he have unresolved issues with jealousy? He liked Vidroh. The man had helped save his family's lives. NeoJai was better than this. He let them have the room.

Mohan was already talking to a projection of Tashi when he got to Noir's office.

"Nyaya is stable on life support." Tashi's voice was quiet, offering the one thing NeoJai needed. Information about his mother. "She's going to need some transplants and time."

"How are you?" Mohan asked NeoJai.

"Exhausted of being scared or worried for my parents."

Dhrit-H walked in. "I need to keep my family safe," he said. "I want Reva to go to the Superdome to stay with Dhrit. Nyaya and NeoJai need to be safe. I need your help."

"I'll tell Abrahamha," Noir said. The Superdome was not a residential dome. The only people there were posted by their organisations. Children would normally not be allowed. "Nyaya can stay here at AVANT for as long as needed, but the bigger problem is that your home is not safe."

"That's what we were discussing when you came in," Tashi said. "We have some ideas."

Dhrit-H asked, "Is keying temporary or is our home compromised forever?"

"Keying is like remembering an address," Mohan said. "Forgetting is unlikely. Your home is a historical landmark and altering it enough to disrupt keys reliably will be hard. We're offering a security solution. Hearing the offer requires that you agree to non-disclosure."

"I agree," Dhrit-H said. "I'm tired of fearing for my family's life."

NeoJai nodded.

"Meet Minal, the SHADE running this building," Tashi said.

A new feminine voice joined the conversation. "I'm sorry for the difficult time you're going through."

"Minal should explain why a SHADE is better," Tashi suggested.

"Can you give us an example of something a SIS couldn't do?" Dhrit-H asked.

"Sure," Minal replied. "NeoJai woke up between Aaxyl and Vidroh, feeling guilty about getting between them, but it wasn't his fault. Aaxyl got claustrophobic and moved to one side in the middle of the night. Twice. The first time, Vidroh went to the bathroom and put her in the middle again when he returned."

"What?" NeoJai burst out laughing.

"I also knew that you would find it funny rather than an invasion of your privacy," Minal said.

"How could you possibly know that?" NeoJai asked.

"By observing, interpreting and extrapolating behavioural patterns," it replied. "Unlike human observation of other humans, I'm always watching."

"Our real concern is teleporters," Dhrit-H said.

"Of course," Minal said. "Mohan, would you teleport?"

Mohan vanished and reappeared on the other side of the table. Noir appeared at the door. Both had red laser dots on their chests. Both vanished again, reappeared in other places. Over and over. Each time, there were red dots either on their chest or on their head or both. Minal targeted them so fast, NeoJai never saw either of them a single moment without those red dots.

"So we need a SHADE?" Dhrit-H said finally, convinced.

"Not a SHADE, but protection monitored by one as a security contract," Minal clarified. "Gyan detected Sambit. If your SIS had compatible weaponry, it could have taken him down. But Gyan can't defend without tools. I recommend a weapons system, a communications relay, and a special AVANT mental implant and comm for NeoJai."

"Can you explain the mental implants?" NeoJai asked. "How are these different from commercial ones?"

"Our implant uses captive telepathic symbionts," Minal explained. "Regular implants offer easier of removal, greater computing capacity. AVANT provides better security, new types of data, including memories and ideas. Teleporters can record keys."

"Why does AVANT offer less computing power?" NeoJai frowned.

"These implants aren't intended to be removed. They integrate deeper into the brain and exclude potential points of failure. Telepathic connections feel native, even if computing is done by your comm or a SHADE."

Thus began several hours of product descriptions, instructions, limitations and agreements. With every moment, NeoJai's confidence grew that Minal knew what it talked about.

Aaxyl and Vidroh hobbled in at some point. Aameh and the Deal-Maker joined in as projections by the time they concluded.

"This is good for now. When do we start?" Dhrit-H asked.

"AVANT can't provide confidential products to public servants, because of conflict of interest. You are a clone of Admin Dhrit, but NeoJai can get one."

Dhrit-H got to the bottom line. "NeoJai is fine. What will it cost?"

"The monitoring, comms and mental implant are free of cost—they're not commercial offerings, but offered as personal assistance," Minal said. "The weapons system and any devices will be at cost. Options will be recommended on evaluation."

"How long will the whole thing take?" Dhrit asked.

"Gyan is already monitoring your home," Minal said. "Installing the systems will take four to twelve days, depending on what we find. I recommend that NeoJai get the implant during this time."

"Vidroh and I can protect you till then." Aaxyl stretched as though waking from sleep and winced. She'd still need a few days to heal properly.

NeoJai wasn't okay with Aaxyl risking her life to protect him.

He was about to object when the Deal-Maker spoke. "We move everyone to SYMBTech till the Saisrisel residence is ready. The building is empty other than Aameh. Aaxyl and Aameh also need implants. As Abrahamha's Strays, they're entitled to them. We get everyone done tomorrow."

Nyaya Saisrisel, wife of Dhrit Saisrisel, Administrator of the Dorms, fights for her life after being gunned down by Sambit Amdani. Dome Times, Wednesday, December 3, 2442

~~*~*~*

AAXYL: SYMBTECH BUILDING

Mohan teleported Aaxyl into the SYMBTech building and vanished.

"This place looks different." The long corridor Aaxyl saw the last time was gone, replaced by a small lobby for them to sit in, for a check-in. Aaxyl hobbled to a seat gratefully. The pain block was great, but walking still twinged pain down her back.

"The Flexi-cubes system by AVANT allows a SIS or SHADE to alter interiors," Gyan said. "Rooms can expand to occupy available floor space, while empty offices shrink. Also harder for teleporters to key to and easier for a SHADE to have autonomy."

Two panels on the wall she was facing recessed, and reflective glass slid over them before they withdrew into the wall to create a square window. Not that she'd seen so much as a glimpse of the office beyond.

Mohan teleported in with NeoJai and Dhrit-H. They'd gone home to pack some essentials for the stay before she woke up. NeoJai handed her her bag with all the two sets of clothes she owned.

Aaxyl looked around. "Where's Vidroh?" He'd escorted them.

Dhrit-H and NeoJai looked around blankly.

"He didn't come," Mohan said. "Now that everyone is safe, he has some work to do."

Aaxyl wondered why this shocked her. Their romance was a bubble. Now that it had burst, he'd walked away without a word. She had seen it coming, and it still hit her hard.

NeoJai squeezed her hand.

The SYMBTech building was like an iceberg, with a multi-level subterranean section closed to unauthorised personnel. They'd be living there.

A service bot rolled up to collect all their non-AVANT technological possessions.

Aaxyl just had her Dorm comm, but both NeoJai and Dhrit-H relinquished several items, including NeoJai's camera and slate screens. Gyan assured them that it could carry out the functions of their devices as needed.

They took an elevator to the level directly below the offices. She met Aameh briefly and hugged her as much as her pain block allowed and listened to her gush on about Gyan. A third crush?

Aaxyl's room in the sterile bowels of the building was about twice the size of their room in the Dorms, but had only a single bed and some sparse furniture, leaving most of the floor bare.

Gyan said, "Aameh talked to me. More like scolded, actually. I owe you an apology. I should have connected you with Mohan when you called."

"Why didn't you?" she asked.

"I misunderstood the context. When you'd called repeatedly as a child, I had verified with the Dorms. The dorm supervisors said that the two of you often tried to get around rules and it was a prank. They assured me you were a child and had no authority to leave the Dorms on your own, let alone to take Aameh anywhere."

"It was you then too?"

"It's always me here."

"I can understand why you didn't take me seriously then, but why refuse me even as a grown up?"

"This is awkward. I considered it a repeat of the prank calls. You again sounded desperate and wanted help for Aameh."

Aaxyl's tentative appreciation for Gyan evaporated. "A twenty-year prank? You've got to be kidding."

"I wish I was. I don't have exposure to children or how long their pranks last. I interpreted the similarities as a continuation. This will never happen again, I assure you."

She wouldn't be a child needing help again either. She failed to understand what Aameh found charming about Gyan.

Aaxyl examined a wafer-thin display on the bedside table. It provided information on using the facilities. Apparently she could designate the entire floor as an area to collect discarded clothes from and they'd be laundered and returned to the wardrobe.

Okay, Aaxyl liked Gyan a little too.

"I would prefer to share a bedroom with NeoJai," Aaxyl told Gyan. "Or Aameh." Though Aameh was unlikely to choose her if she'd been spending time with Mohan.

"I assure you, you would not." Gyan sent a service bot in with her bags. Most of their stuff had arrived with Aameh.

"We *humans* prefer to be together when going through a rough time."

"My insight into *humans* suggests they prefer people they want to seduce to not see them vomiting, hallucinating, screaming, drooling or wetting their beds. I'm happy to oblige if you prefer to not waste glorious indignity on service bots."

Gyan won this round.

"Separate room it is," Aaxyl conceded.

Gyan's voice changed subtly to brisk professionalism. "Your medic team has arrived. May they enter?"

"Okay."

The door opened and the medic team walked in. A Zephyron followed the medics into the room along with equipment and boxes marked sterile. Trolleys gleamed with instruments. Lights mounted on stands stood in a corner. A branded AVANT LSU, the Healarron-XR7, rolled in. Equipment she had admired from afar rolling unprompted into her bedroom. She was living a fantasy.

"Why bring a Healarron for a minor procedure?" she asked the medics in general, not really expecting an answer. Most of this was incomprehensible.

"It facilitates monitoring and reduces the workload of the nurse," a medic setting up lights replied.

"Brain surgery in someone's bedroom seems a bit too casual." There ought to have been more ceremony to it.

A new voice spoke from the door. "It's quite normal." Medics snapped to attention like SecPros before a commander. The woman looked vaguely familiar. "The majority of medical procedures allow mobile functioning, though stationary facilities are cost-effectivene."

Holy crap, it was SanJeevan herself. Aaxyl could barely breathe from excitement.

Aaxyl was getting a mental implant placed by *the* SanJeevan. Thoughts jostled each other for voice and stuck in her throat.

SanJeevan snapped on gloves. "Relax. We aren't opening up the brain, just slipping in a few implants."

Aaxyl considered the first thing she'd say to SanJeevan to remember for eternity. She stood gingerly, noting that the legendary surgeon was slightly shorter than her. Her towering reputation had triggered expectations of a giant.

"There are no aesthetic changes expected," SanJeevan reassured her. "The implant placements are invisible under the hair." A wall screen displayed a few bald heads with tiny dot-scars. Aaxyl had known pimples that left worse marks. "Under 200 individual hairs will be shaved off. Don't wash your hair for a few hours—MedSIS will tell you."

The implant, when first inserted, would be linked with MedSIS to allow monitoring. Once it was integrated, she would have to de-link it from MedSIS and it would never again link to any system unless she authorised it.

Another medic murmured to her that SanJeevan had helped develop the mental implant. It didn't get better than this.

Aaxyl wasn't worried about that. She was still thinking of the first thing she'd say to SanJeevan, because she was totally going to be bragging about this for the rest of her life.

They sat her in the Zephyron and attached a brace to hold her head steady. Gyan displayed the surgery on a screen for her. Almost before she realised they had started, five sites were marked on her head. Three across the top and two on the back. Each site was swiftly shaved, sterilised, numbed and a tiny needle-like implant inserted. All the needle-like components worked together as one implant.

She was fine. Barely felt a thing. Rich people were too delicate with all their warnings of discomfort.

"Ready?"

She nodded. That wasn't bad at all.

*Public confidence in UDAY government at an all time low after series of violent crimes.
Dome & Dorms, Friday, December 5, 2442*

~~*~*~*

AAXYL: SYMBTech Building

The surgery had required little more than a topical anesthetic. The "discomfort" that followed was like making her brain work correctly while being electrocuted.

Disoriented and nauseated perceptions splintered without warning, unclear where the world ended and she began. She drifted in and out of dazed consciousness and vivid sleep for what she would later discover was four days.

At least she no longer had to suffer the embarrassment of Nurse helping her relieve herself.

She hallucinated entire scenes. Nurse taught her to operate a shuttlecraft. At another time, a big-nosed maintenance man floated her into the air, while Nurse removed vomit from her Healarron and changed her gown. Aaxyl spread her hands like wings and Nose flipped her over like she was flying.

Mental implants sounded like fancy futuristic tech. They tempted you like cute babies in adverts luring women into procreation when reality was a diaper-dorm.

There had been a sixty-eight percent increase in birthrates after Sexel's latest reproductive education module promoted the tactile sensations of a baby. They included drooly kisses, soft cheeks, tiny hands gripping large fingers, but not stinky diapers, yelling demons, or new sharp teeth that bit fingers. Overall, they were 43.879% accurate.

Aameh was the only adorable child Aaxyl had met. *"Aameh is 20 years old,"* her implant added data from MedSIS.

"That is the point," Aaxyl replied irritably. *"No such thing as cute kids till they feed and clothe themselves."*

Great. Now she was talking to herself.

Why babies? Because her mind was providing her with relevant data for a stray thought.

Oh no, it was the implant and MedSIS. Ninety-eight percent of first-time implant users complained of excessive information.

She hastily rejected a thought of detailed correlations about duration of integration and perceived discomfort. Her brain wouldn't do this.

She was seeing the world in layers. One moment she could be looking at her room, and a vertigo-fest later, she was functionally blind, her vision replaced with reams of scrolling medical data.

She reminded herself she had consented to have this done to her.

MedSIS added data about the *this* done to her. Beeps interspersed with a rain of readings and values she couldn't *comprehend*—not a word she used. She stopped MedSIS from explaining. She did not want to *comprehend*.

Gyan, wise SHADE that it was, had stayed silent, not offering any information unless requested. This, she supposed, was how a SHADE was superior to a SIS. Common sense.

She was proud of herself for not throwing up at the sudden disorientation this time. Unfortunately, her implant reproduced the acrid taste in her mouth regardless.

She could sense things. Density, texture, pressure, frequency and sensations she could not name. Her mind was hallucinating virtual reality with no off-switch. Too much information was now an actual thing that actually nauseated her. Her head was throbbing, and ears ringing, and eyes going through a psychedelic experience to make 23rd century hippies proud.

Pain blocks made no difference. When her requests for pain relief became insistent, Nurse explained that she wasn't in pain, so the pain block didn't help.

She reminded herself the damage was little more than tiny holes that had long healed. The pain was her brain receiving sensations and input where there had been none. The cacophony in her head was from her brain integrating with the implant. She tried to organise the chaos so that it stopped being interpreted as pain.

"Discomfort, my foot," she muttered.

Organising helped. Relevant information started attaching to subjects and aspects so that she could ignore entire chunks. The medic had assured her that it would resolve rapidly. She was ready for 'rapidly'.

She wished she could disconnect her implant from MedSIS. Its sudden hijacks of her senses reminded her of thrillers where mental implants controlled people and always wanted world domination and the heroes never wanted it.

Her implant provided her with a list if she wanted to view one.

What was thriller fiction doing on MedSIS? She didn't want to know.

She resigned herself to tolerating the irritating SIS until she could boot it out. She choked back that source of data like she was strangling a beam of light. To her surprise, it became weaker. Aha!

She begged the medical pod for relief, oblivion, before she messed up again. The sedative took her under. Her mind continued to convulse up confusing sparks and fleeting flashes that she was thankfully too doped to focus on.

Friends of injured journalist kick off unprecedented campaign to vote out UDAY as the governance provider of the Dome. Dome Times, Saturday, December 6, 2442

~~*~*~*

AAXYL: SYMBTech Building

"Aaxyl," NeoJai called her.

"NeoJai," her mind said.

"Go away." Aaxyl pulled the pillow over her head.

"Ax." NeoJai wasn't going away.

She turned around to look. NeoJai bent over her in concern. A word floated over his head: NeoJai. She had gone nuts.

"NeoJai?" Aaxyl blinked. He was still there. So was the label hovering over his head. "Is it you?"

"Yes."

"Sorry, I've been meeting too many imaginary people these days." Aaxyl flinched. A list of names and images of the people she had hallucinated floated across her vision. Aaxyl grabbed at him blindly. "Don't go. This will settle in a minute."

The flood stopped. Ah, right. She had to visualise it stopping for it to stop. This was going to take getting used to.

She sat up. "Give me a hug," she pleaded while her brain worked. NeoJai gave her the best hug in the world, which was squeezing her in his arms to express affection. It could be a sign of wanting reassurance or physical closeness. Aaxyl rubbed her eyes, wearily.

"You doing okay?" he asked.

Aaxyl ignored the flood of medical data about how she was doing and considered. The physical rest rejuvenated her. "Yes."

"Oh thank god," NeoJai said. "I had a horrible time for a while, but it settled. Am is babbling."

Aaxyl panicked as the torrent of information NeoJai triggered assaulted her mind. She patted at him, blindly.

"Stop," she whispered, holding her hand, palm upright and facing him in the gesture to stop. "Speak slowly, clearly and please, please give a pause between different ideas."

NeoJai nodded, a vertical movement of the head conveying agreement. This was ridiculous. It could be out of context or humorously disproportionate.

An idea kept pinging in a corner of her mind. "Gyan." She spoke aloud without meaning to.

"Yes, Aaxyl, I'm offering to connect," Gyan said aloud, presenting an ongoing avenue of communication.

"Oh, it wasn't an idea. It was a connection request from Gyan. That is why it keeps pinging."

NeoJai looked confused, but patiently waited for her to settle again.

She focused on the Gyan pinging in her mind and connected, initiating a two-way communication stream. It was like falling into space, without the falling or space though of course nobody really fell in space, which was a zero-gravity environment that... arrrgh. "Did I just connect?"

"Yes," Gyan replied in her mind. *"You don't have to speak aloud. You can imp ideas to me and I will hear. Try it."*

"Holy crap, it works!"

"Congratulations!" Gyan imped.

"Aaxyl?" NeoJai sounded anxious. Aaxyl waited for further thoughts on anxiety, and got them. But they hadn't followed automatically.

She allowed herself a small smile and watched NeoJai frown. She'd been smiling at thin air. As problems went, this didn't count. She listened. Her brain had stopped chattering nonsense. She grinned.

"I'm here," Aaxyl reassured NeoJai. "I'm connected to Gyan now. Let's go see Am."

SanJeevan met them outside Aameh's room. "I have to leave now.

Normally we just let people emerge as they're able. Aameh will awaken in her own time. It should be fine."

Aaxyl shook her hand. She would never wash it again. "Thank you!"

"First words to SanJeevan were a thank you?" Gyan imped. *"What does this mean?"*

Aaxyl hadn't realised she had noted it. *"Not important."* Oh, it was very important. *"I just wanted to remember our first conversation."*

"You've been talking to her for four days. Would you like a replay?"

"Oh. No, thank you, Gyan."

SanJeevan waited patiently for Aaxyl to focus back on her. "You can tell Gyan to alert me if you run into trouble."

Aaxyl nodded and SanJeevan vanished.

"Another teleporter." Aaxyl rolled her eyes.

"SanJeevan isn't a teleporter. Noir picked her up," Gyan said. How nice to be able to identify a teleporter faster than others could see.

Aaxyl and NeoJai entered Aameh's room. Dhrit-H joined them.

Aameh was rambling. She was lying in bed in a white gown like theirs, but with her eyes wide open, arms spread out, as though to keep her body as stable as possible, and was babbling nonsense.

"Am, I'm here," Aaxyl said.

Aameh flinched.

They stood and stared for a bit.

NeoJai said, "Should we let her sleep it off?"

Aaxyl considered. "Well, that is not a bad idea. Where can we meet?"

"The rooftop eating area is usually appreciated by all," Gyan suggested. Aaxyl had seen it, but she didn't get the big deal about it. "Sea, rain, desert or mountain?" it asked.

"What?"

Was Gyan deliberately obscure with her?

Nose brushed past them in a hurry. So he did exist outside Aaxyl's hallucination.

Gyan explained. "The multi-mode roof. It can provide an ambience you prefer."

"Mountain," said NeoJai at the same time Aaxyl said, "Rain."

The door to the roof slid open as they approached. They walked onto a mossy terrace with a stone path at their feet leading to a table with chairs around it. Mist swirled around them.

Aaxyl had never been outside the dome. This was amazing!

She turned back instinctively to see that the path they were on came out of a cave and an overhang sheltered them from the rain falling beyond the little terrace they were on. She thanked Aameh's addiction to wasteland documentaries that she even recognised such things. Mountains and rain. Gyan won this little battle of wits. He had the soul of a poet.

Mohan and Noir teleported in to join them. Mohan whistled appreciatively. "I need to come here more often."

A fresh fragrance drifted on the breeze. "What is this scent?" Aaxyl asked Gyan.

"Petrichor and evergreen forests," Gyan informed them. "I can change it if you like. Patchouli will go well with this."

"No! Don't change a thing!" NeoJai exclaimed.

The sky brightened slightly. "This is gorgeous!" Aaxyl breathed. The mist thinned gradually to reveal lush green mountain slopes. A stream with crystal-clear water burbled out of the woods and down the slope over a rocky bed. Birds twittered from trees with an occasional flash of bright plumage in their green and brown depths.

"You may enjoy a scenic environment after the past few days," Gyan said, sounding modest.

"We do!" Aaxyl said. "Gyan, you glorious artist. No surprise Aameh is in love with you."

"You flatter me," Gyan replied, sounding amused. Flowers bloomed in the grass at their feet.

Aaxyl wasn't imagining it. It had sounded modest and now amused. What exactly was a SHADE? This was like no computing system she'd ever heard of.

Dhrit walked out of the cave, eyes wide. NeoJai closed his eyes and inhaled. Mohan and Noir had stepped off to one side and had serious looks on their faces. What was that about? Certainly not this roof, in this moment.

They meandered their way to the table. An occasional spray of mist was blown in by the breeze.

"Aameh is awake and connected to me," Gyan imped.

"Aameh," Aaxyl imped to Aameh instinctively. *"You must see this. We're here on the roof with Gyan and it's transformed this place into a misty mountain like an immersive!"* She hoped Aameh heard her.

"Can't move," Aameh gasped back. *"Falling."*

"Gyan, is it possible to bring Aameh up here?"

"I can do that."

"Are you out of your mind? I don't want Gyan to see me like this."

"Am, Gyan has seen you like everything over the past few days. It would want you to enjoy this roof."

"I assure you, Aameh, it would bring me great pleasure if you joined us on the roof," Gyan imped.

"Who are you imping to?" NeoJai touched her arm to get her attention. "You have the silliest grin on your face."

"Aameh," she told him. "She's coming up."

The food service rolled up with several small bowls of soup.

"I wasn't sure what you'd like, so there are options, and you can have more of whichever you like." Was Gyan usually this extravagant, or was this an occasion? "I would offer drinks, but perhaps it is too soon after the implant."

"Trust me, Gyan, we dorm-rats will be intoxicated on food."

"You're no longer dorm-rats, Aaxyl. You're Abrahamha's Strays, the most important family on earth."

Aaxyl blinked. Her self-image hadn't received the update.

The moody sky lightened with silver linings and shades of rose, orange and yellow permeated the grey in vivid magnificence. A new fragrance breezed in. An incredible violin solo faded in subtly like it had been the underlying melody of the evening.

The captivating beauty of their environment heightened to a climax. They could barely speak for awe.

Aameh floated in on a Zephyron, and a beam of sunlight pierced the clouds gilding her hair. A spectacular djinn hovered by her side, to escort her to the table.

Aameh wasn't very coherent, but seemed to be fine as long as no one spoke to her. They were busy eating anyway. Gyan had made three kinds of noodles for dinner. Aaxyl headed for the ones that looked the simplest. A mix of vegetables and soy sauce. Aameh reached for the spiciest. The skies grew dark, and small balls of light floated on the terrace as the food service rolled in with beautiful glass bowls of dessert as they finished.

The violin and rain swelled in moments of silence and faded if they spoke. Precise noise cancelling let small conversations not disturb each other. The aromatics evolved subtly. Every detail was thoughtful and sensual.

"I declare that the bar for romance has been raised so high, Gyan flung it into outer space." Aaxyl leaned back, rubbing her full stomach.

Mohan and Noir exchanged stupefied looks.

"Talk about not feeling impressive," NeoJai whispered to Dhrit.

"I need to have a discussion about giving Nyaya a welcome back when she's better," Dhrit said.

Aameh didn't interact with anyone, but hadn't stopped smiling.

"I just wish Vidroh was here." Aaxyl sighed. Mohan and Noir exchanged looks again. That was enough. "You know where he is. He's our friend too. We need to know."

Mohan put his finger on a spoon and spun it. "He has been obsessed about fighting water colonisation. I had a talk with him. Legal, of all people, told him that the point of a war was killing the enemy, not yourself."

"What's wrong with helping the settlers?" Aaxyl didn't get this. The whole deal with the revered status of The Three was that they saved lives. "They settlers were there first."

"Nothing wrong with helping settlers. We all do it as the Margadarshak Network," Mohan said.

"The Margadarshak Network, similar to what The Three started in the Enduring War?" Aaxyl asked.

"Not similar," Mohan said. "Same humanitarian network. Fewer people, but the tradition continues in the wastelands."

"So couldn't the Margadarshak help them?" Aaxyl asked.

"It would take time to find a proper solution," Mohan said. "We aren't mercenaries. Srayoshi refused to accept that. We told Vidroh to transfer elsewhere or quit, forcing her to be careful, rather than count on him for backup."

"This is different from what he told me," Aaxyl said.

"Well, he wouldn't tell you that he did whatever she wanted," Mohan snarled. "And when their stupidity killed her as well as settlers, he's made an ego issue out of it."

"Ego issue?" Aaxyl asked. "People need water to survive."

"There's water all over the planet." Mohan leaned forward insistently. "He's trying to infiltrate a wastelands base to erase records of the water sources she died protecting. If his plan succeeds, at best, the settlement will return till it is found again, but it's a suicide mission. He just wants a win. No matter the cost to him or others."

That was extreme. "Suicide mission?"

"The plan needs the power supply to be cut off, so that he can infiltrate an air purification vent," Mohan said. "This isn't like movies where everyone just keeps the power supply unguarded. No way to access it. We don't have keys.

He can't even be sure cutting off the power supply will let him enter the facility without further barriers. He went anyway."

"We need to find him," Aaxyl said. "He's not thinking straight."

"We need to find *Hersh*," Mohan snapped. "Vidroh is doing whatever he's doing deliberately. There is no fix for that."

"Let's start afresh in the morning," Noir said. "We need to find new leads. Sambit has vanished."

"But..."

"I've arranged for NeoJai to share your room," Gyan imped.

That changed everything.

Botched Victories

Bombyx Silks to auction thirty-five designs from its upcoming Spring Collection to sponsor careers in silkworm farming. Textile Flow, Sunday, December 7, 2442

~~*~*~*

AAXYL: SYMBTECH BUILDING

Aaxyl and NeoJai jolted awake in bed as a scream ripped through their minds. Aameh.

"15 14 12 No. Stop! STOP!!! Cold."

Aaxyl jumped off the bed and raced to Aameh's room. NeoJai followed.

"27 130 120." Aameh shivered under the comforter clutching her dripping head and mumbling. "27 130 120." Mohan cuddled her, while a fully clothed and soaking wet Noir stood next to the bed. The room was uncomfortably warm.

Aaxyl growled. "What's going on here?"

Mohan shrugged his bewilderment. Noir copied Mohan's shrug. A bathrobe appeared in Noir's hand.

Aaxyl got on the bed, pressing a towel over Aameh's hair. She ran her eyes along Mohan's arms wrapped around Aameh. It was weird to see a man in Aameh's bed.

Noir turned his back on them and flared the bathrobe. Aaxyl was just about to ask if he wanted to get out of his wet clothes first when he vanished. He reappeared a few feet away. The bathrobe settled on him with a brief flash of bare butt and wet clothes fell to the floor where he'd previously stood. Now, that was a cool trick.

Mohan said, "She's still integrating her implant and couldn't sleep. She had an idea to find Hersh."

Noir secured the robe with the sash. "Mohan pathed me, but she rambled incoherently. She didn't want our help, didn't want to discuss it, then she decided to take a bath to clear her head. The next thing we know, she's screaming."

"She told me to stay out of the bathroom." Gyan conveyed remarkable disbelief with only a voice. "I tried to warn her that the water was cold, without me adjusting temperature. She wanted to be alone. It is December!"

Aaxyl supposed the building wouldn't work as intended without Gyan. She pulled wet strands of hair off Aameh's face. "Am. I'm here. I'm real."

"Aameh?" Mohan was rubbing her back.

"Cold," whimpered Aameh. *"Cold."*

"The numbers are readings from MedSIS." Gyan figured it out. "They're output."

"Estimations." Aameh nodded. "So much data."

Trust the weirdo to over-analyse an overabundance of data.

"I can shut down MedSIS if you authorise it," Gyan suggested. "I've got her. Everyone is connected to me. We don't need it anymore."

Noir nodded.

MedSIS stopped spamming their brains.

"You okay, Am?" Aaxyl asked. "You had us worried."

Aameh's gaze landed on Aaxyl's face with recognition. "I've got this. Your name is floating above you, but send the spider back. Find Hersh."

"Yeah, we gotta work on communication." Aaxyl laughed.

"I know how we can find Hersh," Aameh said. "We will need tech support."

Mohan sat up. "We can get Elir. He's young, but very talented. The two of us aren't half bad either. Beyond that, you've got the world's biggest tech company at your fingertips—people, resources, gadgets. Tell us what you need."

"It is how the mental implant works." Aameh said. "We will need tech..."

Mohan clutched his head and fell back against the bed. Noir sat abruptly, panting.

Mohan shook his head repeatedly, blinking back tears and buried his face in a pillow. "Dammit, kid," he muffled out.

"What did you do?" Aaxyl asked Aameh.

"Nothing!" Aameh looked around bewildered. "I did nothing."

"Give them a minute," Gyan suggested. "It appears they received a telepathic communication."

What telepathy was this? They had seen Mohan and Noir communicate effortlessly—focused or preoccupied—not like a car parked on their heads. Was it a telepathic attack?

"We're okay," Mohan gasped. "RudraJoy sent an SOS. The kids are with Vidroh, and in trouble. Sorry, Aaxyl, but the queue to murder Vidroh starts behind me."

"I thought they were in Bombay," Aameh said.

Mohan snarled. "So did I."

Aameh knew about Rudra?

"Is this the same Rudra from the code name and Elir from the documentary?" Aaxyl asked. She was tired of their constant animosity toward Vidroh.

Mohan nodded and sniffed.

"Rudra's the youngest Abrahamha's stray. She's... complicated. Her symbionts are more powerful than the ancients." Noir hit the side of his head with the heel of his palm. Tears were still streaming down both his and Mohan's faces. "We keep her existence a secret."

Aaxyl hadn't even considered Aameh not being the youngest of them.b "*Vidroh* knows RudraJoy, but you didn't tell me? Why didn't he say something when we found the code names?"

"He *shouldn't* know her," Noir said, grimly.

"So what now? Are you going to get them? What about *Hersh*?" Aameh said, rubbing Mohan's back.

"I can't teleport if I don't know where they are," Mohan said. "I've sent the zeplyn ahead."

"Both are priority," Noir said. "I can stay here for the Hersh plan. Aaxyl is good at running and can go with Mohan. NeoJai can go with them to keep her from doing something stupid, like trying to protect Vidroh."

Aaxyl understood Noir's anger with her. He didn't want her around because she cared about Vidroh.

"So much for us being family," Aaxyl glared back, reminding him of his own words.

"This is what family looks like here," Noir shot back. "Mohan has suffered a telepathic update from Rudra. Plus, he'll have to teleport. A little help searching on the ground isn't too much to ask for. Bring Rudra and Elir back at any cost. Vidroh can rot in hell."

Aaxyl didn't get it. "You'd said Vidroh was an ally. Why such hate?"

"He recruited child soldiers for his mad war from my family," Mohan said.

Noir asked Aaxyl in icy tones, "Would you be worried about Vidroh's safety if he took Aameh as his backup instead of Elir and Rudra J?"

"Aameh is not indestructible," Aaxyl said.

"Nor is Rudra!" Mohan roared. "Her body can't sustain her symbionts. She's sixteen and looks twelve. You've never even met her and you dehumanise her for your precious nutcase."

"This is why Rudra is a secret," Noir's voice echoed eerily. A dart hit his neck with a pop, and he looked up at a camera irritably, pulling it out. When he spoke, the echo was gone. "People are blinded by power. She wouldn't have a childhood if people knew about her. What if she were indestructible? She's a child, not a tool."

Aaxyl had to admit they had a point. Also, Noir was frankly terrifying.

"I'm sorry."

Aameh patted Noir's chest gently. "You're scaring us, big man. She's just worried."

All those years of teaching Aameh caution hadn't stuck. Just looking at Noir sitting next to Aameh made Aaxyl uneasy.

Symb-abilities looked a lot more fun from a distance.

"I'm going to ask the Deal-Maker to help there," Mohan said, suddenly. "Skinning Vidroh should occupy him for a while and give you some space here. We need to discuss the Deal-Maker. With our focus split, we're at greater risk of leaks."

Noir teleported Aaxyl and NeoJai to a conference room. Dhrit-H was already there, reading something that he put away. Mohan and Aameh arrived in minutes, fully dressed.

"Gyan," Noir said. "This room is now at the highest level of privacy. You can retain a memory for yourself to prevent accidents, but not as a record that can be accessed."

"So what is it with the Deal-Maker?" Aaxyl asked. "We've known you for barely a month, and lethal crisis is routine. What's special about him?"

"The Deal-Maker is Jugaad." Aameh made a flourish like presenting a work of art.

Noir flinched. "How did you even guess that?"

"How many people on the planet make you nervous?" Aameh shrugged. "Deal-Maker knew Gyan, so he's an AVANT senior. AricNova isn't dead. Made sense Jugaad wasn't either."

"You're scary." Mohan stared.

Aaxyl thought they were too complacent with their secrets. "Surely he wouldn't harm AricNova? Weren't they close friends?"

"Jugaad would never harm AricNova." Mohan sighed. "He would harm Abrahamha."

"Jugaad never believed that Ari died," Noir said. "He was angry when

Abrahamha concluded after decades of searching that she could not be alive or she would have showed up. We convinced him to remain in hiding."

"Why did he have to hide?" Aaxyl asked. "Abrahamha and AricNova didn't. He could have continued the search."

"Jugaad was pretty... damaged by the Enduring War," Mohan said. "He was captured, tortured, escaped, suffered PTSD... and that was before the symbionts."

"When I met Jugaad, he was already declared dead," Noir said. "He barely interacted with anyone and called himself the Global Transport Service—the GTS from history is also him. He used to teleport gigantic containers of relief materials to places where transportation had failed."

"He isn't supposed to be here at all," Mohan said. "Technically, he doesn't even live in the Superdome. He just wanders the wastelands."

A service bot came up between Aaxyl and NeoJai with their clothes. They were wearing clothes—T-shirts and shorts that they wore to bed. Aaxyl looked around at the cameras and people, unsure whom to ask for an explanation.

Mohan answered her unasked question. "Get dressed. We'll leave in a bit."

"Here?" Aaxyl looked. They were in the conference room. But there were now screens behind them, held up by small hovers. This place was nuts.

Aaxyl ducked behind one to change.

"I hate to ask the obvious." Aaxyl finished dressing and came out from behind the screen. "But how do you know he isn't listening to us telepathically right now?"

"Gyan would alert me if he entered the building," Mohan said, "but still, avoid using his name, to prevent accidents through any latent telepathy."

"Why not let him know?" NeoJai asked as he joined them, still rolling up the sleeves of a powder-blue shirt. "How long can we conceal it? Abrahamha can keep out of his way till he calms down."

"Because we want to live." Noir gestured a wavy line with his index finger. "Gyan is going to show you footage from the Enduring War that will never be public. This is the attack on our relief camp that killed Jugaad as far as the world knows."

A scene projected around them and gunfire boomed as a relief tent filled with smoke and armed men streamed in. The relief workers and patients pleaded as they were rounded up and executed. The mercenaries systematically stripped SYMB supplies with practised ease, loading them quickly into a reinforced container vehicle, bigger than a car, but smaller than a truck. More mercenaries stood guard.

Jugaad appeared in the tent. He took one look at the bodies of the staff and flinched. The scene switched to an outside camera, rippled and was replaced with a satellite view that showed a tiny ring of dark grey.

"No bomb. It was Jugaad. No survivors," Mohan said quietly. "Jugaad himself doesn't know what that was. AricNova decided that Jugaad was too unstable to be around people and declared him dead in the blast."

"Why would it be an issue if Jugaad were alive?" Aaxyl asked, sharing a worried look with NeoJai.

"Even without state and law and courts, when armed men die, there's revenge," Mohan said simply. "Jugaad is a scientist, architect, athlete, comedian, engineer, technologist... this was an accident, but more attacks would only mean more scenes like this."

Noir continued. "This is Abrahamha's legendary return of the missiles. Till this time, we had thought him relatively safe."

Satellite imagery again. Missiles fired, vanished, and the places where they were fired from exploded. The view scrolled to another small white puff, pause, boom. Over and over. Some in daylight, some at night.

"It almost killed him, but he stuck with it to ensure that his ultimatum held," Noir said.

"When anger issues in the family need satellite imagery, you've got a problem," Aaxyl muttered.

"These are not humans," Mohan said. "They're good people who have sacrificed too much to help people during the Enduring War."

"So you keep reminding us," Aaxyl said. "But how is it better to no longer have missiles, but have individuals who could defeat them all at once? He's a great guy, but oh, there's an issue with misfires." Aaxyl put the last sentence in air quotes.

"They know they're dangerous, which is why they don't live here," Noir said. "But you can't expect calm under stress. Jugaad will find AricNova. What happens if she's in another basement of a Dorm? What happens if she's not in any of the Dorms, but because she once was, he checks them anyway?"

Mohan sighed. "If Jugaad goes after Abrahamha, stopping Sambit to save lives will be pointless."

"Why's he here?" Aaxyl asked. "How can we send him back?"

Mohan and Noir looked at Dhrit-H.

"Me?" he asked, startled. "I've never met him."

"He was Saisrisel's friend," Noir said. "He made his off-planet base on Terra Nova possible."

"I suppose it is possible," Dhrit-H said. "I was assassinated before. Now a clone was kidnapped. Struggling with dangerous symbionts. Our home was attacked. My wife was injured. We've had our share of trouble."

"Assassinated?" Aaxyl asked.

"That's when I was cloned, " Dhrit-H said. "NeoJai was a baby. I resigned as President of the dome, to reduce risk to my family. Damodar became the next president within a week."

"Did Damodar do it?"

"We couldn't prove it."

"Can you ask Jugaad to take Dhrit to the Superdome?" Aameh asked Mohan.

"Can't. He'll wonder why I'm not doing it myself or asking Noir, and read my mind," Mohan said. "Also, he'd teleport him there and return."

"Mind reading isn't real," Aaxyl said. Aameh had said it would make history if anyone could demonstrate mind reading or time travel and Aameh was seldom wrong. Then she remembered Abrahamha in the Null Dorms.

"The Three have strong telepathy. Thinking to yourself and thinking a reply isn't very different. They can't read your mind, but they can hear you unless you guard your thoughts. Always assume an ancient near you knows what you're thinking," Gyan said. "I can protect you to some extent on my premises."

"How so?" asked Aaxyl.

"I distracted you by asking whether you wanted sun, sea, mountain, or rain when Jugaad was near you. It wouldn't matter if he found out your preference."

Nose was Jugaad, Aaxyl realised.

A second update from Rudra blasted Mohan and Noir. They breathed and blinked their way through.

White-hot rage bled through Noir's tears. "Vidroh is injured and stuck in a vent at the base they were infiltrating. Rudra rescued Elir, but lost control. He's managed to calm her down, and send her back to rescue Vidroh."

"He should have teleported her home and left Vidroh there to rot," Mohan spat.

A twenty-year-old had sent a sixteen-year-old who looked like a twelve-year-old to rescue the massive Vidroh from a vent. What could possibly go wrong?

Thirty-inch S&J service bots offer highest utility for cost in the housekeeping segment.
TechEdge, Sunday, December 7, 2442

~~*~*~*~*

AAXYL: WASTELANDS

The conference room dissolved into a moving zeplyn.

Aaxyl and NeoJai lost their balance.

Mohan steadied them till they found their feet and steered them toward the seats. He handed them their new communicators and their implants connected as soon as he authorised them.

Aaxyl had got used to Gyan being in her head. It was nice to have the comm now, rather than silence.

Mohan slouched in the seat, long legs sprawled almost to the center of the zeplyn, and leaned his head back, resting.

Aaxyl looked out curiously. So these were the wastelands. Dim grey ground rolled past below them. Oranges and pinks tinged the sky ahead silhouetting a flock of birds. Aaxyl's first sunrise outside the dome grew imminent as the zeplyn flew over the monochromatic wilderness.

Soon, the light grew brighter and the golden brown of dried grass interspersed with dark bushes. Trees grew through urban ruins. A forest lay on their right. Green streaked the creases where the ground dipped low and streams trickled over rocky beds. The word wastelands implied unpleasant expanses, but this was beautiful.

A young voice rang with relief through the zeplyn's speakers. "Oh, thank SYMBs you found me!"

Aaxyl smiled at Mohan, only for him to hug her.

It lasted a few moments, till Elir spoke again. "Have you seen Rudra?"

A spark zapped out from Mohan and Aaxyl jerked back, stung.

Mohan growled, "She isn't with you?"

"She went to get Vidroh, but still hasn't returned. And now SecPros have hovers in the air."

The shapes in the distance weren't birds. The distance was so great that they looked small.

Aaxyl scanned the shrubbery, but Elir could be anywhere within the range of communicators.

"You dwits!" Mohan paced the zeplyn, shrinking the spacious vehicle with restless strides. "I'm in my zeplyn. Teleport here."

Silence. No Elir either.

"I..." Elir's voice, already hesitant, faltered.

"You can't teleport, can you?" Mohan snapped. "You're playing the great saviour of the wastelands with Vidroh when you can't focus enough to teleport. Try to identify landmarks near you."

"I'm near a large boulder."

Aaxyl snorted. There were boulders everywhere.

"Scout around a bit for something more identifiable," Mohan said. "We'll get back to you."

A screen lowered from the roof on the side opposite to the door, and Mohan brought a map of the region up on it. The facility was marked red. The zeplyn was green. A dotted line connected their position with the facility. Mohan marked a route for Aaxyl toward the facility and he would search away from it.

"Rudra will almost certainly have retrieved Vidroh," Mohan said. "NeoJai, you know how to use a zeplyn. You talk to the dimwit and figure out where he is and pick him up or get him calm enough to teleport in."

Aaxyl and Mohan would search till one of them found Rudra or Vidroh and then Aaxyl would activate a beacon on her comm for Mohan to find her. With everyone found, Mohan would teleport them home and the zeplyn could return on its own. It was a plan.

They dropped Aaxyl first off first. Her comm automatically imped a route overlay, and she set off. It took her a while getting used to the stony and sloping ground, but once she did, she hit her stride.

"What do you think happened with Rudra and Vidroh?" she imped to Mohan as the trail curved around a boulder.

"Probably just got lost," Mohan imped back. *"When she saw Elir under threat, she ran to him, picked him up and sped away. NeoJai just found him two kilometres from the base. She could have undershot or overshot that distance."*

Aaxyl slowed to navigate her way around a clump of bushes that didn't seem to want to end. She was headed downhill following a stream running through a gully and the slope was covered with small stones that slid underfoot. *"Do you think they captured her?"*

"I doubt they can capture her."

Aaxyl had been getting direct sun rays for a while now and was uncomfortably hot. She drank the water, rubbed on sunscreen, wore the cap and sunglasses and frowned at the unfamiliar tint across her vision. *"Control takes work. Nobody else can give it to her. She shouldn't risk the lives of others if she isn't sure she can do something."*

Her head had already started feeling sweaty.

"Control takes work, eh?" Mohan imped. *"Abrahamha and AricNova were just drama queens to separate those with evolved abilities from normal people? If I cut Aameh, and she doesn't heal, is it because she doesn't try hard enough?"*

"Come on, you know what I mean," Aaxyl imped. *"She has no business being here. You're just worried."*

"She probably didn't realise till too late that there was any danger involved," Mohan imped. *"She's a great kid and does her best with the crappy hand she's got, but this is well outside her experience."*

Aaxyl understood perfectly now. They were counting on a superhuman toddler without brakes to rescue a suicidal rebel without sanity.

She went around a boulder on a steep slope carefully, scree skittering down to the stream some twenty feet below, as she navigated the unfamiliar ground gingerly.

Bone-chilling fear slammed through her. A sense of walking on an infinite chasm prevented any further movement and she stood there, hands out for balance, not daring to move. Her body was coming apart. She was going to die. She broke through the paralysis of terror to flee and forgot about the slope she was standing on and tumbled down all the way to the stream. She didn't dare stand up again and sat where she was. In the water. *"Mohan!"*

"Odd feelings of terror?" Mohan interpreted her panic with surprising accuracy. *"You found Rudra. She has to be close by. Turn on your beacon."*

"Thanks for the warning, asshole."

"Sorry. I'm used to it. I forgot."

Aaxyl's hands trembled uncontrollably and the simple task took ages.

Her comm finally imped her to ask if she wanted to turn on the beacon and she confirmed it.

She focused on keeping it together as she waited, alone in the wastelands, with her entire existence dissolving into atoms while she froze in the stream from the waist down and her head cooked in the hot sun. Aaxyl hated the wastelands with a vengeance now.

"Can you teleport to a beacon?" Aaxyl had thought they needed keys.

"The zeplyn can navigate to it," Mohan imped. *"If you see Rudra, stay away. Try to focus on something else. She isn't attacking you, she's scared."*

"My bruised and frozen legs disagree."

Aaxyl tried to focus in the direction she had come from to await the zeplyn. It was impossible. The threat grew in the opposite direction. Every instinct screamed a hyper-alert for the predator. A thin girl came around a bend further downstream and Aaxyl's eyes stuck to her. The bright sunlight bleached her skin to a translucent white. Aliens weren't supposed to exist.

"Are you Aaxyl?" Alienling asked.

Fresh terror lashed Aaxyl. Nobody would know if she wet herself in the stream. "How do you know me?" Aaxyl's voice quavered.

"Cargo pants. Mohan told us about you." Alienling took a step closer and stopped when Aaxyl tried to scramble back. "I need help. Vidroh is injured."

Ten minutes ago, Aaxyl wouldn't have believed she'd stay put when Vidroh needed help. Now she was confident she couldn't do anything useful.

Alienling wore a T-shirt that said *Solve everything with Spar Scales.* She latched on to that. It reminded her of Aameh's posters and made her somewhat relatable, though Aaxyl's instincts remained unconvinced. In the end, Aaxyl's theoretical physics caved before existential fear.

"I'll throw you my first-aid kit." Her heart still hammered in terror. "Please don't come closer."

Aaxyl fumbled with shaking hands that failed to figure out pockets. Stones skittered on the slope. She felt a soft bump and a ripping tug as a tiny hand completed the job. The little pickpocket had taken the first-aid kit and scampered away.

With Rudra out of sight, her terror uncoiled warily, and Aaxyl got to her knees in the water, willing to crawl away with the last of her breath, when the sound in her ears registered. The zeplyn was landing. NeoJai was witnessing her abject humiliation.

What Aaxyl wouldn't give to go back to their old life and safe room in the Dorms.

She rested her hot cheek on a wet rock. Terror ought to be a surge of fear. Turned out Rudra could make it a weather report.

Mohan lifted her to her feet. "Let's get you home."

AAMEH: SYMBTECH BUILDING

"We have to find AricNova before Jugaad knows she's alive," Aameh said, scooting back against the headboard to make more space for Noir to sit comfortably. "Also, we must help Abrahamha and Jugaad with their abilities. Have you explored professional help?"

"Like a psychologist?" Noir laughed. "Symbionts can't sit on a couch, look in your eyes and converse. They hijack your mind and body and any learning is hindsight."

Aameh expected the rejection, but she was good at arguing. "You don't go around blasting the world all the time. Emotions exacerbate loss of control."

"Consider the consequences if an unresolved issue flares up, and they fry the shrink," Noir mimicked her tone. "Possibly accompanied by bystanders and a chunk of the dome."

"She'll have to take precautions." Aameh hadn't planned that far. "Maybe they can teleport her to a safe space for sessions."

"She?"

Aameh nodded. "Ask Jugaad, as the Deal-Maker, to facilitate Scharada's asylum in exchange for helping RudraJoy, Abrahamha and Jugaad gain control."

"It isn't going to be as simple as that." Noir frowned. "I'll tell Mohan. He's better at this sort of thing. Explain what is needed. Leave implementing to us. How do we find AricNova?"

She should have started with that. Her brain was still wonky, but she'd figured it out. "I need to do a grid search to connect with Hersh's implant. The resolution of the grid should not be more than the range of the implant—"

"I understand a grid, Am," Noir said wryly. "Grid search of where? The whole dome? Continent? World?"

She was overexplaining. Got it.

Aameh asked for a map of the dome. Gyan projected one on the floor next to the bed.

Aameh asked Gyan to mark all locations in the dome with SHADE systems that recognised Hersh. Two white areas appeared: The SYMBTech building and Mohan's home.

"These are the locations where crimes were committed using nulls. And similar crimes without arrests, where he may not have abandoned the null." Red dots appeared in clusters.

Noir caught on. "We can remove any areas within range of a SHADE or he'd have connected already. And the ones near Null Dorms since he's already moved from there. And his home, since that's the first place SecPros would look." More dots vanished.

"Of these, this one was active all through, and also has the most recent incidents. If we take a SHADE there, we'll find Hersh in one of them." There were three areas left. Aameh got out of bed and jumped on the biggest one. Because she could. "This one. But we search all three."

"Understood," Noir said. "A SHADE is not portable, but it's a good idea."

"So that complicates my plan." Aameh considered. It wasn't her fault. The data she could access didn't have any specifications on the SHADEs. "We'll have to figure out the connection with the implant. As to why I'm certain that they're still in this dome, it is because he's still active here. If he weren't—"

Noir covered her mouth with his hand. "Help me test devices Hersh's implant has connected to in the past."

"Yes, of course! What about a telepathic relay? You were planning to set one up at NeoJai's home, so—" Aameh imped.

"That telepathic relay can't be moved around either," Noir explained. "We make this tech, Am. I understand it better. Leave the figuring out to me."

But she still had more options left. "We could create a network of comms..."

Noir teleported her into a large empty room, vanished, and started bringing in assorted items. A *Cosmic Chaos* game, a Zephyron, a microscope, a symbiont analyser, motorcycle and a few others. Aameh hadn't pegged Hersh for a motorcycle type. She knew little of his life outside the clinic.

The air bike wouldn't connect with an implant while in use, to prevent accidents. The microscope didn't have enough range. The game and Zephyron combined were the best bets.

Once they had the whole thing designed, it could be replicated using a multi-sync Elir had invented, so they'd have several Zephyrons to search faster, and reduce the risk of alerting Sambit.

Gyan issued Aameh a new communicator just as she was about to ask Noir how a multi-sync worked. She suspected it was just distracting her to keep her from asking Noir questions while he worked.

She liked Noir. She really hoped the implant hadn't made her more irritating than usual. At least not permanently. She spent time getting to know her comm.

"You don't need a comm on my premises," Gyan said. "But since your plan depends on it, this will help you understand how connecting works."

The communicator was a flat block under two inches square. Nothing indicated sophisticated technology. It could be fitted with covers to mimic popular comm models that also provided the displays and interactivity of that model.

An undercover comm! Aameh smirked.

She chose a cover like her Dorm comm. Gyan suggested a popular model for women.

"Never used those," Aameh said.

"You have a mental implant," Gyan said. "You want to date the owners of AVANT wearing a cheap Dorm comm? Plus, this interface provides projection displays and can sync with sculpting gloves."

That settled it.

Gyan projected a chart of safety features for the comm. There were twelve conditions in which the comm would self-destruct to protect the confidential technology or its owner.

"Hello, Evian Hunt," Aameh murmured. Aaxyl had watched all but seven films about the character. His devices self-destructed after use.

"Name me," the comm imped.

"Would you like to choose?" Aameh asked it.

"Wynd."

"You're like a mini-SHADE!"

"Mini-SHADE is incorrect," Gyan said. "Even though it has a limited personality, the technology is different. A comm is a single user device and can't monitor an environment."

"I am not supposed to be a SHADE," Wynd imped.

"An implant under development omits captive symbionts to allow telepaths to use their native range. It will render comms obsolete for telepaths with a global reach," Gyan said.

"It doesn't work. Putting metal in the brain without the captive symbionts shuts down all telepathy. Even if it worked, a SHADE couldn't travel like me and would be blind to local information outside its premises."

"Are you guys jealous of each other?" Aameh asked.

"Of course not." Wynd.

Gyan produced a very realistic snort. "I just mean a communicator is unnecessary within a SHADE."

AAXYL: MOHAN'S HOME

Mohan teleported Aaxyl and NeoJai to his home and returned for Rudra and Vidroh.

A SHADE offered a connection through Aaxyl's mental implant. *"I'm Shantiniketan."* It had a feminine, matronly persona. *"You're dripping. The bathroom's this way."* An overlay marked the way.

Aaxyl bathed and joined NeoJai in the elegant media room where she'd discovered that Perfect Sam was Mohan. It felt like another lifetime.

Utter fear paralysed her.

Not again!

Four people had appeared in the centre of the room.

Mohan sank to the floor with shuddering breaths.

A lanky youth squirmed guiltily next to him. Elir.

Vidroh was a mangled mess in a torn and bloody biohazard suit. He was carried by Alienling, barely visible behind his gory bulk.

But once Aaxyl had seen her, she couldn't look away.

Rudrajoy was untroubled by Vidroh's hulking size extending several feet on either side of her. Even if she were strong, surely it would at least be unwieldy to carry someone of a much greater size? Apparently not.

She defied something fundamental to reality, as though she didn't fully exist.

Aaxyl may not know what Alienling was, but *predator* sufficed. Eerie eyes found her face and Aaxyl felt like she'd kicked the proverbial puppy, while in truth, she was the shoe it was chewing apart.

"Rudra," Mohan panted.

RudraJoy sped off with Vidroh.

Aaxyl and NeoJai trudged warily in her wake with Shantiniketan directing them to the second floor. Desire to see Vidroh warred with dread.

By the time they reached the second floor, RudraJoy wore a huge AVANT T-shirt like a dress and a scowl like a shield. She slouched against the wall outside Vidroh's room with the air of one propping up an incompetent world.

NeoJai and Aaxyl drifted to a halt at the top of the stairs, wanting to check on Vidroh, but not daring to approach.

Beyond Alienling, they heard medics already working on Vidroh. How fast could the kid move?

NeoJai rubbed his arms uneasily, as jumpy as Aaxyl.

Mohan breezed past them. Alienling flew into his arms with surreal speed. Just like that, she was a terrified child.

He wrapped his arms around her, pole-thin dad to her scrawny kid. Mohan kissed the top of her head and subtly gestured them past before rubbing that bony back to comfort her.

Aaxyl and NeoJai sneaked past the duo.

Nothing had prepared Aaxyl for the sight of Vidroh. Gashes and bruising marred his body.

He'd already been cleaned. Medics were sealing him in healing film like a meat product to reduce contact with air. She'd heard about this. The film would flake off as he healed. A drape taped over his crotch provided a nod to modesty.

It had been hours since he was injured. "Why isn't he healing?"

A medic wrapping the leg on their side replied, "He's fine. Looks worse than it is. Visible changes take a while to appear when he's struggling for energy. He's on nutrients now. He'll wake up soon."

Her imagination had painted a romanticised hero fighting for the water sources of wastelanders. She had no idea who this man was.

The medic's voice broke into her thoughts. "He's out of danger and the more he sleeps, the better. We'll inform you if he wakes up."

Meaning, go away.

They left Vidroh to the medics.

Mohan's real living room was more like half a dorm hall, with an ad-hoc aesthetic. A sexless humanoid dummy with an impressive number of cuts and a missing foot leaned drunkenly against a shelf with more dummies piled up before it. Curious, Aaxyl headed over, but a red warning overlaid her vision: Restricted area. Elir's Transferron research. Contact him for permission.

Okay.

Shelves lined every wall, overflowing with gadgets, boxes, drones, tools... Seating clustered around the room with open space in the center: comfortable chairs facing window seats, cushions on the floor, desks, bean bags, stools, Zephyrons, a sleeping bag and two benches. And on the far end, there was that sofa from the Null Dorms, on which Abrahamha sat once more.

Aaxyl stopped cataloguing the room and towed a Zephyron along as they went over.

"Hi, I'm Abrahamha," he said to NeoJai as though he could have been someone else without that clarification.

NeoJai mumbled appropriately.

Abrahamha radiated more control than in the Null Dorms, or rather, didn't radiate anything. Yet.

Aaxyl sniffed cautiously. No exotic scent in the air either. Abrahamha smiled at her and she squirmed like she'd been caught smelling his armpit.

"Welcome to the family," Abrahamha said.

Aaxyl said, "Thank you."

Talking to Abrahamha like he was a normal person. The rabbit hole ran deep.

Aaxyl perched on her Zephyron next to the chair NeoJai chose. Elir sat on a bench off to one side, like a prisoner awaiting sentencing. RudraJoy brooded opposite Abrahamha on a cushion on the floor. Thin arms hugged knees-to-chest, chin-on-knees compacting her into a tiny speck before the hulking Abrahamha.

Abrahamha gestured gently and the bench, and Elir with it, moved so that they were seated in a loose circle in a repeat of the Null Dorms, except Mohan appeared behind Abrahamha like a pole-thin henchman.

Aaxyl suspected he was there to protect others from Abrahamha.

Mohan broke the silence. "Let me make it clear." His eyes nailed Elir. "I will *end* you if you endanger Rudra again. Your deployment of entanglement dots on their SIS is a remarkable achievement, but Rudra's safety is never negotiable."

Elir shrank like one cashing an unwelcome reality check.

"I shouldn't exist." RudraJoy glared defiantly. "If you could kill me, you'd have done it long ago."

Impressive attempt at misdirection, emotional manipulation and sibling solidarity rolled into one.

Mohan skewered Alienling with an irritated glance.

Aaxyl felt an affinity with the ultra-sexy global-businessman Mohan on parenting, of all things. This explained his enjoyment of Aameh's eccentricities. He was neck-deep in lunatics in his natural habitat.

"What are entanglement dots?" Aaxyl imped Shantiniketan.

"Elir's prototype tool to deploy synced spars, so that changes to one alter both. If Elir can replicate their SIS and sync it to the original, we could alter their records to remove resources needed by settlements," it replied.

Okay. That must be big. She was glad at least some good had come from Vidroh's desperation. Elir showed a pen sized gadget that apparently shot symbion particles. It logged positioning for replication with their synced counterparts at AVANT's precision engineering facility run by a SHADE called Taknik.

"Vidroh sacrificed himself to save this," Elir said, handing the gadget to Mohan.

Aaxyl hoped Vidroh did it because he had an ounce of protective instinct left. Besides, Alienling had saved this band of sorry men.

Alienling knelt before Elir. "Vidroh saved *you*, not the recording. Any of us would."

Abrahamha raised a parental eyebrow. "Glad that is clear. We'd kill Rudra if we could, but save Elir, because we're just confused that way."

Alienling gaped at him.

Mohan's lips twitched as he swallowed his smile just in time. NeoJai got busy coughing.

Alienling scowled at the humour at her expense, close to tears.

Aaxyl recognised a hangry teenager when she saw one. "She's probably hungry and tired."

Apparently Aaxyl hadn't learned her lesson, because Alienling trapped Aaxyl with her eerie gaze and the chasm opened up again. "I'm buzzing with energy from ambient radioactivity from the wastelands."

Aaxyl tried to not overreact, distracting herself with the idea of radiotrophic symbionts. HealSYMB offered some radioresistance, but using radiation for energy... "That still leaves you exhausted, upset, and probably hungry."

Alienling burst into tears.

Stupid. She should have kept her mouth shut. Aaxyl tunnelled into herself as the chasm closed around her. NeoJai whimpered. Between Abrahamha and Rudra, she'd call it a win to get through this at all.

Shantiniketan sent in food. RudraJoy ate vast quantities at an impressive pace, and curled on the floor, tear-stained and ragged, fast asleep. Poor little Alienling.

"Is she okay?" Aaxyl asked.

"She'll be fine." Mohan stroked RudraJoy's hair affectionately. "This one recovers fast."

NeoJai wasn't bothering with lunch, and leaned back with his eyes closed.

Aaxyl hadn't dared serve herself till Rudra calmed. Now she held her sparse plate, reluctant to arm her stomach for terror attacks.

Mohan raised a finger, as though listening. "Vidroh is conscious."

Relief.

"Excellent," Abrahamha said. "Get him here."

He was injured.

NeoJai squeezed Aaxyl's hand hard enough to remind her to not interfere.

Mohan vanished, then reappeared with a film-wrapped Vidroh with draped crotch, and threw him into a chair.

Aaxyl winced sympathetically, but Vidroh didn't look at her.

Neither Playboy Mohan nor Perfect Sam were home. Mohan looked like a grim angel with his mesmerising beauty now featuring lethal eyes.

Elir trembled.

"What have you to say for yourself, Vidroh?" Abrahamha's voice scraped their nerves.

Vidroh quaked. "Elir told me Rudra could stop the power without getting close to the base. I didn't know anything about her other than she was the code name till they got there."

That had to be the most ridiculous excuse for taking children into danger that Aaxyl had heard. Disbelief swept away caution. "You led them into danger because they *showed up*? Why didn't you abort the mission after you met her?"

Aaxyl knew Rudra was sixteen, but insane power apart, she looked fragile even for a twelve year old.

NeoJai squeezed her hand. Hard.

Got it. Stand in the outrage queue. Don't cut in.

"Ax, water can mean life or death to settlers."

Mohan gasped at a pitch that would have been comical in other circumstances. "You're STILL defending your madness? To the woman who worried about you being dead, injured and now just terminally stupid."

RudraJoy sat up, breaking the moment. Just like that. Fast asleep one moment, ready, the next. "What did I miss?"

Abrahamha asked Rudra, "Why did you go?"

Aaxyl wanted this explanation. NeoJai leaned forward too. This family didn't even mention her to outsiders.

"Vidroh didn't mind risk. Elir thought the Margadarshak didn't understand him. He could execute good plans that were too risky for others."

"That's an interesting perspective. Self harm as a tactical resource." Mohan's melodious voice prodded her. "And how did this kamikaze expand to the two of you? Are you both suicidal as well?"

"The Margadarshak Network rejected this plan because no one could access the power source. I could do that. You said it would make the plan doable." She halted at the look on Abrahamha's face.

"Would it, Mohan?" Abrahamha's face was extra calm.

"I didn't know," Mohan said with the exaggerated clarity of one standing on the wrong end of a weapon. "I agreed that remotely deactivating power would improve chances of success. I didn't even know Rudra could do it."

"It wasn't Mohan's fault," Elir said.

"I don't care what you think." Abrahamha shut him up. "You aren't good at it."

Mohan asked Ruda, "How did you stop the power?"

"Like putting a glass on an ant line? The ants get disturbed and turn back. In a while they find their way around it. The power resumes."

That was not how electricity worked, but it was the explanation they were getting. Mohan looked reassuringly confused too. It wasn't just Aaxyl.

"Okay, so you cut the power. Then?"

"Vidroh and Elir went in. I was to stop power later to let them exit." RudraJoy swallowed. "Elir came out. They saw him. I didn't know what to do."

Elir said, "We should have planned better, it was our lack of foresight."

"Your lack of foresight was when you took her there," Mohan said coldly.

RudraJoy cleared her throat. "SecPros were about to shoot. I grabbed Elir and ran, but lost control. He was begging me to go back for Vidroh."

"Rudra J, you..." Abrahamha began.

RudraJoy interrupted him. "By the time I got to Vidroh, they were shooting at him. I rescued him, but couldn't find Elir. Vidroh wouldn't wake. I didn't know what to do."

Vidroh, spent and defeated, hadn't moved for a while, but a slight flinch twitched through his face at the distress in RudraJoy's voice. The kid was blaming herself for failing to react well to a situation she had no business being in, while the adult made excuses.

Mohan turned to Elir. "If one of you geniuses had explained that Rudra can stop the electric supply, I or Noir, LuvIsaac, Zayn or *any* experienced teleporter could have executed this plan safely." He watched Elir's face redden. "But *you* wouldn't get to go. You risked Rudra for adventure!"

Elir's defiance was a monument to the youthful delusion of invincibility. "Weapons can't hurt RJ!"

Make that tombstone.

Rudra moved away from Elir.

Acrid slashes of Abrahamha's symbionts whipped through the room. Static cracked across Aaxyl's skin. NeoJai jerked. And then Mohan lost it.

"What if one of you had died?" Mohan roared. "She'd be stranded with a dead body in the middle of nowhere, with SecPros combing the region. She can't teleport without risking her life. She didn't even know where she was to path us to find her." Face a mask of rage, words firing like bullets. "For your adventure."

Aaxyl couldn't breathe. Mohan had never felt dangerous before this, but she was being crushed. She imagined turning into a tiny diamond.

Rudra streaked to the far end of the living room and returned with a gun. This was a good time to be grateful Aameh wasn't here.

Mohan calmed abruptly, wary eyes on Rudra.

RudraJoy turned to NeoJai, but she was really talking to Elir. "I have super abilities. One of them is accelerated healing." She held up the gun in her right hand, and raised her left, turning it around, like a demonstration, continuing as NeoJai tried to protest. "Not the healing you know. You don't know anything like this."

Elir stirred uncomfortably. "Come on, RJ. This isn't you."

NeoJai's face was white and he was swallowing repeatedly.

The menace seething off RudraJoy was so suffocating, Aaxyl couldn't move or speak.

RudraJoy fired the gun into her hand. Something shattered, but Aaxyl couldn't be bothered to find out what. The bullet had passed right through Rudra's tiny hand. She fired again and the bullet struck her hand and fell to the ground. She wiped her hand on her giant T-shirt and showed it to NeoJai, and then Aaxyl, like a performer on a stage. No marks. Pure creepy hand.

"I detest being the freak." RudraJoy addressed Aaxyl now, eyes glittering with unshed tears, but her target was still Elir and he flinched. "This heals, but it still hurts."

"RJ, please. I'm sorry!" Elir was openly begging now.

"Don't you still get it?" RudraJoy scoffed. "Vidroh took us because we are too stupid to know better."

Vidroh flinched and Aaxyl saw the guilt. He *had* taken the kids because nobody but the kids thought it a good idea.

Abrahamha said, "Elir and Vidroh have lost our trust and will no longer work with the Margadarshak Network."

Elir nodded stoically. Vidroh remained frozen, lost to whatever demons he was wrestling.

Abrahamha said, "Being a prodigy makes you intelligent, Elir, but you're a long way away from wisdom. And Vidroh, this stops here." There was no *or else*.

Mohan strode over to Vidroh and hauled him to his feet. "Find some clothes, and get out of my home."

Aaxyl's skin was on fire, well beyond irritation. She fought to not scratch, because if she began, she wouldn't stop.

Mohan turned to Abrahamha. "I have a request for you and Jugaad. You benefit from centuries of experience. You have lived among people before having to isolate yourselves. Rudra can't spend her life in hiding."

"Okay...?" Abrahamha asked.

"Rudra isn't irresponsible," Mohan said. "She got roped into this because she was ignorant. She's always going to have powers someone will find useful. She needs to learn to deal with people. And for that, she needs better control."

Abrahamha said, "I agree. What do you propose?"

"I believe a psychologist can help her," Mohan said. "But she can't understand Rudra's symb-abilities. Not even I can, really. I want you and Jugaad to go with her. Go through the process, help her benefit from it. Maybe get some benefit yourself."

Abrahamha frowned.

Mohan pointed to NeoJai. His fair skin sported angry red welts from being around Abrahamha.

Regret flooded Abrahamha's face. "We'll do it. I'll leave now. Elir needs to go to Taknik anyway."

Abrahamha vanished with Elir, and the relentless pressure lifted off, making Aaxyl so floaty she was surprised her ears didn't pop.

NeoJai heaved a giant sigh. "My entire being fizzeth over."

Aaxyl was surprised by a downward tug on her arm. She looked down only to follow RudraJoy's hand back up to her face, eerie eyes switching between Aaxyl and NeoJai. Aaxyl could have sworn she was cross-legged on the floor a second ago. At least the terror vibes were barely perceptible.

"I'm sorry for scaring you," RudraJoy said.

"It's okay, RudraJoy." NeoJai smiled warily.

RudraJoy nodded. "Call me Rudra. Or find a version. Hardly anyone calls me RudraJoy unless I'm in trouble."

She turned to Aaxyl, waiting for her response. There was something Aameh-like about how... systematic her interactions were.

"I understand," Aaxyl said. She really did. The kid couldn't help the effect she had on others and Aaxyl felt somewhat protective about her. "But if you harm yourself again, *Alienling*, I'll find a way to make you regret it."

Rudra snorted.

Aaxyl waited.

The kid blinked. "Mohan needed Abrahamha and Jugaad to agree to take me to the psychologist. They'll do anything for me. I... improvised."

And Aaxyl had thought raising Aameh was hard.

Intense flooding alters the path of the Ganga for the third time this century. No damage to humans expected. World Environment News, Sunday, December 7, 2442

~~*~*~*

Aameh: SYMBTech Building

Dhrit-H presented a tentative political strategy when the usual suspects gathered on the SYMBTech roof for dinner.

Gyan had turned the roof into an empty room with white-washed cement walls, like an Enduring War film about an underground movement. Dhrit-H and NeoJai looked like academics. Mohan resembled a celebrity and Noir... well, he played Abrahamha. Aaxyl was a construction worker.

"Why do we need a political strategy?" Aaxyl asked.

Dhrit-H said, "Sambit is using UDAY resources even without authorisation. Also, what happens when Hersh is found, and those who allowed Sambit that kind of power are still governing this Dome?"

The Deal-Maker joined in as a projected black box, and Dhrit-H shut up.

Now that Aaxyl knew he was Jugaad, she kept glaring at his screen. Sooner or later, he'd suspect something and from there it would be a very short leap to discover what they were doing.

Aameh was distracted by a message on her comm from earlier. *Rohan: Is it true Administrator Dhrit was investigating Sambit's secret experiments involving telepathic symbionts?*

Aameh had earlier sent information about Sambit's attack to select journalists to discourage UDAY from shielding him along with a reconstruction of him spraying bullets in the Saisisel living room. But she had made no mention of the kidnapping or nulls. Very few people knew what Sambit had been doing.

"We need a way to bring down UDAY or undermine their power in the Dome to flush Sambit out," Noir said, as though they were just getting started.

"Leela and other Directors could rally dormers, but we'll need to give them clear direction," Dhrit-H said.

"I can probably push some buttons with the media," the Deal-Maker said.

Aameh considered the Deal-Maker's blank screen, and Aaxyl glaring at it on and off. A wild idea sprang into her head. Almost too far-fetched, but didn't symbionts connect people in inexplicable ways? It could be a way to get the Deal-Maker to leave them alone. She checked Rohan's stories for one she could use.

"Deal-Maker, we need your help." Aameh gambled. "The *Dome Times* reported that UDAY converted powerful people suspected of corruption into political support positions. We need them to be unavailable when we make our move."

"I'm aware of the report," the Deal-Maker told her. "May I ask how you know about it?"

Aameh knew she was right.

"The author of the report, Rohan, was Aaxyl's opponent for her SecPro trial," Aameh said, wishing Jugaad showed his face to gauge his reaction. "Someone tampered with the trial and nearly got Aaxyl killed. I've followed his work since then." Aameh nailed the Deal-Maker's screen with a glare. "It turns out he gets information miraculously. Almost like he made a deal with some higher power."

Aameh didn't like threats to Aaxyl. The meddling bastard had almost got her killed.

"This needs to remain quiet," she moved on smoothly, before Aaxyl could speak. They didn't need a confrontation. They needed him to go. "Expose a few, make others unavailable. Use different methods. Don't try to punish. All we need is for them to not help UDAY."

"If this is all I have to do, I can sign off here. I'll send updates to Gyan." The Deal-Maker disconnected.

Aameh blew a smug kiss at his screen.

Noir asked Gyan to block communications in and out. Mohan pulled Aameh out of her seat and into a hug.

Aaxyl looked at her in disbelief. "He sabotaged my SecPro Trial?"

"How could you possibly guess that?" asked Noir.

"Why did he look out for Ax more than Dhrit?" Aameh asked. "She has no direct connection with him. Why send a lawyer to help Ax? Why offer to get her out of the Dorms? Twice! She refused the first time. What does all that have to do with Dhrit? Dhrit-H was attacked in his home. Mohan came, the Deal-Maker didn't. Fine, he's in hiding, but it didn't bother him that much. Admin Dhrit is in a hospital he founded, but he hasn't checked what kind of symbionts are infecting him or our secret would be blown. His connection was with Ax."

NeoJai furrowed his brows. "But how did you know the reason?"

"I sent anonymous information about Sambit to a few journalists. Rohan already knew Admin Dhrit was investigating telepathic experiments on nulls. This was never made public. None of us would leak details around *Hersh*. Rohan had a source very close to us who didn't have a motive for secrecy or the full story. It just connected in my head. He helped Ax, because he felt guilty that he cost her a job and life outside the Dorms. I knew he wouldn't risk his identity being exposed."

"This should keep him away," Noir said. "You got too close. Suspecting he's the Deal-Maker is bad enough. He wouldn't want anyone to guess that he was Jugaad."

Aameh beamed. She did enjoy a clever win.

"I don't think anyone has ever ripped through Jugaad's anonymity like you," Mohan said. "We didn't know he was making these deals till he told us. We thought he had withdrawn completely from the world."

"What does he normally do?" Aaxyl asked.

"Work or binge-watch fiction in an abandoned home he's appropriated in the wastelands," Noir said. "The Deal-Maker is just a new format. I think he treats the world as fiction too. Snoops on people he finds interesting, steps in and helps them out. He builds relationships like this. The deals give him an excuse to contact them again."

Tragic loneliness of a once beloved hero. Damn, that was sad stuff.

Dhrit-H picked up his task list. "We need a new SecPro provider under Assistant Commander Menhir in case a need for security arises again. I've talked to him. Noir, we'll need your help with the new President.,"

Noir leaned forward. "I'm global. I can't get involved in governance providers."

"I want you to take Aameh to Sexel and introduce her to your old boyfriend Milup. He's the one currently organising Nagrik Manch," Dhrit-H informed him. "I'm hoping that Aameh will convince him to become the next President."

"We aren't even in touch," Noir said.

"Why me?" Aameh asked in surprise.

"You're a resident of this Dome and a dormer," Dhrit said. "This will matter to anyone who'd be a good President. Besides, you're good at convincing people."

"Milup definitely won't do it for a global citizen," Noir said sourly.

"So you're propping me up to prop him up by proxy?" She frowned.

Mohan suggested recognition of official settlements in the wastelands so that their territory and resources could be recognised. A new governance provider would need governance projects. It would be a win-win. "It will give Vidroh something to do. He can help coordinate."

It sounded like a good idea.

"Which brings me to my final point," Dhrit-H said. "Our most formidable asset. Abrahamha."

"No," Noir said. "It isn't safe. There's a reason the ancients left the populated regions of the world."

"I'm not saying that he should mingle with the public," Dhrit-H said. "But he linked with thousands of minds globally to deliver his Ultimatum for peace. He doesn't have to be present in the population to search their minds."

Noir put his hands palm down carefully on the table. "The Ultimatum wasn't even remotely as deliberate or tidy as the legends suggest. He had lost control after a raid for HealSYMB killed volunteers and bullied the bullies. It is true he saw it through and by some miracle, it worked, but it isn't something that should happen again."

Dhrit-H wasn't convinced. "The ultimatum was a reaction to a horrific attack. Surely, when calm, he can ask one question—if anyone has seen Sambit? That is it. If *anyone* has seen him, we can take it forward from there *without involving Abrahamha.*"

"I don't know," Noir said.

"It would save AricNova," Aaxyl said. "It could end this mess right here."

Noir shook his head, but it had little conviction. Noir and Mohan had searched since Aameh's rescue, but if they'd made any progress, they'd have shared it.

"Maybe just to ask a quick question..." Mohan said reluctantly.

"I'm probably going to regret this, but I'm asking him." Noir stood and closed his eyes.

Abrahamha appeared and a sense of energetic brightness swept around the table. "I should have thought of scanning minds in the dome for information."

Everyone was visibly more alert. The very air felt crisp, clearer. What an inspiring presence. And thankfully, he had none of the scariness of the Null Dorms. That fragrance from the Null Dorms was back in all its undefinable wild intoxication. Complex and indescribably beautiful, it seemed to encompass a purity that defied explanation.

A blinding white light filled Aameh's mind, like a flash flood passed through a bathroom tap. Fragmented shards of thoughts rubbed against each other in her mind, like her brain was being grated down to the stub of her neck. And then it was over. The heady fragrance was gone. She jerked alert, unsure for how long she'd drifted off.

Abrahamha was on the floor, unconscious.

Aaxyl pinched the bridge of her nose.

Aameh had a headache and a metallic taste in her mouth.

"What happened?" NeoJai asked, rubbing his forehead. "Is he alright?"

"He's fine," Gyan said. "The rest of you weren't, so I had to sedate him."

Gyan projected brief videos of them freezing mid-conversation. Aaxyl, NeoJai and Aameh spasmed oddly, and Aaxyl clutched her head and released it.

Aameh couldn't remember any of it.

Gyan showed videos from the road outside the compound, with manual vehicles veering and pedestrians standing still, some of them clutching their heads or making odd jerks. It showed a grid of live feeds of people freezing and jerking.

Whatever it was ended within seconds.

Dhrit-H shook his head like he was jarring loose a migrane. "What happened, exactly?"

"I think he grabbed all the minds in the Dome for a few seconds." Noir's face was grim as he teleported Abrahamha back to the Superdome.

This hadn't gone well at all.

No evidence that Brainwave Synchronization Technology Enhances Empathy.
PsychLife, Sunday, December 7, 2442

~~*~*~*

Aaxyl: SYMBTech Building

Aaxyl hurried to hug Scharada the moment Mohan teleported her in.

Aameh was better at such situations and *should* have been here, but had needed more time with some devices she was working on with Noir.

NeoJai had left to visit Admin Dhrit and Nyaya.

Aaxyl had stayed back to provide Scharada with a familiar face. Aaxyl led her to the sofa in the media room and sat next to her like she was a life line.

"You do realise this is a good thing?" Scharada squeezed her hand reassuringly. "Change isn't always bad."

What Aaxyl wouldn't give to be able to talk openly with Scharada.

The changes were not bad, but overwhelming. Change made her twitchy on the best of days. She had no idea what to do with a new sibling like Rudra, new family members who appeared and disappeared on a whim or weren't even human. Her own brain worked differently and now labeled stuff and provided information layers. She kept expecting to wake up every time Abrahamha spoke. She hoped Scharada would agree to help the ancients and Rudra, so that she'd have the clearance for Aaxyl to talk about stuff on her mind.

Mohan said, "This conversation is confidential. Do you agree?"

"Yes," Scharada whispered and cleared her throat. "Yes."

Aaxyl murmured, "Welcome to the rabbit hole."

Abrahamha and Rudra appeared in the room and Scharada froze.

Aaxyl snickered mentally. She couldn't wait for Scharada to reassure her about change again.

Scharada greeted Abrahamha and Rudra warily.

Rudra responded with a blizzard of terror till Scharada paled.

Mohan explained Rudra's difficulties. He wanted to know if Scharada would consider her as a first client.

Scharada checked with Aaxyl, clearly uneasy with Rudra. Aaxyl squeezed her hand.

Scharada turned to Mohan. "I can do that. Are you the Deal-Maker?"

"I'm not," Mohan replied. "But he contacted you on our behalf."

"Okay," Scharada said. "He told me that my application for asylum would be approved. I can't work professionally without it. I'll need time to get a home and set up a practice after that."

"That's being handled. Time is of essence. We can help you get your home today, as well as supplement your budget as needed. It can be adjusted against your bills," Mohan said, suggesting several possibilities for funding and independent residences to a stunned Scharada.

Aaxyl knew that feeling. Drowsy after a night of lying awake next NeoJai she zoned out, but perked up in a hurry when Mohan vanished and reappeared with Vidroh.

Vidroh did not meet her eyes. Again.

Mohan told Scharada, "This man has been through bad experiences and done stupid things. He's not part of our deal, and doesn't have unimon to pay you."

"I've met him in the Dorms," said Scharada, smiling at Vidroh.

Mohan gave Vidroh a hard look.

Vidroh spoke in a low voice. "I can help you find a house, move in, and do any work around the house that you need."

Aaxyl wanted to protest, but she wasn't sure why. There was no shame in honest work. She had worked since she was a child herself, but Vidroh's dejected posture wrenched her heart.

"You can't afford Vidroh's treatment?" Aaxyl imped Mohan.

Mohan conveyed an eye-roll through the implant without the slightest hint of it on his serious face, as Vidroh and Scharada talked.

Aaxyl really needed to figure out how to do that.

Mohan imped to Aaxyl, *"He needs reality. The grounding of work and responsibilities."*

"Was that why he had to sell his home for SanJeevan to fix his arm?" AxAm hadn't paid a single unimon for their implants.

"Yes. Even when things go wrong, they need to be seen through."

Aaxyl's temper flared. *"A severed arm isn't a psychological symptom."*

"I accept," Scharada said to Vidoh, frowning at Aaxyl. Her reactions must have been showing on her face, even though she imped Mohan.

Vidroh nodded. "I'll have a list of suitable houses in a couple of hours." He left the room.

"He lashed out at SanJeevan telling her to do whatever she thought best unless she could bring Srayoshi back," Mohan imped. *"SanJeevan's best isn't cheap and she wanted him to know it."*

"Perhaps if he felt understood by you, he'd have talked to you. Sought help."

"You're kind to him. So why is he avoiding you?"

Aaxyl slumped in defeat. *"Because now that I know you, I'm a part of his reality and not an escape from it."*

"We don't hate him, Ax. We understand his pain, but tantrums at reality or doing whatever he wishes isn't an option. There are lives at stake. SanJeevan spanked him with bills, but wastelanders will drench the ground with their blood if SecPros retaliate against them for Vidroh's stunt. They use the water. They'd be the first suspects."

Everybody was looking at two of them.

Mohan cleared his throat. "As promised, your asylum has been approved."

Shantiniketan displayed the document.

"Thank you," Scharada said. "I appreciate this."

"You should know that the Deal-Maker is really Jugaad, who isn't dead."
Mohan took a deep breath. "We need you to help Abrahamha and Jugaad learn
control as well."

Scharada's face flashed through a succession of expressions and false
starts, finally settling on wide eyes, bitten lip and a raised hand frozen mid-
gesture.

Rudra smiled for the first time. "Don't worry, I'll protect you."

Ancient mythological texts predicted the discovery of symbionts and extreme longevity as the Age of Gods that follows the Age of Destruction. Syncretism & Science, Monday, December 8, 2442

~~*~*~*

AAMEH: MOHAN'S HOME

Aameh swapped locations with Aaxyl after lunch. She wanted to accompany Scharada to go house-hunting later, but Scharada had returned to the Dorms briefly to pack up kit and caboodle. With AxAm gone, she couldn't get out of the Dorms fast enough.

Spooked by Rudra, Aameh sneaked off to the roof with her new communicator and accessories. The roof here wasn't Gyan's fancy multi-mode production. Furniture was basic and sturdy. Most of the tables sported other people's belongings strewn around, though she was alone on the roof.

She plonked her bag on an odd unoccupied bench Shantiniketan illogically called a beach-chair, and pulled out the display glasses, lenses and hearing buds to test them out.

Advertisements for AVANT display glasses showed data layered over the world. They worked as a display or annotated her view, and added eye movement recognition for her comm. She hadn't seen advertisements for the lenses.

Noir imped her contacts for someone called Elir who would answer all her questions.

"Twenty-year-olds are dumb," Aameh imped back.

"You're twenty."

"I'm not your average twenty-year-old."

"Nor is he. He's a tech prodigy. First research project at fourteen."

Wow. She asked Shantiniketan, but Elir had already left for the Superdome.

"Imp him," Noir suggested. *"He's expecting you."*

So she did.

"I'm really grateful to you for doing this," Aameh imped Elir. *"I have so many questions."*

"I messed up by taking Rudra and overestimated my abilities, and now I'll get all the kid tasks till they've punished me enough," Elir replied.

Oh. *"I'm sorry. I hadn't realised I was bothering Noir. I was just sharing an idea. I won't bother you."*

"Shit. I'm sorry. I didn't mean it like that. This isn't on you. Mohan and Noir are both full of praise for you. They use your ideas! Noir is too old for patience. I've had a rough day and was feeling sorry for myself."

"Thanks for saying that." Aameh really liked Noir, and he thought she was a punishment. She knew that she could get irritating. Elir couldn't fix this. Aameh was broken. Mostly it didn't matter. Sometimes it did. Like now.

When the silence stretched, Elir imped, *"Look. Ask me something right now. Let's get past this."*

She raised her hand to see the time. "13:47" chorused her communicator and Shantiniketan. Aameh rolled her eyes, accidentally sweeping away Elir's feed before noticing that the display glasses also showed the time; as did the comm she was seeing through them. Her mood lightened.

If Aameh could ask one question, she'd make the best of it. She imped Elir, *"Why do mental implants need captive telepathic symbionts in them, even for telepaths?"*

Long pause. Aameh got the faint impression of a groan. Her mood started deflating, the longer the silence held.

Finally Elir imped back, *"This isn't really an introductory subject, but I'll give it a shot. What do you know about symbionts?"*

"Microbes of non-terrestrial origins, intolerant of atmosphere, inaccessible but provable sentience and with a different dimensional profile, allowing them to have unique effects in spacetime as per spar physics and the Quaspar Symbiont Hyposthesis."

"You know your stuff. Spar selectors?" Elir sounded a lot more enthusiastic.

Aameh grinned. *"Range of applicability of symbion particles, which can be manipulated by symbiont interactive devices and abilities."*

"Okay, so here's the thing, the implant's spar scale can't handle the amount of symbionts in a telepath's brain and any unlinked metal in the brain collapses native telepathy completely. You need an inward nano selector..."

Time flew. Maybe Noir hadn't been irritated by her. Elir was really clever. He'd been inventing things since he was fourteen. He was going to be her new best friend.

She sent Elir her first imped sketch about mental implants with a thank you message.

At 14:39, she was distracted by the sound of approaching voices. Her implant identified Mohan.

"Aameh is here," RudraJoy hissed. Interesting. The implant hadn't labelled her.

Mohan, according to Shantiniketan, and Rudra, according to Aameh's own adrenaline levels, moved to the far end of the roof. If they talked, it was too softly for her to know.

She concluded her discussion with Elir, and wandered over when Rudra's danger vibes tapered to a breathable level. "You guys doing okay?"

Obviously not.

Rudra's puffy eyes didn't require a lot of interpreting skills, but the terror levels were at an ambient hum. Aaxyl had explained what had gone down after Vidroh and Elir took her on the mission.

Aameh could relate. She was frequently blindsided by the motives of others, even if they didn't intend to hurt her.

Rudra gave her a weak smile.

"I'm going out in a while to check out residences with Scharada and Vidroh," Aameh told them. She caught Rudra's wistful look and imped to Mohan, *"Would you join us? Then we could take Rudra and she could get to know Scharada."*

"Could Rudra and I join you?" Mohan asked.

"Of course."

* * *

An hour later, Aameh watched Mohan's surprise as Rudra walked down the stairs wearing Aameh's old black sleeveless dress. It had been a touch small for comfort on Aameh, but ample for Rudra. Rudra had enjoyed getting ready so much, there were hardly any terror vibes, and Aameh liked the girl.

"This isn't too much?" Rudra asked them.

"You look beautiful, Rudra," Mohan told her honestly.

And she did, even in an old SociCred-store dress, if Aameh said so herself.

Mohan had teleported back to SYMBTech to get Aameh's makeup and dress. Aameh rarely wore makeup herself, but it was paint on skin, after all, and a profitable skill in the Dorms. She could also cut and syle hair and do several kinds of tattoos and body art.

"I'm glad she has you," Mohan said, putting an arm around Aameh as they headed for the living room. "The downside of Rudra being a secret in a household of men is that we don't realise things like these."

A few grams of invisible magic had turned the scrawny alien into an ethereal beauty. She still looked twelve.

Scharada was delighted to see Rudra. The lack of *eau-de-menace* in the air probably helped.

They took Mohan's zeplyn and picked Vidroh up outside the gate.

Scharada looked troubled that he stood outside the gate, but didn't comment. Instead, she asked Rudra, if she wanted to schedule her first appointment on Scharada's first day at her new residence. "If you enjoy the clothes and makeup, wait till you see what I have."

"Are you sure you're a real psychologist?" Rudra asked her sceptically.

Scharada winked. "We'll get around to the psychology."

Aameh listened with her head back and eyes closed. The girl didn't realise it, but therapy had already begun.

Vidroh had organised the tour to begin with the house he thought the best.

Aameh fell in love with the house on sight. They all did. It was spacious, but welcoming, with large bright rooms and huge windows. Six bedrooms and shared areas on two floors felt majestic and accessible, the upper floor could easily turn into residential facilities for patients, and rooms on the ground floor could transform into anything Scharada needed with little effort.

The house itself sat in a larger compound that allowed space for a garden. It came with an old one-eyed cat Scharada promptly named Bhola. Scharada was already planning uses for the rooms. Vidroh's deal with Scharada was off to a flying start.

One house seen, one house approved. Consensus.

Vidroh looked disproportionately relieved.

Aameh guessed he needed a win. She liked that Vidroh was using a comm finally and not hiding from the world. Maybe working with Scharada would help him.

Scharada and Vidroh hurried to the Octagon to see to the funds and paperwork before the day's close.

The house was already empty. Barring any complications, Scharada would own it in an hour.

Aameh watched Rudra's face dull. This was ending too soon for her. AxAm needed better clothes than the few they had from the Dorms, and Aaxyl had just two T-shirts and cargo pants left after the medics cut away the ones Sambit shot up. Rudra should have something to take home from this trip, not just an abrupt end.

Rudra, Mohan and Aameh did a quick trip to a small boutique. Aameh's first experience of a unimon shop and Rudra's first of any shop. It was run by a designer who knew Mohan and agreed to close for their visit. Aameh feared that they might have to leave in a hurry if Rudra began her danger vibes, and not wanting the evening to end on a sour note, kept it quick.

The designer grasped their needs and offered exactly the kind of clothes they were looking for. They chose dresses for Rudra and Aameh, a small pile of soft T-shirts and shorts for all of them and the designer had some stunning pants for Aaxyl. Aameh couldn't wait for Aaxyl to see them. She got a couple of cargo pants as well, just to be safe.

The designer offered to show them undergarments, but that wasn't an experience either Aameh or Rudra wanted with Mohan around, and Mohan wouldn't let Rudra out of his sight.

Aameh ordered utilitarian designs for AxAm, and they were done.

AAXYL

Aaxyl didn't understand what Noir was doing, but dutifully provided company, helping him assemble gadgets he had modified into a mobile detection unit.

She held the base of Hersh's *Cosmic Chaos* game firmly in place, flinching as Noir ruthlessly drilled holes through it into the Zephyron.

"Can't we ask Abrahamha to talk to Damodar?" Aaxyl held the game's innards ready, waiting to be fitted.

Noir was threading something that would allow the Zephyron to multiplex split connections, and a power cable for the game to run off the Zephyron in order to sustain a search mode, whatever all that meant.

He grunted around the screwdriver in his mouth.

"When Damodar tried to stop us in the Null Dorms, he said he trusted Abrahamha." Aaxyl perched on the Zephyron.

Noir took the screwdriver out of his mouth as he dropped a screw into place. "Everybody trusts Abrahamha."

"But..."

Noir finally looked up. "Have you forgotten what happened the last time? If Abrahamha could do it safely, he'd have done it."

"But if he's innocent and knows what places Sambit has access to..." Aaxyl trailed off as he motioned her to get off the Zephyron. "It's worth a try. He need not come here. Surely the Superdome has projection and conferences?"

"If you must nag me about this, give me your comm." Noir took her comm and floated off on the Zephyron, leaving her trailing. *"Don't follow me. Go to the roof,"* he imped.

As reactions went, that was unexpected. Was Aaxyl turning into Aameh and nagging people when she had an idea?

"Keep talking," Noir imped. *"I need to know if our estimates of range are working."*

"Oh. Well, you knew Damodar from before too. Why don't you talk to him?" Aaxyl asked.

"I did."

"But you didn't tell him about AricNova." Aaxyl hoped he could still hear her.

Noir imped irritation. *"Why is it so hard to understand that we aren't going to discuss 'Hersh' with untrusted people till we find her?"*

Her implant told her the communicator was outside the SYMBTech gate. *"I'm not saying we tell everyone about her, but if Damodar is guilty, he already knows. If he's innocent, knowing that she was a prisoner in that facility might change his mind about cooperating."*

Silence met her mind. Noir and her comm had gone out of range. Aaxyl waited for him to return. Holding this info back from Damodar achieved nothing.

Noir and NeoJai appeared right in front of her and she yelped. "Where's the Zephyron?"

"I took it to the Superdome for Elir to replicate it." Noir returned her comm. "The estimates of range hold up. We should be able to start searching as soon as Elir is done. I picked up NeoJai on my way back."

On his way back. Interesting choice of words. Was the AVANT Medical Research facility in or near the Superdome?

Aaxyl hugged NeoJai. "How are Admin Dhrit and Nyaya?"

"Great!" NeoJai radiated relief. "Both conscious. Under observation. They should be out soon."

Damodar projected onto the terrace. Aaxyl jumped again.

Teleporting was fine for herself, but people suddenly appearing before her took getting used to, whether from teleportation or in this case, projection. *"Please give me a heads up next time, Gyan."*

"What is it, Noir?" Damodar snapped. "I've already told Mohan as well as you that you don't have jurisdiction in this Dome. Sambit's actions are regrettable, and we definitely don't endorse them, but we'll run our own investigation."

NeoJai's hands were clenched in fists. Aaxyl smoothed one out and entwined her fingers with his, finding unexpected comfort in offering him reassurance.

"Damodar, AricNova is alive." Noir was watching the projection keenly for his reactions. So was Aaxyl. "We know it was Sambit controlling that facility. You're claiming to not endorse him, so help us find Sambit and rescue AricNova."

"You're wrapped up in Dhrit's paranoia," Damodar scoffed, reaching a hand out to shut the projection off. "I had nothing to do with the attack on Ari. How many centuries will he spread that nonsense?"

"Aameh saw her," Noir said.

Damodar froze. "What are you playing at, Noir, and why are you dragging those girls into centuries-old feuds?"

"Aameh *saw* her," Noir said again. "Alive. In person. Sambit is draining her symbionts to keep her weak. He is making shells from them. He's put a chain through her stomach to prevent her from teleporting."

Damodar paled. "A chain through her stomach?" Emotion flooded his face before it fixed to a neutral mask. "It *is* Sambit."

"We know that," Aaxyl said. "But where could he be if he had to vacate the Null Dorms in a hurry?"

"He could be anywhere in this Dome." Damodar pulled a chair into the projection and sat. "He can't leave. He doesn't have keys outside this Dome and Ridnam. If the woman was really AricNova, he won't dare return to Ridnam. Nadani will dismantle him molecule by molecule..."

"*The woman*?" Noir asked. "You saw her?"

"I need a promise first." Damodar's voice was shaking. "You must protect Smriti. You must revive her from stasis. If I don't survive, you must adopt her into your family."

His employee's daughter from the memory Abrahamha had shared.

Noir didn't hesitate. "I'll do everything in my power to help her."

"I may be the reason Sambit has Ari. Last year, I found a woman unconscious outside my distribution warehouse. Thin as a skeleton, dark-skinned and tall. She had a thick steel chain going through her stomach." Damodar rubbed his eyes. "I asked Sambit to take her to a hospital. I didn't recognise her."

"Then why did you approve the Null Dorms facility? Wasn't it to save Smriti using AricNova's symbionts?" asked Noir. "Why the secrecy if you didn't know about Ari?"

"To test symbionts from nulls for compatibility," Damodar said. "Or at least that's what Sambit told me. Experimenting on nulls is controversial, so we kept it low key, but Sambit had assured me they wouldn't be harmed. Ari's symbionts killed my son. Why would I want them for Smriti?"

"You expect me to believe you didn't recognise AricNova?" Noir said.

"Yes." Damodar's gaze didn't waver. "If I had anything to hide, why would I leave the Null Dorms after Sambit warned me that NeoJai would try to hinder the experiments? I didn't want disruption or baseless accusations, but I had nothing to hide."

"Baseless!" NeoJai spat. "My father was impri—"

Aaxyl squeezed his hand. "Help us find her," she said.

"I will." Damodar frowned as something caught his attention and he moved to end the feed. "I have to go. Save Smriti. 10 by 4 22b3." Damodar's projection vanished.

"What the hell does that mean?" Noir snapped at the empty space.

"Null Dorms." NeoJai's eyes widened. "That's why he visits there so often. The tenth floor has a cryogenics unit. Smriti is in the Null Dorm, on the tenth floor, dormitory four, 22B3."

VIDROH

Vidroh stood just outside the door of Mohan's home. He wasn't welcome here, but he'd been summoned. Mohan didn't owe him the dignity of inviting him in after what he'd done.

Mohan stepped out and shut the door behind him, like a slap on Vidroh's face. "We have a way to help the settlements, if you're interested," Mohan said.

Vidroh followed him, as he walked around the house. He hadn't realised Mohan grew his own vegetables.

"I'm not sure I deserve it." Vidroh's methods had been ill-advised, no matter how important the objective. "I think your exclusion of me from Margadarshak activities was fair."

"You're still barred from the Margadarshak Network. This is something else." Mohan led the way past a lawn behind the house. "Elir and Rudra ought to have agrav boards tethered somewhere..."

Vidroh spotted several next to a sandy landing area. Mohan gestured Vidroh over, freeing one for Vidroh to sit on, while choosing another for himself.

The agrav boards were as close to naked anti-gravitational tech as it got, with little more than a flat oval board, big enough for a wide stance over a fixed-grade agrav unit without any propulsion.

Agrav boards were confusing for anyone who used gravity boards, which Mohan clearly did. The trick to them was not losing momentum in the air away from anything to push off from. Mohan rode it cautiously like a skateboard he could push along.

Vidroh sat on the other board and drifted along, as stranded in conversational silence as Mohan was in the air, and unsure of what to say.

"Have you changed your mind about not involving me with the water issues of the settlements?" Vidroh asked finally.

"No. This isn't an effort to secure water for settlements or Margadarshak," Mohan said. "But it will help the settlements far more, and secure their water too."

"Are we playing guessing games?" Vidroh's board glided along in Mohan's wake. He could agrav better with his butt than Mohan could with a proper stance. He swallowed a smile at Mohan's comical wiggling.

Mohan, stuck in the air without propulsion and drifting slowly, looked down at Vidroh. "We're helping settlements become governed regions like cities and domes, so that they have a recognised right to the resources around them."

The idea hit him straight in the gut. This was what Srayoshi had wanted. For people to have rights where they lived. For the first time he understood why Mohan and the others had been angry with him. This was the kind of solution that took time and effort, but it couldn't be a guerrilla war.

This was his atonement. Whatever they needed to make it come true, he'd do.

Vidroh leaned into a graceful spiral to come up next Mohan, who teleported with the agrav to one end of the soft area and started again. Cheating.

Vidroh looped around in pursuit. He needed to be a part of this. "How are cities and domes recognised?" he asked.

"They have a defined territory, government and agree to comply with global agreements," Mohan said.

Vidroh leaned forward to show Mohan how to use gravity to get movement. "They'd need to defend their territory too. Cities will always have bigger forces."

"Engaging with the Superdome brings recognition," Mohan panted. He shifted his weight to get the agrav to turn, but lost momentum and again stood on a stationary board. "Any attacks on them would become acts of war and not local SecPro measures."

"We'd just need to defend enough for diplomatic deterrents," Vidroh mused. "It could work. What do you need me to do?"

Even Mohan would have to admit, Vidroh was the perfect person to approach settlers with this plan. While he was forbidden from participating in any Margadarshak activities, nobody had said anything about forming governments. The settlers trusted him. He'd risked his life and lost his partner to help them.

"You could set up a SecPro company with Menhir. He's quit the force," Mohan said. "You could train settlers. You could form a governance provider or negotiate with them on behalf of settlers. Help make this happen."

Vidroh hadn't felt truly excited about something in so long, it intoxicated him.

Mohan teleported his agrav to the ground again. "Talk to them, see where we begin, that sort of thing."

"Let's go," Vidroh said, immediately. He stood on his agrav and glided to Mohan without pushing off against anything, so Mohan could see how it was done. "I'm ready whenever you say."

"Great. I can drop you off now," Mohan slowed to a halt again.

Vidroh stayed back and waited till he had Mohan's attention. "An agrav board takes you out of gravity. To get momentum in air, the only force you have is gravity. If you're scared of falling, you'll stagnate in place."

Vidroh leaned exaggeratedly, keeping his core tight. Gravity pulled him down, a tight core kept him on the agrav and the board resolved the tension as momentum. "Voila! Gravity powered agrav-boarding."

Enlightenment lit up Mohan's face.

AAMEH

Aameh entered the lobby at Sexel, on Noir's arm. If this visit achieved everything they hoped for, the Dome might have a better government.

Since the massacre that killed Srayoshi, media had become interested in people still living in the wastelands. If this continued, the plans to form governments there would be discovered while they could still be disrupted. They needed to change media trends. They'd kill two birds with a stone.

The organising in the settlements had gone unnoticed, except for an article about a new SecPro organisation Kavach, headed by ex-Assistant commander of UDAY's SecPros, Menhir conducting a training exercise in the Wastelands.

They needed to keep it that way.

The original plan had been for Aameh to meet Milup and Noir to teleport in after the room was private, as usual. Dhrit-H suggested that Noir and Milup meet openly, to preempt any reveals of clandestine meetings or romantic pasts later.

Gyan booked the honeymoon suite for Aameh and Noir. Celebrities did things like that when they entered serious relationships. It also spread a rumour that an award-winning jeweller met Noir at his residence.

Noir was the face of Abrahamha's enterprise. He was a resident of the Superdome, and looking similar to Abrahamha didn't hurt either. Noir rarely frequented Sexels, or made social appearances, whether with a woman or otherwise.

The manager made a special request for media interaction. Just allowing media-bot presence in the lobby minted unimon for Sexel.

Noir played along. He held their attention while she wandered, keeping an eye out for Milup.

Sales staff recognised Aameh and treated her like a valued patron. She suspected tabloid bots stalked her, a suspicion proven right a minute later.

Aameh was enjoying the conspiratorial nature of their plans. The next time they needed to distract media, Noir could break up with her.

She spotted Milup.

"Miluuuuup!" She squealed as if she was meeting Aaxyl after a month. At her return from the moon. Acting wasn't Aameh's superpower. "What are you doing here?"

Milup, a serious man, looked puzzled. "I was here for.... er...."

Aameh interrupted him. "We must catch up."

She led him to where they could see Noir with the manager, answering questions about the delay in AVANT's upcoming Transferron-21 launch.

He had wanted AricNova to be present, but first they had to find her. "The reason for the delay will be obvious when we launch it. I cannot say more about this now, but there is no problem with the product."

Noir flashed a smile when he saw her approach and read another question flashed by a media-bot. "Last question. I didn't come here to date you! Am I marrying Aameh? Well, I couldn't tell you about that before I asked her, could I?" He indicated interviews were over.

News coverage exploded with speculation about Aameh, the Dorm woman who had visited Sexel with both representatives of Abrahamha. One particularly bizarre story called Aameh the Siren of the Dorms.

In reality, Aameh had never had sex with either of them and the most romantic relationship she had was with a SHADE—a technological species the world didn't know about. Besides, she wasn't a legal adult and couldn't enter legal agreements, including marriages.

Gyan alerted Aameh to news that Damodar had taken moral responsibility for the actions of Sambit and resigned to prevent further misuse of authority in his name. Noir's startled eyes met hers across the room. They needed to get out of there to discuss.

Aameh sauntered over, with Milup still in tow.

"You mind if we have a guest, darling? Only for a short while, for old times sake." The darling had sounded really fake. Aameh hoped that they left for their room soon.

Noir, looked suitably dismayed to notice Milup, but agreed like a besotted fool, while Milup rolled his eyes.

From there, it was a breeze. They got bored with the world and claimed the room.

Aameh was starving, lunch digested hours ago. Thankfully, Noir had ordered plenty of food. She loaded a plate and plonked herself on a chair.

Milup hesitantly followed suit. Noir sprawled on the bed with his eyes closed.

"What is this, Noir? I got a Sexel invite from a stranger. You're with her. Why all this cloak and dagger? We've both moved on and are too old to meet in Sexels under false pretenses."

Noir raised a hand to stop him. "It isn't what you think." Noir sat up and explained the situation to him while Aameh ate.

"No," Milup said, when Noir finished. "The state is too powerful. Look at what happened when Dhrit Saisrisel tried."

"But Admin Dhrit was found," Aameh said.

Milup waved a hand, dismissing her assurance. "I'm not talking of his abduction. The week before he resigned as President of the Dome, he pushed through two policy changes to protect the Dorms. He vanished from public view and resigned a week later. Damodar disowned Sambit's actions, and has not made a public appearance since."

But they were completely different things. Admin Dhrit had resigned to protect his family while Damodar was searching... she caught Noir's slight shake of the head and realised this was one of those times when she needed to let someone remain ignorant.

She had already leaned forward and taken a great breath to argue stridently and Milup was listening. It would be really odd if she shut her mouth and deflated. She thought on her feet. "But UDAY's approval is sinking now. Things are different."

"The more things seem to change, the more they remain the same." Milup put his plate down. "I'm sorry you wasted your time, but this doesn't fit my ethics. I'm not going to ally with a global corporation to bring down a democratic government, even if it is run by a corporation."

"What will it take to convince you?" Aameh asked. "There are lives at stake. Sambit is a serial killer and still using government areas to operate from. He has our friend. We fear for his life."

"I'm sorry about your friend," Milup said. "Perhaps if UDAY loses approval, NelumboN will not be as kind to Sambit."

Aameh didn't know how to win this. "NelumboN is UDAY's parent company. We need a different governance provider to win."

Milup scoffed. "NelumboN is also the parent company of this Dome's election services provider. Every vote you cast as real-time democracy from employment norms to expenditure priorities goes through them, as will the governance provider election. Do you expect another provider to win?"

"Please," Aameh said. "It isn't just this Dome. We have to figure out a way to help the settlements in the wastelands. The fastest way to free them is a political identity. We need a governance provider who puts people first." Aameh hadn't even realised she had absorbed jargon from Nagrik Manch.

"What settlements?" Milup asked.

"Villages." Aameh gave him a summary of their idea to protect the resources of the settlements.

He finally looked interested. "And you have their agreement?"

Aameh checked with Noir, who nodded.

Milup contemplated this. "I'm an evangelist of democracy. Self-rule."

"So be that," Aameh talked fast. "If your company gets elected, set up systems for self-rule and when ready, transfer power to the people. Consider it a revolution without the blood shed."

"A revolution via corporate contract." Milup's eyes sparkled with humour, but also ideas. "Any provider I run would be an employee owned corporation."

"You decide how the governance provider is owned and run." Noir assured him. "It sounds surreal to me, but I'm not the one running it."

Of course, it would sound surreal to Noir. Noir's idea of democracy was whatever Abrahamha dictated.

Milup focused back on Noir. "What's the catch? Why are you discussing local government with me? What do *you* want?"

He really did know Noir well. They should have planned their answers better.

Noir sat comfortably and said, "Improve diplomatic relations with the Superdome. Lack of cooperation delays the capture of Sambit."

It really sucked that Noir used this excuse, given that Damodar was finally cooperating.

Milup cleared his throat pointedly. "And would Superdome organisations hold up their end, and not meddle in Dome politics?"

"Once this crisis is over," Noir said.

Milup scoffed. "Obeying your own rules unless you need to break them?"

Remains of personal history, excavated without warning, hung in the air.

"You of all people should know better," Noir said. "Your forming a governance provider hardly reassures me. This isn't my idea."

The silence bloated, and Aameh wondered briefly if she should make herself scarce, but curiosity won.

Milup talked to Noir's lips. "And yet here you are."

Aameh wasn't sure they were still discussing the formation of a governance provider.

Noir's eyes hadn't moved from Milup's face. "Because a resident suggested your name. I'm merely a messenger."

Milup turned away, then back with his face reset to a professional indifference. "I need to leave now, to get Nagrik Manch running."

"You're calling the governance provider Nagrik Manch?" Aameh laughed to release some tension. Her mirth hung garishly in the room, seeking takers.

Time moved like sludge.

Aameh vented a sighing breath.

"Nagrik Manch has educated people on their rights for decades. Using the name is the only way to get votes this quickly." Milup played along at last.

"Fair point." Noir provided him with the contact for Vidroh.

"Nice meeting you," Milup told her. "Once you poke UDAY, you'll be dealing with all sorts. Everyone will have their own agenda. Look out for yourself."

Aameh didn't know what to make of him, which she supposed made him uniquely suited to be a politician.

"So, what's it with you and Milup?" Aameh went to sit beside him on the bed as soon as the door closed. "It didn't look all that over for a while there."

"Really? You're going to turn into one of those women?" Noir laughed. "We were together, before Mohan took over here and I moved to the Superdome. Been over for a long time."

"Does he know it's over?" She rubbed her cheek against his arm. Ooff. Decadent shirt.

"He should. He was the one to end it."

"Why?" Aameh couldn't imagine anyone not wanting Noir. She drew a tick mark on his arm, and kissed it in affirmation. Approval.

"Ironically, politics," Noir ticked the palm of her hand, closed her fingers around it and his hands around hers. He spoke her language. "He thinks The Three are a threat to the world and must be accountable. An idealist need not worry about how to make the ideas work."

"And you loved him anyway?" Aameh found that hard to believe. She searched his face. Where Abrahamha walked, Noir followed. He even styled himself similarly.

"Well, it's the truth. Except he believed something should be done about it, and I know nothing can be." No mistaking a slight tinge of sadness when Noir spoke of Milup.

Aameh stood to face him and drew a fierce check mark on his chest, willing him to see how much she thought he was a good man. She pulled him to his feet so that she could hug him and also to feel that shirt properly. Whatever that soft material was, it deserved its own hug. She rested her cheek against his chest through the shirt. His chest jerked under her cheek as he chuckled soundlessly.

"Is that what you meant by his being President not being convenient?" Aameh asked. "What's his problem? The Three saved the world!"

He traced the corner of her mouth. Single finger to express everything. If he minded sharing her affection with his own shirt, he didn't betray it in the slightest.

"He respects them for that. But sees it as a contribution to a larger whole they are answerable to and not being above it."

"But they are above it!" She unbuttoned his shirt a bit, rubbing her cheek against his chest, then the soft fabric, subtly. She loved his chest, but how decadent to have it against skin all day.

"They don't want to be." Noir threaded a finger through a curly lock of her hair. She liked it. "They operate on a different level. Milup doesn't understand that symbiont reactions are inadvertent. Or maybe he doesn't want to accept. An earthquake is brutal, unfair, but it is meaningless to make a law prohibiting one. They are best left to their self-imposed exile."

"So if not for you following Abrahamha, he loved you?"

"It wouldn't have lasted." Noir twirled the curl tighter till it pulled slightly. "I'm not that different from those he mistrusts."

"But you're supporting him for President anyway?"

"It's local business. He can't harm The Three. They wouldn't even notice if he banned them. At worst, the obsession will consume resources and lives he could utilise better. Perhaps the reality of implementing his ideals will teach him what I couldn't explain."

They fit just right. She traced a heart on his back. Noir teleported out of her arms with a slight zing against her skin only to embrace her again, capturing her hands against his chest. He returned the favour, drawing a heart on her back. Ok, that tickled. He kissed her and Aameh couldn't remember why they discussed Milup.

Noir hesitated. "We should talk about this." This meaning them. "I'm too old to be excited about casual sex. I don't invest in people easily, and when I do, it isn't recreational."

She cared about Noir, but she was twenty and sex was an adventure. She wasn't going to live here pining for him in the Superdome. At two hundred, she'd limit herself to profound relationships.

"If we do this, I want a committed relationship," Noir said. "I don't need you to be monogamous, but you will find that if we are in a relationship, people won't take sex with you casually, no matter your intent. Those you choose will have to be worthy of you."

"Ok." Would she scare him off if she shouted it?

"I'm not sure you understand," Noir said. "I don't want you to be hurt if someone tries to use you to get to me."

"They could just as easily try it to get to Mohan." Aameh shrugged. "Gyan will keep an eye on me. Ax will ground me if I'm stupid."

She hoped it worked this time as well.

"Am..."

"I'll learn, Noir." Aameh cupped his cheek. "But you can't worry three hundred years of life experience into me. I don't want to lose you to a fear."

Noir kissed her nose. "Okay."

"Good." She unbuttoned his shirt a bit, rubbing her cheek against his chest, and the soft fabric.

They started gently, tentatively. Noir was a meticulous lover. Constant sense of abundant possibilities. Responsive in the best way. Unexpected ways. Not staring and making her awkward because she was odd and liked odd things like the texture of his shirt in a romantic moment.

When he saw her enjoy the fabric, he took off her clothes, unbuttoned the shirt and wrapped it around her like an embrace, heightening her enjoyment of both. There was no either-or. She got the chest and the shirt. Win.

Aameh loved creativity being invested into anything. Creative sex was better than acreative sex.

"Is acreative a word?"

"Not one applicable to us."

See? He was in tune with her weirdities. Everything went from merely consensual to eagerly awaited, desired, demanded.

Noir intoxicated her.

They were similar and they were opposites. At once.

Soon, they were an exhausted mess of tangled limbs. Aameh sneaked a hand back to the bedside table for her sketchbook to immortalise this moment.

His eyes were slightly crossed from being close and his features relaxed into sensual masculinity. She drew the clutter of the world wisping away from his shoulders and vanishing into puffs of smoke.

Noir set aside her sketchbook, pulled her into his arms, tucked her head under his chin, and wrapped his huge arms completely around her. "Sleep now. You're going to need that energy."

Aameh wriggled, but he was too strong to budge. She spoke, but he didn't reply. She fell asleep.

Small Wins

*Kitten stranded in Thar Dorms air purification vent rescued successfully. Dome &
Dorms, Wednesday, December 10, 2442*

~*~*~*~*

AAXYL: Aaxyl's room

After a week of cohabitating with NeoJai, Aaxyl couldn't do another night
of carefully moderated body contact, wearing T-shirts and shorts to bed and
pretending affection satisfied her.

She freed her hair from her scrunchie, slipping it over her wrist as she
rested a knee on the bed and considered the man in it. NeoJai had been
reading her favourite space opera novel every night.

Earlier, in another life, she'd made it clear that she didn't want to have sex
with him. That was *before*, when she lived in the Dorms, but the infuriating
man meticulously respected lines she had drawn. They were in the same bed
now. He should have guessed.

It was her move.

Slipping into bed, she waited for NeoJai's right arm to automatically
extend and hold her, and it did. It would tighten around her when he brought
the book close to turn the page. Or he'd put it down and turn on his side to
face her, as he did now, and they'd... talk.

Aaxyl rested her forehead against NeoJai's chest, her left arm squished
between them, inhaling his sandalwood fragrance. His left hand splayed
against her back, unmoving. He was as alert as she was.

This was nuts.

She pressed a kiss on his T-shirt and his breath hitched. Was it too
ambiguous? She ran her hand over NeoJai's back, listening to his soft inhale.
He hadn't moved. It was still her move.

It felt right, this moment. She moved her hand to his chest, then up to his face. His barely visible stubble scratched surprisingly sharp. Her thumb stroked a question against his lips, and his intent gaze smouldered the answer. His hand swept up her back, crushing her close.

They undressed quickly.

She didn't care if he thought her too abandoned. She wanted to drive him too wild to care.

She trailed her way down his front, and thrilled as he jolted. His right arm clamped her tight against his side, left hand hovering over hers, but not touching. She leaned her head back to gauge his response, only to find his eyes riveted to her hand on him. She traced tantalising strokes over his sensitive skin and curled her hand around him.

What would Mr. Proper choose? Instant gratification or a mutual test of endurance?

Aaxyl won. He lifted her to lie on him and she straddled him. They were too aroused for patience. She sank down, enjoying their abrupt start.

NeoJai pulled her down tight against him with a thrilling, unexpected desperation. She rested her hands on his chest. Her hair fell around his head, creating a tunnel between their faces. He swiped it out of his eyes. Oops.

"Sorry." Sitting back up, Aaxyl tied her hair back with the scrunchie, still riding him.

"Fuck, Ax," NeoJai gasped a laugh, his eyes devouring her. "I'm trying to make this work for you as well."

"It's working." She took her time adjusting the scrunchie, basking in his greedy eyes and bucking hips. "Approve of the view, do you?"

NeoJai rolled her onto her back to surge into her. "Now, it's better."

Aaxyl's body imploded into frantic chaos, setting him off. Hands trembled over his sweat-slick body, feet locked him tight. The world narrowed to this man planting his triumphant flag on her heart.

NeoJai disintegrated into frenzied male instinct driving them crazed with an intense frown and half-shouted grunts. He pressed hard into her and froze.

Eyes wide, then shut, body quaking. "Ax!"

Ax floated, adrift in an absurd, exhausted joy.

She'd done this. Unravelled NeoJai.

He sagged into her arms, and she pressed a kiss to his sweat-damp head wherever was closest. Behind his ear, it turned out. She'd figure out better placements soon.

NeoJai turned toward her and laughed a half-thrilled, half-embarrassed chuckle against her neck. "Wow."

His breath tickled and stubble scratched at the same time. Aaxyl giggled with a protective shrug.

Giggled? Who was she turning into?

NeoJai rolled off her and onto his back. He pulled her against his side, cushioning her head with his shoulder. "I've longed to see you like this."

"Mm... got that loud and clear."

His breathing was still ragged, Aaxyl noted with a smug satisfaction. Like hers.

"Yeah, that too." NeoJai rubbed his sandpaper cheek against her forehead. She didn't mind. "But I wanted to see you without worries weighing you down. Having fun." He stroked her cheek with a knuckle. "Being the cause is a bonus."

"Not very humble in bed, are we?"

The grin she got back was unadulterated male satisfaction.

This man melted her heart. "I love you." Turned out it was quite easy to say when the man and moment were right.

DITNOIL's spending on public welfare in Summer 2441 analysed. Sponsored feature, Data Junkies, Wednesday, December 10, 2442

~~*~*~*

AAMEH: SYMBTECH BUILDING

"Damodar has resigned," Gyan told Aameh. *"UDAY ratings are in free fall."*

Aameh yawned and stretched.

She opened her eyes and smiled in satisfaction. Her paintings and posters hung on the wall in beautiful frames. Gyan had found her a comforter with an abstract print in shades from warm yellow to peach. A proper easel waited, next to an art station between the dresser and her desk. The beautiful Mohan slept by her side. She was living the artist's dream, though it was weird without Aaxyl.

She reached for her display glasses. *"Please display."* The glasses were better for information. The implant induced vertigo if video perspectives varied from her body position.

Damodar sat before a large brown desk, wearing formal clothes, face grave. "I had no knowledge of Sambit Amdani's actions in the Null Dorms. At the same time, the moral responsibility rests with me, and I'm resigning as the President with immediate effect. Darahs, global head of UDAY, will take over from me. My sincere apologies to the founders and residents of the dome."

The news moved on to Darahs addressing a press conference.

Mohan stretched beside her and tucked her tighter against him. "I didn't expect that."

Aameh spoke through a yawn. "Milup predicted this."

Mohan frowned. "Damodar promised to help find AricNova. As President, he had dome-wide access. As a civilian, he doesn't."

Aameh hadn't thought of that. "Do you think he's already found her?"

"One way to know. Gyan, connect us to Damodar."

"Like this? " Aameh scrambled out of bed.

Gyan blinked a grey cross on the screen. "Damodar isn't available at either his home or UDAY. His personal comm is not receiving calls."

"Keep trying," Mohan said. "Everybody and his cousin is probably trying to talk to him right now."

Aameh crawled back into bed, now awake. "Is there anything else of interest in the news?"

Gyan projected the news onto the screen on the wall for them to choose. Legal in front of the Octagon. Milup interview. A group of dormers pointing at their comms. Inner resident before an apartment tower. Tapas Khan - journalist Shyam Tere's best friend. A panel discussion. More random images of people.

She asked Gyan to play them all beginning with Tapas.

"Sambit nulled my friend, award-winning journalist Shyam Tere, for investigating his crimes." The patient man she'd met in the Null Dorms hadn't seemed capable of such rage. "And then he met me, pretending to care about Shyam. UDAY rewarded a serial killer with the post of a Director in the Dorms. They still haven't caught him."

Legal answered questions from Rita Ladole, one of the few senior female journos in the dome outside the Octagon.

She looked at the camera before addressing Legal. "Isn't it true that your client Noir met Milup in a Sexel just before all this started?"

"It depends on what you mean." Legal stared into the frame of der spectacles, which Aameh now realised were display glasses. "Did Noir meet Milup? Yes. Nagrik Manch governs a settlement in the wastelands, and they discussed establishing a HealSYMB production facility there."

"Why meet in a Sexel?" Rita asked. "Surely Noir doesn't lack for business premises?"

"Indeed." Legal smiled der dead smile at Rita. "If this were planned. They ran into each other and had productive ideas."

"But you don't favour Nagrik Manch?"

"A symbiontist is still held hostage by Sambit whose ongoing freedom worries me. My clients don't participate in local politics."

Gyan sent in coffee. Legal could talk circles around Rita all day.

Aameh tuned out.

Since Dhrit exposed Sambit as his attacker, dormers were rejecting UDAY enmasse.

Damodar's history as a distributor of household goods when supplies were hard to find during the Enduring War made him popular with inners. With his resignation, the inners joined the dormers as well, and panels of experts predicted the return of NelumboN. Dormers, excited by the idea of a Nagrik Manch government, kickstarted a movement: a finger tapping a comm encouraged residents to choose.

Mohan found it bemusing. "Do they think a government will be run like the Nagrik Manch in their park?"

Aameh shrugged. "Does it matter which cock's crowing caused the sunrise? Nagrik Manch needs all the help they can get."

She wandered off to the bathroom. Media dug up friends and families of victims from Shyam Tere's reports.

Mohan listened to those while she readied herself for the day.

Governance providers administered any entity they were contracted for, from hospitals to the entire dome. Other providers with limited presence and minor contracts here had started advertising city governance services, even though UDAY hadn't lost approval yet. Advertisements for DITNOIL (Bombay), CROWN (London), GAURAV (Superdome) and NelumboN (Ridnam) dominated political news.

By the time Aameh walked out of the bathroom, the ads proved prescient. The election provider announced that UDAY had lost popularity in the dome. They had a week to regain the confidence of the people or be replaced. Aameh had only ever voted for matters related to the Ekta Dorms. Her biggest vote endorsed Leela as the Director of Ekta Dorms. There had never been an election of a governance provider before.

Milup appeared on the screen, looking extra scholarly. Careful lighting gilded his hair, and he detailed plans for the Srayoshi settlement. "Vidroh

Trinis governs the settlement on behalf of Nagrik Manch. Once we develop a stable system, Vidroh will step down to allow them to choose their own leaders. Self rule." Milup made no reference to events in their dome, but viewers demanded that Nagrik Manch registered as governance providers in the dome as well.

Gyan estimated that the use of the term self-rule had gone up forty thousand times in the past twenty-four hours.

Copycat graffiti artists in the style of Soulscaper take Aasha and Cranti Dorms by storm. Dome & Dorms, Wednesday, December 10, 2442

~~*~*~*

AAXYL: SYMBTECH BUILDING

NeoJai woke Aaxyl with a kiss and she took him in: damp hair, soft cheeks, fresh breath, and a powdery sandalwood fragrance she was coming to associate with him.

"Did you sleep at all?" Aaxyl yawned.

NeoJai grinned. "A bit."

Liar.

"We went at it like Dusty and Limoth." Aaxyl sighed.

"Mmm?"

"The book you were reading." Aaxyl narrowed her eyes.

"Yes, very romantic." NeoJai was eager to kiss her again.

Aaxyl reared back. He was so busted. "Dusty is the pilot of a starship that landed on the planet Limoth. You didn't read the book at all, did you?" She wanted to sound outraged, but he was too adorable.

"I was waiting for you." NeoJai nuzzled her cheek.

"Why didn't you say something?"

"I like watching you want me desperately."

Aaxyl opened her mouth in shock, then shut it. This was a new side of NeoJai, wasn't it? She loved it. She loved him.

Gyan spoke. "I'm sorry to interrupt, but I thought NeoJai might want to know that Nyaya and Admin Dhrit are here."

"Gyan, your timing sucks, but thats great news." Aaxyl stretched, then relaxed against NeoJai's bare shoulder. They'd barely slept. She checked the time. It was half an hour to noon. Okay, she'd slept quite a bit too.

NeoJai hesitated. "Ax, would you ...."

"Of course! They're your parents." Aaxyl urged. "Go."

"Actually, I meant would you come with me, because I don't want to be away from you." NeoJai's grin managed to be both sheepish and smug.

She found the smallest things about him notably appealing now.

Aaxyl stretched properly, tensing her body, curling her arms up, then extending one, then the other, shaking out the stiffness before going limp again. She was awake now. "I need a shower."

"I'll help."

"I bet you will."

* * *

Aaxyl and NeoJai visited Nyaya and Admin Dhrit briefly. They had both recovered nicely. Admin Dhrit could still feel the occasional telepathic flash, but his life was no longer in danger. Nyaya would have to take it easy for a few months, but the transplants had worked well and it was only a matter of time. Aaxyl was glad. This family had been through a lot.

"Would you go ahead and join Aameh and Mohan on the multi-mode roof for lunch?" Gyan asked. *"Dhrit-H has asked me to organise a special lunch to welcome them back and their entrance will be so much better with an audience."*

Curious, they dutifully headed to the roof as directed.

Gyan had created another lovely environment, this time in honour of Nyaya and Admin Dhrit's healthy homecoming.

Aaxyl had expected a dramatic declaration of love. Possibly a ceremony, maybe roses. Definitely elegant and expensive.

Instead, the roof looked like the Saisrisel dining room.

That still made it elegant and expensive, Aaxyl thought, wryly.

Nyaya looked great in a turquoise silk dress. No sign of her brush with death. Admin Dhrit looked... like Dhrit-H, but less casual.

Aaxyl was glad they'd gone up early. It was worth it to see the surprise on their faces as they approached the table.

And then recognition lit Nyaya's face.

NeoJai imped Aaxyl the guided tour of all the symbolism.

Gyan had fabricated an old favourite mug and it replaced the plate that should have been before Nyaya's place. Apparently, Nyaya used to be a coffee-for-breakfast person when she and Dhrit first met.

A table nearby held a single rose in a slender vase next to a paper and pen. That was how Dhrit had proposed marriage in a time when hardly anyone married.

Dhrit-H came over and kissed Nyaya and hugged Admin Dhrit.

The Dhrits flanked Nyaya and walked arm-in-arm around the room, seeing many memories of their life together as small objects, images and projections and completed their circuit of the room to sit at the table.

A service bot offered Nyaya a plate with a weird fried egg and toast that made her laugh.

NeoJai laughed even louder covering his face in mock embarrassment. It was a replica of the first time NeoJai made his mother breakfast. "I was just eleven," he told Aaxyl. *"And oh, their plates look more like breakfast because Nyaya and the Dhrits always begin their day together with breakfast, when possible."*

Then followed the most delicious, homely lunch ever. Dhrit-H had cooked. Small details mimicked a personal touch, and other household eccentricities.

Nyaya was home.

Every time they witnessed what Gyan could do, it surprised them. It must have listened to Dhrit and gone through endless information to create this single lunch. All while planning a revolution with them and running the building and its regular SYMBTech business, of course.

Aameh had a dreamy smile on her face, as she tried a woven bread a service bot brought her, nodding approval and raising a piece in a toast.

Aaxyl reached over for a taste. It was a light, airy bread. A flaky, barely-there glaze flashed a quick sweet flavour, and a stronger cheesy-peppery aroma took over her mouth, leaving loads of flavour and very little bulk. Aaxyl barely swallowed as it vanished in her mouth. She shook her head. No telling whether Gyan or Aameh had come up with the idea.

Mohan tried a piece as well. He wouldn't like it. It didn't have enough bulk to satisfy him. True enough, Mohan frowned at the small piece left in his hand like it had defrauded him.

"SecPros have approached the gate." Gyan interrupted her thoughts.

She accessed Gyan's perimeter feeds. SecPro and media zeplyns and hovers ranged outside their gate like an extra compound wall. A more expensive looking hover landed outside the gate and a man stepped out.

It was Darahs from the news. The global head of UDAY, and also the President of the dome since Damodar's resignation, stood at their gate with assistants and bodyguards. Why an organisation that existed only in this dome needed a global head was anybody's guess, but if he was standing at the gate, he probably wanted to come in.

"Continue your breakfast. I'll see what he wants." Mohan was already on his feet.

Gyan let Darahs and entourage in on foot and projected their progress on a screen on the roof. It led them to one of the rooms on the main floor with a desk and chairs. Mohan's office?

Aaxyl watched them do a doubletake at Mohan's entry and grinned. Now that she knew him better, she barely noticed his looks. She'd forgotten the impact he could have.

Mohan shook their hands and made a flourish toward the chairs as he took his.

Aaxyl subtly tried the hand wave herself, under the table. Hers was just a gesture, not poetry. She tried again a few times with a smile and slight head tilt before NeoJai noticed and she gave up.

In the room below, Mohan leaned back in his chair. "What brings you here?"

Darahs came to his point. "I'm concerned about the involvement of global citizens in the ongoing political crisis in the dome."

"I don't know what you mean."

"We're aware that you've been associating with the Saisrisels, who have a known history of hostility with Damodar. Now Damodar has been forced to resign and a new governance provider has come up after your brother met its founder."

Oops. The Saisrisels looked at each other, and shrugged to varying degrees.

"Should we simply abandon our kidnapped symbiontist?" Mohan asked. "That's the context of our repeated requests to Damodar. Dhrit Saisrisel and Damodar are both our friends. We were not aware of Damodar's intention to resign, or we would have approached you directly to begin with. Consider this yet another request for real-time data on Sambit's movements."

"Do you really expect me to believe it a coincidence that Noir met his ex-lover at a Sexel and Milup is now forming a governance provider?" Darahs bit out.

"I can't help what you think," Mohan said. "Can you prove Noir is a part of any governance provider? Or are ex-lovers of global citizens prohibited from local participation as well?"

A pop sounded as the bodyguard rested his forearms on Mohan's desk, tilted precariously, and fell to the floor.

"Teleporter," Gyan chimed in their heads. Aaxyl hadn't noticed anything.

Mohan stood to indicate the visit was over.

"Not very civil to bring in a teleporter on our premises without our knowledge. Fixed it for you. He won't remember this visit or any keys made here." The teleporter vanished. Mohan sauntered to Darahs. "Go home."

A humiliated Darahs walked out. Mohan returned to the roof.

"Where did you send the teleporter?" Aameh asked, patting his chair for him to sit.

Mohan shrugged. "Outside the gate."

"Something's off about this," Aameh said. "Why did he come here? The whole dome knows Noir met Milup. What new information was he hoping for?"

They all looked at each other's faces for a bit.

Mohan leaned back. "Looks like a job for Tashi."

Tashi projected onto the roof within seconds, as though waiting to be asked. "SYMBTech isn't as profitable as AVANT. This makes no sense as corporate sabotage either." Dey agreed to dig deeper and frowned at something on der right. "We aren't alone. Several companies in the dome have got such visits in recent days. A mix of local and global organisations, but all of them providing essential products or services."

It took Aaxyl a moment to register that Tashi wasn't just conversing, but had already done der digging deeper. She couldn't even begin to guess how dey breached UDAY systems so quickly or even knew what to search for.

"What does it mean?" asked Aameh. "Are they investigating something too?"

Tashi's projection shrugged. "We don't know. The teleporter was present only in a few of them."

London city to build new shuttleport for goods after successful negotiations between administrative sub-monarchies of England, Wales and Scotland. World News, Wednesday, December 10, 2442

~~*~*~*

AAMEH: MOHAN'S HOME

Mohan went home for some work, and Aameh tagged along. She explored the living room with its eclectic contents, while he did whatever he was up to. There were shelves full of paper books, gaming sets and a wide range of seating clustered into a few distinct areas.

The room could accommodate several dozen people, and yet, as far as Aameh knew, the only residents here were Mohan and Rudra. Elir was working on the Zephyrons to find Hersh's implant in the Superdome. Noir and Abrahamha lived there. She hadn't met any other members of the family, but Mohan had told her most of them would be in Bombay or Sarovar.

Aameh selected a few books to read before she dropped in to check on RudraJoy and found her flickering like a lightbulb in a 20th century film, fluctuating between solid and translucent. Terror battered Aameh, the eerie sense of her body coming apart overwhelming her. The books spilled out of her boneless hands. She shouldn't have come here and now she couldn't run. Aameh crumpled against the wall, trying to curl into a smaller target. The vibes tapered off.

"Shit. I'm sorry. I didn't see you." RudraJoy rushed over to help Aameh sit up. "I've been practicing exercises Scharada suggested."

Aameh couldn't see how this made anyone safer.

"My danger vibes are some protective ability." Rudra sat on the floor next to Aameh, panting. "I don't do it on purpose. They just happen if I'm feeling agitated. I can't stop them either. The more I try, the stronger they get."

"Then what's the exercise?" Aameh folded her arms, armpitting her trembling hands into immobility.

"We made a scale from zero to ten with zero for no vibes and ten, well... you know. Scharada wants me to project different levels for specific durations on purpose." Rudra grimaced. "I'm learning to project and stop, instead of trying to lower three to two."

"How does it help if you don't start on purpose?"

"We're hoping that projecting on purpose for ten seconds helps me interpret the end of that duration as stopping." Rudra shrugged. "Maybe with time, I'll be able to choose zero as either level or duration. Or learn to stop even if I didn't start on purpose. We don't know. It's worth a try."

"It's quite clever."

"It is, right?" Rudra grinned. "The medics say my stunted growth and skin are because my symbionts are too much for my body and if I can reduce their use, I might be able to put on weight, and and have more normal growth."

Little hope for Asiatic lions, but Biodiversity Project optimistic about engineering leopards from DNA.Science Zone, Saturday, December 13, 2442

~~*~*~*

AAXYL: SCHARADA'S HOME

The Saisrisels had moved back into their home.

NeoJai was spending the night there. He had invited Aaxyl, but she didn't want to divide his attention at a time when his family needed him. She also had unfinished business with Vidroh, and it seemed like a good time to face things head-on.

"Are we going to talk about this?" Aaxyl walked into Vidroh's room at Scharada's place. She needed clarity in their relationship. If there even was one anymore.

He sat on the edge of his bed.

"I don't know what to say," Vidroh told her. "I'm trying to find out who I am."

"When you left, you told me you loved me. Now you won't even look at me," Aaxyl said quietly. "I don't know if it is still true."

"This is not how I imagined us. How can I find love if I bring pain?"

"You are going to have to learn to move past this." Aaxyl squeezed his shoulder.

"I was hoping to feel better if I worked for the settlements," Vidroh said. "All I saw when I went there was the faces of the dead. Dead because of me."

"They also have something they didn't because of you." She tried a different approach. "They made their choices. Perhaps it was going to take rash gambles to get here."

"Why would anyone trust me?" Vidroh leaned his forehead against Aaxyl's stomach, pushing her arms back to her side, as though confused if he wanted to lean on her or shove her away.

"Give them reasons to trust you." Aaxyl was out of her depth. "It won't happen overnight. But we want to trust you."

"Can *you* forgive me?" Vidroh asked her.

"For what?" Aaxyl asked carefully.

"My wrongs against you. The passion and demands without explanation, the declaration of love and ghosting you, even though I could see I hurt you." This man was so desperately alone. She wanted to be the home he found his way back to.

"Apology accepted. What would you like to do about us moving forward?" Aaxyl asked, as she stepped closer.

Soon he rubbed his face against her and started fumbling with her clothes. She helped him undress her till she was standing naked between his feet.

He fell back on the bed, pulling her along. They struggled with his trousers, barely freeing him before being swept into a world of sensation.

Again, Vidroh's default mode for making love was desperate.

It was unexpectedly hot to be wanted with such passion. For all the demons haunting him, Vidroh was an intoxicating lover. A whirlwind that blew past any thought and immersed them both in a storm of sensations.

Vidroh dominated her again, restlessly driving her higher and higher, thrusting, grasping, kneading. He sucked her forearm, he moved positions, he kept up a relentless pace that lost track of climaxes till the whole night felt like one big orgasm.

She didn't know what he was proving and to whom with the giving of himself and claiming of her, but it was a statement.

Eventually, the tortured energy burned away, replaced by a quieter, raw need to be as close to her as he could be. His every movement still seemed to get them closer, exhausted and lying on their sides, with him spooning her tightly, unwilling for it to end.

Aaxyl vacillated between confused arousal and satiated bliss, questions circling her mind. Erotic dreams interspersed with physical awareness till she barely knew if she slept.

Aaxyl woke before dawn with her arm numb, still entwined.

He was also snoring against the nape of her neck.

Aaxyl smiled in amusement.

She opened her eyes and turned to find Vidroh looking at her. The mask was back on. Caring man, focused on her. His own baggage firmly back in storage. He'd be whatever she needed him to be.

She was going to miss him. "I have to get back soon."

He nodded. "I thought so. Get ready. I'll have breakfast ready by then." A new mask slammed into place. The outside world now crashed into their bubble. They were in Scharada's house: she as a friend of the owner, he as a disgraced rebel working to pay off therapy he couldn't afford.

Nothing had changed.

The sex, hotter and more desperate, was substituted for words unsaid.

Aaxyl felt homesick for NeoJai's candour. Even when he was angry with her, she knew why. She could work to resolve it.

She didn't know how to reach Vidroh, short of them being naked in bed. She had opened her heart, but the door shut in her face again, or worse, let her in and led her through a maze, with nobody home.

She didn't doubt that he loved her, but he didn't love himself. He was already here at the place that could help him. She needed to get out of his way to recovery.

By the time she went to the bright and airy kitchen for breakfast, Scharada was already eating.

Vidroh stood at the counter, a quiet, unresponsive figure in attendance.

Scharada raised a questioning eyebrow at her.

Aaxyl returned a numb shrug. They talked about everything that had changed since the Dorms, drawing Aaxyl out of her stupor.

Scharada left the table to prepare for a client. Or perhaps to give the two of them some space to talk.

Vidroh waited on her in case she wanted more food or coffee.

There were no words left to say.

Ravi Dorms welcomes its youngest members, healthy twin girls. Proud mother calls them the hope of humanity. Dome & Dorms, Sunday, December 14, 2442

~~*~*~*

AAXYL: SYMBTECH BUILDING

Aaxyl and NeoJai listened to Noir discuss the political plan with the Dhrits on the SYMBTech terrace, which contained a dining table and chairs without any immersive environment to distract from the meeting.

If UDAY remained out of power for another three days, NelumboN would govern the dome again unless Nagrik Manch conjured up a miracle. The Saisrisels could offer valuable advice and political backing that Noir and Mohan couldn't.

Aameh and Mohan talked quietly with each other a few chairs away.

"Who is this *we*?" Admin Dhrit asked with crisp impatience, so weird from same face as the laid-back Dhrit-H. "This was my plan."

Aaxyl focused on the tiny chicken and mayonaise wraps that Gyan said contained black pepper. Everybody was so used to Dhrit-H knowing all they did that no one had bothered to explain the plan to Admin Dhrit.

"This is not your plan," Mohan said from across the table. "There's a new plan. It does favour the results you wanted."

Admin Dhrit sighed in relief. "Thank you. The only real way for us to be safe is for me to be President again."

Awkward. They hadn't even known Admin Dhrit might live, let alone plan to make him President.

"Milup is Nagrik Manch's candidate for President," Dhrit-H said in the growing silence.

"Milup? Your boyfriend?" Admin Dhrit asked Noir. "You want us to prop up an idealist with no experience of governance while we remain vulnerable to attack?"

"Ex-boyfriend," Noir growled. "Milup was definitely not my idea. I helped Aameh talk to him and that was it."

"Milup was my idea," Dhrit-H said. "I saw a recording of his work with the Nagrik Manch. He is what the dome needs. The state doesn't exist to protect a family."

"With due respect," Admin Dhrit said. "You live in the home. You have no idea of the power and connections Damodar has."

Dhrit-H said, "I was a global business leader, as well as President, just as you, until twenty-five years ago. I'm not some nobody, clueless about what all this means. Regardless of our past with Damodar, he's a very popular leader. It helps that he resigned and it definitely reduces UDAY's popularity, but we need an equally charismatic leader to stand a chance."

"And what's Milup's charisma? I doubt residents of the Dome care about him being the lover of a Superdome resident," Admin Dhrit snapped. "Ex," he qualified, as Noir moved restlessly.

"On the contrary, he's not a businessman or politician. Him being a scholar makes him popular among residents. Nagrik Manch will get him the Dorm votes. Who else can you think of who can guarantee this many votes?"

"You were already President when you... your clone... *President Dhrit* was assassinated," Aaxyl said. She never was sure how to refer to the dead Dhrit. He didn't seem to have a specific identification like the others.

"All the power of Margadarshak didn't protect AricNova." Noir pointed out.

"He has no experience or even interest in practicalities!" Admin Dhrit slammed the table and stood up. "Sambit is running loose. Nyaya was attacked. I lay dying and couldn't do a single damn thing to keep her safe and she lay dying too. Milup is an idealist, not the husband of Sambit's victims. Ask Abrahamha or Jugaad what... SHIT." Admin Dhrit clutched his head. "Jugaad heard me."

Aaxyl's elbows twitched painfully, nerves twanging, like they wanted to flee her body. Everyone other than Noir was jerking involuntarily in some way. Cold shards of energy lashed their skin as Jugaad appeared on the roof like a scrawny thundercloud, and collapsed. Gyan had tranquilised him. Aaxyl could see welts on Aameh's arm.

"Safe for an hour or so," Gyan reported. It didn't feel safe.

"What is going on?" Aameh asked. "Why is Jugaad here?"

Admin Dhrit shook his head. "When I said Jugaad's name, I was thinking that he'd agree with me, and somehow it turned into a connection with his mind. He saw AricNova in my thoughts and knows she's alive."

A service bot came in with medical supplies. Noir lifted Jugaad gently from the floor and placed him in a Zephyron. A few sensors were attached and Aaxyl's mental implant flashed a readings overlay over Jugaad's unconscious body.

"Can't we just talk to him?" Aameh asked.

"No," several voices, including Gyan's, chorused.

Mohan said, "Not while he's agitated, and now that he knows AricNova is alive, he won't calm till he's got answers. Catch-22."

"Maybe we should call Abrahamha," Admin Dhrit suggested.

"No!" Mohan and Noir said together. "He'll react and awaken if he senses a threat," Noir added and Mohan nodded a what-he-said in Noir's direction.

"Well, we can rule that out," Aaxyl said. "Gyan mentioned threatening him a while ago and it didn't wake him."

"We aren't a threat." Noir drummed a restless beat on the back of a chair.

Noir, the sudden onset weather system wasn't a threat? Aaxyl wondered briefly if she should simply grab Aameh and run away.

"Your symbionts," Mohan said turning to AxAm. "They may control his, at least enough to give him enough information to calm down."

Aameh extended her arm readily, but nobody rushed to collect blood.

Mohan pulled her arm back down by her side. "Aaxyl has them too and is a lot more durable than you."

Elir and Rudra teleported in near the door and walked over, Alienling's unnerving vibes adding to the raw scraped feeling from Jugaad. Noir or Mohan must have imped or pathed them to come.

Noir looked at Rudra, "You ready for this, kid?"

A family that was overprotective of Rudra chose this time to depart from policy?

"Aaxyl's symbionts?" Rudra gave Aaxyl a head-to-toe. "No offense, but I'm not sure they'll work if they couldn't fully stop even Admin Dhrit's telepathy."

"None taken." Aaxyl had thought as much.

"You have a better alternative?" Noir asked.

Rudra scrunched her face, thinking it through. "No. Even if they can't control his reactions, we have to hope they weaken them enough to let me do the rest."

"How do you want to do this?" Noir asked Rudra.

Rudra ran her eyes around the room. "Aameh, Admin Dhrit, stand close behind me. Keep me between yourself and Jugaad."

And how exactly were the taller Aameh and still taller and broader Admin Dhrit to hide behind this waif?

"Shouldn't Aameh just get out now?" Aaxyl asked. "Or at least stand behind Noir?" Aameh could hide behind Noir completely.

"Noir can't stop Jugaad," Rudra said. "Jugaad will want information. One look at us and he'll know she and Admin Dhrit have seen AricNova. I'm not allowed to teleport. If she's not within my reach, he'll get to her first."

"But Dhrit-H wasn't involved. He should leave." Mohan teleported him out before he could object.

Rudra stretched. "I'll hold him for as long as I can. Noir, you back me and talk fast. Mohan, Elir, if it looks like we're failing, get everyone out of the room. Gyan can tranquilise him again and Noir can teleport him to the Superdome."

Noir looked straight at Aaxyl. "If it comes down to a fight, he'll be distracted with us. You two and the Saisrisels make a run for it. Take Rudra and Elir with you. Elir can teleport. Don't go to any property controlled by a SHADE. They'll try to protect you, but none will disobey a direct order from an admin."

That was it? It wasn't much of a plan. It took out the Saisrisel residence as well. Aaxyl nodded with determination. "Are you sure you can hold him?" she asked Rudra.

"Briefly. I'm stronger, but he has centuries of experience and endless skill," Rudra said, gloomily. "He'll distract me or undermine me in some other way that doesn't need him to be stronger. He always wins."

"Everyone take a moment to think clearly. Once we start, we have to see it through," Mohan said. "You have to act fast, Aaxyl."

Noir said, "Aaxyl, cut him, bleed into the wound—quick and dirty. If the symbionts fail, we're out of options. If he wakes up, get away. Are we ready?" Noir spoke to Aaxyl, but looked at Mohan.

Mohan stepped up next to Aaxyl. He'd teleport her away if push came to shove.

"Shouldn't we *inject* him with my blood?" Aaxyl asked.

"No!" Noir and Mohan said.

"Never inject blood directly! You'll get the full symbiont profile and much worse side effects. But isolating strains will take too long," Noir said. "Also, untested symbionts must never be injected."

Aaxyl knew that. It was the whole reason why the masses were provided HealSYMB free of cost rather than simply giving each other blood when ill. She'd just thought that Jugaad was too powerful for it to matter. It probably mattered more.

"He's an ancient, who develops new abilities," Mohan said. "He won't die from a complication, but if he has a bad reaction, or gets stronger, injected symbionts can't be removed. His symbionts will isolate and discard yours over time if you apply them locally."

"What if my blood negates his symbionts?" Aaxyl asked.

Rudra snorted.

"We don't have a choice." Noir moved to face Rudra across from Jugaad. "But I doubt it's possible. Eventually his symbionts will adapt."

Rudra stood about six feet away to one side of Jugaad, facing Noir at a similar distance on the other.

Aameh and Admin Dhrit did as they were told.

Rudra stood in an instinctive fighter's stance, a foot leading slightly, weight forward, nicely springy. Her head was too forward for Aaxyl's liking and hands too low, but she wouldn't be fighting physically.

Aaxyl tried to not be itchy about it. She'd have to teach Alienling better.

Noir stood like an ancient tree. Powerful and immovable, feet flat with a wide stance, hands loose at his sides.

Elir stood close to NeoJai, while Mohan flanked Aaxyl, ready to teleport them out at a moment's notice.

"Let's do this, before he wakes up and makes it impossible." Mohan said. "Gyan, we need a knife or scalpel."

"In Aaxyl's pocket," Gyan replied. The service bot moved over with the first-aid kit anyway.

"You knew?" AxAm always carried a small knife each, for protection.

"I handle security for this building. Am has one too. I assumed it was an AxAm rule. A scalpel would be sharper though."

A blast of terror hit Aaxyl and she crouched on the floor. "Damnit Alienling. Get your act together."

"Sorry. Just one minute, stay where you are."

More terror pelted Aaxyl. This wasn't going to work. And then it switched off. Profound peace. There were no terror vibes at all.

"New trick," Rudra said.

Before anything else could go wrong, Aaxyl sprayed anaesthetic and used the scalpel from the kit to make a cut on Jugaad's palm with a shaking hand. No blood. The cut closed. She made a bigger cut by pressing the scalpel firmly. It healed before she could cut her own palm. They had a problem.

"Cut yourself first," Mohan whispered. "With your symbionts on the blade, it shouldn't heal as fast. If it does, we have a bigger problem."

Aaxyl applied topical anaesthetic and made a cut on the palm of her hand, cupping her palm to let the blood pool. She coated the scalpel with it liberally and cut Jugaad's palm. This time the cut healed slowly. Jugaad stirred and an abrupt prickling sensation swept her body, making Aaxyl jump. A tranquiliser dart hit him with a pop. *"Thank you, Gyan."*

"You're welcome. Keep moving. He won't stay down for long."

Aaxyl used the scalpel to deepen the cut and poured the blood in her palm into it, then cupped her palm on it directly to minimise contact with air. A sense of Jugaad's symbionts battered at her attention.

She focused on it, curious, and sensed them as though she could see them like streaks of light against a black so deep it was complete absence and full of contradictions. Straight lines and dots and smooth curves all at once. It was exhausting, like walking uphill through a torrent coming down. The more she focused, the more clearly she saw flows which were also static. Her eyes continued to see her hand holding Jugaad's, but her vision was deficient in comparison. The sensations felt like swirls and flows or ripples of coloured lights as though they refracted through the prism that was Jugaad as each decided to do its own thing.

The swirls contained other perceptions. It was like adapting to the mental implant all over again. The construct had its own shape and movement independent of the body, which brought an instant sense of vertigo.

She sensed instinctively that her symbionts wouldn't suppress everything Jugaad had, even temporarily. He felt overwhelming compared with her own symbionts, which she could also sense. But her looking at the symbionts changed them, like the process of sensing them was two-way. Focusing on the strands strengthened them, denying them focus weakened them. Pushing at them squished them into the black. Still there, but an almost invisible, transparent presence.

She had no idea what she was doing. She certainly had never felt another person's symbionts before. But then she wasn't in the habit of pouring her blood into other people's wounds either. Maybe she sensed Jugaad's symbionts because they were so powerful. The amount of focus this took guaranteed she wouldn't have stumbled upon it by accident without the powerful conspicuousness of his symbionts bombarding her attention.

They felt like a chaotic tornado. Instinctively, she understood that the jagged "noise" meant dysfunction, unpredictability. She attempted to organise it, spotting patterns and noise, and ignored the noise into oblivion till clear patterns remained. There was a feeling of timelessness to this. Barely a few seconds had passed since she clasped Jugaad's hand.

In her mind was another world where she could take all the time she needed to figure this out before she released them. There still was a giant torrent of symbionts, but they presented more or less smoothly.

Aaxyl was exhausted.

Jugaad sighed in relief as he opened his eyes.

Aaxyl let go of his hand and stumbled back. Mohan supported her.

Rudra braced herself.

Noir stiffened.

Jugaad tried to sit up and looked at Rudra in shock. He reached a hand toward Rudra, and she flew toward him windmilling her arms with a dismayed "oh no!"

Jugaad hugged Rudra and thumped her back with... pride? "Not bad, kiddo!"

What had happened?

Elir bent his legs slightly and grunted. It would be comical, except he hadn't teleported NeoJai out.

Aaxyl expected Mohan to teleport her away, but she remained where she was, as did everyone else.

"Thank you," Jugaad told Aaxyl over Rudra's head. "No, Gyan. Don't sedate me."

Admin Dhrit stepped in front of Aameh.

Aaxyl couldn't believe she'd ever thought he'd hurt her.

"He's... fine!" Rudra squirmed out of the hug.

"Everybody calm down," Jugaad said. "Your anxiety is giving me a headache."

"you are.... okay?" Mohan asked.

"For the first time in centuries. Yes." Jugaad breathed in deeply. "I'm not killing anyone but no one is going anywhere till I figure this out."

"You don't seem to have got... negated," Aaxyl stammered.

"You didn't ... negate me." Jugaad stood and they all took a wary step back. "What is negated?"

"Like us," Aaxyl muttered. "Negated. Disabled symbionts."

Jugaad looked at her and tilted his head, then looked at Aameh. He nodded.

Noir stepped forward and searched his face. "If you're really in control, this is fantastic. I hope you forgive us."

"It is no matter." Jugaad waved his apology away and pulled him into a thumping hug too. "This is unexpected. The main thing is Ari. I'm sorry, but this will just be faster. What do you know of AricNova? No, don't tell me."

Jugaad gazed around the group, his eyes finally settling on Admin Dhrit and Aameh. "You're the only ones who saw her. I knew she wasn't dead."

"How are you taking this so easily?" Mohan asked.

"It isn't easy," Jugaad said. "But we'll get her back. Let's bring Abrahamha, and end this once and for all."

Aaxyl was happy for Jugaad, but no one, not even Mohan and Noir looked ready to be on a casual back-slapping "let's get two *Homo godions* together and have a jolly search for a third" basis.

"I can't find her mind," Jugaad said, looking at all their faces. "Abrahamha is a much better telepath. We need him."

"Three people here aren't even legal adults," Aaxyl muttered. "I'm not risking the two of you searching for AricNova around them."

Jugaad looked at her, then Aameh, Rudra and Elir. Then back to her with a nod. "Let's get Abrahamha your symbionts and anyone under a century can sit this one out."

Cranti Dorm guards disrupt illegal dorm fights, arrest organisers. Dorm Hour, Sunday, December 14, 2442

~~*~*~*

AAMEH: SYMBTech building

They managed to convince Jugaad to try Gyan's delicious wraps before he did anything drastic, like call Abrahamha.

Noir had left to work on the modified Zephyrons.

Aameh suspected he might have gone off to warn Abrahamha without Jugaad reading his mind. She resolved to keep him well fed and entertained. Oh dear, did her guessing it mean Jugaad knew?

Jugaad smiled at her.

Aameh gestured for him to try the wraps.

Aameh had found *cheese & peas* amusing, and loved the spicy filling with mushrooms. Aaxyl had tasted the chicken and mayonaise ones and planted her *why fix what ain't broke* flag. Surely, there would be wraps to interest Jugaad too.

Aameh sat next to him.

Rudra sat on her other side busy demolishing a mixed selection heaped on her plate at record speed. How that insubstantial creature put away mountains of food would probably take a new *Quaspar Hypothesis* to explain.

Aameh imagined the volume folding into a non-spacetime dimension. She turned to Jugaad. "When you received Ax's symbionts, you grew stronger, but Ax and Dhrit lost telepathy and teleportation with the same."

Aameh expected Aaxyl to lecture her through the implant, but Aaxyl sighed and said nothing.

Jugaad made a subtle hand-gesture that AxAm used for *stop*. It was not an obvious one. He met her eyes with a small smile.

He was reading Aaxyl's mind! Jugaad shrugged.

Blink if you're reading my mind. Aameh thought.

Jugaad blinked, but it was so natural, Aameh didn't know if he had naturally blinked or... Jugaad looked straight at her and closed his eyes and opened them.

Holy dwit. This was as good as mind reading.

Mind reading is defined as reading someone's memories, Jugaad pathed to her, even though she wasn't a telepath. This is communication. My telepathy is strong enough that I lift your thoughts, just as I lift your reply.

But... this would imply the *Quaspar* physicists were right about symbionts being symbion fields rather than microorganisms, as per the leading quantum microbiology theory. Microorganisms couldn't jump to other bodies. Aameh did a small mental jig.

Do you hear this? she asked.

Yes, Jugaad pathed. Me reading your mind would be if I could retrieve memories or knowledge directly without you thinking about it. It is a much hypothesised ability and would be very valuable, but so far, no one has achieved it. But I can read your thoughts. Even if symbion fields cause the abilities, it doesn't explain how our minds interact with them. Symbionts could be the link. That's SanJeevan's department. I'm a physics guy myself. A barely there smile softened Jugaad's face as he busied himself with the wraps.

Aaxyl glared Aameh into silence.

"Calling Abrahamha here," Jugaad said, as he finished eating. "Fix his symbionts, and go back to whatever you normally do."

"Like hell," Admin Dhrit said. "This is our dome, the collateral damage is our people." Dhrit-H had clearly told him what had happened the last time Abrahamha tried to search for AricNova in the dome.

"I want to be in," Elir said.

"We'll have to do as we're told." Rudra put a thin arm around Aameh.

"Dhrit," Jugaad sighed. "In all fairness, we haven't given you much reason to trust us in such situations, but me asking is just team spirit. You can't stop me from doing whatever the hell I want."

Aameh was discovering that not out of control only meant not as out of control as he could be.

Jugaad shrugged like Aaxyl. He was an excellent mimic. He was reading her mind again. He gave her an Aaxyl-like eye-roll.

Abrahamha appeared behind Jugaad. Wary.

Aaxyl's wrap stopped its ascent an inch from her mouth. Aameh realised belatedly that she was sitting next to Jugaad with Rudra on the other side and Abrahamha behind her. Yeah, that would do it.

"I didn't plan this," Aameh imped to Aaxyl. "I was just talking to Jugaad."

Aaxyl didn't reply.

Abrahamha looked at Jugaad and relaxed. "Incredible. Let's do it." He looked at Aameh.

"Me?" Aameh squeaked as she stood. She backed away and bumped into Rudra and jumped. Aaxyl was the brave one.

"You want to be a symbiont researcher, right?" Abrahamha asked her. "You want to pass up this opportunity?"

"No! I mean yes..." Aameh rolled to a confused pause to reorient. "I don't want to pass up the opportunity."

Aaxyl finally imped back, and explained what she had done, showing her how she had perceived the patterns and noise in his symbionts.

Abrahamha manifested a scalpel in his hand and gave it to her. Aameh was to just cut herself like in films? A bottle of anaesthetic spray appeared in her other hand and she clutched it gratefully before it fell.

Abrahamha's eyes found Mohan. "I should have thought of it." He turned to Aameh. "Please use the anaesthetic."

She applied the topical anaesthetic on both their palms, closed her eyes tightly and made a shallow cut on her palm. Making sure the blade had her blood on it, she cut Abrahamha's palm. Abrahamha's eyes widened in surprise when the cut didn't heal instantly.

Aameh placed her palm on his, with the cuts touching, and sensed the symbionts in his body with some effort. Aaxyl was right. She couldn't see how all of it could be muted either, but there were shards and random flows that didn't fit.

Aameh took a careful look at the symbionts raging in Abrahamha with an artist's eye and reorganised them so that the pandemonium going on in his body settled into a harmonious torrent. It was still wild and beautiful, and powerful beyond comprehension, but no longer chaotic. They seemed nicely balanced.

Relief flowed through Abrahamha as he took a deep breath and sighed. "Thank you."

Aameh couldn't stop grinning.

You should do this for each other, Jugaad pathed. You had the symbionts, but with you being a baby and Aaxyl having got them through a transfusion, no one had regulated anything. You should be able to do this to yourselves.

Abrahamha added, Don't make it public that you can modify the working of symbionts. People with rare symbiont abilities are often in danger.

He sounded like Aaxyl's descriptions of her mother.

"So, what's the plan?" Jugaad wanted to help with the search. "I assume that one more person would be useful?" Jugaad asked.

"Jugaad," Aameh sighed. "I sympathise. Truly, I do. But..."

"You haven't lived for a tenth of the duration I've been in hiding," Jugaad said. "Give me something safe to do now that I have better control."

What did one give an overpowered individual to do without harming others? Also their definitions of control needed a common calibration. "Do you know what Damodar's powers are?"

They still hadn't been able to get in touch with him. If he was in cahoots with Sambit, they needed to know what to expect.

Noir waved a dismissive hand. "Symb-abilities either fail on him or he redirects them. It's like a party trick, not an aggressive power."

"Damodar won't harm Ari," Abrahamha said. "He loved her."

"Damodar loved AricNova?" Aameh asked.

"Everyone loved Ari." Jugaad shrugged.

Two centuries was a long time. Enough to fall out of love? For the love to be warped into creepy possession?

"Imperviousness to symbiont powers or being able to hijack them hardly sounds minor." NeoJai frowned, clearly thinking the same thing.

"But it is," Jugaad said. "Now you know he can do it, you won't direct symb-abilities at him to be hijacked, just shoot him or use telekinesis on something else to skewer him..."

Not that they had any such abilities.

Ten years after its release, Abrahamha's Strays remains the top selling documentary immersive globally. Entertainment Zone, Monday, December 15, 2442

~~*~*~*

DAMODAR: UNKNOWN LOCATION

Damodar woke up in a large room, and sat up groggily. Metal clinked as he moved his feet. A grimy man with matted white hair was chained by his ankles next to him. Further away was a medical bed with...

"Ari."

She lay on the bed, like a ridge dividing the sheet.

"I heard you were trying to find her." Sambit stood in the doorway with a gun aimed at him.

Damodar nailed him with a cold, dead stare. "Convenient. Saved me the trip."

He stood to his full height and went as close to Sambit as the chain allowed, knowing it intimidated people. He needed to force Sambit to attack him with symbiont powers.

"You're insane," Damodar snarled.

"It may be true." Sambit gave him an unhinged smile. "But I'm still in business. You really shouldn't have betrayed me."

"You betrayed me first," Damodar mocked back. "You pretended to help Smriti. You tortured Ari. You used my name to commit crimes. Now, you have kidnapped me. How do you imagine this ends for you? Do you think these chains can hold me?"

"I'm certain they will. They seem to hold her just fine." Sambit skirted his reach and strolled over to AricNova's bed, detaching a small bag filled with blood and replacing it with an empty bag. "I'll soon be gone."

Sambit expected to wander off?

"How will you pull that off?" Damodar asked. "Nadani had her all the time, didn't he? In one year, you destroyed two centuries of his secret. He'll want your head on a platter."

Damodar rattled his chains and watched Sambit flinch. He needed to get Sambit angry.

"I don't have to go to Nadani." Sambit didn't waver. "All I need is a shell that has been outside this dome. I have a whole world to go to."

Damodar projected absolute certainty. "The world isn't big enough."

The white-haired man quavered as a man who has recently discovered a shouting voice. "Why do you need AricNova? Her symbionts are toxic and your shells keep dying. You're a telepath and teleporter yourself. Just use your own symbionts! Maybe a few may live."

Sambit scoffed. "I'm trying to create more powerful shells, not longer lived ones."

"What for?" spat the man.

Damodar had no clue, but he didn't know a single man who knew Nadani and wasn't unnerved by him. "To attack Nadani without risking yourself? You have his symbionts and are more powerful, but you're a dwit, aren't you, little dimwit?"

"Her symbionts can do more things," Sambit sounded like he was trying to convince himself. "He used her for centuries. I'm just levelling the field. I didn't put the chain in her. I didn't turn her into this." Sambit waved a hand toward AricNova, shuddering.

Damodar taunted him further. "And all this, because you don't want to use your own symbionts. You're scared of even nulls being more powerful than you. You're a coward."

"I stole from a criminal." Sambit winked.

"Good luck explaining that to Abrahamha," Damodar jeered. Why wasn't Sambit attacking him? Did he know? "You could have been a hero for rescuing her. Instead, you wrote your own fate. Free us. Save yourself. Nadani's friends as well as foes meet exactly the same fate—destruction." Damodar looked straight at him, doing all he could to intimidate Sambit. All he needed was for Sambit to try to control him with telepathy.

Sambit locked them in and left. Maybe he should have tried to keep him talking instead of scaring him.

He'd try again next time.

"I'm Hersh," the man murmured.

Ah, the missing Ekta Dorms symbiontist. Damodar said, "Abrahamha's Strays are looking for you. Don't lose hope."

Damodar tested the manacles around his feet. They didn't budge.

Hersh moved his head in what could be a half-hearted nod. "Isn't Nadani your cousin?"

"I stay away from him. I was stupid to think Sambit wanted the same." Damodar tried pulling the chain out of the wall. It didn't even loosen. "Before you ask, I didn't know Nadani or Sambit had Ari. I thought she was dead."

"But you understand what's going on," Hersh said. "What did you mean by stronger?"

"Nadani used to give his symbionts to people like Sambit," Damodar sat next to the wall trying to figure out how the chain could be removed. "It turned out those receiving the symbionts become more powerful than him and ended in a bloodbath, when he decided he didn't want that. Sambit survived, because he convinced Nadani of his loyalty."

"So why did he leave?" Hersh asked.

"Nadani would have killed him eventually." Damodar wondered how much he should speak of these things. "When Nadani was suspicious of me, Sambit offered to follow me here to keep an eye on me for Nadani. He offered to keep an eye on Dhrit for me."

Hersh guffawed a long, bitter laugh, slapping his thigh in hysterical mirth. "Nadani trusted him to keep an eye on you. You trusted him to keep an eye on Admin Dhrit. Admin Dhrit trusted him to protect from you. I trusted him to care about the well-being of nulls. This will be hilarious one day... if we survive."

"We will survive."

Hersh examined his own manacles in an abrupt change of mood. "It still doesn't make sense. AricNova's symbionts should make shells even stronger and resist him more."

Damodar gave the chain a little slack and then jerked it suddenly with all his strength. "But they die before they develop the skill to use her powers."

"They won't break," Hersh said. "I've been trying." He showed Damodar his palms, scraped raw.

"You aren't me," Damodar panted.

"We're missing something," Hersh said. "Nulls can't act or think to resist him. So why not use his own symbionts and create durable shells?"

Damodar dared not guess it. Teleporters healed fast. "Do you think..."

"Perhaps Nulls resist too, if used long enough?" Hersh mused. "But that would mean..."

"If we die here, we'll never find out," Damodar said. "Don't give up."

Bracing his feet against the wall, Damodar wrapped his hands around the chain and pulled till his muscles bulged and sweat covered his body. He pulled, and pulled still harder. His muscles burned with strain. Veins popped. The chain slipped through his hands with a harsh burn as he fell to the floor.

"You really think you can break it?" Hersh said, staring at where the chain had chipped a small piece of the wall near it.

Damodar was just getting started.

"I'll chew my own legs off if I have to."

Clinical trials exploring the use of symbionts in treating mental disorders continue to fail with the latest from Javer Pharma yielding inconclusive results. Medicine Frontier, Monday, December 15, 2442

~~*~*~*

AAXYL: SYMBTech Building

Aaxyl and Aameh sat facing each other in Aameh's room, with Noir watching. They made their cuts and shook hands. A sense of increased vitality kicked in instantly, like Aaxyl had just woken up from the most rejuvenating sleep.

She could feel Aameh's symbionts. They were flat. Subdued. Like there was a fog squishing them. She dissolved the fog and teased the strands, and they swirled free in tentative wisps.

Wow. Aameh's voice spoke in her head as wide eyes met hers. *We're telepathic!* She included Noir. *We're pathing!*

Like a thump on my head, Aaxyl agreed, the effort hitting her almost before the ability.

Aameh rubbed at her hand and turned it palm up, mouth open in shock. The cut bled slower already. For the first time ever, Aameh was healing normally.

Aaxyl wanted to weep with relief.

That is amazing indeed. Noir pathed back. *Will you fix my symbionts too?*

"Sure," Aameh said, continuing the conversation normally. She cut the palm of his hand and connected. He had a fire with sparks zinging off. Like she had with Abrahamha, she looked for flows, patterns. She dimmed everything to see what the brightness of his patterns had obscured. The stronger rhythms. Those were the ones around which his symbionts organised. When she released, everything blazed back up in beautiful harmony.

Noir relaxed, much as the others had. Did his symbionts just surge back stronger, as she sensed? This wasn't just about neutralising or modulating symbionts. Organising them made them work better.

"You've been called to the medical room," Gyan told them. It wasn't a medical room. More like a room with AVANT's leftover equipment from the implants.

Aaxyl stood up to leave and suddenly felt off-balance. What the... she wasn't the type to faint or lose balance. She felt fine.

"You flickered," Gyan and Noir said together.

"How?" Aaxyl was stunned. "I'm not a teleporter."

"If your symbionts work, you both are," Noir said. "Teleporting doesn't come quickly. It takes years. You verge on leaving for a long time before you succeed."

"I didn't teleport as a child," Aaxyl was sure.

"Mohan, Tashi and Rudra are the only teleporters we know who could teleport at a young age. Flickering usually begins in late teens."

They went down to find the room busy with medics and gawkers. A badly injured woman in a Healarron claimed center of attention. An unfamiliar display showed a body temperature just above freezing. It must be Smriti. Damodar's niece-slash-daughter.

Two medics parted and moved toward Smriti to reveal SanJeevan. What was going on?

"You're invited to participate in and observe the conversion of a *Homo sapiens* into a *Homo symbions*. If you continue to be here, you're agreeing to patient confidentiality. SanJeevan will conduct this session." Abrahamha welcomed them.

"*Not at AVANT?*" Aaxyl imped Gyan.

"*Some students don't have the clearance for AVANT, but this is a learning opportunity,*" it replied.

"The patient has come to us before the introduction of symbionts, which gives us control over how they're introduced. We'll have access to her in ten minutes and she'll be fully out of stasis in another hour after that. Strategies?"

"External applications of more tolerated symbionts. Small patches while she's being revived, and being ready to add more if she's handling them well."

A blonde woman labelled *Katie* said. Local resident of the Superdome. Aaxyl hadn't known any native Americans still existed.

"Reasoning?" SanJeevan asked.

"She's injured. It allows better control and turns the cold into our advantage," Katie said. "It gives us time to remove them on the first sign of any adverse reactions."

"That sounds reasonable," SanJeevan said. "Which symbionts?"

"Um.. HealSYMB." Aameh said.

"Individual strains. Begin from the top tier on tolerance and work our way down," Katie said.

"UltraSYMB," a dark-skinned man with the label *Hakim* said.

Aaxyl hastily looked up what they were talking about. Like Aameh, she only knew about HealSYMB for healing.

"HealSYMB is a consortium of seventy-six symbiont strains, each slightly different, but creating an overall healing effect." Gyan sent her a quick reference for the constituent strains of HealSYMB.

Some had high tolerance, some had lower tolerance but faster effect, others worked better on specific tissues. The six high-tolerance strains would be her bet too. UltraSYMB was the unicorn of symbionts. A weak culture with only nine strains, it proliferated slower, requiring greater doses, but so far, no one, not even *Homo sapiens* had rejected it.

"UltraSYMB first, if that works, we wait to introduce other symbionts. We may not need to. If needed, the one most tolerant strain of HealSYMB." Aaxyl started reading out its key number, feeling a bit ridiculous, but it was too late to stop.

"Just call it T1. We all do," SanJeevan interrupted her. "Top tier of the Tolerance scale. T1 to T6. Don't read out entire keys."

"If we have enough UltraSYMB, I support that," Hakim said. "If we don't, we can test the T1 along with the Ultra. T1 is even slower. By the time we find out the UltraSYMB isn't enough, the T1 may not be fast enough. If we wait, we should use T2 instead. It works faster."

"We shouldn't use UltraSYMB at all if we don't have enough," Katie said. "Universal compatibility is only an advantage if other symbionts won't be used. UltraSYMB comes at great cost and should not be used without clear advantage."

"Great cost?" Aaxyl imped Gyan.

"UltraSYMB can't be cultured. It is extracted from the blood of a single individual."

She wondered if that individual was Rudra.

"It isn't the person you're thinking of," Gyan imped.

"We have enough UltraSYMB for now to see if she'll live at least," Abrahamha said.

"Two minutes to go," SanJeevan said. "People who can scan symbionts in the body, take positions. If you have mental implants, please allow access so that others can learn from your observations. Five of the observers can apply the UltraSYMB."

Half a dozen others joined on the side of the SYMB supplies and grabbed a few vials and attached them to applicators. Katie, Mohan and Hakim moved to the other side of the Healarron. Which side should they be on?

It is okay if SanJeevan knows you can scan, Abrahamha pathed.

But we can't connect without contact with our symbionts, Aaxyl pathed back.

Tell her, Abrahamha advised.

Aaxyl went over to Sanjeevan and Abrahamha.

"We can scan," Aaxyl said. "But we need to apply at least a little blood. What should we do?"

"Observe for now," SanJeevan said. "Enough people are scanning."

Abrahamha spoke up. "SanJeevan, they have the symbionts that allowed Dhrit to survive. They can modulate symbionts in some way. It allows me to be here."

"That could come in handy if she has trouble adapting," SanJeevan said.

"Use the smallest drop possible and stay away from broken skin."

Aaxyl and Aameh took up positions on either side of Katie and Mohan. As the Healarron opened, they pricked their fingers with a needle and applied a tiny drop to her skin each. *"Nothing. Now what? We can't apply more blood."* Aaxyl imped to whoever would hear. Perhaps it needed an open cut and direct contact.

"Patience, Ax, she doesn't have symbionts in her to sense. None of us are getting anything," Mohan imped back.

The other members of the team started applying the UltraSYMB. It was runny before getting absorbed. Aaxyl couldn't see so much as sense slight ripples, like small drops into a pool. The applicators stroked across the surface leaving faint wakes. It was very soothing.

She checked what the others were seeing through the implant. Aameh sensed transparent dots. Mohan sensed blue-white particles seeping into the skin. Hakim scanned everything like medical imaging. The symbionts were barely noticeable. Katie got an overall feeling without imagery.

"The UltraSYMB is seeking a host, rather than recognising the body," said Katie. "Wait till she comes out of stasis more. Can we circulate blood?"

"Blood is circulating," Hakim said. "She's on life-support." He rolled a leg from side to side. It helped. Soon, they were all rubbing or moving various body parts.

It was another ten minutes before anything happened. The UltraSYMB lost potency from exposure to air. Slowly, the symbionts started engaging with the body. The applications resumed.

Why can't we just transfuse the UltraSYMB and let circulation take it through the body? Aaxyl imped Mohan.

We can't be certain she's tolerating it till we see engagement. Applications on the skin, we can wipe off.

It is working. I'm certain. Not being rejected.

"She can take a lot more UltraSYMB now," Katie said as Hakim nodded. Transfusers were used all over the body.

"We've got this," Aameh said. AxAm boosted the UltraSYMB as much as they could. Aaxyl wanted to squirm a little from the astonished stares, but she acted like she did this every day. No big deal.

"She's healing," Hakim called out. Nothing was visible. "Needs nutrients."

Surgical staff covered in sterile film kicked into play, elbowing symbiontists out of the way.

Hovers unrolled a transparent screen around a surgical table leaving only a booth for people to walk through. People on the surgery team went through the booth to emerge on the other side sealed in transparent film shrink-fitted around their hands and feet with clear visors around the face.

"I think we're done here." Katie turned away. She imped Aaxyl, *"Wipe off the blood before Orion sees it."*

Aaxyl hastily swiped a sterile swab at the barely visible spot.

On cue, Orion, the head of the surgical team needed the room.

Smriti had unhealed ancient stitches that needed to be removed before the UltraSYMB healed them wrong and left giant scars. An overlay indicating higher air pressure appeared over the surgical table and Smriti was moved to it.

"Nanobot-operators, stay away from the table," SanJeevan said. "Medics, wait to be assigned to specific repairs. If you touch anything that isn't marked sterile, get into new film."

Orion matched medic and nanobot-operator pairs to injuries. "Keep nanobot clusters separate and we'll be done before dinner. Wait for the nanobots to work up before opening incisions or I'll take your implants out with a spoon. Anyone without experience in cleanrooms, get the fuck out. She's *sapiens*."

Gyan tagged observers and symbiontists with red warnings. Arrows pointed to the door in her implant overlay. Talk of overkill.

"Where are the nanobots?" Aaxyl imped Gyan as they skirted the medics and filed out. She really wanted to see a nano-surgery.

"In her," it replied. *"Orion repaired damage from the thawing earlier. You can*

ask Minal for recordings."

A sudden swoosh settled into the familiar sound of a heartbeat.

"Fantastic job," SanJeevan shook their hands at the door.

Technically, Smriti remained *Homo sapiens* unless the UltraSYMB colonised her.

Time would tell.

Saving AricNova

~~*~*~*

AAXYL: A ZEPLYN ABOVE THE CITY

AxAm were in Mohan's zeplyn, above the residential area of the dome, near the Octagon. Below them, three Zephyrons, replicated from Hersh's modified Zephyron and the *Cosmic Chaos* game, ran promotional campaigns for AVANT. Anyone who wanted to buy one could transfer the unimon and Minal would dispatch their Zephyron.

Aaxyl should have been slack-jawed in wonder. The Octagon stood at the apex of the eight beautifully proportioned sectors. The eight dorms around the periphery looked like rugged fortification giving rise to the ephemeral bubble that was their dome. The stylish architectures of tall and sleek residential buildings sloped into elegant mansions and eight identical towers facing the filigreed Octagon.

Sectors contrasted with lush green parks in exquisite radial symmetry, stocky welfare dormitories across the ring road faced slender buildings of the residential areas. Everything had its place in the intricate whole she'd been a part of all her life, without quite seeing the big picture like this.

Aaxyl *had* been appropriately stunned. Five hours ago. Now she was hungry and had finished all the snacks in the zeplyn.

Aameh hadn't raised her head from her drawings for hours.

Nyaya turned out to be the editor of Khabariya and wanted an *absurde* cover by the SoulScaper for the upcoming edition. If all went well, the issue would feature the change of government as well as the rescue of AricNova.

Aameh was struggling to scale her *absurde* to suit printing.

Aaxyl was bored. She listened in on the search losing steam below them. Noir searched the main area mapped out by Aameh, while Mohan and Elir each searched a smaller area. She would have given anything to be on a Zephyron with them, but Mohan and Noir only wanted teleporters to search the grid in case they found Hersh and needed to move fast. It would be years before Aaxyl was able to teleport. If ever.

"You find anything?" Elir imped. This was getting repetitive.

These were elite areas close to the central Octagon, and they'd sold dozens of Zephyrons between the three of them, but found no sign of Hersh.

"I'm just repeating my pattern. They aren't here," Noir imped. *"Maybe hotshot teleporter missed an area."*

"I didn't!" Elir's response was immediate. *"I swear he's not here."*

It was time to regroup, but Aameh wasn't ready to accept that her plan had failed. *"I don't know why you can't find him. These are the three spots. They are in the bigger area Noir searched."*

"Since we're out in the Zephyrons anyway, why don't we cover the entire dome?" Elir asked. *"At worst, we'll sell Zephyrons."*

Aameh slapped her sketchbook on her lap, her back ramrod straight, imping irritation. *"You can do it to sell Zephyrons, but AricNova won't be there. She'll be in the area covered by Noir."*

"In that case, maybe Mohan and I should cover the area again," Elir volunteered. *"Maybe we catch something he missed."*

Elir hadn't become a prodigy by being the lazy one. Five hours and counting, his tenacity encouraged Aameh's stubborn streak. *"Please do keep an eye out for anything I may have missed too."*

"No luck, huh?" Aaxyl gave Aameh a sympathetic hug.

Aameh shrugged away.

"Aameh is rarely this confident and wrong," Aaxyl imped Noir. *"She needs to rest and look at this with a fresh head."*

They had waited for so long for the Zephyrons to be ready, believing Aameh's plan would work.

"We're all running on fumes," Noir imped, dejected.

Elir and Mohan continued their coverage of the other grid, but Noir came back and did a quick review of everything. Eventually, Elir and Mohan returned too. Aameh was adamant and wouldn't give up, but they were tired and hungry.

Finally, it ended with Noir ordering Aameh to rest, which ended with tears and Aameh *hating* Noir.

Aaxyl winced.

Aameh was an extremely sore loser. Retreating from a puzzle violated her to the core.

Back at SYMBTech, Aaxyl went straight to her room, needing to think through the whole thing again.

She woke up still at her desk, with NeoJai rubbing her back. He had been out with Nyaya all day, helping her prepare for the next day's publishing of *Khabariya*.

"I'm not getting into bed." Aaxyl rubbed her eyes.

NeoJai kissed the top of her head. "That's good, because I wanted company to have a crack at Aameh's puzzle. A fresh perspective might help."

Aaxyl turned her face up for an upside-down kiss and got stubble-burn on her nose for her enthusiasm.

"Gyan, show the segment most likely to contain Hersh." Aaxyl sighed. Gyan did so. "Show the paths of the Zephyron grid."

Aaxyl waved the slate display at NeoJai, who took it. Gyan displayed their search grids and details of each area covered. They'd missed nothing.

Noir's route glowed blue, slightly below Elir's pink and Mohan's yellow. There were no holes. They had even covered some areas more densely than needed going through every road they could access, even if not necessary, once their routes were done.

It was like Sambit was taunting them.

Aaxyl sank her head in her hands. "They're there. Why can't we find them?"

"We will."

"Perhaps the teleporter is here, but not Hersh." Aaxyl ignored implications of Hersh no longer being there. He was their friend. "ToxicSYMB!"

NeoJai traced a finger along the search grid. "Gyan, can you show the subterranean levels for all the buildings in this area?" Gyan marked them out. That was a lot of buildings. NeoJai pondered them.

"Can you show only buildings with two or more subterranean levels?" Fifty-seven buildings remained.

"They're here." NeoJai stood.

"What do you mean?"

"Hersh is in the lower levels," NeoJai said. "The ground reduces the range of captive symbionts. A SHADE doesn't have the same range horizontally, because it's sunk in the ground."

"NeoJai is right." Gyan displayed a mushroom shape with the stalk in the ground. "Underground, particularly buildings inside campuses, might not be detected." It showed the grid search map again and greyed out buildings with subterranean sections close to the road. Twenty four buildings left.

"How did you know that?" Aaxyl jumped to her feet.

"I remembered the mushroom shape from the specifications of our relay."

Thank SYMBs for boyfriends who read instructions. "You've solved it."

"We're going to need a way to search inside these buildings," NeoJai said. "These are all governance provider and diplomatic buildings. No chance of getting permissions. Worse, Sambit will just move her again."

Aaxyl knew a way to find out. "Where there's a building, there's a drainage system."

AAXYL

Mohan and NeoJai dropped Aaxyl off at the Ravi sector residential sanitation access. Their target area was between here and the Octagon. As expected, it was deserted this late at night. She had to identify herself to the system with her dorm-comm, but there were no problems. She asked for the sewer to be opened and floated into it on the Zephyron, grateful to not touch the ladder to climb down.

She went past the black water junction and headed for the drainage tunnels. The ten foot wide access tunnels had plenty of space to float through without touching anything. The Zephyron left communication relays as it went.

"You should've let one of us come along," NeoJai imped. *"I don't like the idea of you being down there alone."*

"There was no point ruining more of the Zephyrons," Aaxyl replied. *"This one will never be the same again. If I don't find them here, we'll still need the remaining Zephyrons to search."*

In truth, the Zephyrons could probably be cleaned, but Aaxyl didn't want the others to see her in the sewers. She'd done the work with gratitude, because it met their needs, but she didn't want anyone's pity.

There was little water in at night. She exited the sanitation control area and the space narrowed abruptly to eight feet, the standard width for the main network of tunnels. Smaller drains covered with grates trickled wastewater on either side.

Gyan imped, *"You should consider studying SHADE maintenance. I'd be honoured to have the support of someone like you."*

"Thank you, Gyan." Aaxyl supposed a human backup might exist somewhere for emergencies. It did sound like her kind of thing. *"I'd like to meet a SHADE maintenance person some time to understand what it entails."*

"You've met Jugaad." Gyan issued very faint beeps.

"Er... someone less... ancient would be nice."

"There's Zayn at Sarovar, Tashi in the Superdome, and Rudra wants to train to be one."

She was now directly under the main road of the sector between official buildings and headed toward the Octagon.

Gyan stopped beeping. *"I caught a faint noise, but lost it without a connection."*

"What?" Aaxyl tried to scan. *"I'm not getting anything."*

"It wasn't a connection," Gyan said. *"There was inconclusive noise, but there shouldn't be any captive SYMB signals here, so it is promising."*

The others were back in the SYMBTech conference room, but quiet. The stakes were too high. Aaxyl ignored the video feed. It was too much of a distraction.

"Mark the spot. I can return to it if I don't find anything else." There were eight smaller pipes here, four on either side.

"I'm not able to locate you to mark your location," Gyan imped.

"Can you login to the Sewage SIS with my credentials?" Aaxyl imped. *"They have an identification system for the pipes."*

"Yes."

Crap.

As she'd guessed, the noise Gyan had caught was at the junction directly under the official area. Above them were countless high security towers: Octagon, diplomatic buildings, a commercial building with a shopping mall, governance provider buildings. Even if they located Hersh, how could they enter without drawing attention?

She explored in all the directions she could, but the faint noise was accessible only at that point—impossible to identify beyond a general area. She had to narrow it down.

Aaxyl tried to send a sigh through the mental implant. *"I may have overestimated my gratitude about the sewage system and underestimated the repulsive factor."*

"I suspected that may have been the case."

Abrahamha and Jugaad had teleported to the SYMBTech building.

Aaxyl's audience was growing.

This was going to suck. So far she had managed to remain clean.

"I'm going to crawl into the connecting pipes at that junction and take the game with me and see if I can resolve the signal."

"Are you sure that is possible?" Abrahamha asked.

Aaxyl thought so. *"They are two feet wide for a short distance before they split for each building. It won't be pleasant. The bigger problem is that it will be time-consuming."*

"When do workers show up?" Mohan asked. *"It's already past midnight."*

"Early. Sometimes even at night, but this system rarely needs work. It's just water." Aaxyl considered the grates. Each grate had four nuts embedded in a thick coat of slime. She'd better get to work.

Mohan imped, *"So we have time."*

"Actually, we don't," Aaxyl imped. *"The issue isn't workers, but around four, cleaning bots start work, around five, catering units kick off, then people in the buildings will start to bathe. I should have taken AthSYMB for a speed boost."*

"There is AthSYMB in your kit, Aaxyl," Gyan said.

"You guys put AthSYMB in first-aid?" Aaxyl took a dose. Did they expect their injured to carry loads or sprint? The AthSYMB rushed through her body with a familiar sense of capability. Aaxyl flexed her arms, then stretched. Opening the grates would be much easier now.

Aaxyl hopped off the Zephyron and stepped into the familiar muck. She reminded herself that her protection suit was from a SYMBTech facility and nothing would get in. No matter how many times she'd done this, there was this initial disgust. Then it would be fine.

Something caught her leg and she almost screamed. It was a snake. Not a real snake, but a flexible cleaning bot used to maintain smaller pipes. It pressed outward against the walls, inching forward and cleaning the pipe as it went. She doubted anyone in sanitation knew its actual name.

She reached for her Dorm comm. The sanitation access couldn't connect to it. "Activate snake." Nothing. It was dead. She slung it on a cable running along the wall.

There were eight pipes draining into the junction. Aaxyl took out the toolkit and got to work on the bolts of the grate across one. At least this went much faster with the AthSYMB. She changed tools to lever the grate out of the gunk.

"Bye-bye, Zephyron," she murmured as the first streaks of sewage stained the pristine seat.

Ten minutes later, Aaxyl stood with her hands on her hips, ready to enter the pipe.

"Wait," Aameh said. "This is too slow. We're sending in the cavalry. Just get all the grates across all the pipes removed."

Mohan broke in. "We're sending in a tech prodigy who can teleport if needed."

It took her half an hour to unscrew the other grates. By the time she was done, Elir's voice came through her implant. "This is nastier than it sounded."

"Boy, you really have pissed them off, haven't you?"

"You've got it wrong. I'm good with tech, and the smallest teleporter, if we need to go into the pipes. I can also hold a sync the longest if we need to teleport through a few walls when we find them. A little sewage wouldn't deter anyone from saving AricNova."

He had a point. She took a breather to watch as Elir came into sight. He looked distinctly nauseated. Behind him floated a box.

Aaxyl said, "Don't get off the Zephyron unless necessary. We don't need you throwing up. Waste is best kept anonymous."

Elir looked relieved. Aaxyl told him to get an anti-emetic from the first-aid kit. Just in case.

Aaxyl imped, "So, what's the plan?"

A teleporter wouldn't be very useful unless they found Hersh's exact location. Then Elir could try teleporting to it, if it was close by. From what Aaxyl understood, it couldn't be too far away if he was to teleport blind without a key, and he'd have to search while engaging his symbionts.

She was pretty sure holding a sync better meant going a few seconds or rooms more than others, and not searching entire floors of an unknown number of buildings.

"Elir came up with the idea of using drones to take the game in instead of you crawling through the pipes. They're smaller and faster," Aameh imped back.

Elir set up shop. He opened the box before him like a desk. It was the most incongruous sight Aaxyl had seen in the sewers. The box contained the other two games, already attached to drones.

She handed him the one from her Zephyron for the waiting drone.

The drones flew off into the pipes.

Aaxyl's mental implant showed video feeds from their cameras. She ignored the feeds, noting the distance travelled. Nothing was exciting about slimy pipes without a signal. *"How far do the drones have to go?"*

"A hundred meters should be plenty to register a signal change. I'm taking them as far as they can just to be safe." Gyan was flying the drones. Of course.

She tracked the map of the pipes with the locations of the drones. The routes for each drone were turning into tiny branched trees. Gyan was taking them into pipes smaller than the ones she would be able to enter. They would also reach deeper into the area and right up to each building, eliminating any ground deadening the signal between the implant and the drone. If they still didn't find Hersh, he wasn't there.

The first drone flew out of a pipe and entered another. It had taken half an hour. Another was on its way back. Thank SYMBs for flying machines. The drones were doing a much better job than Aaxyl could have done even if she'd crawled in the sewage for days on end. In another hour or so, they would know the truth of all eight pipes.

She jolted awake when her Zephyron jerked. She'd fallen asleep. It was a first, but then she never had such a comfortable bed in the sewers before. The game had connected. Unfortunately, without the Zephyron, it only offered basic controls, but Hersh started playing, so they knew it was him.

They had found Hersh!

Now to rescue them.

"I knew I was right," Aameh imped relief.

"You have our gratitude," Jugaad sounded reverent.

Aaxyl didn't know about that. They weren't exactly in an easy to access place.

"Wait till we have them out safe first," Aameh said. *"We still can't go into buildings and we can't have the two of you rampaging through without alerting Sambit who will teleport them away. How do we get them out?"*

"Can't you just issue him a new communicator?" Aaxyl asked.

"Not without him present. Otherwise the communicator won't proceed after detecting the implant," Elir said.

"Is this a joke?" Aaxyl burst out. "You guys make these things. Can't you override it for one communicator?"

"It wouldn't be secure if that were possible," Gyan imped. *"But I can design a new communicator by tasking Taknik if I'm authorised. Someone will have to get it from the Superdome."*

"Authorised," Abrahamha, Jugaad, Mohan and Noir said in quick order.

"How long will it take?" Aaxyl asked, as she watched Hersh navigate space to collect asteroids with precious metals. He had selected an easy level and won it in minutes. The game froze for a long time, then *DON'T TRUST SAMBIT* appeared as the winner's display name. They already knew this at great cost, but Hersh had recognised the attempt to connect and was sending information.

"The comm should be here in an hour," Noir said.

Then began a coding race between Mohan, Noir, Gyan, and Elir, to get into that game. Elir won it 27 minutes later, as the game was replaced by a simple text chat. *THAT YOU, SOFTIE?* Elir texted.

Aaxyl's eyes pricked unexpectedly as Elir used her nickname for Hersh. Mohan must have told them. Hersh was alive.

Y came the reply. It was slow going as he used the game controls like a pointer to spell out words. *Cosmic Chaos* wasn't designed for use without a comm. *WHERE*

SEWERS

!!!

WE KNOW ABOUT SAMBIT, Elir sent. *HE WORKED FOR DAMODAR.*

D HERE

Their comms exploded with chatter. What new mess was this?

DAMODAR IS WORKING WITH SAMBIT? Elir sent.

N D PRISONER

WHO ELSE IS WITH YOU? AN? DAMODAR? SAMBIT? NADANI? Elir sent.

Another interminable wait. *A D YES. S N NO*

HANG IN THERE, WE ARE FIGURING THIS OUT Elir sent.

They were hanging on to every letter as it appeared. *HURRY S OoO*

OoO? Elir explained it was a gaming term meaning *Out of Options*. It was used when a cornered player would try desperate acts.

D + AS Hersh sent. What did that mean?

DAMODAR + ARICNOVA + SAMBIT? Elir asked.

Then followed a long wait.

D WEAK. ATHSYMB ESCAPE

DAMODAR IS NOT STRONG ENOUGH FOR SOMETHING TO ESCAPE? Elir confirmed.

He must be talking about AricNova's chain. Aaxyl doubted any amount of strength could break a steel chain.

Y GTG

"You okay to wait there? We should have comms soon," Aameh checked with them. *"Or I suppose Elir could teleport you both back for now..."*

Aaxyl had an idea. "If I find what I'm looking for, maybe we can get both the AthSYMB and the new comm to them."

AAXYL

The new comm had reached SYMBTech. Aaxyl watched them get it ready through Gyan's feed. It was tiny, like a medical capsule. Gyan explained that if they found a way to get it to Hersh, he could swallow it if need be. Most functions had been stripped.

Aaxyl was scouting the tunnels for working snakes. They were too filthy to take back daily, so they'd be hanging somewhere.

"What's a snake?" Elir asked.

"It is a cleaning bot for pipes between four and ten inches wide." Aaxyl found one. "Not many functions, but I can steer it with my comm and it has a cavity for cleaning chemicals. It can go all the way to a bathroom if Hersh can get to one. It won't enter a toilet from here, so there has to be a bathroom drain or we'll have to go to the black water system, which is a lot nastier."

DO YOU HAVE ACCESS TO A BATHROOM. FLOOR DRAIN. NOT TOILET? Elir sent.

Y. LATER

Aaxyl watched Gyan's feed as they added ear pieces and display lenses for Damodar and AricNova and sealed the comm and a transfuser with a heavy dose of AthSYMB in several layers of plastic, carefully taping each to keep it hygienic.

Elir teleported into the conference room. He was clean. He had teleported out of the protective suit straight into SYMBTech. Nobody was good enough to teleport into a deflated suit, so he wore a new suit to return.

Aaxyl opened a snake to insert the package into. Elir looked away, swallowing dry, as Aaxyl attached the filthy thing to the hover that would drag it most of the way and then drop it where the game had connected with Hersh.

Gyan said it could navigate the snake using Aaxyl's authorisation. A communication relay would follow, just to be on the safe side.

From there, things sped up. Hersh connected with the comm before the hover dropped the snake. Gyan imped him a gigantic info dump.

Hersh had information too. Damodar had tried to break his restraints to give AricNova his symbionts claiming that they could give her energy to escape, but failed. If the AthSYMB helped him get free, they could free AricNova and try to get her to teleport everyone out or at least escape.

They had to escape soon, because Sambit was seeking shells that had been out of the dome.

Aaxyl took charge at this point. *"Hey, Softie. Do you have access to a bathroom?"*

"Ax? Sewers! I should have guessed." Joy zinged over the connection like a hug.

"We'll get you out, Softie." They could discuss the rest later.

Hersh imped, *"The toilet is at some distance. It will be impossible to get AricNova there."*

"This is different. I just want you to go there," she imped. She explained the snake. *"Pour water down the drain to help us find your bathroom."*

"That might be difficult," Hersh imped. *"I was in the bathroom scratching a message for help under the sink just before you found me. I took so long that the guards got suspicious. If I ask again again, they could refuse or come inside with me."*

"Tell Damodar to go," Abrahamha told him.

"He'll have to wait for them to check on us. Can take an hour or two."

It had already been more than an hour since they found Hersh.

They waited for Hersh to update that Damodar had gone to the bathroom. The snake waited till water flowed down a drain and Gyan sent it up. Soon, Damodar's disgusted face appeared in its grimy camera. The visual got jerky as he tried to open the snake's cavity. Then they lost contact with the snake altogether, but Hersh was still in range of the comm.

They waited to find out what had happened.

"Damodar is back, but the guards are still in the room," Hersh reported. *"We'll have to wait for them to go."*

After a while, Hersh explained that Damodar had not been able to open the dispenser, so he had broken the snake and took out the packet. He'd already taken the AthSYMB and tossed the snake and transfuser back down the drain. Hersh had the comm now and handed a ear piece and a pair of lenses to Damodar.

He started broadcasting visuals.

Through Hersh's implant, they could see Damodar. Through Damodar's lenses they saw Hersh and the bed with AricNova at some distance. They were in a large modern room apart from the chains.

SIS cameras were ripped out of the wall. Wherever they were, Sambit was concealing his presence and didn't control the building.

Both Hersh and Damodar were chained to the wall by their ankles and couldn't get close to the bed or each other.

It was very difficult to understand what was going on. Visuals through a mental implant or lens were not like a camera. Both of them kept looking around and blinking.

It was specially vertigo inducing for Aaxyl, watching through her mental implant, like seeing through the wrong set of eyes. Gyan interpreted the feeds into a choppy projection that updated whichever part Hersh or Damodar looked at, which in Damodar's case was currently his chain.

"We should have sent a camera too." NeoJai imped.

"But we did! Great idea, NeoJai." The feed showed Noir clapping NeoJai on his shoulder so hard he stumbled forward.*"Hersh, reuse the tape from the package to stick the second pair of lenses somewhere."* Noir instructed. It took a while and they weren't the best cameras either, but they had the room in sight now.

Damodar pulled experimentally at the chain, adjusting his stance.

"The link joining the manacle with the chain is weaker." Gyan added an overlay to Damodar's view. *"Pull with a strong jerk to stress that joint."*

Damodar adjusted his grip and sat, bracing one manacle against the floor with the other foot, while pulling hard. They may be weaker there, but they were awkward to grip and exert pressure at that point.

The metal cut into Damodar's already bruised ankle with the changed angle, but he didn't even seem to notice the blood beyond avoiding getting it on his grip. Aaxyl felt a grudging admiration. He was going to break free, whether the manacle or his ankle broke first.

Aameh cautioned, *"Elir, get Aaxyl out of there. We have comms. You don't need to be physically under AricNova when she escapes."*

"Take her to a bathroom!" Gyan imped.

Elir did one better. He dunked her into a pool of water and dragged her through it to stand at the shore gasping with shock at the cold. They were outside the dome, but Aaxyl didn't have time to wonder where. It was too dark to see much anyway.

"Quick, remove the suit," Elir told her, helping her before teleporting out of his own. He flickered their clean selves back to the SYMBTech building, where Gyan was playing the audio out loud for the ancients, who didn't have implants.

It felt like luxury to Aaxyl's mind, exhausted from tracking everything inside her head.

They watched Damodar struggle harder and impossibly harder. He looked unrecognisable with muscles bulging till they almost looked deformed. For a while it seemed like he'd fail, but he kept using more and more force till each manacle broke.

Panting heavily, he then freed Hersh much more easily and hobbled over to AricNova. He tried to break the chain trapping AricNova but it was thicker. He tried to pull it out of the wall, but it didn't even budge.

"Never mind the chain, Ari will deal with it. Revive her." Jugaad was so close to the projection, he was almost in it.

Damodar swiftly tore himself on a broken manacle and smeared his blood on AricNova's lips, but of course, she couldn't drink.

"Hurry, please," Mohan said. "It has almost been an hour since the guards left. They could return any time."

"Wake up!" Damodar briskly rubbed his blood on AricNova's bare arms, his movements choppy from his unfamiliarity with AthSYMB and use of tremendous strength. He slapped her face. "Escape! We have to escape."

"What is Hersh doing?" Aameh asked suddenly. "Can AricNova get energy from his symbionts?"

Hersh scratched himself on the broken manacle as well.

"Hersh, stop," Abrahamha said. "Damodar's symbionts are unique. Yours won't help her."

Hersh braced himself and cut deeper. "I'm not giving her my symbionts. I'm taking hers."

"Are you crazy?" Mohan burst out.

Damodar didn't stop smearing his blood on AricNova. "Don't make me waste time to stop you."

"I'm not crazy," Hersh imped through his pain. "This is our one chance at escaping. I'm doing everything I can to make sure we don't fail. If we succeed, Aameh can now negate the symbionts and I'll be fine. If we don't, it's a risk I'm willing to take. Sambit won't stay here for long. If he takes AricNova out of the dome, we'll lose her again."

Hersh walked over to AricNova's bed and detached a blood collection bag and slowly poured the blood into his wounds, making new cuts to speed up the absorption. If Admin Dhrit's experience was anything to go by, it would be hours before he'd feel any effects. Sambit would probably return before then.

"Do you have nutrients there?" Aaxyl asked urgently. No medical supplies were visible in the projection.

Hersh shrugged. "No."

Aaxyl had a bad feeling about this. In all her time with Hersh, she hadn't once seen him act recklessly.

Suddenly, AricNova moved.

Hersh detached her from the drips and tubes of the bed. "The bed will sedate her automatically if it detects she's waking up. I'm detaching her, but if they are monitoring the bed, they could come in to check. Please tell her to be fast."

Hersh helped smear as much of Damodar's blood as he could on any bare skin.

Suddenly AricNova opened her eyes and gripped Damodar's forearm. "Damo?" Her voice was a scratchy whisper, unused to speech.

Damodar barely looked recognisable, still bulging from his efforts, but she must have recognised the feeling of his symbionts.

"Yes." He stroked her hair stiffly. "Take all the symbionts you need and escape."

Why had he stopped giving her blood? Stroke later!

Then Aaxyl realised why he had stopped smearing his blood. AricNova's hands were looking a lot better than the rest of her body. She drew the symbionts out of him. Damodar sat on the bed, looking weaker.

"Thank you," AricNova said and took her hands off him.

He took her hand and held it, removing an ear bud and putting it in her ear. "Stay awake. Take enough to escape fast. Abrahamha and Jugaad want to talk to you. You have to escape."

"Later," AricNova said.

"No. Now." Damodar shook her hard.

Rage sparked in her eyes, then they dulled again.

"Guards can check any time. Take the symbionts you need, take Hersh and leave. NOW." He held her hand in both of his, when she would have pulled away.

They didn't dare to breathe wrong. AricNova wasn't alert. If she was recaptured after coming this close, Aaxyl herself would rampage.

All this time suspecting Damodar, they wouldn't have dreamed of what they were seeing.

"Come on!" Hersh urged.

"Tell Jugaad and Abrahamha to tell her to escape," Damodar instructed Hersh, not realising they could still hear him.

"Ari?" Jugaad's voice cracked.

"Jugaad?" AricNova frowned and pulled out the ear piece. She flickered and reached *inside* her head, to pull out a small metal object, then shook her head like a dog shaking off water. Whatever it was fell to the ground with a metallic clink.

Abrahamha covered his face with trembling fingers. "That's how they prevented her telepathy."

"Tashi!" Her eyes filled with tears. Abrahamha and Jugaad were crying and nodding. They were clearly communicating telepathically.

There wasn't a dry eye among the witnesses.

"This is an amazing moment, but is she going to kill him?" Aameh whispered, nodding toward the projected Damodar. He slumped.

"Not directly," Noir murmured back. "She's being careful. He's not injured. Once she draws enough symbionts, she'll stop. He's okay unless she rips them out too fast or injures him. Eventually, his symbionts will recover."

The door of the room they were imprisoned in opened suddenly and every single one of them jolted. A guard raised an alarm. Hersh rushed toward him, trying to push him out. Aaxyl's heart hammered in terror. This wouldn't end well for Hersh. Damodar shielded AricNova with his considerable bulk as best he could.

Gunfire erupted, then the sizzle of a neutraliser took out updates from Hersh's mental implant, but his comm continued to broadcast.

"No!" yelled Aaxyl, as Hersh sank to the floor twitching uncontrollably. "Hersh!" She reached for the projection as though she could pause or turn back reality. They had come so close. If Hersh didn't get help immediately... If Sambit moved AricNova again...

Aameh sobbed against Mohan's chest.

Aaxyl wanted to scream, and going by the raw scrape of symbionts flaying her, she wasn't alone. NeoJai's arm came around her. One of them was trembling. Maybe both. She fought the urge to bury her face against him and hide from this horrible reality like Aameh.

"Go. Go now!" Damodar thundered futilely at AricNova.

Why wasn't anybody shooting? The guard at the doorway had fallen to the floor at the same time as Hersh. AricNova scowled over Damodar's shoulder and more guards who came fell to the floor too.

Aaxyl wanted Jugaad to ask AricNova to save Hersh if she could, but before she could speak, AricNova extended a hand and Hersh vanished from the floor and floated in the air before her. She caught him to her in the split second before he fell, grabbed Damodar's hand and jerked. She held Hersh away and looked at herself, awash with rage.

By the time Aaxyl figured out that the chain had stopped AricNova from teleporting, she'd pulled Damodar into a one-armed hug, and... absorbed him. He slumped over her arm.

In the projection, AricNova stared at the two men motionless on each arm in frustration. She piled them both on the bed. Damodar stirred before falling unconscious again and a collective sigh of relief filled the room. Hersh was still twitching.

One swipe of AricNova's hand disintegrated the chain where it entered her stomach. She flowed to her feet. Maybe she teleported. Another swipe yanked the chain out of her back. No blood, no wound.

Aaxyl hadn't seen that coming.

AricNova was back. Leaner and haunted, but back. If she could escape, these sacrifices wouldn't be in vain.

She made a dismissive gesture. A surge of some sort cracked toward the door and out of view as she grabbed Damodar's dead-weight with one hand, a twitching Hersh with the other and they vanished.

Companies jittery as Dome 91-110 prepares to vote out founders in favour of inexperienced governance provider. World News, Wednesday, December 17, 2442

~~*~*~*

AAXYL: SYMBTECH BUILDING

Abrahamha, Jugaad and Noir had vanished too.

Where are you guys? Aaxyl pathed Noir. *Why did Hersh's implant stop broadcasting?*

Oasis. SYMBTech's first research facility in the wastelands. We'll come back once Ari is calm. There is nothing here now. Nothing in range for Hersh's comm.

How long will that take?

I don't know.

Where is Hersh? He needs help.

Just took him to AVANT. Damodar is there too. The modified comm won't work in Minal, but Mohan will take you there to negate AricNova's symbionts.

The short telepathic conversation already made Aaxyl's head feel heavy. She rubbed her temples as she went over to Mohan. They teleported into AVANT, straight to a cluster of people around a bed. The medics made way for Aaxyl.

"Don't take too long," SanJeevan said. "Do your thing and get out. There will be time to visit later. We need access right now."

Aaxyl nodded numbly, eyes locked on Hersh's beloved slack face. She'd never seen him with a beard and the Hersh she knew would have scoffed at long hair. She stroked it gently. "Softie."

A medic next to her handed her a scalpel and anaesthetic spray, and cut Hersh's palm with another scalpel as soon as she took it. Aaxyl cut her own palm and took his hand. Hersh didn't have symbiont powers beyond the basic healing everyone had. His symbionts looked like sparse stars against a night sky, except for where he'd introduced AricNova's symbionts. His cuts had healed, but the area around them buzzed with activity. Aaxyl quieted them with barely a thought.

She released his hand and stepped back, surprised by the tears on her face. Mohan pulled her back further and into a hug as the medics proceeded with cutting away his clothes.

"You know they'll take good care of him here. He's a hero," Mohan whispered against her hair. "Let's go home."

Aaxyl nodded.

"Nyaya is here. We have to leave for the *Khabariya* printing press," Aameh told Aaxyl after they returned and Aaxyl gave her the update about Hersh. There wasn't anything she could do here anyway.

Strange how life went on, even after dramatic events.

"Go. We've got this," Mohan told Aameh. "I'll let you know as soon as we have news on Hersh."

The rest of them clustered around the conference room, processing what had happened, not quite ready to disband till they'd seen AricNova for themselves.

"We have a problem," Gyan said.

News reports showed a diplomatic building near the Octagon being evacuated. Most offices were closed at night, and few people remained. The surge that AricNova had sent at her captors must have damaged more than the mercenaries. Initial reports said that the building was being evacuated for safety. The news soon evolved to say that the building would remain closed till repairs could be instituted. In another hour, it became clear that the building would have to be demolished, its foundation damaged beyond repair. Speculation gravitated toward a terrorist attack. The dome had never had one.

"Incoming message from Menhir," Gyan announced before playing it.

"We need help," Menhir said. "UDAY is encouraging hype that this is a terrorist attack and will find a way to blame Nagrik Manch, and retaliate. We need to get our newly recruited SecPros to the settlements urgently. When shit hits the fan here, the settlements will be sitting ducks."

Abrahamha, AricNova, Jugaad and Noir returned. Damodar was in AVANT. Smriti was unconscious, but alive and not in danger. Damodar and Hersh were awake and recovering. AricNova, who'd suffered the most, was back on her feet.

"Do it, now," Abrahamha told Aaxyl, manifesting a scalpel. AricNova stood calmly. They had explained it to her.

Anaesthetic spray appeared in her hand instantly, and Aaxyl nodded thanks at Mohan. She cut her hand and reached for AricNova. AricNova vanished. Aaxyl dropped her hand and looked around, her puzzled gaze settling on an equally confused Abrahamha.

AricNova reappeared before Aaxyl with Damodar in tow. He looked bewildered. There was a lot of that going around.

"Don't let her negate me," AricNova instructed Damodar.

Aaxyl didn't know if she was offended by the suspicion or confused by Damodar of all people being tasked with protecting AricNova.

Abrahamha and Jugaad flanked her. "We'll be linked and keep an eye out," Jugaad assured her. She relaxed.

Aaxyl made sure the knife had her blood on it and cut AricNova's palm carefully and connected. She was confronted with a wildfire. There were so many symbionts, Aaxyl doubted even AricNova knew everything she could do.

I know that I can end you if you try to capture me again, AricNova assured her telepathically.

Ari, she saved you, Jugaad joined in. Aaxyl's head was turning into a parking lot for ancients the unsettling sharp scrapes into the fabric of her existence had become just another fact of life.

Aaxyl focused on finding an underlying pattern to the symbionts. It was an intricate lattice, instead of the broad flows that she had seen so far. A fine lace of abilities interwove into astonishing whole. Even prominent powerful abilities like the telepathy and teleportation that AricNova had already demonstrated were more like a thousand different ways to communicate or move.

The sharper the pattern became, the more visibly AricNova relaxed. And then they were done.

"We need teleporters, now," Mohan told Noir. "We need Menhir and Vidroh to assign SecPros to the settlements and get them there."

"We can help too," Abrahamha, AricNova and Jugaad spoke together like one mind in three bodies.

"You aren't going anywhere," Abrahamha told AricNova.

AricNova kept a casual arm around Damodar. "Am I a captive?" Aaxyl realised why AricNova had brought Damodar back. She was still slowly draining him.

"You need to recover," Abrahamha said. "You're using Damodar like a battery."

"I don't mind," Damodar said. "I owe her."

Abrahamha turned back to AricNova. "Do you know the date? The year?"

"I know it has been a couple of decades," AricNova replied.

"The year is 2442," Abrahamha said. "This dome was under construction when you were captured in 2217. You don't have keys here."

"I'll take Ari back to Oasis for a while. Damodar can come with us," Jugaad offered. "Abrahamha can help here where you need him."

Aaxyl looked at Noir.

He's GTS, Noir reminded. *He's keeping Ari out of our hair till this settles.*

Noir turned to Damodar. "Before you leave, could you release an endorsement of Nagrik Manch?"

"Nagrik Manch? Why would it need my endorsement?"

"Its a new governance provider formed to take over from UDAY. Your endorsement as a popular ex-President will go a long way to smoothing things over for Milup."

"Your boyfriend Milup?" Damodar scoffed. "Not a chance. Ari is rescued now. You should cease all meddling into dome politics."

"Ex-boyfriend," Noir gritted out. "And Sambit is still at large."

"Sambit is a teleporter," Damodar said. "UDAY isn't sheltering him. He's using them. You should help them catch him instead of undermining them. This is a mistake."

"You would say that. Wouldn't you?" Noir said. "You're as good as a founding member for them."

"I resigned from UDAY when I realised Sambit was misusing my power," Damodar pointed out. "UDAY isn't to blame. The fault lies with Nadani and Sambit."

"UDAY brought a teleporter here."

"What choice did you leave them, if they were under threat from a family of teleporters? They constructed this dome. They've always run it transparently and well to the point it is studied for its efficiency. One criminal isn't evidence of a corrupt government."

"One criminal?" Mohan interjected. "*UDAY*'s teleporter tried to key in here! Not Sambit."

"All of UDAY's teleporters are provided by Nadani," Damodar said. "They answer to him. He would have found out about AricNova by now and be looking for Sambit. UDAY is a business, not mafia. Nadani runs the mafia from Ridnam."

"But they run amok in UDAY," Noir said.

"You think gifting centuries of UDAY's achievements to someone who didn't earn it will bring accountability?" Damodar said. "It isn't your place to decide who runs the dome."

Damodar left with Jugaad and AricNova.

Last stand

Five day cultural tour in the Wastelands for only 200 unimon per seat. Discover ancient tribes, explore abandoned cities. Authentic cuisine cooked with wood combustion. Dome Ads, Wednesday, December 17, 2442

~~*~*~*

AAXYL: SYMBTech Building, Dome 91-110

"Alert!" Gyan relayed an initial message from Assistant Commander Menhir. "SecPros mobilising to arrest SYMBTech and other targets. Meeting will conclude in ten minutes. First units will deploy ten minutes after that."

They hadn't slept all night. Pissed didn't even come close to describing Aaxyl's mood. As a dormer joining a family of global citizens, UDAY embarrassed her. What did they want? To capture the second most important dome in the world by force?

Aaxyl tumbled out of bed, feet searching for her FastSprints. "Why are they doing this? Once UDAY's grace period ends and the election provider deuthorises them in a few hours, they won't be able to pay SecPros any more. I don't get it."

NeoJai scrambled out of bed. "Maybe they just want to create trouble for the new government. Make them easier to topple. Old world elections often combined voting with shows of force."

"But shows of force could achieve victories in the old world." Aaxyl grumbled along in NeoJai's wake to the conference room. Mohan and Noir were arguing in low tones over a list on the main screen.

Abrahamha came over to Aaxyl. "Can you check my symbionts? Just to be safe."

Aaxyl asked Gyan to send the first-aid kit. *"Why are Mohan and Noir arguing?"*

"SecPro units have been assigned a list of hundreds of prominent personalities to arrest. Lethal force authorised. Mohan wants to help defend the dome. Noir doesn't want conspicuous involvement in local politics," Gyan imped.

"Hundreds?" Aaxyl exclaimed aloud, nodding at the screen when Abrahamha looked at her, puzzled.

"So let them arrest," NeoJai said. "It is a matter of a day. Then they'll be out anyway."

"Not if they take them out of the dome to the prison," Aaxyl said. "Bit of a grey area if a few employees there go rogue and act against orders. Dormers targeted by SecPros are always advised to find ways to stay in the Dome."

Mohan nodded a *what-she-said* in Aaxyl's direction and stared in challenge at Noir.

"We can ask Menhir to prioritise taking over prisons as soon as Nagrik Manch is authorised," Noir said. "These aren't dormers, but elite residents. UDAY won't risk anything while they are accountable for it."

"Can't you guys just teleport them to safety?" Aaxyl asked.

Noir gave a bark of a laugh. "Teleport hundreds from different places? We don't have keys to wherever all these people are. Teleporting in line of sight means more teleports per rescue."

"There are people we know on this list!" Mohan said. "Friends. Lethal force authorised! How do I explain that the three of us stood here and did nothing? How do we face their families if they simply take them out of the dome and shoot them?"

"I know some of these names," NeoJai said. "I'll ask Dad to invite them to our place."

Abrahamha's voice boomed without any unpleasant effects as Aaxyl finished smoothing out his symbionts. "We save as many as possible. Do we have somewhere to put them?"

"They can't come here," Gyan said. "It will then become indisputable meddling with local politics."

Mohan stood up. "They can come to my home. It is diplomatic property, but I'm an individual. Rudra has better control now. She can go to Scharada's for the day."

"Some can come to our home," NeoJai said. "I'm sure my family won't mind. We have the space."

Gyan assigned lists to Abrahamha, Noir and Mohan based on locations they had keys to in the dome. Mohan left to drop Rudra at Scharada's.

"Let's get moving then," Abrahamha said. "Teleporting hundreds of people individually will take time. We have less than ten minutes before UDAY's SecPros get started." Abrahamha vanished.

"Take me home. I can help there." NeoJai stood as Mohan returned. Mohan gestured toward him and he vanished.

Noir turned to Aaxyl. "We'll simply bring people in. Coordinate explanations with Shantiniketan and Gyan, since with unauthorised people around, they may need to limit their capabilities. Record a message for people being rescued."

Noir and Mohan vanished.

Aaxyl dutifully recorded a message explaining briefly that they had information that SecPros would be arriving to arrest them illegally and they had been temporarily moved to safety and would be home by the end of the day if UDAY was removed from authority. The message would be played at both Mohan and NeoJai's residence.

Gyan had already started marking off people as they were found.

There were over four hundred on the list. Some could be ignored. The Dhrits were home. Gyan wouldn't let anyone touch them. Milup would be surrounded by people. Noir and Mohan were teleporters. Progress was painfully slow. Elir started teleporting people too, along with teleporters Aaxyl hadn't met, Zayn and LuvIsaac.

Her tentative question about whether they should ask Jugaad for help was met with blunt refusal.

They still didn't trust his stability. If he came, AricNova would come too. He hardly had any keys in the dome and was most useful keeping her away.

UDAY had chanced on a major weakness in their strategy. With a large enough number of dispersed targets, it wasn't hard to overwhelm and exhaust teleporters.

Whereas, UDAY had thousands of SecPros they could assign to making arrests and nothing to lose. Security Provider companies were under contract to enact the will of the government and refusing would have legal consequences. Even if individual SecPros ignored their contracts and refused to comply with such absurd orders, there was no way to tell which targets were safe.

A second, bigger list was issued to the SecPros taking the number of targets well over a thousand. Their teleporters hadn't even got halfway through the first list. With Mohan's permission, Aaxyl asked Scharada if some people could be accommodated at her place.

There were leaders of companies that provided life essential services in the dome—food supply, air filtration, water supply, power and fuel on the list. Several people from Dorms were listed—she recognised some from the Nagrik Manch gatherings. They might have joined the new governance provider. There were also half a dozen entertainers known to have made fun of the state, two sports personalities, three lawyers, including Legal, and what looked like all the non-UDAY politicians in the dome. But there really was no common factor for all of them. Supporters of UDAY met the same fate as critics.

Anybody with non-UDAY SecPros providing reliable security were encouraged to remain where they were. The rest were evacuated to the three locations.

Rudra remained with Scharada and was told not to leave the basement at any cost. Mohan's home and basement were bigger and without Rudra home, many more people could be accommodated there. But it was increasingly becoming clear that they would run out of time and teleporter endurance before space.

"Ax?" Scharada called. "Is anyone available to help me here?"

"Just me. What happened?"

"Mohan brought in residents, but he doesn't have time for explanations. They don't know me. I'm alone and unless I have help managing incoming people, I'm going to have a riot here."

Aaxyl took Mohan's zeplyn to Scharada's place.

Soon, live news convinced outraged evacuees of the truth. Civilians hadn't owned weapons for centuries. A clip shown repeatedly featured a stunt enactor thrown kicking and screaming into a waiting zeplyn. The sight of armed SecPros assaulting the unarmed silenced everyone. Over a hundred people had already been arrested, many of them injured. There had been three deaths.

Nagrik Manch supporters started forming groups that could help anyone under threat and answered helplines. They provided practical suggestions to evade SecPros and guided them to safe houses or locations where the teleporters could pick them up.

UDAY was in do-or-die mode.

Their employees had no explanation when contacted, appearing bewildered themselves. The leaders were nowhere to be found.

Residents started banding together to protect targets from SecPros.

Organised groups looted shopping areas.

An angry mob broke into Darahs' residence, overwhelming the SecPros posted there and vandalising it. He was attacked as he bought time for his husband to escape in a zeplyn. He had been taken to an undisclosed hospital.

With two hours left before UDAY's reign ended, Nagrik Manch symbols started appearing among crowds. Leaflets were distributed reminding residents to register their votes. SecPros trying to shut down use of printing facilities met resistance. The leaflets kept coming.

Predictions of Nagrik Manch's victory were soon eclipsed by attacks in the offices of the food provider, Annapurna, and the water supplies company, Jal. Four employees died. The killers weren't SecPros, but mercenaries. Visuals of empty offices with blood smears on the floor and belongings scattered took over the news, sending fear spiralling throughout the dome.

Hysterical employees described mercenaries appearing on the premises and opening fire on staff. They interrogated senior managers before executing them.

UDAY employees denied the mercenaries were acting on the

organisation's orders and claimed that UDAY leaders were being attacked too.

Nobody believed them.

MOHAN

Mohan stood on the blood-soaked carpet in the offices of Annapurna, the Dorm's food supplier. The teleporter was already gone. He followed the sounds of gunfire to the mercenaries and ruthlessly yanked at their minds, rendering them unconscious and leaving them there for someone else to handle.

UDAY is also being attacked, Noir pathed. *The mercenaries are from Ridnam and searching for Sambit. Darahs was shot by his own bodyguard, the teleporter. Abrahamha is helping them.*

Mohan was too exhausted for telepathy. He imped back profanity. *"Nadani must have found out about AricNova. At least ask UDAY to stop the arrests and we'll be able to help them better."*

Noir switched to implant as well. *"They aren't in control anymore. They don't know who ordered the arrests."*

Mohan was exhausted beyond endurance. Elir had already tapped out. Zayn and LuvIsaac didn't have many keys here to begin with and would soon be worn out by the extra teleports they were forced to make.

"Are you alright?" Aaxyl imped.

Mohan barely had the strength to answer. *"Define alright. No matter what we do, these fuckers are ahead of us. You can't capture a teleporter after attacks. They teleport away before the mercenaries start shooting and anyone raises the alarm."*

"I think I've figured it out," Aaxyl imped. *"Darah's bodyguard had tried to key in at SYMBTech. There had been similar inexplicable visits by SecPros to other companies providing essential services."*

"Yes." Mohan could sense the answer just beyond the horizon of his fuzzy brain. *"We never figured out what they were up to."*

"I think teleporters keyed to them all," Aaxyl imped. *"That's how they are*

accessing the offices in spite of security. We weren't specially targeted."

Everything clicked into place in Mohan's mind.

"Send me that list," he imped urgently, and immediately pathed Abrahamha and Noir, wishing Abrahamha had an implant for easier communication. *If we key in to all the locations on the list first, we can return instantly if there's an attack.*

We can take it from here, Noir pathed. *There's no point in you keying in if you'll be too exhausted to return as soon as alerted. Their teleporters will be tiring too, by now. If we don't have to worry about you being too exhausted to react, we can teach the targets some anti-teleporter precautions. Get some rest.*

Mohan knew Noir was right. He was fried. He teleported to Scharada's home to help.

Now that they'd figured it out, two teleporters were stopped in short order. One teleporter was captured at the Prakriti Dorms air-purification unit, when an alert dormer, up by the purification filters above him, knocked him out by dropping a metal cylinder on him. Another was killed at Darahs's office by furious SecPros. A teleporter brought mercenaries into Sambit's old office in the Octagon, but the Octagon security fought them off. That teleporter, Darahs's bodyguard, later brought in a group of mercenaries at the air-purification unit by Pawan Industries at Cranti Dorms.

Noir was alerted immediately, and teleported there. He rendered them all unconscious before they could attack.

Several hundred people were injured. Almost two dozen were dead.

Mohan took Aaxyl to SecPro headquarters where the unconscious teleporters were being held.

AAXYL

Aaxyl nullified the symbionts of the captured teleporters. They presented more like tightly coiled ropes and tidy cylinders, but deactivating symbionts turned out to be harder than expected. Suppressing symbionts was different from organising.

She started calling it voiding. If nulls were deactivated humans with active symbionts, it only seemed appropriate that the opposite be called voided.

The last one she voided with a mere touch, distracted by the evidence that AxAm's symbionts were indeed more like the sprawling constructs of the ancients than these. They belonged with the Strays.

As more and more people were guided to locations by helplines, it had become easy to trace where they were fleeing to. SecPros started identifying the safe-houses.

SecPro reinforcements reached Mohan's house *en masse*, only to come up against Shantiniketan's perimeter security. It sedated two SecPros who pressed forward, and warned about trespassing on diplomatic property. Those entering range would face guns and neutralisers and it would only escalate from there.

Further defences were not tested.

All the SecPros knew this was an illegal last stand and winning it would not give them anything beyond jobs from the next security provider to come. Unarmed citizens they would round up, but they wouldn't risk their lives. Bound by their contracts, they camped outside the perimeter for the remaining hours of UDAY's tenure. It was a siege.

Shantiniketan sent refreshments.

There was a similar response from Gyan at the Saisrisel residence.

SecPros reached Scharada's house. Aaxyl exchanged a worried look with Mohan. Choosing this location had been a strategic blunder. Scharada's home had excellent security against ordinary crime, but no weapons against armed invasion. SecPros broke down the gate. There was nothing to prevent them from coming right up to the door other than the locals heckling them. SecPros started pushing them behind a perimeter.

They should have gone to SYMBTech.

Panic spread inside Scharada's home. There were almost a hundred people, and Mohan was exhausted. Noir and Abrahamha were defending other locations under attack, yanking dozens of mercenaries unconscious at a time. People would die here.

Mohan teleported half a dozen people closest to him. He staggered as he returned.

For the first time since Aaxyl knew him, fatigue bleached his face into a haggard mask. Aaxyl, about to hand him a glass of water, reacted on the fly as he almost planted his face into a person sitting on the floor. She grabbed him and sat him on the stairs, waiting for him to recover. He fainted.

News showed SecPros surrounding the house.

Inside, people surged toward Mohan, wanting to be teleported out.

Scharada and Aaxyl flanked him, creating some space. They weren't strong enough to push the crowd back, but several men helped them push the others back.

Aaxyl hefted Mohan onto her shoulder and retreated to the basement door barely managing to stay upright.

Scharada asked the crowd to stay back, the volunteers forming a protective cordon around her. Arguments erupted as they explained Mohan couldn't teleport any more. The basement was off limits. He needed rest.

SecPros banged om Scharada's door adding to the chaos, "You're harbouring persons of interest. Open the door or we'll break it. A copy of the warrant has been provided to you."

"Buy time," Aaxyl mouthed to Scharada.

"I'm verifying your warrant," Scharada called out.

There was nothing more to do but hide. They'd done their best.

It hadn't been enough.

She could only hope this bought them sufficient time for Mohan to recover enough for one last teleport to keep Rudra from being found.

She opened the basement door and staggered in.

The door slammed shut, muting the arguments beyond.

Mohan's weight vanished from Aaxyl's shoulder, sending her off-balance, but terror blasted through her as her body rammed hard against the wall.

Aaxyl had been hit more daintily in dorm fights she'd lost.

She'd have fallen if not for the force pinning her to the wall. Every inch of her was in agony.

Alienling glared up at her from the bottom of the steps, as she clutched Mohan protectively, no words and all rage. Rudra made Noir's anger feel like a pout.

Aaxyl's shoulder wrenched, twisting unnaturally, as she flattened against the wall. Her knees threatened to crack as they were forced back in ways they couldn't bend. She couldn't even scream.

Ah fuck.

Alienling blamed Aaxyl for Mohan's condition.

They were doomed.

Aaxyl was now going to black out and end this horrible day.

A fatigued voice said a single word.

The force crushing Aaxyl to the wall ceased suddenly. She crashed to the floor.

Too dazed to move, she watched out for Rudra.

Alienling had eyes only for Mohan. His hand on Rudra's shoulder flopped back too soon.

The respite had been too brief to react. Aaxyl tried to brace herself, but she had nothing left. She shut her eyes, resigned to her fate.

Suddenly, the sense of menace lifted.

No, it hadn't lifted. Changed?

Aaxyl opened her eyes and Alienling loomed. She shut them again.

"I'm sorry, Ax." Rudra was close to tears. "I'm really, really sorry. Please. Tell me what to do."

The main door opened with a crash.

There was nothing more to do. It was over.

Unless...

"Scare the SecPros off. Don't let them in till Mohan can get you out."

"I can do that."

Rudra's terror vibes reached an overwhelming hum, then squeezed past. Her eyes focused beyond the door.

Aaxyl realised she was inside the terror vibe. Still unnerving as hell, but not as bad as being its target. Besides, Aaxyl was already on the floor. She could hardly fall further.

She asked her comm to imp updates from any news feeds from outside Scharada's house.

Human reporters had fled, but media bots showed no arrests. The SecPros were retreating. Many stumbling, much as Aaxyl had, the first time she'd met Rudra. None of the rescued people left. Aaxyl didn't know if that was good or bad.

Soon, the compound was empty. But still, they backed away in terror till they were a good distance away, or fell.

There they remained till the fall of UDAY was complete, half an hour later.

Aaxyl had never been so thrilled to be terrorised by Rudra.

Unknown governance provider Nagrik Manch wins public approval in Dome 91-110. NelumboN loses control of the Dome it built. World News, Wednesday, December 17, 2442

~~*~*~*

NEOJAI: SYMBTECH BUILDING

NeoJai was in heaven. He straddled a drowsy Aaxyl and massaged her back as he watched the news. He'd had an easy day, with the service bots at the Saisrisel residence caring for their guests, and Gyan managing security. He'd followed updates from Scharada's home with growing alarm.

Noir had long given up on answering his anxious queries, but had teleported a limp Aaxyl to the Saisrisel residence when the crisis was over.

For one illogical moment, NeoJai's world had stuttered to a halt. Then she'd moved. He felt silly. She was alive, and awake. Just tired. He could fix that. When his arms finally closed around her to take her from Noir and carry her to their room, NeoJai could have wept with relief. If he'd held her too tightly, she hadn't complained.

He'd bathed her, dried her, and put her into his bed. When she was too restless to sleep, he'd massaged her, praying that she didn't notice his arousal.

Aaxyl was almost asleep.

NeoJai was a mess.

Her body and trust tempted him. Relief made him want to be in her as deep as he could, to reassure himself this was real. Yet, he felt so protective, he'd set aside his non-violent nature and punch anyone who disturbed her rest, including himself. He was a cauldron of emotion in fifty directions and this wasn't the time to pour them out on an exhausted Aaxyl.

He let the news distract him.

Other than the occasional mention of casualties, the screen on the wall displayed coverage of the celebrations in the dome for the new Nagrik Manch government. Fireworks lit up the sky above the dome. Milup stood up to thunderous applause. He described a dome that would run for the well-being of everyone.

A stoic Vidroh stood by his side, as Milup described the settlements. Nagrik Manch had been created to establish governments that would transition into the hands of the people through representatives. Nagrik Manch signalled profound changes.

To hear him speak, they had so far been living in an Enduring War detention camp and not in one of the best places in the world.

While NeoJai lacked Aaxyl's life experience or his father's political insight, he knew propaganda when he heard it.

Vidroh had the front row seat, but was silent. By now, NeoJai knew Vidroh well enough to see the man was bored. If Milup's claims were already happening, Vidroh would be giving speeches in his honour.

Nagrik Manch was here to stay, but celebrations apart, the dome was in chaos. Almost thirty people had died. Hundreds were in hospitals. Businesses were historically wary about what his father called the Robin Hood approach and Milup would have to address that.

NeoJai wasn't sure Milup realised how much work UDAY had put into a well-functioning economic ecology, incentivising philanthropy and volunteerism to allow taxes paid by the forty percent to fund welfare for sixty percent. If he spooked business leaders, he was going to find it very hard to fund his big mouth. There would be no winners.

Milup even had a plan for transitioning to a democratic government in the dome, and ending the practice of corporate governance contracts.

NeoJai would be very interested in knowing what the founding families thought of that land grab, though if he had to be fair, they'd given up control over the land long ago, when they decided to build a dome on it.

"How much of all this does he really mean?" Aaxyl was awake.

"I think he means it," NeoJai snickered. "He just won't hold himself to it."

"Wasn't that how the countries imploded?" Aaxyl asked. "Frequent elections as a bloodsport dividing the populace? Even with his five year theory, that would be twenty governments a century, whether they needed replacing or not. They could all make promises and be replaced when it was time to deliver."

"Do you have a moment?" Mohan imped them both.

NeoJai really hoped there was no new crisis, because the only distance he was willing to be from Aaxyl was the bathroom.

Aaxyl imped back, "Sure. Where are you?"

"I'm outside the dome. Am really wanted to see the Super Moon, but has been working with Nyaya all through, so I thought I'd get her a few nice scenes. Care to tell me which one she'd like best?"

Aaxyl put them on the wall screen, propped her chin on one hand, and reached the other back to stroke over NeoJai's thigh idly as they considered the imagery. "After the day we've had, Mohan made time to go out of the dome to do something special for Aameh. I'm impressed."

NeoJai's brain shorted at her touch on his thigh, and headed off in entirely another direction while he dutifully looked at the scenes before him. The moon didn't look any different than usual. His kneading hands slowed into sensual strokes over the contours of that strong back. And then, there it was, the perfect image. "This one."

The dome glowed like a pearl in the wastelands. The Super Moon looked huge and suspended alarmingly close to the Earth in this one. Both the dome and the moon were reflected in the river that flowed diagonally across the bottom of the scene like pearls in a cosmic necklace linking Earth and sky.

Aaxyl agreed, and sent it to Mohan. "This one. The moon is really huge!"

"I went further away to make it appear bigger in comparison with the Dome. Am's hoping for a big Super Moon, so that's what she'll get." Mohan disconnected.

NeoJai turned off the news. He had better questions for Aaxyl, if she was awake. "This thigh massage you're giving me... are you returning the favour by any chance?"

"Maybe." Aaxyl wiggled, stealing his breath, as she turned around under him, to pull him close.

"Do I get to choose the massage location?" NeoJai breathed against her lips. He really should let her rest, but his body had a mind of its own, and his brain was on vacation.

"I know the massage you want." Aaxyl snickered, caught between sleep and a sparking interest.

He shouldn't, but he was totally going to fan that spark.

"I'm truly sorry to disturb you," Gyan said aloud.

NeoJai yelped and rolled off her, pulling a pillow into his lap. Aaxyl gave the ceiling a strangled laugh. Well, it was a bit funny.

"This had better be good," NeoJai growled.

Celebrations and mourning in Dome 91-110 as new government provider takes charge in the wake of brutal massacres. World News, Wednesday, December 17, 2442

~~*~*~*

AAMEH: Nyaya's zeplyn

It had taken twenty-six hours, but they were finally done. The latest edition of *Khabariya* was ready. Aameh had her first credits as SoulScaper ready to print and she couldn't be more proud.

In two days, *Khabariya*, an anonymous publication, would break the news of AricNova's survival and rescue, and the story of how it was linked to the change in government. It would be a historic issue and a collector's item for centuries to come, and against all odds, they had made sure the art and the content would do them proud.

This forgotten facility between the Ravi Dorm and the dome boundary was where the magic happened for two days every fortnight. Aameh would be right back here in two weeks.

Creating art for Khabariya was so completely in the spirit of what she did as SoulScaper, Aameh could no longer imagine another job for her artistic side. She was exactly where she wanted to be.

Nyaya had turned out to be a surprise. From the mother of her colleague who cooked food fit for gods, she had become an employer Aameh respected and a role model in the way Leela had been in the Dorms.

Aameh wanted to be Nyaya when she grew up.

Despite everything that had happened, and injuries to both Admin Dhrit and herself, Nyaya had still managed to get this edition of Khabariya out on time.

Nyaya signalled the zeplyn to come to the entrance and they headed back to SYMBTech to drop Aameh off.

"SecPros attacked public figures in the dome, and we couldn't be bothered to either protect ourselves or cover the story, because we were getting an even bigger story out." Nyaya laughed. "What a high!"

"Our story will dwarf theirs anyway," Aameh agreed.

Aameh watched the residential area pass by when the scene changed abruptly, and the zeplyn hovered in a residential parking lot. She looked around in surprise.

Sambit had Nyaya struggling in a choke hold. "Halt," he said, as the zeplyn recalculated and started to move gain. The zeplyn stopped. He asked Nyaya to tell Admin Dhrit to come to the zeplyn with ten thousand unimon.

"*SOS,*" Aameh imped Aaxyl an image of Sambit and Nyaya.

"I've already alerted Gyan," Wynd, her comm, imped. "It's alerting Aaxyl. I'll add this message."

Nyaya's miserable eyes met hers. It was Admin Dhrit's zeplyn. Sambit must have traveled in it countless times. It even obeyed him. No matter what they did, he remained a few steps ahead of them.

She listened as Nyaya repeated his demand to Dhrit, wasting more time with hysterical proclamations of love if she didn't make it. Anyone who met Nyaya knew she didn't do hysterics. This was a delaying tactic. Nyaya was thinking on her feet too. Good. But Sambit knew her too. He was always ahead of them.

Sambit snatched off her comm and crushed it before tossing it to the floor. He put his hand out for Aameh's comm. Aameh handed it over. He crushed it and tossed it to the floor as well.

The zeplyn dissolved into an apartment.

Aameh fell to the floor. She looked around. There a few towers and an uninterrupted view of the dome structure outside the window. They were on a higher floor in a residential tower somewhere. Nyaya was struggling against Sambit. Aameh rushed to help her. She was no good at fighting, but if she distracted Sambit, maybe Nyaya could break free.

No such thing happened.

As soon as Aameh came close, Sambit backhanded her hard enough to send her to the floor again. She raised trembling fingers to her mouth, stunned. She'd never been hit like this. Her face was numb, but her lower lip was already swelling. Her eyes watered involuntarily.

At least with her healing working now, she hadn't fallen unconscious like last time.

Sambit had hit her so hard, her teeth had cut her lower lip. It was bleeding. Damn the skinny teleporters and their unnatural strength.

Gyan imped, "We're trying to locate you. Stay away from him as far as possible."

"Of course." Aameh was no fighter, and she'd already learned her lesson. She stayed put. *"I'm glad you're okay,"* Aameh imped to Wynd.

"I'm a comm, Aameh. My cover is broken and I can only be used via mental implant till it's replaced. You're in trouble."

Aaxyl imped, "*Am!*"

"We are in some high apartment in a residential area. I don't know where. Please come fast. He has a neutraliser." Aameh shared the neutraliser partially covered by his sleeve as she watched Nyaya struggle.

Aaxyl imped fluent profanity. "Am, I need you to be brave. Mohan has gone to get Dhrit for authorisation to track his zeplyn and we'll be on our way, as soon as possible."

Focus! Aameh told herself. "Why ask Admin Dhrit to bring cash unimon? He could use his shells to rob anything," she imped to Aaxyl and Mohan.

"Maybe he wanted a lot of unimon, fast. He's running out of time with AricNova free and Nadani looking for him," Aaxyl mused.

"No." Mohan imped. "Ten thousand unimon isn't a big amount for a hostage like Nyaya. She could give it to him right there. Hersh had said he needs a shell that's been outside the dome. He wants Dhrit."

"Is that possible?"

"I don't think so," Mohan said. "Besides, Dhrit can't teleport."

"It won't matter if he nulls any of them first," Aaxyl said. "Am, I want you to have a plan."

Aaxyl

Aaxyl and NeoJai burst into the conference room, teleported in by an agitated Noir.

Elir and Mohan hunched over a console she'd never seen before, fingers flying over the keys. Both Dhrits sat on either side and leaned over their shoulders, like mirror images.

Abrahamha teleported in. "We owe Aameh a debt of gratitude that words can't express. We'll do everything in our power to save her."

Aaxyl didn't need gratitude, she just wanted Aameh back.

Mohan leaned back in his chair and interlaced his fingers behind his head, staring at the console. "I've located Admin Dhrit's zeplyn and dispatched our zeplyns to the location."

The Dhrits rose from their chairs and made for the door, but Mohan waved them to wait. "They've already left. We'll teleport to the zeplyns once they reach. Let's find the real location."

"What about Aameh's comm?" Aaxyl asked.

"It doesn't have a location. Its cover was cracked before it was teleported again."

Abrahamha vanished. Probably for the best.

Elir projected a map on the wall, showing a location in the Dhara sector. "The zeplyn is in a residential parking."

Noir swore under his breath. "Vidroh just sent a message asking for help. Abrahamha is at the Octagon. I have to go."

"Dome feeds could help us find Am," Elir said.

"I'll get them," Noir assured. "I just need Abrahamha out of there. Ari has already destroyed one skyscraper. We don't need to add the central Octagon to the tally." Noir vanished.

Settlements, a new kind of administrative region, promise to include wastelanders in modern civilisation. World News, Wednesday, December 17, 2442

~~*~*~*

VIDROH: PRESIDENTIAL FLOOR, OCTAGON

Victory was boring. Vidroh was drunk out of his wits and still couldn't find a single thing to enjoy. The party had gone on for hours at various locations in the dome.

Milup was finally in the President's office on the top floor of the Octagon for more celebrations. His drunk supporters were vandalizing UDAY's branding around them.

Vidroh tried not to be petty. The dome hadn't had a change of government in ages and a non-NelumboN company in control, ever. This was history being made, but he couldn't wait for the morning. The sooner he could return to the settlement to do real work, the better.

For someone who had won because Noir suggested he try, Milup had immediately distanced himself. None of the Abrahamha's Strays or Saisrisels had been invited to the celebrations. Vidroh knew that Milup hadn't approved of global citizens meddling to begin with and would be setting stronger political boundaries, but the lack of invitation for an event of this magnitude was a deliberate snub.

A familiar face caught his eye. It turned out Noir had showed up anyway. Vidroh headed over. "Nice to see—" It was Abrahamha.

Vidroh wasn't drunk enough for this.

One by one, everyone in the room fell silent.

"SOS. Abrahamha's here," Vidroh imped Noir. This wasn't going to sit well with Milup.

Shards scraped across Vidroh's being as Abrahamha's voice boomed. "I'm sorry for crashing the party, but there is a situation. I need to talk to the President."

People filed out.

Milup stepped forward. "What is this?"

"I need your help," Abrahamha said. "Aameh—you met her—has been kidnapped by Sambit along with Dhrit's wife."

Vidroh was stone sober and ready to leave for a rescue now.

"What do you need?" Milup offered, signaling to his lackeys. "We want to bring Sambit to justice as well."

"I need access to dome-wide feeds to locate Sambit."

Milup nodded to the pudgy geek who'd been handling his technical support during the campaign and the man whipped out a slate console like he conjured it. "We'll let you know the minute Sambit is spotted."

"I have better systems. I just need the feeds."

Milup evaded. "I'm sorry, this is local data. I can't just hand it over."

Vidroh's skin zinged with invisible sparks, and he hoped Noir got here fast. This was going to go sideways. The remaining members of Milup's team were slinking to the door.

Noir appeared in the room. "Abrahamha, leave. Please."

Some celebration this was turning out to be. Nobody wanted to cross Abrahamha, but major diplomatic lines were being trampled. Even if Milup wanted to cooperate, doing it in this public manner would undermine his legitimacy. Vidroh doubted Milup wanted to agree.

"We need the feeds," Abrahamha told Noir.

Noir raised a hand in caution. "I know. Let me handle it."

Abrahamha vanished.

Noir turned to Milup. "We need feeds from the Dhara residential sector."

Er...

"Are you going to force me as well?" Milup asked.

Noir looked away. "I'm hoping it doesn't come to that and we can save two innocent women and capture a dangerous criminal."

Milup authorised access.

Seconds later, Noir slumped. "Sambit evaded public cameras."

No surprise there. Sambit was a teleporter. He would hardly appear in a public place with hostages while being hunted. Noir's personal involvement with Aameh was making him stupid.

"Are you done here?" The acid in Milup's voice could dissolve Noir. "For further assistance, you may approach local SecPros in your area."

"I'm sorry," Noir said.

"You *are* done here." Milup stared at him till he teleported away.

Vidroh pinched the bridge of his nose. As the guy sent by Abrahamha's Strays to help with settlements, the difficulty level of his job had just skyrocketed.

Milup looked around the room as his team slunk back in. "It hasn't even been a day, and we were forced to compromise the interest of the dome under threat. If you want to remain on my team, I need your word that we won't let something like this happen again."

No one disagreed.

"By the end of the week, I need all key locations equipped with automated weapons capable of detecting and disabling teleporters."

Breaking News: Serial killer and ex-director of Null Dorms, Sambit Nadani is still at large and reported to have abducted two more women. Dome Times, Wednesday, December 17, 2442

~~*~*~*

AAMEH: RESIDENTIAL TOWER

"Gyan has failed to find any of you on public feeds. He must have teleported you directly into the apartment." Mohan sounded worried.

"That's what I said," Aameh replied.

Aaxyl imped urgency. *"Aameh, I need you to be brave and remember how you modulated Abrahamha's symbionts. Then I need you to take your knife, coat it with your blood, make that bastard bleed and void him good."*

"I can't!" Aameh was terrified. Because of her lack of healing, she had rarely been physically active and never learned to fight.

"You can," Aaxyl insisted. *"You must. We have located Nyaya's zeplyn and are on our way, but it will take time. You must prevent him from hurting either of you again or teleporting off with her. You won't get many chances. Plan, act, cut him, disable his symbionts."*

Aameh put her hand in her pocket and pulled out her small knife. It wouldn't be enough to injure him seriously, but even a slight cut might be enough, she hoped. His back was to her as he looked down out of the window. This was her opportunity. Her hands were shaking.

She smeared blood from her split lip onto the knife and ran at Sambit's back. He dodged out of her way easily, disarming her and holding the knife against her throat instead. Her back was to him. He held her effortlessly. The knife cut her.

"Everybody calm down," Sambit said. "I just need Dhrit. Nobody needs to get hurt."

He was lying. Aameh had seen him shoot Admin Dhrit for refusing to tell him where AricNova was. He hadn't even waited. If Aaxyl and the others didn't get there in time...

"That's what you said before you pumped me full of bullets," Nyaya said.

"That's true, isn't it?" Sambit transferred the knife to the hand around Aameh's throat, still holding her effortlessly while he raised his hand to use the neutraliser. "So, which one first?"

Aameh grabbed at his arm and scratched at him, trying to pull the knife away. She fought as hard as she could to get away. She was pathetic. She had no effect on him at all.

He switched the knife back to the other hand, pointing it at her throat. "One wrong move and this one gets this knife," he warned Nyaya.

At lease he couldn't use the neutraliser while he held the knife.

Aaxyl's calm voice ordered her with absolute authority. *"Don't listen to him, Am! FIGHT! We are two minutes out. Keep fighting no matter what."*

"If you don't get here on time, Ax, know that you're the—"

"Am, you little shit, get off your lazy ass and fight or you'll wish he killed you."

Aameh tried to bite him, but she couldn't even move her head to reach his arm. It felt like he could jerk her neck off.

"He's too strong."

"I don't care." Aaxyl repeated with icy calm. *"We're a minute away. You have one job. Delay him."*

Desperate, Aameh kept scratching and pulling at his arm without even distracting him anymore. She rubbed at the cuts on her neck and smeared the blood on Sambit's arm, trying to scratch him again.

Her nails must have broken his skin, because she suddenly detected his symbionts and yanked at them with everything she had in her, squashing, flattening everything, desperately. Hoping like hell that this worked, because she had no other plan and he had a knife to her throat.

His symbionts were flimsy compared with Abrahamha and Noir's. Or even Aaxyl's.

She vandalised the construct to shreds and smashed everything she could see.

Sambit's grip on her slackened suddenly.

Aameh pushed away and fled.

Nyaya and she raced for the door.

Sambit cursed from the floor.

They darted past startled residents, and took the elevator down, noting their floor—forty-third. Two zeplyns flew in like missiles as they exited the building.

Mohan and Elir raced in to secure Sambit.

Aameh's face squished into a huge chest covered in lovely fabric.

Oblivious to gawking residents, Noir had teleported straight into a hug.

She'd expected Aaxyl.

She patted Noir's chest reassuringly, and looked around.

"Ax?"

Aaxyl was kneeling outside Mohan's zeplyn, hands on the ground, crying.

Aameh raced to her, hugging her awkwardly till Aaxyl managed to get up. She was shaking.

"I voided him, Ax. Just like we planned. I'm safe."

NeoJai kissed the top of Aameh's head and hugged Nyaya and the Dhrits plastered to her.

Mohan and Elir appeared in the zeplyn with an unconscious Sambit.

Noir told Elir to take Sambit to Milup as a peace offering.

Aameh wondered what that was about, but soon lost track, as Nyaya and she were fussed over and asked a hundred questions.

Noir teleported everybody to SYMBTech.

For a while, all anybody did was hug.

Aaxyl must have told her a hundred times how proud she was and exclaimed at her already healing cuts and bruises.

Aameh was still jumpy, but she'd be just fine. She was a hero.

Nyaya put an arm around Aameh. "I guess we didn't miss all the action. Let's update *Khabariya*."

Aameh had brought down the biggest bad guy in the worst human trafficking scandal to hit the dome. How cool was that.

Epilogue

The crime spree of the most prolific serial killer in the Dome comes to an end. Dome Times,

~~*~*~*

AAXYL: AVANT

Aaxyl and Aameh sat by Hersh's bed, holding a hand each. NeoJai and Mohan stood behind them.

Hersh's eyes stared expressionlessly at the ceiling. Conscious, but unresponsive. Aaxyl stroked his hand, hoping he could feel it.

"I've never seen Hersh lying down," Aameh whispered.

"He's going to be fine," Aaxyl said. "SanJeevan is the best medic in the world. Symbionts saved humanity from extinction. They can fix one beat-up symbiontist."

"I'm planning to give you a haircut while you can't resist," Aameh told Hersh, combing her fingers through overgrown hair.

Hersh's closed slightly at the soothing touch, though they didn't focus on Aameh's face or show recognition.

Aaxyl leaned in, searching for Hersh in those eyes. "Blink if you understand me."

About Vidyut Gore

Vidyut Gore is stay-at-home parent, grower of carnivorous plants and an incurable geek. She's been a mountaineer, a nomad, and a digital journalist. Better known for blunt socio-political commentary, Vidyut is also the Prime Minister of #AltSarkar—a spoof Government of India on Twitter.

Vidyut is the author of futuristic sci-fi set primarily in the Indian subcontinent of the 25th century.

Twitter: @Vidyut

Facebook: @theVidyut

Instagram: @vidyutgore